*Tomorrow at sun-up, one of you will fight Krusha the squatch. We drew straws for the pleasure. He won.*

"I'll fight," said Wulf.

Berlaze raised an eyebrow. *Not you. Krusha has chosen who he will fight.*

"Who?" Wulf demanded.

*Another question and I will kill you with a thought.*

Wulf kept his mouth shut but held his ground.

*If your warrior wins, I will give you half a day's head start up the mountain. Then we will hunt you.*

Sofi looked up to the mountains. With two children and the likes of Bodil in tow, half a day was no head start at all.

*If Krusha wins, you will get one thousand of our paces' head start. Then we will hunt you.*

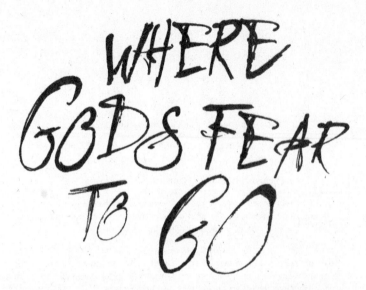

# WHERE GODS FEAR TO GO

West of West: Book Three

# ANGUS WATSON

orbit

www.orbitbooks.net

ORBIT

First published in Great Britain in 2019 by Orbit

1 3 5 7 9 10 8 6 4 2

Copyright © 2019 by Angus Watson

Map copyright © Tim Paul Illustrations 2019

Excerpt from *The Grey Bastards* by Jonathan French
Copyright © 2015, 2018 by Jonathan French

The moral right of the author has been asserted.

A CIP catalogue record for this book is available from the British Library.

ISBN 978-0-356-50760-6

Typeset in Apollo MT Std by Palimpsest Book Production Ltd,
Falkirk, Stirlingshire
Printed and bound in Great Britain by Clays Ltd, Elcograf S.p.A.

Papers used by Orbit are from well-managed
forests and other responsible sources.

MIX
Paper from
responsible sources
FSC® C104740
www.fsc.org

Orbit
An imprint of
Little, Brown Book Group
Carmelite House
50 Victoria Embankment
London EC4Y 0DZ

An Hachette UK Company
www.hachette.co.uk

www.orbitbooks.net

*For Oliver Papps*

AVALANCHE

WORMSLAND

FLASH FLOOD

GREAT DIVIDE

THREE SISTERS
CANYON

ERIK'S
BRIDGE

AYLA'S
CASTLE

OLA WOLVINDER'S
LONGHOUSE

RED RIVER

POTHOLE
PEOPLE

MASSACARE

WALK OUT OF

WASP
MEN

BIGHORN
ISLAND

S H I N I N G   M O U N T A I N S

COPYRIGHT 2019 © BY TIM PAUL

# Part One

## Mountains

# Chapter 1

## The Squatch Chief

Berlaze the chief squatch was twice the height of a tall man and built like a family of buffalo stitched into a single skin. Apart from his leathery face and the palms of his enormous hands, he was covered in coarse black fur. Sofi Tornado had expected him to smell like a bear that's been dead for a week, and he did.

She'd met one squatch before – Ayla, who'd helped the Calnians and the Wootah escape from the Badlands. Ayla had been fearsome enough, but compared to Berlaze she was about as scary as a baby chipmunk. He looked down at Sofi with his wide nose, thin lips and black eyes squashed together into the sort of expression you might find on a parent who's caught you trying to abduct their child.

Sofi tried to think of something to say, but it was pointless. Berlaze was going to kill them. One of the few facts that Calnian scholars knew about squatch was that they always killed humans. The mystery here was why the Owsla and the Wootah were still alive.

The desire to fight – the *need* to fight – fizzed in her limbs. She was Sofi Tornado, captain of the Owsla. She longed to smash Berlaze's knee with her hand axe and jam her dagger-tooth knife through his eye. Despite his size, it would have been easy. If it weren't for the fact that Berlaze could kill her with a thought.

The squatch had appeared from nowhere and slaughtered their guide without touching him. Sofi, Paloma Pronghorn and Wulf the Fat had attacked. Sofi was meant to be unbeatable, Paloma was the fastest person on earth and Wulf, although nothing compared to the alchemically enhanced Owsla, was a capable warrior by normal measures.

Sofi remembered only attacking, then waking with the feeling that her skull was squeezing her mind. Wulf had called it a mind crush, which was about right.

The giant squatch gathered around their chief didn't ease the situation at all. A few were taller and a couple were stockier than Chief Berlaze. They made the Wootah and Calnians, standing a few paces behind Sofi, look like infants. Even mighty Chogolisa Earthquake, taller than any man and strong as two dozen, looked slight next to a squatch.

The squatch's gods, it seemed, had collaborated with their hirsute worshippers to humble Sofi. All around the pastureland that the squatch called home, black cliffs soared from green, forested slopes to impossibly high snow-coated, jagged peaks. Even if Sofi could persuade Berlaze to release them, her women and the immeasurably less capable Wootah would have to scale those summits.

For the thousandth time, Sofi wished she was back in Calnia, killing at the empress's behest, blinded to moral qualms by the daily dose of dried rattlesnake. Sofi slightly enjoyed the paradox that if she still had rattlesnake in her diet, she would have killed Yoki Choppa for taking the rattlesnake out of her diet. But only slightly.

*The pale male said we needed to let you live,* Berlaze thought at her. Every word pressed inside her skull, each one a mini mind crush. *He said you are on a quest that will save us all. I cannot believe for a moment that it is true, but do amuse me by trying to explain.*

"Have you been troubled by disasters and monsters?" she asked.

*Squatch business is not your business,* boomed Berlaze into her mind.

Sofi winced – these louder thoughts squeezed her skull all the more – then continued. "As I'm sure you know, there has been a rash of tornados, storms like we've never seen before, earthquakes and other disasters recently. We've heard that monsters roam the far side of these peaks. We have seen one ourselves – an impossibly large flying beast that burst and unleashed a swam of killer wasps."

*What of it?* sneered Berlaze.

"Our prophet Ottar the Moaner—"

*The idiot boy?*

"The boy, yes. Both he and our warlock, Yoki Choppa, agree on the cause of the monsters and the disasters."

*Enlighten me.*

"At The Meadows, several hundred miles beyond the Shining Mountains," Sofi nodded towards the westward peaks, "there is a force causing all of this. It means to exterminate all life."

*What is this force?*

We don't know.

*How will you stop it?*

"I—"

She was interrupted by a yell from Ottar. She turned. The boy was flapping his arms and gabbling at his sister.

"What's he saying, Freydis?" Sofi asked.

"He can feel the rage of the force at The Meadows. It's stronger. He says—"

Ottar grabbed Freydis's arm and spoke earnestly. Sofi was finding the boy easier to understand and caught the odd word – monsters, death, more death – but couldn't decipher the whole.

Ottar finished talking and nodded hard.

*What did he say?* asked Berlaze.

Sofi felt a glimmer of hope. Maybe Berlaze hadn't completely dismissed them.

Freydis skipped over, blonde hair blowing about her face, button nose jutting bravely up at them. "Sofi Tornado, do you remember the tornado that killed Chnob the White, and the dragon that burst into wasps and killed Gunnhild Kristlover?"

Sofi nodded. She was glad the girl was addressing her and ignoring Berlaze. The Wootah might have had very little experience outside the narrow world in which the Goachica had confined them, but they were usefully unflappable.

"Ottar says those were nothing," Freydis continued, big blue eyes widening. "The disasters are going to get bigger and there are going to be more of them, and there's an army building in The Meadows. Herds and herds and swarms too of monsters like the wasp dragon, and bigger monsters, too. Much bigger! They will kill everyone."

*And we will rejoice when they succeed,* Berlaze thought at them.

Freydis treated the fourteen-foot-high, thickly muscled ogre to the same look she'd given Ottar the day before when he'd cried after jamming a stick too far up his nose.

"The squatch will also die," she said.

Berlaze loomed over the little girl. Keef the Berserker and Erik the Angry started forward. Wulf stopped Erik. Sitsi Kestrel, the Owsla's big-eyed archer, placed a restraining hand on Keef's arm.

*We will destroy the Warlock Queen's monsters!* Berlaze mind-bellowed.

"You can fight them, Chief Berlaze." The girl held her ground and the beast's gaze. If his words pained Freydis's mind the way they pained Sofi, she didn't show it. "But they'll kill you all. Easily and quickly." The child nodded as if agreeing with herself.

Berlaze stared. Sofi worried he was going to mind-crush her, but then he shook his head and walked back to Sofi.

He seemed more relaxed. She wasn't sure if that was a good thing.

*There is a lot to hate about humans,* he thought at her, less boomingly now. *It's difficult to say what aspect of your foul characters I loathe the most. But it may very well be your arrogance. Have you considered for a moment that we might have our own prophets and alchemists? No. We have fur on our bodies. How could we also have minds in our heads? Well, we have, and they are far superior to yours. We can do more than kill weak creatures like you with them. We have known since last winter that the troubles are caused by a force in The Meadows. We know that the force is the Warlock Queen.*

"Warlock Queen?" Sofi asked before she could stop herself.

*You see, you insignificant fool? We know more than you. Several moons ago I sent twelve of my best across the mountains to find the Warlock Queen and put a stop to her ruin.* Berlaze looked at the gathered Wootah and Calnians, black nose creased in distain. *What can tiny, weak, stupid humans hope to achieve that my own squad cannot? Each of my squatch is worth all of you and more.*

"Ottar the Moaner will stop the Warlock Queen," said Sofi. She wanted to ask Berlaze what he knew about the Warlock Queen, but checked herself. "Before any of the Wootah knew The Meadows existed, the boy said he had to get there. Before we met the Wootah, our warlock Yoki Choppa's alchemical bowl showed the same."

*Why?*

She glanced back at Yoki Choppa for help. He shrugged. Verbose as ever.

"The prophesy is not clear," she admitted.

Berlaze looked at Sofi, then each of the Calnians and Wootah in turn.

*It's no good,* thought Berlaze. *Maybe there's something in your prophesy, but I hate humans too much. I am going to have to kill all of you, now.*

Sofi leapt at him.

Her mind exploded and she fell.

*STOP!* she heard as she landed. The pressure released in her head. She rolled and came to her feet.

*STOP!* the voice in her mind repeated. A squatch was running towards them. She was a long way off, but Sofi recognised the sound of her steps from when she'd fled the Badlands.

"'s'Ayla," confirmed Ottar.

Ayla slowed to a walk.

*Hello, Ayla,* thought Berlaze.

*Hello, Father.*

Ayla is Berlaze's daughter? Well, that's a lucky turn of events, thought Sofi. Possibly.

*Where have you been?* asked the chief. *We haven't seen you for, what, a year?*

*I was captured by the Badlanders. I escaped a moon ago. These people helped me.*

That wasn't quite true, thought Sofi. If anything, Ayla's intervention had saved the Wootah and Calnians from Beaver Man's clutches. But she wasn't going to argue the point.

*Without them,* Ayla continued, *I would be dead in the Badlands. So please will you give them whatever provisions they require and send them on their way?*

*No,* thought Berlaze. *I am about to kill them.*

*But they saved me!*

*They are humans. They are selfish and cruel. If they did save you – which I seriously doubt – it was only incidental to saving themselves. They will die.*

*Father, no. These are good creatures. They are on a quest that will help us all. Let them go.*

Berlaze's facial features wrinkled and pulsed in thought.

In a way, thought Sofi, it would be easier if Berlaze did kill them all. Ayanna, Empress of Calnia, had dreamed that the Wootah – or Mushroom Men as they'd been known – would destroy the world. She'd sent Sofi Tornado and her Owsla to kill them all. Yoki Choppa had stopped them, and said that Ottar the Moaner was in fact going to *save* the world and they must escort him and the rest of the Wootah to The Meadows.

Sofi had believed the warlock and was doing what he asked. However, she was trying to keep her distance from the Wootah because, when the quest was over – if they succeeded – Sofi would have to decide whether the empress's orders still stood. She didn't see why they shouldn't – a prophecy was a prophecy. So, if they did make it to The Meadows and stop all the terrors, she would have to slaughter the Wootah to prevent them destroying the world.

She looked at them, as they waited to hear if they were to die that day. Thyri Treelegs stared pouty defiance. Keef the Berserker was smiling with genuine swagger. Sassa Lipchewer, Erik the Angry and Wulf the Fat were all trying not to look scared, and succeeding to a degree. Finn the Deep was trying not to look scared and failing, but he was gripping the hilt of his sword and was probably ready to use it. Bodil Gooseface was looking about with her mouth open, more perplexed than scared. Little Ottar the Moaner was splay-legged on the grassy ground, poking his finger into the soil and singing.

No, Sofi wasn't looking forward to killing them all, so it would be something of a relief if Berlaze did the job, even if he took her life too.

After an uncomfortably long time, the hulking hominid looked back down at Sofi. *I will give you my decision at sunset. You will wait by the lake. If any of you try to escape, you will be killed.*

*Thank you, Father*, thought Ayla.

Berlaze smiled at his daughter, then turned to Sofi. His face was still twisted in a smile, but it wasn't a kind one.

# Chapter 2

## An Objectionable Face

Sun sparkled winningly on the water and the mountains were a spectacularly proud yet broody backdrop. The still day was almost silent, other than the splashes of water-fowl and riparian mammals, the odd ploop of a surfacing fish and honks from the numerous elk which wandered about with no apparent fear of squatch or human.

In other circumstances, thought Sofi, the land might have been beautiful.

However, the watching squatch, sitting hairy and hunched, ready to kill them with a mind crush the moment they looked like they were trying to flee, did rather spoil the effect.

"Let's ignore the buggers and make use of the day," Wulf the Fat had said as they walked towards the lakeshore, and it seemed that everyone agreed.

Yoki Choppa sat on a rock, hunched over his smoking alchemical bowl.

Wulf, Keef the Berserker and Thyri Treelegs sparred, hammer against long-handled axe against blade. Sitsi Kestrel, Paloma Pronghorn and Chogolisa Earthquake – the other three remaining Owsla from the ten that had set off to kill the Mushroom Men – watched them, calling out advice. Sofi probably should have made her women train, but, whatever Berlaze decided, they were going to need all their energy later.

\*   \*   \*

The two children, Ottar the Moaner and Freydis the Annoying, pootled about on the lakeshore with Bodil Gooseface, throwing stones into the water and marvelling at animals.

Finn the Deep (formerly Finnbogi the Boggy) and his father Erik the Angry gathered wood, then sat on the grass making pair after pair of the racket-like shoes that Erik had devised to enable Paloma Pronghorn to run on water. Sofi wondered why they might need more than one pair of water shoes – if Erik was thinking they might escape across the lake it was a non-starter, since only Paloma Pronghorn had the pace to run on water – but she didn't really care.

"Wouldn't it be more useful for everyone if I spent the time training with Thyri?" Finn asked, for the fifth time.

"More useful for you, maybe," Erik replied. "But I am sorry, I need your help."

"Why?" Finn whined.

The way Finn hankered after Thyri Treelegs was pathetic. The girl wasn't interested and he should have moved on. Even worse, Finn was also in never-to-be-requited love with Paloma Pronghorn, ever since she'd got drunk and made the mistake of kissing him. So whenever he wasn't embarrassing himself with Thyri, Finn spent his time practically begging for Paloma's attention.

Sofi wondered if she should have a chat with the boy, then checked herself.

She didn't care about the ways and whims of the Wootah.

Yoki Choppa, Bodil and the children made lunch. Afterwards, Chogolisa went to sit with Erik and Finn, and they chatted and laughed and continued to make water shoes. Chogolisa's relationship with Erik was against Owsla rules, and it was going to be a complication when Sofi had to kill the Wootah after their quest. However, the chances of Chogolisa and Erik – of any of them in fact – living to the end of the quest were so slim that she let the big woman have her fun. Erik was Chogolisa's first and Sofi had never seen her so happy. Maybe it was the lack of rattlesnake in her diet, but she couldn't bring herself to deny Chogolisa her first taste of love. Not yet, anyway.

Bodil and Keef sat nearby, looking out over the lake, while Sassa and Wulf paced the shore. Both Bodil's and Sassa's growing babies had been conceived at around the same time, judging by the tiny, fast hearts Sofi could hear beating away. But the difference between the couples was striking.

Sofi and Wulf exuded a proud-parent air, walking in contented silence. Keef and Bodil's silence seemed awkward, like two Calnian nobles who've been taught that one must converse the entire time, but found themselves forced together with simply nothing to converse about. Keef started to sharpen his long-handled axe, Arse Splitter. Bodil sat, mouth open, as if her mind was empty. Sofi sometimes suspected that it might have been, but every now and then Bodil did something useful or said something insightful. None of the Wootah were simple. Even Finn, pathetic with women, had proved himself brave and even impressive in other ways. Controlling the crowd pigeons who'd carried them all away from the Badlands had taken great mental strength and stamina. In the two moons or so since they'd met the Wootah, Finn seemed to have grown up a lot. One might even say he was progressing from boyhood to manhood and –

She stopped herself. She didn't care about the Wootah.

Paloma Pronghorn jogged up faster than others ran, dropped onto the grass next to Sofi, and followed her gaze.

"I don't get it," said Paloma. "Surely Keef knows the baby isn't his? She told us she was pregnant about three days after she and Keef shagged. Sassa told me Finn and Bodil got it on by the Rock River on the day they killed Sadzi Wolf. It has to be Finn's child."

Sofi remembered the day. Erik the Angry had struck the killing blow. It had been self-defence, but remembering that the Wootah killed one of hers was going to make it easier if she did have to finish them off.

"That makes sense, timing-wise," she said.

"Yes," continued Paloma, "Keef can't be so thick that he thinks the baby is his."

"And if the baby is Finn's—"

"Why isn't he doing the decent thing and claiming it?"

Sofi shrugged. She didn't care.

"Because," Paloma continued, "Finn is in love with Thyri Treelegs and would much rather have babies with her."

"Or you."

Paloma reddened. It wasn't the first time Paloma had got drunk and kissed someone she regretted, not by any means, but she'd never had to travel in the same group as her mistake day after day immediately afterwards. Sofi almost smiled.

"Well, maybe, but isn't everyone a bit in love with me?" Paloma grinned, then leapt up to go and bother someone else.

Sofi watched the beautiful, vibrant and super-fast woman dance-run away. She'd been joking, but most people probably were at least a little in love with her.

Sofi walked down to the lakeshore where Yoki Choppa was poking about for insects and plants to add to his alchemical bundle.

"How can we beat the mind crush?" she asked.

"Can't," he said, without looking up.

"Do you know how they do it?" she asked.

"Maybe."

"How?"

"I'm not certain, and knowing won't help." He carried on poking about.

"Why did our guide die instantly when the rest of us were knocked out?"

"Maybe because he was old. Maybe they hated him more."

"What do you think the range is?"

"It would be a guess."

"Let's hear it."

"Maybe ten paces."

Sofi nodded. The squatch had been about that far away when they'd killed their guide Weeko Fang. "Can you block it, even a little?"

Yoki Choppa shook his head sadly.

Sofi walked away, feeling two further new and irksome emotions that had been unleashed by the denial of daily rattlesnake: guilt and compassion. She shouldn't have asked Yoki Choppa if he could block the squatch mind crush. She'd known he wouldn't be able to.

Yoki Choppa could use herbs to enhance nature. His alchemy was powerful. It had created the Owsla, for example, but that had taken years. The warlock's immediate abilities were far from spectacular. Using people's hair to track where they were over dozens of miles was the most impressive, and that had its limits.

Since the Owsla and Yoki Choppa had left Calnian territory, they'd joined up with a small boy who was destined to save the world using powers that none of them could even guess at. Beaver Man and his warlocks had used ancient magic to revive long-dead monsters and create the Empty Children. They'd been trapped by spiders attached to their necks, controlled by the Empty Children. They'd heard that Chippaminka had taken over the minds of the Calnian rulers and made them go to war. They'd seen Finn the Deep guide a millions-strong flock of crowd pigeons. They'd been protected from ghosts in the Black Mountains by Tatinka Buffalo's strange, deep magic. And now they'd met the squatch who could kill them with a look.

Yoki Choppa's alchemy had been unable to compete with

any of the abilities of their foes and it had been overshadowed by the magic of their allies.

He *had* made a powder which melted the faces of Beaver Man's Owsla and possibly saved them all by doing so, but that was one small act of alchemy – little more than a clever trick – in the midst of all sorts of more powerful magic, and he'd been too late to save Luby Zephyr. Arguably, the shoes that Erik the Angry had made to allow Paloma to run on water were more impressive than any of Yoki Choppa's contributions to the quest.

So Sofi guessed Yoki Choppa must be feeling redundant. He prepared the Owsla's power animals, true, but they required such small quantities that the batches he'd already made would last for years. After he'd denied them their power animals to let the Wootah escape, then told her the power animal secret, Sofi had insisted that each woman carried her own. So now the warlock didn't even have the role of slipping their medicine into their food every day.

She could have gone back to the lakeside and told him that she respected and valued him, that she was grateful for their powers, and that she – and her women – loved him like a father. But she wasn't going to. She'd have to have a lot more than rattlesnake taken out of her diet before she got that soppy.

He'd be fine.

Innowak the swan god had pulled his sun chariot almost to the horizon when Berlaze appeared again. He came alone, striding with a swaying, powerful gait. His confidence rankled. Sofi longed to destroy it.

*I do not want to let you go,* thought Berlaze. *There is nothing you can do at The Meadows that my squatch cannot do a hundred times better. However, my daughter insists that you saved her. So I will indulge her. First, you will spend the night by the lake.*

Calnians and Wootah looked at one another. Keef and Sitsi were beaming. Sofi was wary.

*Then*, continued Berlaze, *tomorrow at sun-up, one of you will fight Krusha the squatch. We drew straws for the pleasure. He won.*

"I'll fight," said Wulf.

Berlaze raised an eyebrow. *Not you. Krusha has chosen who he will fight.*

"Who?" Wulf demanded.

*Another question and I will kill you with a thought.*

Wulf kept his mouth shut but held his ground.

*If your warrior wins, I will give you half a day's head start up the mountain. Then we will hunt you.*

Sofi looked up to the mountains. With two children and the likes of Bodil in tow, half a day was no head start at all.

*If Krusha wins, you will get one thousand of our paces' head start. Then we will hunt you.*

Wootah and Calnians looked at each other.

*Krusha chose the one of you whose face he liked the least,* thought Berlaze with a smile.

Keef was bouncing with excitement, hoping it might be him.

Berlaze raised a hairy finger not much smaller than Ottar's forearm and pointed at the boy. Several people gasped, but the squatch smiled and moved his finger to point at Freydis, then Paloma, then Chogolisa – make it Chogolisa, thought Sofi. But he lowered his finger.

*Actually, can you guess who's got the most objectionable face?* Berlaze asked.

There was a pause while everybody looked at each other.

"It's me, isn't it," Finn broke the silence.

*It is!* thought Berlaze.

"Thought so," said Keef, shaking his head and scowling.

"Pigfuckers," said Finn.

# Chapter 3

## Foe Slicer

Finn the Deep ducked. Krusha's claws swished overhead. Nice duck! the young Wootah man told himself, but his flash of self-congratulation was cut short by the creature's follow-up backhand slamming into his midriff. The Wootah man staggered backwards across the boulder-strewn fighting field.

He tripped on one of the smaller rocks, spun and fell face-first into a large heap of freshly shat elk dung.

The watching squatch hooted weirdly.

"Ha ha!" came from Keef the Berserker, who might have been a little more supportive. *"No matter how seriously you take yourself or your situation,"* said his dead aunt Gunnhild Kristlover in his mind, *"there is always the danger that others will find you hilarious."*

Spitting shit, Finn pushed himself up onto all fours. On the bright side, it was herbivore crap. If you absolutely had to have turds in your mouth, herbivore beat carnivore every day.

His opponent lumbered towards him, blocking the mountain sun, blocking everything with his hairy bulk. A thin-lipped muzzle twisted into a mock-concerned smile and the beast winked. An inhuman roar would have been a lot less distrubing.

Finn's father Erik the Angry had told him that one could learn nothing about fighting from animals because animals were idiots. Bears, for example, had three fighting styles: tooth and claw rip-the-other-fucker-apart raging, tentative ready-to-flee swiping, or fleeing. Given the relative size and power of humans and bears, the best tactic for people who had some ability of persuasion over the animals, like Finn and his father, was to scare the bear into running away.

Squatch, however, were larger and stronger than bears and at least as intelligent as humans. Finn could not think of any possible move or combination of moves that would see him walking away from this fight, and he couldn't get into his opponent's mind.

*Which arm would you like to lose first?* The squatch towered above and Finn regretted lying there musing when he should have been leaping to his feet.

*I'm quite attached to both of them,* he thought back.

*Not for long, you're not.*

He'd walked into that one.

The monster reached down. Finn tried to roll clear, but powerful fingers grabbed his arm and hoicked him off the ground. Finn hurled a handful of elk crap into his attacker's open-mouthed face. The beast yelped and dropped him.

Finn landed in a crouch, sprang up and ran.

*FLIGHT IS NOT AN OPTION!* Finn felt his thoughts cloud and his head swim. He slowed, stopped, and stooped, hands on his knees, eyes closed and shaking his head. He was well aware that Krusha might be running at him, winding up to take his head off with a punch, but he also knew that he'd pass out if any more light got into his eyes.

Finally his mind cleared. Krusha was ten paces off, smiling at him, hands on hips. Waiting.

Finn turned to Chief Berlaze, standing next to his daughter Ayla and a few other squatch at the opposite end of the fighting field to Finn's gang. "You said mind crushes weren't allowed!"

*Neither is running away.*

"I was going to loop round and attack him."

*Then do it.*

Krusha smiled and beckoned. The monster's arsehole-faced confidence, annoyingly, wasn't even a tiny bit misplaced. Finn didn't have a hope.

"Are you sure I can't have my sword?" he asked Berlaze. "I'd still have no chance, but you might see a better fight."

*Nope*, the great beast thought back.

*Oh, go on, Father, give him his sword*, implored Ayla.

*Why?*

*They believe they go to a superior afterlife if they die with a weapon in hand.*

Finn blinked. He hadn't thought of that. He looked at Krusha, twice his height and, what, five times his weight? Sword or not, he really was about to die. He felt sick.

*Idiots*, thought Berlaze.

*I would be dead without them*, Ayla beseeched.

*I agreed to let this one fight for their freedom. Nothing more. You told me that he defeated two monstrous serpents with no weapon.*

*That was different. They were snakes so he was able to out-think them. These people have done nothing to harm us and –*

*Give him the weapon*, interrupted Krusha. *It won't make any difference.*

*That's not the point*, Berlaze argued. *It is the human arrogance that they should be considered above all other animals that is in question here and . . .*

Finn realised with a start that he shouldn't have been able to hear the squatch talking to each other. Previously he'd only heard them when they'd directed a thought at him. But now he was eavesdropping while they thought things between themselves.

He must focus on their words, he told himself as the squatch carried on thinking away at each other. He might learn something life-saving.

Because Finn was Finn, however, telling himself to focus had exactly the opposite effect and he found himself having a good look at his surroundings.

The Calnians and Wootah were gathered a little way uphill of the fighting field, guarded by a group of squatch who'd promised to kill them with mind crushes if they tried to intervenc in Finn's fight.

Wulf nodded manfully, Sassa smiled support and Keef grinned at him. Bodil waved. Erik looked the most fraught, which was nice, but also what one might expect from a father. Paloma Pronghorn could have pretended to be more upset. Still, at least she was looking him in the eye for about the first time since they'd made love back in the Black Mountains. Actually "made love" was probably a bit strong, but they'd certainly kissed and had a serious fumble. Thyri Treelegs, who also hadn't looked at him much since he'd kissed Paloma, wore a stony-faced scowl. No change there then. Ottar the Moaner was playing with the fur on a surprisingly compliant squatch's paw as if it was just another humdrum morning.

All around the mountains menaced, brutes of black rock and snow towering over the inconsequential events below. Finn had thought that the mountains were lovely when he'd first seen them, but now they filled him with bowel-loosening dread. "Even if you defeat Krusha by some miracle," they seemed to say, "there's no way you're getting across us."

*Focus, focus*, Finn told himself, *focus on Krusha's mind*.

He heard a flash of squatch thoughts, briefly found himself pondering how difficult it was to focus on something when there were so many distractions, and then he was back in.

*Fine*, Berlaze was thinking, *he can have his little weapon, Krusha is still going to punch him into a greasy spot*. As well as his conversational thoughts, Finn could now hear the chief's private musings. Actually, it was more feel than hear, but he could definitely understand them. He was pondering whether to kill his daughter for challenging him in public again. He'd avoided having to kill her before by arranging for her to be captured by the Badlanders, but the annoying child had escaped.

*Thank you*, thought Ayla at her father, telling herself that this was a sign of his goodness that she knew was hidden deep down.

Yes, thought Finn, hidden so deep that he wants to kill his own daughter because she's nice.

*He's giving him the sword!* Krusha was thinking. *I've never seen anything as beautiful as that sword and I want it. How did these weak fools make something so wonderful? If I take it off the human and kill him with it in a spectacular way then Berlaze will have to give it to me, won't he? If I win it and I own it, surely Gabi will finally see that I have more to offer than that smooth-haired dickwad Nairda . . .*

Finn, who sometimes caught himself seriously thinking that if he did stuff like getting a butterfly to land on his hand then both Thyri and Paloma would finally fall for him, was glad to discover that squatch were as idiotic as humans.

*Come and get your sword*, Berlaze thought at Finn. He was meant to hear that one.

He walked over. So he could hear their private thoughts now, but he hadn't learned much. Krusha was planning to take the sword off him and use it, rather than clawing, biting or stomping him to death. How could he use that knowledge to defeat the monster? Nothing sprang to mind.

He looked at Thyri Treelegs, hoping for inspiration from the person who'd taught him all he knew about fighting. She glowered back. How could she still be angry with him? Why was she angry? If she'd ever shown any interest in him, he'd never have kissed Paloma.

He looked at Paloma. She looked away.

*For the love of Tor . . .* he thought.

His eyes settled on Freydis the Annoying. The girl smiled encouragingly and nodded. Well, thank Loakie someone on my side seems to be on my side, he thought.

Berlaze handed him his sword Foe Slicer, hilt-first. Think what you like about the murderous, human-hating squatch, thought Finn, but they had manners.

He hefted the wonderful weapon and walked towards Krusha, still no nearer working out how in Hel he was going to beat the bugger.

Sassa Lipchewer watched Finn advance on the squatch. The core Wootah philosophy – from when they'd been Hardworkers on the bank of Olaf's Fresh Sea and in the old world before – had been *you die when you die*. Recently, however, she was coming to think that the phrase and the entire fatalistic philosophy had been thought up by men, and stupid men to boot. Having thought that, she'd bought into it for a long while. Life was a lot easier when you weren't scared of dying and didn't mourn the dead.

Pregnancy had changed everything. She straightened her crest of hair and placed a hand on her growing stomach. Now that her son or daughter would die if she died, she really really didn't want to die.

*You die when you die* was based on the idea that the after-life was awesome. Since they'd left Hardwork they'd seen so much that was amazing – mournful and majestic landscapes, monstrous and beautiful animals, people behaving wonder-fully, extraordinarily and awfully – that Sassa wanted her child to see this world first, no matter how great the next one was.

She looked forward to a time when her child was old enough to understand the adventures he or she had lived through in the comfort of the womb, and be inspired to find their own adventures. That was at least part of the reason that she wasn't interested in dying when she died.

She also wanted to live beyond pregnancy. She looked forward to a time when she felt a little less nauseous, headachy and not forever plagued by the need to pee. At least she wasn't actually vomiting any more, touch wood, unlike Bodil.

She chewed her lips, gripped Wulf's hand and prayed to Fraya to help Finnbogi the Boggy, or Finn the Deep as they were meant to call him now. She could feel all of them, Calnians and Wootah alike, holding their breath, as man and beast approached each other.

The squatch lunged.

Finn leapt back, surprisingly sprightly, slashed overhead, and it was the squatch's turn to dodge. Foe Slicer clanged onto a boulder. Sparks flew.

Erik, Wulf and Keef cheered. Sitsi Kestrel brought her hands together in a little clap and Sassa found herself bouncing on her toes. It was hardly a battle-ending blow, but the fact that the squatch had had to dodge it surely meant that Finn had a chance?

The squatch swung a fist. Finn leapt out of range, parried, thrust and . . . sliced into the squatch's wrist!

Krusha roared. Sassa heard herself squeak.

The squatch lifted its hand to inspect the injury, then looked at the human. It looked very, very unhappy. Sassa gulped.

Finn took a few steps back, holding his sword aloft. He did not look threatening. It looked like he was trying to hide behind the blade.

Krusha roared and charged. Finn swung his weapon, but the squatch kicked the sword from Finn's grip, sending it spinning away.

The young Wootah man looked at his hand as if thinking *where's my sword?* The squatch swung an arm and punched him in the chest. Finn flew like a hurled toy, landed on the grass and tumbled over and over. He missed all the boulders but came to rest face up, limbs spread in a star and prone. He looked finished.

Wootah and Calnians groaned.

"Idiot!" shouted Keef. "Get up, get your sword back and shove it up his arse!"

Finn didn't move.

Sassa longed to run to him, but the nearest squatch captor seemed to read her thoughts and shook his head.

If Finn lost this fight, they'd only get a thousand paces' head start before the squatch gave chase, which basically meant that the squatch would kill them as near immediately as made no difference. If, by some miracle, Finn won, they'd get half a day. Sassa thought that probably wasn't nearly enough, but at least it would give them hope.

"Finn!" shouted Thyri Treelegs.

Finn roused. He tried to get up but fell back. His ribs must have been broken by the punch, thought Sassa.

The squatch lumbered over. Finn tried to scrabble away on his back, but the squatch picked him up by one foot, swung him round and round his head, and threw him.

Finn flew twenty paces. All the humans gasped, even Sofi Tornado.

Somehow, he missed the boulders again and landed rolling on the grass. He came to rest near the sword. He clambered up and looked around.

"Your sword's right there!" called Wulf.

"What?" Finn asked, cupping at ear.

"Foe Slicer's right next to you, dummy!" shouted Keef.

Finn looked down. "Oh!"

He picked up the blade and held it aloft. "Thanks!" he shouted.

"Now get on with killing the animal!"

All the squatch turned to look at Keef. They did not like being called animals. Keef grinned back at them, his remaining eye twinkling.

Krusha loped up to Finn. Finn slashed, Krusha swung a fist. Finn dodged and jumped back, then back, and back again as Krusha continued to swing punches.

If one blow connected with his head, thought Sassa, the fight's over.

Krusha punched and punched. Finn jumped further and further back. It was just a matter of time before a hit connected. Sassa felt a sharp pain as she chewed too deep into her lip, but she kept on chewing.

Finn leapt backwards, up onto a broad rock platform. It was surely a fatal error.

What the Wootah and Calnians could see, but Finn couldn't, was the four-pace drop at the other side of the platform, where he was headed.

"Watch out behind you, Finn!" cried Sitsi.

"Look out!" shouted Wulf.

"Stop jumping backwards, you prick!" advised Keef.

Desperately avoiding Krusha's blows and jumping backwards towards his doom, Finn didn't hear.

Sassa put her hands over her face.

"Oh no," she heard Paloma say. She opened her fingers.

Finn was teetering on the edge of the drop. He waved his arms. Krusha drove a fist. Finn fell.

The humans groaned. Even Sofi put her hands over her face.

Finn landed on his feet, bending his knees to absorb the impact. For a moment Sassa thought he was fine, even though it had been a long drop, but he wobbled, slumped back onto the grass and lay still.

The Wootah and Calnians deflated like holed waterskins. The squatch roared triumph. They would get their thousand paces' dash, then there would be slaughter.

Krusha roared gleefully and dived headfirst off the rock platform after the doomed Wootah man.

Sassa was never sure how Finn moved so quickly, even

managed to move at all after falling such
the monster dropped, Finn leapt into a crouc
sword around so that its hilt was braced agair
blade pointing at the falling foe.

The squatch warrior saw his fate but could or
arms and yell. Foe Slicer pierced the screaming,
like a knife into a snowball and burst from the ba
head with a spray of gore. Finn leapt one way. Th
squatch fell the other.

Sassa whooped and jumped up and down. She cou
help it. All around her the Calnians and Wootah were do
the same, shouting, "Woo-tah! Woo-tah!". Even Sofi Tornac
and Yoki Choppa were smiling.

Meanwhile, Finn was trying to heave the squatch's head
over to retrieve his sword, but the beast was too heavy and
Finn gave up, flinging up his hands in flouncy resignation.

Good old Finn, thought Sassa. Not many people could
manage to look that shit only moments after killing a monster
with such a cool and clever move.

a long way. As
h, whipped the
st the ground,
ly wave his
hairy face
k of his
e dead
ldn't
ing
o

...in the Deep to the kindly squatch, *your*
*s to kill you.*

*gantic female squatted so that her black eyes*
with Finn's. She smelled of warm, woolly musk.
..ded pleasantly with the fresh scent of the pine, as
..ie two were meant together. *He may seem like a monster,*
*but you must understand that, from the squatch point of*
*view, humans are the monsters. You eat other animals even*
*though —*

*I'm sorry,* Finn interrupted, *but I heard him think that he*
*means to kill you. I can hear squatch think.*

*Yes, Finn, that's how we talk.*

*No, I can hear your inner thoughts. It's how I beat Krusha.*
*You disagreed with Berlaze in public and he means to kill you*
*for it. He arranged to have you captured by the Badlanders the*
*last time you pissed him off.*

*Inner thoughts?* she asked.

*When your father agreed to give me the sword, you thought*
*that proved that he has some good in him, right?*

Ayla stared at him.

*How?*

*I can hear animals think.*

*But we're not—*

*Okay, sorry, I can hear the minds of creatures that aren't*
*human. At the same time that you were thinking he was good*

*deep down, your father was thinking that he'd have to kill you, since his arrangement with the Badlanders to kidnap you had been screwed up by you escaping. He doesn't like you embarrassing him.*

*What?* Her eyes filled with tears.

Finn tried not to listen, he didn't want to intrude, but he couldn't help hearing her thinking that an agreement between her father and the Badlanders explained a lot about her capture. But how could he have done it? Her own father? Her earliest memory was laughing with him while they hurled boulders into a lake. Surely he loved her as much as she loved him?

Finn regretted his blunt honesty.

*Sorry*, he thought.

*You're sure? What am I thinking now?* She furrowed her brow and stared at him.

*You're thinking about ripping my leg off and beating me to death with it as punishment for suggesting your father had anything to do with the Badlanders catching you, but only as a test to see if I can hear what you're thinking. You wouldn't actually do it. You're also remembering your big sister saying that your father was evil when she left the tribe.*

*I see.*

*Yes. Now you're wondering if you should head west to join your sister even though she used to annoy you. So do. Come west with us. None of us want to kill you.*

*I don't suppose I have much choice.*

*We're not that bad.*

*Sorry, I'm grateful for the offer. It's just—*

*I understand.* Finn nodded, trying to convey hope. *It'll all be fine. Things generally are in my experience.*

*Really?*

Finn thought about Bjarni Chickenhead dying slowly. He remembered Wulf waking him with the words "Gunnhild is dead". *Well . . . no. They're either fine or they're not. But you can't do anything about what's going to happen, so why worry? You die when you die.*

"Come on, Finn!" shouted Wulf the Fat. "We're off!"

*Well*, asked Finn, *coming?*

"Snowline's a mile ahead!" Paloma Pronghorn cheerily reported back to Sofi Tornado when they'd been going half the morning. "It's thin enough on the ground while there's tree cover, and there's a path up the southern side of this valley that'll suit us. A mile further on, however, the trees stop – I guess it's too high up for them – and we're fucked. The snow is hip-deep to begin with. Then it gets deeper."

Sofi looked back. Sitsi Kestrel, Yoki Choppa and Chogolisa Earthquake were behind her, followed by the Wootah tribe, puffing as they paced up through the trees. Chogolisa had Ottar on her shoulders and Ayla was carrying Freydis, and that was about all that could be done to speed things up. Everyone had two of Erik's sinew and wood water-running shoes sticking up from their backpacks. He'd insisted that everyone bring them. Sofi hadn't had the time or inclination to ask why.

The Wootah's fitness had improved markedly after twenty days' hard walking from the Black Mountains. However, the path was steep and strewn with boulders and fallen logs, the Wootah were only unenhanced humans and they were not making fast progress. Sofi pictured squatch sprinting up the hill, leaping over the obstacles with ease. Half a day head start was not enough. Not nearly.

"Head back down the hill, Paloma," she said. "See if the squatch are following, but be careful. Don't get close enough—"

"They said they'd give us half a day."

"Did Berlaze strike you as the sort of fellow who keeps his word?"

*Don't trust him*, thought Ayla from her place next to Ottar and Freydis at the back of the walkers.

*Oh, hello*, thought Paloma. *How close do you need to be to do that crush thing on our minds?*

*About three paces.*

*Your paces or mine?*

*Squatch paces. So maybe ten of yours.*

*Great, thanks.* Paloma liked this communication by thought business. It left more time for running.

"Okay, I'm off!" she told Sofi.

And off Paloma was, hopping downslope between the Wootah. Keef the Berserker nodded to her. Sassa and Wulf smiled. Finn . . . she avoided his inevitable moody glare. She regretted kissing him, but she knew she'd probably do it again if they got through this and got drunk again. She liked a snog after a drink or five, and he was the least bad option in the group. And that was that – the sum of her affection for the man. He was the least unappealing of the available males. Why couldn't he see that, and stop pouting at her like a bullied trout? Most annoyingly, she felt bad about it. She cursed Yoki Choppa for the thousandth time for taking away their rattlesnake. Life had been more fun when they'd been cruel.

Ayla was a furry blur flashing by and Paloma was on her own again, bouncing down the wooded mountainside with huge springing leaps. Elk, chipmunk, a couple of humped bears and other animals heard her coming but didn't have time to flee until she'd flown by.

The tight gorge became a valley, then widened out into meadow. A family of yellow-bellied marmots was looping about next to a splashing stream. Paloma paused to watch them.

The moment she stopped running, she heard squatch thundering across the meadow below. So they hadn't even waited a quarter of a day before beginning their pursuit, the cheating fuckers.

Paloma zipped into the treeline on the valley's northern flank and sprinted between trees until she could see them.

Some three dozen squatch were loping along the valley floor at a serious pace, following the Calnians and Wootah's tracks.

She ran back to the others. Actually, she ran a little past and uphill of them, then bounded down the slope towards them like a bighorn in spring, because she knew it would look better.

"They're coming," she told Sofi.

"How far behind?"

Paloma looked at the sky. "They'll catch up by noon."

Sofi nodded, then yelled: "The squatch are after us already. We have to speed up, a lot. Sitsi, take the lead. Keep the pace as fast as you can. I'll take the rear. Keef, you're with me. Paloma, run back and keep an eye on the squatch. If you can slow them down or lead them off-track, do, but you are not to go within twenty paces of them."

"Ayla said their mind crush only works from three paces."

"You'll stay twenty paces clear. It's not a request."

Paloma opened her mouth to complain, but saw the look in Sofi's eye and closed it again.

The Wootah, Calnians and Ayla the squatch headed off. Were they going any faster? If so, Paloma couldn't tell, and it certainly wasn't nearly fast enough. They were definitely going to be caught, probably before lunchtime.

Yoki Choppa, bringing up the rear, stopped and gave Paloma a meaningful look. She knew what he meant, but she said: "What?"

"Don't go near the squatch." He held eye contact until she had to look away.

"Okay!" A heartbeat later she was a hundred paces away.

Paloma Pronghorn stood on a rock high up on the valley side, legs wide, hands on hips. Her long, loose, dark hair wafted in the refreshing wind flowing down from the snow-caps above. Way below, clouds rolled like smoke over silhouetted, tree-fringed ridges. She'd been in the clouds a few times, but never before had she been above them. It pleased her.

She pressed the balls of her bare feet into the rock and stretched her calves. Half a mile below elk scattered as the squatch galloped across a clearing.

Paloma reckoned her friends might make it to the deep snow before the squatch caught up. Then it would depend on how good squatch were on deep snow. Probably much better than humans. As things were, the Wootah were all going to die, the Owsla too if they tried to save them.

Their quest was to get Ottar the Moaner to The Meadows, so if all else went to shit Sofi would make Paloma take him on her own. The idea of crossing the mountains and then the Desert You Don't Walk Out Of and facing more and more monsters and natural disasters was unappealing enough, but the notion of doing it with a snotty boy for company was unacceptable. So she had to slow the squatch. But how?

A chipmunk scurried onto a nearby juniper log, perched with a pine cone in its paws and looked at her. Paloma wrinkled her nose at it. It dropped the cone, ran in a circle, picked up the nut and resumed its vigil. A rotund little bird with a black and white head watched her from another branch, chirping out a plaintive ditty as if it had something important to say. Below, the leading squatch reached the trees and disappeared.

Sofi had told her to stay twenty paces clear. However, given the element of surprise and a run-up, Paloma reckoned she could sprint in, crack a squatch or two over the head with her killing stick and be twenty paces away before any of the others realised what had happened. A couple of deaths, or serious injuries, would surely make the charging beasts more cautious through the trees and buy a little time?

Of course, last time she'd tried to attack a squatch it had flattened her with a thought before she'd landed a blow. If this lot knocked her out and caught her, they'd rip her apart like a wet leaf.

But this time would be different, she told herself, because she'd surprise them . . . At least she hoped she would. Point was, she had to do it.

She nodded her leave to the chipmunk and the fat bird, took a deep breath of pristine mountain air, leapt from her perch and bounded down the slope towards the running squatch, killing stick in hand.

Sitsi Kestrel, leading the march up the mountain, had started off as fast as she thought the Wootah could manage, then sped up when Paloma had said the squatch were coming. So far the Wootah had kept up.

They were jogging uphill, along a spine between two higher ridges. A forest fire had ravaged the area recently and the trees were blackened, branchless spurs. A variety of fresh green bushes and skinny plants had seized their opportunity and burst from the burned soil.

Hopefully they'd be clear of the trees before the squatch were on them. Then, hopefully again, out in the open she and Sassa would be able to keep the squatch at bay with their bows. But maybe they wouldn't? A moon ago, Sitsi had thought that, given plenty of arrows and an open field, her bow could deal with anything. Since then she'd met the lizard kings and Beaver Man. Both had been impervious to her arrows. Chances were that the squatch were, too.

They couldn't flee any faster, not least because Sassa Lipchewer and Bodil Gooseface were pregnant. A thought that she wouldn't mind too much if Bodil lost her baby flashed into her mind and she banished it instantly. She really did not want Bodil's baby to die, she really didn't. If she did want to split up Bodil and Keef she only need tell him what everyone else knew: that the child was Finn's. But she would never do that.

Their path dipped in and out of a stream which had halted the progress of the recent fire, and they were back into the lush pine forest. The air was fragrant, the light dappled, and there could have been a thousand squatch hiding behind trees. Sitsi's eyesight was enhanced by her power animal, the chuckwalla lizard. She could see the freckles on a frog from a mile away. In thick woods, however, her ability was about as useful as a bent arrow.

The path steepened. The trees were thinning, revealing more glimpses of the snow-capped peaks towering above. They had a long way to go, and if the squatch were already following . . . She looked back. The Wootah were pink-cheeked and sweating, breath condensing in the colder air. How much longer could they keep going?

Keef the Berserker was holding Bodil Gooseface's hand and helping her along. Sitsi quivered with unbidden pique. Finn should have been helping Bodil, but he was too busy lusting over all the other women. At the very least somebody ought to put the three idiots straight over who was actually responsible for the baby. Surely Keef didn't think it was his? Surely he was far too fine a man to be tangled up in Finn and Bodil's nonsense?

She looked past them.

Thyri Treelegs ran next to Sassa Lipchewer. The stocky girl looked the spryest of all the Wootah, prancing along, blade bouncing on her bare thigh. She wore a pouty *I'm just as good as an Owsla* expression. Sassa looked warrior-like, too, especially with the fin haircut Paloma had given her, but she looked like she was about to collapse.

Chogolisa seemed fine with Ottar bouncing on her shoulders, as you'd expect, and Ayla, by her easy gait, was untroubled by carrying Freydis.

Yoki Choppa was next, head down, lower lip protruding,

alchemical bundle jiggling on his shoulder and the surplus fat of his chest and stomach wobbling as he ran. Sofi and Wulf took the rear, like the good leaders they were. There was still no sign of the squatch pursuit behind them, nor of Paloma.

The sudden roar of squatch from lower down the mountain startled her. It was more triumphant hooting than roaring, like hunters who have caught an elusive prey. Sitsi gulped. She hoped Paloma hadn't done anything silly. It would be just like the Pronghorn to disobey Sofi's orders, attack the squatch and get herself killed.

Paloma realised she was holding her breath and made herself exhale. By Innowak, she felt awful. She was crouching in a narrow dry valley in the woods, waiting for the squatch to appear along the path below. She was actually sweating with fear. Sweating with fear! Curse Yoki Choppa yet again for denying them the rattlesnake that made them brave. Bravery was fun. Fear was miserable and made her guts churn. What use could it possibly be?

Then again. She was about to attack an enemy that had defeated her with ease last time she'd attacked them. Perhaps her fear was trying to tell her "what you're about to do is very stupid and you will be killed. Don't do it." Back in Calnia, Paloma had assumed that the Owsla could defeat any opponent in a fight. That view had changed as they'd come west. If one looked at it objectively, Yoki Choppa had removed their fearlessness so that they'd be able to judge when to fight and when to run away. Objectively, it was a good idea.

Objectively, this was a time to run away.

But were pronghorns objective? Actually, she didn't know. It didn't look like there was much at all going on behind their bulbous eyes. Point was, she wasn't running away.

The first squatch pounded onto the path below. By Innowak's burning balls, it was *huge*. Paloma swallowed.

She watched the first few pass, then, before she could persuade herself it was a bad idea — a suicidal idea — she leapt up and sprinted down the gully. Within a heartbeat she was going too fast to stop. If they saw her coming, she was dead.

As she'd hoped, their attention was focussed on the rough track. She skipped off a stump, jumped off a rock and flew, swinging her killing stick.

Her target turned and he (or she, it was hard to tell) was greeted by a faceful of killing stick.

Paloma felt and heard the beast's forehead crack. But at the same moment her head clouded and her vision spiralled.

"No!" she told herself, "you mustn't . . ." and she passed out.

She came to.

She was tumbling. She bounced, ploughed face-first through a pile of pine needles, rolled arse over tit and whumped, upside down, into a fir tree. She fell to the ground, spitting needles.

Roars from above made her jump to her feet. The squatch were crashing down the slope towards her.

She struggled clear of the tree. Thin branches tore at her exposed flesh, but that was way down on her list of worries.

A screaming shout rang out, far too close. She turned. A squatch was diving at her. She leapt away, across the slope and the beast tumbled past. She felt it reach into her mind, but then it was out of range, unable to stop its fall.

A squatch-hurled boulder flashed past her face. She tensed to run, but another rock caught her thigh, hard. The impact knocked her over like a skittle. Roars of triumph rang out.

*We are going to tear you apart!*

*We're going to eat you!*

Paloma sprang up. A squatch was right on her, so close that it didn't need to mind-crush her. It swung a fist. She ducked, then ran.

She was out of its mind-crush range in a hundredth of a heartbeat. One of the great things about being the fastest person in the world was the ability to get out of trouble smartish.

She'd been lucky. She instructed future Paloma to be more careful, knowing full well that future Paloma had no respect whatsoever for the decrees of past Paloma.

There was a dusting of snow on the woodland path. Ankle-deep patches heralded a lot more to come. It was steeper and the Wootah were walking now.

Sofi Tornado joined Sitsi Kestrel at the front to try to increase the pace. A noise high above startled Sofi for the blink of an eye, but she recognised the sound of Paloma skipping swiftly through woodland.

The springy Owsla bounced onto the track ahead of them and waited. She was bleeding from small scratches on her face, legs and arms. There was a bloody bruise on one thigh.

"I think I've slowed them down a bit, but we have to speed up," she said, matching Sofi's walking pace. "Is this really as fast as you've been going?"

"You attacked them," said Sofi.

"Not really, I just—"

"You disobeyed me."

They walked on in silence.

Discipline was becoming increasingly lax with her three remaining Owsla. Paloma Pronghorn had always been cocky, but she'd never disobeyed a clear order before. Even toe-the-line Chogolisa Earthquake and Sitsi Kestrel weren't the dependable followers that they'd once been. A moon or two ago Sofi would have beaten their wilfulness out of them in the practice arena. For disobeying an order, she would have banned Paloma from the arena and missions for a moon and had her performing menial work with the Low.

However, the further westward they marched, the less of a crap Sofi gave about discipline. She didn't think it was her rattlesnake-free diet making her softer. There was no need for the level of control that she'd required for women like Morningstar and Caliska Coyote. Sitsi, Chogolisa and Paloma were simply nicer people.

Sofi's captaincy had become more like Wulf the Fat's lead over the Wootah. It was still effective, but the chasm of authority between her and her troops had narrowed. She'd never have admitted it to the women, but she was becoming less their leader and more their friend. A dominant friend who'd take no shit, but a friend nevertheless.

Sofi fell back to join Ayla.

"Berlaze said that the force at The Meadows was the work of the Warlock Queen. Do you know what he meant by that?"

*No. There is a legend of a Warlock Queen who won a war and united the Warrior and Warlock tribes, but she's long dead.*

They emerged from the trees onto bare mountainside. The snow was ankle-deep and the path was gone.

*Head towards the peak on the left*, thought Ayla.

The snow was soon knee-deep. The Wootah puffed plumes of white exertion. Their pace slowed.

Paloma looked over her shoulder, first at the Wootah, then at Sofi. A squatch roar reverberated from the trees, much louder now. "You're going to ask me to carry Ottar to safety, aren't you?"

Sofi nodded.

"You should come, too. I'll put him on my shoulders and tie his feet, freeing up both arms to pull you, then—"

"No." There was a dark rock outcrop ahead. Sofi reckoned that if they could reach that, Sitsi's arrows and hurled boulders might keep the squatch at bay. Possible but not likely. The odds of finding a helpful pile of boulders were not far

off zero and she doubted that even Sitsi's arrows would slow
a squatch.

They were in trouble. The best they could do was press
on and hope for a miracle.

They waded on through deep snow. Sofi looked back. Falling
away to the east behind them was a series of ever lower
wooded ridges, draped in scraps of wet cloud that reminded
Sofi of dew-sodden spider web on the Ocean of Grass.
Somewhere in those hills' shadowed folds was the plateau
where the squatch had held them. Beyond were endless miles
of plain leading back to Calnia and Hardwork. Those two
places that had seemed so far apart were now clumped
together geographically in her mind, the distance between
them made to seem like nothing by the vastly greater distance
that they'd travelled west across the Ocean of Grass.

A squatch emerged from the trees. Berlaze. He stood,
roaring and beating his chest.

Bodil screamed.

More squatch poured from the trees and joined in Berlaze's
triumphant bellowing.

"Spunk on a skunk," said Sassa.

"Sitsi, shoot. Everyone else, run," said Sofi.

Sitsi strung her bow, nocked an arrow, aimed and loosed
it in a heartbeat. It was a marvellous shot. Berlaze dodged
it, moving at a speed nor far off Paloma's.

"Fucknuts," said Keef.

"Run! Run!" called Wulf.

They waded on.

Sofi looked back.

The squatch were walking calmly. And catching up.

She looked ahead. The snowfield stretched on and on, up
and up. The squatch would be on them before they were a
tenth of the way up it, if the Wootah could keep going. But
they were already slowing.

"I can't go on!" wailed Bodil.

"Everyone stop!" shouted Erik the Angry.

"Yeah, great idea, Erik," said Keef.

"Seriously, stop . . . I've got a . . . plan," Erik panted.

"Everyone stop!" shouted Wulf. "What is it, Erik?"

Erik put his hand on his knees and puffed out a cloud of condensation.

The squatch were closer and closer.

"Anytime now would be good, Erik," said Sofi.

"Everyone take out their . . . rackets from their packs!" Erik managed. "Strap them onto your feet. These are for you, Ayla." He held up a larger pair of rackets.

"Rackets on our feet? Why?" asked Bodil Gooseface.

"Do as he says," said Yoki Choppa.

Sofi could see it, too.

"Owsla, strap on your snow shoes," she ordered.

Sassa attached the wooded frames with half an eye on the approaching squatch. There was no way they were going to get away.

She finished strapping the first shoe. The squatch were maybe a hundred paces away. The one next to Berlaze tapped the chief's arm and pointed at the Wootah and Calnians. Berlaze nodded.

The squatch started running.

Sassa scrabbled at the straps of her second shoe. A squeak of fear escaped her chewing lips. She was not far from sobbing.

They were closer now, fifty paces.

Finally, she got the shoe strapped on. Chogolisa had finished too and was swinging Ottar up onto her shoulders.

"Come on!" said Wulf, taking her arm.

*We're going to catch you and tear you apart!* a squatch mind-shouted. More threats followed. Horrible, ugly threats.

Sassa tried to ignore them and focus on moving as fast as she could on the weird shoes. It felt unnatural. It felt precarious. The broad frames crunched through the crust of snow maybe the breadth of a little finger, but sank no further.

"Keep your feet apart!" called Erik. "Don't step on your own shoes!"

"Faster, faster!" Wulf cried. Sassa looked about. Everyone else was ahead of them. How come they'd got their shoes on so much more quickly than she had, she wondered. Legs wide, arses out, they were running up the hill like a squad of duck people. It would have been funny if it wasn't for –

*We will eat your brains!* mind-shouted a squatch.

She looked back. The squatch were a dozen paces behind. An arrow zipped over her shoulder. Berlaze ducked it.

*You, human with the yellow crest of hair!* Sassa heard, loud and unpleasant as if someone was shouting in her ear, *I'm going to rip your leg off and beat you with it! I'm going to snap your neck and bite the top off your head and drink your brain!*

Another couple of heartbeats and they'd be in mind-crush range.

"Come on!" shouted Sofi. "Faster!"

Sassa put her head down and focused on running, driving her legs like a mad woman.

The squatch had stopped hurling insults, but she could hear their heavy paces and grunting. Maybe, just maybe, their perusuers were tiring. She didn't want to turn. She thought of the baby growing inside her. She had to run, run run.

She had a flash of memory; as a girl maybe eight years old wading through the snow at her parents' farm in Hardwork to fetch food from the very shed that the Calnians had burned down at the start of all this. That had been the cold but sweaty arseache to end all arseaches.

She looked up. Sofi was waiting for them. She dared to turn. The squatch were now fifty paces behind. Sassa's relief at realising they might actually make it gave her another burst of energy.

"We can slow down a little," said Sofi. "They're tiring."

"Can I stay and fight them?" yelled Keef.

"Sure, go for it," called Wulf.

Keef leapt around and landed wide-footed like a giant frog, Arse Splitter at the ready. He was grinning, but it was a worried grin.

"Wow," he said, "there must be fifty of them."

"Sixty-one," said Sofi, jogging past. "Good luck."

"Are you sure you'll allow me to fight them, Hird leader Wulf?"

"On second thoughts, Keef, no. I command you to run with the rest of us."

"Is that your final order, Wulf? There's no way you'll let me stay?"

"Don't push it, Keef."

"Okay! I'll do as ordered!" Keef the Berserker leapt back round and ran.

Sassa jogged on. Next time she dared to turn, the squatch were two hundred paces behind, labouring through waist-deep powder.

"Snow's deeper!" chirped Sitsi. "It's slowed them!"

Well, obviously, thought Sassa, but she didn't say anything.

A few paces ahead of her, Keef, Erik, Wulf and Finn stopped and saw how far back their pursuers had fallen. They pulled down their trousers, waggled their bare arses at the squatch and shouted "Wooooooo-TAH!"

# Chapter 5

## Suffocation

On the one hand, Finn the Deep had had quite enough of trudging uphill. How come it was so much harder than just walking along? On the other hand, he was stupefied by the wondrousness of the snow-capped peaks. It had been summer on the plains, but up here, surely near the top of the mountains now, it was like the middle of winter. Despite the cold which hurt his ears and made his eyes water, the sun glared off rises and valleys, blinding white and sparkling as if the snow had been sown with billions of tiny crystals. Rising out of the white here and there were great, wet, dirty-looking craggy brown cliffs.

Surely this was where the gods lived? Finn half expected to see Tor bounding over the nearest brow, great hammer in one hand, huge mug of ale in the other.

As if to prove him wrong, chubby little birds, very similar to the ones that had filled the woods of Hardwork, flitted about, perching on wooden poles that poked out of the snow here and there. *Look,* they seemed to say, *this is simply more of the world, just like Hardwork. It's nowhere special, so don't think you're special for being up here.*

Finn reached out into their minds and made a connection, but all he found was the joy of flying and a sense that the humans and the following squatch were interesting and probably not threats, but an eye should be kept on them nevertheless.

He looked back. The squatch were a very long way away.

"Can we slow the pace?" Finn asked nobody in particular.

"No," said Sofi. "We don't know how long we're going to be in snow. It may have all blown off the west side of the mountains. So let's get as far ahead as we can before they start catching up again."

"Good point, got it." Finn grinned. She'd bothered to explain. Time was she would have just said "No". Having this wonderful-looking warrior – wearing only her scant battle gear despite the chill – treat him with respect made him forget the cold.

"What are the poles?" he asked Ayla, pointing at wooden posts.

*There are fences and a few huts under the snow,* she answered, *left behind by the people who lived here before we did. The poles are remnants of their largest constructions.*

"People lived up here in the snow?"

*It's not usually snowy this low down at this time of year. They say the freak weather is the work of the force at The Meadows.*

So The Meadows can make a tornado over a thousand miles away, send a weird, enormous insect dragon that bursts into wasps a few hundred miles, and cover these mountains with snow, Finn mused. On top of that, Ottar the Moaner, who'd never been wrong before, said that this was nothing, the force was building up monsters and disasters for an onslaught that was going to kill every creature in the world.

And they were planning to take it on with a few pieces of sharpened metal, a smattering of stone weaponry and a boy who was a good few nuts short of a full basket.

Ayla led them up and along a crescent-shaped ridge. There was a drop of a couple of hundred paces to the right, down to a flat area which Finn guessed was a frozen, snow-covered lake. The cliff on the far side of the lake was fringed with a skirt of dirty snow, which had presumably fallen from the top, collecting dirt as it tumbled.

"You see?" said Erik, "it's just like Beaver Man said. The water, or snow in this case, carries the land downhill bit by bit."

Finn looked back. Sitsi Kestrel was at the rear, a hundred paces behind, bow ready. The cloud shifted and he caught a glimpse of the following squatch. They were spread out a long, long way below, further behind than Finn had dared hope they might be.

But they were still following. He'd been lucky against Krusha. If the beasts caught up, all of them, well, all of the Wootah anyway, were going to be ripped to bits. And it wouldn't take much. All it needed was a couple of snow shoes to break, or Ayla to lead them up a dead-end valley, and they'd be caught.

Finn felt sick with fear.

As if they'd spotted him watching, a few of the squatch stopped and opened their arms. It took a heartbeat for the sound of their roars to reach the walkers on the ridge. The other squatch stopped and joined in, roaring and roaring. Waves of sound washed over the fleeing Wootah and Calnians.

"What are they doing?" he asked Erik.

"I'm not sure. Maybe – oh, fuck."

A deep rumbling rose out of the very snow they were standing on.

The ground shook.

"Run!" shouted Erik.

"I thought you said—"

"Shut the fuck up and run!"

Finn felt the ground drop below his feet. He ran and ran over the shifting snow. The land was falling away, as if it had suddenly decided to flow downhill.

He clipped one snow shoe against the other and stumbled, but righted himself. He ran, keeping his legs wide.

Soon he was exhausted but the ground was firm. He dared to turn. The ridge was tumbling away behind them, sending up huge clouds of snow. Sitsi Kestrel was a good way back, running duck-like on her snow shoes, arms pumping like weird little wings. Magnificent plumes of snow exploded behind her. Right behind her. She was never going to make it.

Finn made to run back but Erik put a hand on his shoulder. "You can't help her."

He was right. Even if he reached her before the avalanche caught her, which he wouldn't, there was nothing he could do to speed her escape from it. Trying to help would be suicide.

The cloud of swirling snow overtook Sitsi and she disappeared.

Something thundered past Erik and Finn, kicking up its own clouds of snow. Paloma Pronghorn.

She was too late.

Sitsi was gone, but Paloma shot into the swirling snow anyway and disappeared.

One moment Sitsi Kestrel could see blue sky, snow, mountains and the Calnians and Wootah fleeing with Erik and Finn bringing up the rear. The next, a cloud of snow exploded around her and even her alchemically enhanced eyes couldn't penetrate the whirling white.

She tried to accelerate. It didn't help. It was like trying to run up a waterfall.

She was near panicking, not because she was about to fall to her death – chances were she'd survive the fall with her toughened Owsla bones – but because she couldn't see. She hated not being able to see! Suddenly she was falling. If felt like she was tumbling backwards, somersaulting head over heels, but it was impossible to know. She *hated* not being able to see.

She realised she might not survive the fall because the avalanche surely was going to deliver her directly to the squatch. One of them would probably grab her like a bear hoiking a salmon out of a river. The analogy probably didn't stop there. It would beat her brains out on a rock and eat her. Or maybe eat her alive! Feet first, then –

She waved her arms and her legs. Could she fly clear of the avalanche? It seemed like she'd been falling far too long. It was maybe a hundred paces from the ridge to the frozen lake below. She hoped the ice was thick.

Whump! She halted with a sickening thud as something whacked her head like a mallet.

She was alive. She still couldn't see. Neither could she move her arms and legs. Was her back broken? No. She could feel the wood of her bow still gripped in her hand. She could shift her shoulders, clench her buttocks and move her toes.

She was buried.

She tried to move her limbs again. No good. She was immobilised by the weight of the snow piled on top of her. The simple problem had a simple solution. She had to dig to the surface. If badgers and groundhogs could do it . . .

She shushed the voice that told her that she didn't have digging claws and powerful forelimbs, and that burrowing mammals generally started at the surface rather than entombed below it.

One leg was bent, the other straight. The arm holding her bow was above her head – or possibly below, it was impossible to tell – and her other arm was pressed into her chest, her hand by her mouth.

She opened her eyes and felt snow push against her huge pupils, scratchy and cold. She closed them again. Her eyes were no use to her here.

She told herself to be calm. She had to think. Snow pressed into her ears, a loud, painfully cold silence.

First priority was air. She wiggled her fingers in front of

her face, clearing a space around her mouth and nose. She sucked in a cold but delicious breath. An achievement. A good start.

Calm, calm, she told herself, exhaling gently. She dribbled a little saliva. It ran down her right cheek. So now she knew which way was up. Her straight left arm, the one holding her bow, was nearest the surface.

Slowly, so as not to exert herself and use up the little air she had, she pressed down on her bent foot. There was the tiniest give but no more. It was the snow shoes. They were really very good at not going through snow. She wrenched her knee towards her chest, hoping to snap the twine binding them to her foot. No good.

She tried her other leg. Same thing. It was held fast by the snow shoe.

She couldn't move. She might as well be encased in rock. There was no hope! She was going to die!

Don't panic, she told herself. Don't panic.

Her legs were deepest, so the compacted snow would be most dense around them. With the added hindrance of the snow shoes, it was no wonder she couldn't move them.

So she should focus on her upper arm. For all she knew, it was at the surface. It could even be sticking out. Although given the pressure in her ears, she doubted she was near the surface.

Rotating her wrist from side to side, she found she could wiggle her bow, then her whole arm. Unfortunately, this sent snow cascading into her precious breathing space. She wriggled her fingers to clear the space again, but it was tougher this time. Power had sapped from her fingers. It was the cold, she realised. Her extremities were stiffening.

It was a very annoying situation.

She could move her arm a little, but any more and it would fill her breathing hole again, and what would it achieve? Her legs were stuck, her torso was stuck, her head was stuck.

She was stuck. She'd been a good hundred paces behind the others. Anyone who'd run back to help her would have been caught in the avalanche, too, and be buried nearby, maybe even beneath her.

So no Calnians or Wootah would be digging her out. Where she'd fallen, she'd be much closer to the chasing squatch, anyway. She'd rather die under the snow than be dug out by them.

So she was going to die.

No. She had to get out. She twisted her hand. Suddenly, her bow flicked free. Her bow and her hand were above the surface!

She should wave it for help, she thought.

If she wanted the squatch to help her.

She pulled down on the bow, trying to use it to lift herself . . . no. It was like trying to pull herself up one-handed onto a slim branch, with someone heavy holding her feet.

The bow pressed into the snow and, if anything, she sank a little deeper.

She drove her elbow outwards. If she could clear a tunnel above herself, maybe that would relieve pressure on her . . .

The little cave around her mouth filled again. Snow pressed on her lips and up her nose.

She almost swore. It really was vexing. She was going to die!

She couldn't move the fingers of her right hand now. She couldn't clear her hole. She tried to bend her left arm, but the collapsing snow had stuck it fast. She could no longer move her bow.

Perhaps more snow had tumbled off the ridge onto her. Maybe the squatch were standing above, piling on snow, enjoying her suffering?

She heaved with everything she had. Nothing. She could not move at all.

Her nose was clogged. She pursed her lips – she wasn't completely immobile! – and tried to suck in air. She got snow.

She could not breathe.

She had maybe a hundred heartbeats, maybe two hundred. Then she'd be dead.

There was nothing to do but wait.

She thought about her boring, sensible parents, who'd tried to teach her to be sensible and boring, then been proud and horrified when the Emperor Zaltan had chosen her for the Owsla. She thought about her simple-minded older brothers, so annoying when she'd been younger, then so heart-burstingly adorable in their guile-free cheerfulness. She'd been so proud when her place in the Owsla had helped them and protected them.

Innowak knew what state they'd find Calnia in when they got back from their quest, with the empress dead and the army destroyed by Beaver Man's monsters. Sitsi had been hoping to swing by and save her family from whatever dire circumstances they were suffering. Shoot a few baddies, whisk her parents and brothers to safety, earn their eternal gratitude and adoration. That had been the plan.

She was going to miss Sofi, Chogolisa and Paloma, Yoki Choppa and the Wootah, too. She hoped they were going to be okay without her. She was going to miss shooting food for them, being their lookout and long-range protector.

Most of all, she regretted that she wasn't going to spend any more time with Keef the Berserker. She wanted to hear more of his jokes, laugh at his antics and simply be with him, watching the sunset or preparing to face a foe.

Tears welled. No. She wouldn't cry. She was Owsla. She would die with her head held high, metaphorically at least.

She could feel her heart beating against her contracting lungs. How many more times would it do that? She wanted to breathe so much. She didn't want to die. She wanted her mum and dad. She wanted Keef.

There was movement above her, crunching in the snow. The squatch! They were going to dig her out and rip her to bits, like a coyote digging out a hibernating groundhog.

Something grabbed her wrist and pulled. Something very strong. The snow shoes were torn off her feet. She could move her legs now and – she could breathe!

She sucked in sweet air as she fell back onto snow, so overjoyed with its marvellous taste that she thought her heart might burst and kill her anyway. Then she looked up, ready to fight.

Paloma Pronghorn was standing over her, hands on hips, grinning.

"Hello!" she said.

"Hi."

Paloma reached down. "We don't have much fannying around time."

Sitsi shook snow from her hair and let Paloma pull her up. The avalanche debris was churned in clumps all around. Above them was a newly exposed brown-black, rocky ridge. A hundred paces down the slope, the lead squatch was headed for them, annoyingly fast over the rough ground. More were following. They had no fannying around time at all.

"My snow shoes are buried," said Sitsi, brushing snow of her bare skin, teeth chattering. "I'll never—"

"Stand on the back of mine," said Paloma, turning. "And hold onto my waist as tightly as you can."

Sitsi did as she was told. And they were off.

Paloma leapt across the avalanche's jumbled debris like a happy mountain goat, as if Sitsi's extra weight was nothing.

Moments later they were heading back up the mountain, which happened to be towards the squatch.

"Um, Paloma?" said Sitsi.

The lead squatch saw his chance and speeded up. He was twenty paces away, fifteen.

"Paloma!"

The speedy woman veered away, over a pile of snow

and then on up the mountain. The squatch roared behind them.

Sitsi hugged Paloma tighter and pressed her face into the taller woman's back. "Thanks," she said.

"Any time!" Paloma yelled.

"Hopefully it's not going to happen again." Sitsi looked back. The squatch were already so far behind that they could have stopped for lunch and still escaped.

Soon they spotted the others, already heading away across the mountains. Sitsi didn't mind that they'd carried on without her. What else were they going to do?

Sofi heard them coming and told the others. They all turned and cheered and shouted "Wootah!" Keef waved Arse Splitter around his head and danced from one foot to the other.

Sitsi beamed as they crowded around the pair of them, and almost cried with happiness when Erik handed her a spare pair of snow shoes. She knew she looked very emotional, very un-Owsla, but she didn't care. She really was very glad to see them all again.

"Welcome back, Sitsi," said Sofi. "Well done, Paloma."

The group set off together again, tramping up across bare snow, clouds boiling up in wisps around them. The going was flat for a while, then downhill. Sitsi guessed they had reached and passed the summit, or at least the highest shoulder of mountain that they were going to climb. She regretted the clouds. Perhaps she'd have been able to see all the way back to Calnia if it had been clear.

Keef the Berserker dropped back to walk beside her.

"Squatch catch up, I'll help you split their arses."

"Great, thanks," said Sitsi.

They walked on together in silence. Sitsi found herself smiling. She felt deeply and deliriously happy. For the feeling it gave one afterwards, it was almost worth facing certain death.

Soon there were trees all around again, but they mostly walked along clear fields of snow, which Sitsi guessed was grassland in summer.

Ayla stopped the others and waited for Sitsi and Keef to catch up at a low rise, where, judging by the young trees poking out, the snow was about a pace deep.

*This*, thought the squatch, *is the Great Divide.*

"Doesn't look that Great," said Keef.

"That's what I said," agreed Finn.

Ayla stood with her legs spread. *We are standing on the spine of the world*, she thought to them. *The snow under my left foot will melt and flow eastward, to the Water Mother and eventually the Great Salt Sea. The snow under my right foot will melt and flow westward, into the Red River, through the baking desert and into the Endless Ocean, thousands of miles away.*

*A snowflake that lands by this foot*, she pointed at one of them, *will end up the farthest imaginable distance from one that lands by the other.*

"Wow," said Sitsi. "Amazing. Can you feel it?" she asked Keef.

"Do you mean can I feel the weight of destiny, here on the Great Divide?" Keef jutted his chin heroically. "Can I feel the pull of the great bodies of water that lie hundreds of miles apart? Are you asking me whether it feels like I'm on a rope swing and it's the moment when I've reached the highest point and, just for a heartbeat, I've stopped, but I can feel the inescapable force that's going to drag me back?"

"Yes!" Sitsi bounced on her toes. "That's exactly it!"

"Nope, can't feel that at all," he grinned. "But Arse Splitter is going to split the arse of a world. Hiiii-ya!" he leapt and swung his long axe to chop into the snow.

Sitsi shook her head.

Wulf, Thyri and Paloma were jumping from one side of

the divide to the other. Yoki Choppa was standing with a
foot on either side, looking thoughtful. Sassa and Bodil were
watching the jumpers, smiling. When they thought nobody
was looking, Erik and Chogolisa kissed with pursed lips
across the divide. Freydis and Ottar changed the destiny of
a few snowballs.

Sofi was standing back, watching them all, a troubled
look on her face.

They headed down the mountain, along a valley with wooded
sides and finally onto a muddy path. They stopped to remove
their snow shoes then splashed along, Calnians barefoot,
Wootah in their green tribe boots. The mammals that had been
scarce on the mountain's bare summit reappeared in multitudes.
Shaggy but majestic mountain goats regarded them suspiciously
from craggy grey outcrops. A group of humped bears bided
their time threateningly on the mountainside ahead, then
ambled into the trees when Chogolisa charged them.

A stream bounced down out of the mountain, then flowed
away, then back again, as if flirting with the path. Water
splashed off rocks, spraying rays of dazzling sunlight. Ayla
said that the happy little torrent would become the mighty
Red River that ran all the way to the Endless Ocean.

A manic child becoming a stately ruler, thought Sitsi.
The hills were alive with metaphor.

"The squatch will catch us on this terrain," said Sofi when
they paused to eat.

"You think they're still following?" Sitsi looked back up
the slope. "The avalanche would have slowed them a lot.
Surely they've given up?"

*There are other routes*, thought Ayla, *and squatch do not
like to be thwarted. They will be chasing.*

"Then we build rafts," said Erik.

"This stream wouldn't take a canoe, let alone a raft," Sofi
replied.

Erik looked up at the high valley sides. "Give it a while," he replied. "This stream will be a river soon and we'll be able to float away."

Erik was both right and wrong. The stream did broaden rapidly into something that an optimist might have called a river, and it would probably have been navigable, had it not been for the beaver dams every few hundred paces.

"We could smash the dams as we go?" suggested Keef.

"Nope," said Yoki Choppa.

"Do you worship them or something?" Keef rolled his eye.

"We don't worship beaver any more than you do," Paloma replied for the warlock, "but we do know a lot more about everything. Smashing the dams wouldn't speed our passage, because the part you can see is only the top. Under the water the beavers' homes are strong enough to survive a flash flood or a hunger-maddened bear. You'd be quicker crawling backwards down the hill than to canoe and smash every dam on the way."

"Even with Arse Splitter?"

"Tell you what," Paloma suggested, "why don't you and Arse Splitter stay here and destroy this dam, then catch us up and tell us how long it took?"

"Can't do that. Only Arse Splitter and me can save you from the squatch."

"We could carry the rafts around the dams?" suggested Erik.

"We could," said Sofi, "but it would be quicker to walk."

So they half walked, half jogged along the widening river. Paloma ran back up the mountain to see how their pursuers were doing.

When the sky was beginning to pink in the west, Wulf jogged up to join Sofi and Sitsi.

"Let's make rafts." he said. "We haven't passed a dam for

a good mile. We can walk round any that we do come to. Plus there's good wood around here." He nodded at a stand of fir trees.

"We're making reasonable progress," said Sofi. "Building rafts will take time."

"True, but on rafts we'll be able to go all night. We can sleep and steer in shifts."

"That," said Sofi, "is a good point. Any squatch in sight, Sitsi?"

Sitsi looked back the way they had come. She caught a glimpse of Paloma a few miles upslope, chasing a herd of elk around a grassy knoll.

"I think we're okay for now," she said.

Paloma joined them before they'd cut down more than a couple of trees.

"The squatch turned back before the divide," she said.

*How do you know?* asked Ayla.

"Tracks."

*Squatch don't tend to give up. They do tend to falsify tracks and follow a different path.*

They looked around. To the west the sky was fiery red. The tree-lined river was busy with humming insects and feasting birds. There was no sign of squatch, but they'd already seen how good the creatures were at concealing themselves.

# Chapter 6

## A New Hope

Wootah and Calnians floated through the night. The air warmed as they bobbed downstream, the woods were increasingly fragrant and the screeches and growls of nocturnal wanderers ever more frequent. Some of the Wootah slept briefly, but all had to wake a few times to carry the rafts round dams, to push across gravel shallows and to circumnavigate a waterfall. The going was, however, relatively easy and they covered many more miles than they would have done walking tired in the dark.

Ayla ran alongside the river, proving, Finn the Deep couldn't help notice, how easily squatch could keep up with rafts.

In the morning they stopped for breakfast, to improve the rafts and construct one more, and to provision so that they wouldn't need to stop again for a while.

Returning from relieving himself in the bushes, Finn met Ayla.

*I am going back now*, she thought.

*I thought you were going to visit your sister?*

Ayla sighed and looked towards the mountains. *That's not why I left my father's tribe. I want to be with the children. Ottar is a very special boy. And Freydis . . . perhaps Freydis is even more special.*

*Why do you say that?*

*No one reason.*

*So come with us and see if you're right.*

*No. My father won't give up. His pride has been stung and he has nothing else to do. He and the other squatch will chase us. They'll enjoy it, they won't tire and they will catch you. Unless I go back and stop them.*

*But they'll kill you,* thought Finn.

*I don't think so. My father will remember that I am his daughter. I may be able to persuade them that you're not worth it.*

*Thanks!*

*I think you're worth it.*

*What if you can't persuade them?*

*Then I will fight my father. He is old. I will defeat him.*

*But you know this territory, we need you.*

*Ottar knows where you're going. He knows where to find my sister Taanya. She has lived over here for a while and should know what's happening in The Meadows. She might even know how you can defeat whatever it is. She is difficult, but she is intelligent.*

*You can speak to Ottar?*

*Yes.*

*Directly?*

*No, I have to go through Freydis, same as everyone else.*

*That's strange.*

*I'd love to stay and wonder about it with you, but I've got to go. Please say farewell to the others for me. I would do it myself, but I don't like goodbyes.*

*But . . .* thought Finn, but Ayla was off, loping up the hill.

Finn returned to the riverbank to find Bodil standing by a tree, shaking her hands, looking like she didn't know what to do with herself.

"Ottar's found a monster in the bushes," she explained, pointing shakily downstream. Finn headed off.

He met Keef. "What's Ottar found?" He asked.

"Big insect."

"An insect?" Typical of Bodil to get in a tiz about nothing, thought Finn.

He climbed a rise between leafy trees and found the others on a flattened area of reeds. By the stink that assaulted his nostrils, it wasn't an insect. It took a sizeable dead animal to produce that level of ming. Chogolisa heard him coming and stood aside so he could have a look.

"Ah," he said.

It did look like an insect, but it was bigger than a man. It had hands like a man, on the end of insectoid limbs. One limb was thrown over its head. This one ended in a huge black pincer.

Flies feasted on the goo that leaked from its smashed head.

"That pincer could cut me in half," said Finn.

"It's the wings I'm worried about," said Thyri.

*Fuck, yes*, thought Finn. He'd thought it was lying on a leathery black sheet, but Treelegs was right. So the thing could fly.

"If I was as slow as you lot I'd be worried about its stinger too," Paloma shoved the beast over with a foot, to reveal a long, pointed, black sting protruding from its lower back.

"I hope there aren't any more of these wasp men," said Sassa, looking west.

Everyone followed her gaze. Nobody said anything, but Finn knew what they were thinking. You don't get just one of any animal. There were likely to come across a whole lot more, and a whole lot worse, before they got very much further.

"We'll be ready," said Sofi. "Come on, let's get going before the squatch catch up."

They walked back to the rafts, debating who'd go on which now that they'd made an extra one.

Back at the river, Finn saw Ottar grab Wulf and look around with his hands open. He seemed to be asking *where?*

"Anyone seen Ayla?" asked Wulf.

"Oops, sorry, I meant to say," said Finn. He'd been thinking about the wasp man, specifically how much he didn't want a flock of them flying at him, and had forgotten about Ayla leaving. Not great.

"What?" asked Wulf.

Ottar looked at him, blue eyes huge and worried.

"She's gone."

Ottar blinked tears.

"She said we've got to find her sister. She says you'll know the way, Ottar. Do you know the way?"

Ottar's glare was so full of rage that Finn took a step back. The boy screamed at him, and Finn braced himself for an attack, but instead the little Wootah threw his head back and wailed.

"Don't cry!" Finn tried. "We'll see her again, I'm sure, and maybe her sister's even nicer and—"

He felt a gentle pressure on his arm and looked down.

"Let him cry," said Freydis. "He'll stop soon."

Ottar the Moaner was still snivelling several hours later. Finn knew because, surprise surprise, he was on Ottar's raft. His other boat mates were Freydis the Annoying, Yoki Choppa and Paloma Pronghorn. At least Paloma was meant to be on their raft, but so far she'd been running alongside the river, scouting the nearby hills, and hadn't so much as laid a toe on the raft that she was meant to be crewing.

They had a brief stop in the early afternoon next to a large pile of washed-up timber to repair and improve their craft. Finn took the opportunity to ask Wulf if there could perhaps be a warrior on his raft, in case they came across living wasp men or any other nasties.

"You've got Paloma," he replied.

"Theoretically, but she hasn't actually been on the raft yet. She's always scouting."

"Then you've got you. Finn the Deep, wielder of Foe Slicer, slayer of the squatch, giant serpent scarcer, and pigeon-controlling saviour of all of us. What's to worry about?"

"Giant insects with claws that will take your head off and stings that'll do Loakie knows what?"

"Can you see any of those around?"

A gold-tinted, striped squirrel stretched out on a nearby rock. Behind it was a grassy meadow filled with yellow flowers where a herd of elk peacefully grazed.

"It's too quiet," said Finn.

"It's not. If it were too quiet, there'd be no squirrels or elk."

"It probably won't stay like this. Can you ask Paloma to stop running about so much and stay on our raft?"

"No. She's scouting, and, anyway, I can't tell her what to do."

"How about putting Thyri on our raft?"

"Finn." Wulf put a hand on his shoulder. "Neither Thyri nor Paloma want to be on your boat. And you don't need them. Come to terms with that, my friend, and you'll have a happier voyage."

They travelled on, rafts bobbing along on the current. Night came but Finn was awake, thinking about what Wulf had said. He sat with Foe Slayer on his lap all through the dark and watched the sky become grey, then pink, then fiery red.

The others woke. Ottar seemed happier.

They floated past grassland and woods draped over low, craggy hills. Otters and muskrats plopped into the water as they passed, the odd bear and wolf watched them go by and Freydis said that she saw a lion.

The sky seemed lower and bluer than it had been to the east of the Shining Mountains. Perhaps, Finn thought with a shudder of fear, it was caused by the force at The Meadows. He scanned for flying monsters but saw only chubby bank-side birds and eagles wheeling over hills.

Wulf, Keef and Erik didn't seem too worried. They spent most of their time in the water, larking about and swimming from raft to raft. Finn felt no urge to join them. He was ready to protect his raft – which Paloma didn't ever set foot on. Who knew where she slept, but it wasn't on the raft. She appeared on the bank every now and then, shouted that there was no sign of the squatch, wasp men or any other evils, and ran off again.

By mid-morning, Finn was beginning to relax and even considering taking a nap. Of course, about twenty heart-beats later, they passed a destroyed village. Only one hut remained intact, and that had a smashed human skeleton hanging upside down from its roof. Freydis and Ottar were already gawping at it by the time Finn thought to cover their eyes.

"Animals have eaten the flesh, fat, muscles and brains," Freydis told Ottar, "so that it can all go back into the ground and become life again."

"Should we stop?" Erik yelled from the rearmost raft.

"There's nobody living." Sofi called back from the leading craft. "And we have all the kit we need. Let's carry on."

By the third evening they'd passed several more broken and deserted settlements, but seen no more monsters, dead or alive, nor any sign of squatch pursuit. They beached the rafts on a grassy island crowned with a copse of broadleaf trees. Sofi declared that they would sleep on dry land to give everyone a proper rest. They arranged the rafts so that they were ready to launch in a heartbeat and set double watches.

After three days' almost constant motion, none of them could walk straight. Ottar and Freydis squealed with delight to see elegant Sofi, mighty Chogolisa and prim Sitsi zigzagging from place to place. Wulf hammered it up with "whooahs!" and "whoopses!" and the children laughed so much that Finn feared they might choke.

Ottar and Freydis were still laughing long after everyone was walking normally again.

"Sofi was like this!" laughed Freydis, pouting sombrely, sticking out out her arse and wiggling it from side to side.

A raised eyebrow from the captain of the Owsla stopped the mimicry but not the giggling.

After they'd eaten, Finn steeled himself to ask Thyri if she would train with him.

"Sure thing," she said, even smiling a little as she did so.

They rafted across the narrow channel, found a flat area of grass and sparred, watched from a treeline some hundred paces distant by a couple of foxes. They trained hard. Finn focused on all he'd learned and almost succeeded in not considering how wonderful Thyri looked in her scanty battle gear, jumping about with her sax blade flashing in the low sun.

"You've imporved," she said after he'd blocked a dozen of her thrusts.

"I guess I've realised that we might be fighting some serious monsters soon."

"We've fought thunder lizards and dagger-tooth cats."

"Yeah, but then I just had to make friends with some birds."

"Don't do yourself down, Finn. You beat a squatch with your sword."

"I tricked him."

"Trickery is a major part of it. If you—" she swung her blade upwards and wapped him in the bollocks with the flat of it before he even knew it was coming.

It wasn't hard, but it was hard enough. He dropped his sword, spread his knees, cupped his balls with both hands and opened and closed his mouth in a silent scream.

"As is staying on your guard," said Thyri, smiling at him properly for the first time, it seemed, since Garth Anvilchin had died.

When they returned, the Owsla were wet-haired, sitting by the fire to dry. None of them looked happy. Even Sitsi was scowling.

"What happened?" Finn asked Chogolisa.

"Talisa White-tail died in the Water Mother because she couldn't swim. Sofi doesn't want the same thing happening to us."

"Why so glum? Swimming's fun."

"Not when you can't do it," said Chogolisa.

"But it's easy."

"Everything becomes more difficult when you're old," said Thyri. "Swimming, fighting, not being a dick – it's all much easier to learn when you're a child. I'm sure you agree, Finn?"

She walked away, not even sparing him a glance to see if he agreed.

"You're not a dick," said Chogolisa.

"Thanks."

He sat next to the big woman, in comfortable silence, watching Yoki Choppa teaching Freydis how to cook, and showing her how he burned things in his alchemical bowl.

All things considered, Finn didn't think he was a dick. Not any more, anyway. Not any more than everybody else.

Back on the rafts the next day it was markedly warmer. There was a section of faster water, which Finn enjoyed, then the river entered a high-walled, precipitous grey canyon. The current calmed, seemingly as awed by the scenery as the humans.

Bighorn sheep picked their way across the cliff sides and great birds circled. Still they saw no people. They'd seen no other living human beings since Eagle's Bluff, half a moon before and east of the Shining Mountains. Were there any people left this far west, Finn wondered. And what had happened to everyone who'd lived in the villages they'd passed?

On they floated. Yoki Choppa taught Freydis combinations of herbs to use in the alchemical bowl. Finn listened for a while, but it was mind-fryingly dull, so he went back to watching the world go by.

The grey rock valley sides gave way to steeper and redder canyons, which closed in claustrophobically on the churning brown river, then opened again to an increasingly weird red rock landscape sparsely decorated with strange plants.

The river became bucking rapids, then calmed, then accelerated again. There was the odd shoal where they had to step into cool water and heave the rafts along, but generally the going was easy. Every now and then Finn thought he saw something spying from crags, but whatever it was darted away before he could be sure. He tried to reach out to nearby animals with his mind, but found nothing. His ability to communicate with creatures seemed to have waned since his battle with the squatch.

"Mine comes and goes, too," said Erik on a broad stretch where the rafts floated along together. "I try not to worry about it."

Sitsi told Finn that the stark red rock was the typical landscape in the Desert You Don't Walk Out Of and that there'd be a lot more of it to come.

*The Desert You Don't Walk Out Of* . . . thought Finn. The name didn't exactly fill one with hope.

On the fifth evening, which they also spent ashore, Keef finished the birch bark canoe he'd been working on since the Shining Mountains. It was big enough for two.

"Can I paddle it with you?" asked Finn.

"No, man, it's going to be a lot more awesome with just one of me."

"Oh, okay."

Finn walked up the riverbank a little and found a fish skeleton lying on flattened grass. Back in Hardwork, his Uncle Poppo had taught him how to make fishing hooks from fish bones. He smiled and squatted to pick out the best bits.

The following day, while Keef showed off by paddling his canoe backwards, sideways and fast, Finn and his raft mates Yoki Choppa, Freydis and Ottar filled their bobbing-along time competing to catch the largest fish. Finn forgot the constant danger of giant flying insects and enjoyed himself. They caught plenty of fish, predominantly a silver-green creature with swollen lips which they called a fatlips.

Shortly after dawn on their sixth day on the rafts, Finn and Ottar were fishing while Yoki Choppa taught alchemical mixtures to Freydis. Watching his line fizz along through the calm water, Finn was thinking that it had all been a crock of bollocks. The Desert You Don't Walk Out Of was meant to be . . . well, it was meant to live up to its name. Sure, there'd been some ominous signs – the dead monster, the broken villages and the skeleton, but there was no denying that every day this side of the Shining Mountains had been easier than any of the other days since they'd left Hardwork a couple of moons before.

But, of course, because the gods didn't like Finn to get complacent, they rounded a bend and Finn's mouth opened in wonder, with a dash of terror.

Hewn from headlands on either side of the river were two impossibly huge carvings of men. Each must have been a hundred paces high. One was muscular, brandishing a thick spear. The other, dressed in a bobbly stone jerkin, held his hands out towards them in a mystical "I'm going to do a spell now" pose.

They stared, awestruck. Finn marvelled at the collective ability of humans. How had they made something so huge? The planning, the hours of work, the skill involved in simply ensuring such large structures remained standing. Was there anything, he wondered, that humans couldn't achieve when they worked together?

Keef paddled back up the river towards them. He hoiked a thumb over his shoulder to indicate the colossusi behind him.

"Who are these cunts then?" he asked.

"I suspect that we are entering the territory of the Warriors and Warlocks," chimed in Sitsi Kestrel, one admonishing eyebrow raised at the profane Wootah man. "They are the dominant tribes in the Desert You Don't Walk Out Of. They started as two tribes, but around a thousand years ago there was a great war. The Warlock Queen . . ."

Finn stopped listening, too busy staring at the colossi. The size of them! It must have taken thousands of people thousands of hours – *moons*. No, years! And how had they known that it would work? What if they'd been going for ten years and one of the arms had fallen off? Finn's philosophy thus far had been that if a project was difficult and time-consuming and might go wrong, then there was no point in even starting it. These Warriors and Warlocks were clearly different people. The statues were a wonderful, inspirational combination of effort, organisation, intelligence and collaboration.

They drifted nearer, silent and tiny before the two massive figures.

Finn became convinced that the carvings were going to come alive and smash their craft. It wouldn't be that weird, given what they'd seen. He held his breath as they passed under the shadow of the Warlock's arms, expecting an unimaginable, life-ending weight of stone to fall.

And then they were through, drifting along as before, silenced by the majesty.

"As I suspected!" shouted Keef, following behind and peering upwards. "No cocks!"

There were no more statues, but soon it was hotter than Finn had ever known. He was very glad that they weren't walking. It was sweltering enough sitting on a raft, feet dangling in the cool river.

"Welcome to the desert!" said Sitsi, floating along next to them.

"And and!" shouted Ottar, pointing at the bank.

"What does he want?" asked Sofi.

Ottar pulled at Freydis's shirt and pointed to the bank.

"He says we need to get off the rafts in a while. We have to head south across the land to find Ayla's sister."

"In a while?" asked Sofi.

Freydis consulted Ottar, then said: "Soon we'll see high red cliffs a way off to the south. That's where Ayla's sister lives."

"There are high red cliffs everywhere."

"These are higher."

Sassa Lipchewer was probably more pleased than she ought to have been when, not long after Ottar had predicted them, high red cliffs appeared to the south, two or three miles from the Red River.

The Calnians might be their allies, but Wootah and Calnians were still different teams and it was satisfying to show the beautiful, powerful Owsla and the intellectually superior warlock Yoki Choppa that the Wootah had their uses; not least a route-finding little boy who was the key to their mission.

Sassa was also bored with being on a raft all the fuck-a-duck day. Sure, it was hotter than she thought possible, and she probably shouldn't be walking in heat like that with a baby growing inside her but, to her surprise, she'd discovered she didn't enjoy indolence. Maybe she'd changed. Perhaps it was becoming a mother, but she simply wanted to get on with things. Sitting ineffectively on a raft all day made her itchy.

"Here, Ottar?" shouted Sofi.

There was a pause, a bit of jibber-jabber from Ottar, then Freydis yelled back, "A bit further, I'll shout when we're there."

Sassa kept her eyes on the cliffs. They were high and they were red, as Ottar had predicted, stretching in a wall from east to west. Here and there in front of the cliffs were pillars of red rock, higher than any pillar of rock should ever have been.

*Why had the Hardworkers never travelled?* Sassa wondered. Surely all of the people who'd lived and died in Hardwork would have given their right tit to see such a landscape? The splendour of it filled her with joy and hope. Surely any dream could be realised in a world that threw up such wonders? Surely the gods who'd made this magnificent land wanted to see good deeds done, worthy quests to succeed against the odds, and lovely, healthy babies be born to the sort of selfless women who went on these worthy quests?

The sun was low and the air cooling when Ottar indicated it was time to land the rafts and head across the land. They poled the crafts over to the reed-lined southern bank and stepped ashore.

"Anything to report?" Sofi asked Paloma, who chose that moment to reappear from her scouting.

"Few lions near the cliffs – which are spectacular, even better up close – but no people. There are human footprints everywhere, but all at least a moon old."

"We'll camp the night here then, and head for the cliff in the morning."

"I'll just double-check for enemies or any animals that might want to eat us." Paloma spun round.

"No, you won't," said Sofi. Paloma turned back, an eyebrow raised. "The Owsla will make the camp. Wulf, would you mind getting the Wootah to scout the immediate area?"

"Sure," said Wulf.

"Can I fish?" asked Freydis.

"Do you mind taking her, Finn?" Wulf asked.

Finn looked at Thyri then back to Wulf. "Freydis could fish from the bank."

"But the fish are bigger in the middle of the river," Freydis implored. "Please can I go on the raft? We can anchor it right in the flow, that's the best place."

"What do you mean they're bigger in the middle?" Finn said suspiciously. "The biggest one we caught – which I caught – was right by the bank."

"*Please* can I go on the raft?"

Thyri was already heading off into the reeds. Finn watched her go, then sighed. "Okay, fine, let's take the raft out again."

Sassa smiled, then followed Wulf through the reeds and into the darkening shade of a stand of trees.

Erik, Bodil, Keef, Ottar and Thyri were waiting on the other side, by a narrow lake.

"Funny place for a lake," said Wulf.

"That's beavers for you," said Keef, nodding at its dammed end.

They set off around the beaver-made body of water. Sassa fell in next to Bodil.

"I *love* beavers," Bodil began. "Did you *see* the baby ones next to that stream that we walked along coming down from the mountains? I loved that stream, too. I wish we'd never left it. When I have my baby I'm going to make sure I live somewhere nice. Not as hot as it is here and not boring like the plains and not weird like the Badlands. Oh why did we leave that stream?"

"We didn't leave the stream," said Sassa. "It became the river that we've been rafting along."

Bodil looked at her as if she'd said that buffalo could fly, blinked, then continued. "Maybe I'll live in the hills with my baby? I liked those hills on the way down from the mountain. I like it when the land's a bit uppy and downy but not too uppy and downy and you can see where things are and it's not such hard work to go everywhere because . . ."

They walked on and Bodil talked, startling ducks and muskrats from their lakeside perches. They were nearer the cliffs here and Sassa could see that they were stratified into red and yellow bands of rock, their layers curved as if the very land had buckled. Towers stood at the end of most of the red promontories like horns on the nose of a dragon. Some were stubby, some slender, but all were jaw-droppingly bizarre and beautiful. To a woman who'd spent almost all her life confined in a ten-mile circle of flat land next to a lake, the place was jab-it-in-a-rabbit amazing.

They rounded the lake and headed up a small hill, following Wulf, Keef, Erik, Thyri and Ottar.

"Shush, Bodil." Sassa had heard a far-off cry as they picked their way between green bushes.

"Why?"

"Just stop talking for a moment, please."

Bodil shut her mouth and looked about like a mildly surprised deer.

"Get back! Off the river!" came a distant shout. "Finn! Get back now!"

"Sounds like Sofi," said Bodil. "I'm good at telling people's voices and—"

"Shush, Bodil." Sassa strained her ears to hear Sofi's shout.

"Fast as you can, Finn!" Sofi yelled.

Wulf and the rest turned and ran back down the hill.

# Chapter 7

## Taken

"**W**hy are we doing this?" Paloma Pronghorn asked Sofi Tornado. She was gripping a tree, as ordered.

"I can hear a flash flood."

Finn was poling the raft back to shore. Freydis was lying on her front, kicking up a small fountain in an attempt to speed up the craft. There *was* a distant roar, now that Paloma listened for it.

"Then what are we doing here? I'll put on my water shoes," said Paloma.

Sofi put a hand on her arm. "No time."

"Will they make it?"

Sofi shouted, "Faster, Finn! There's a flash flood coming!"

"A what?" the young Wootah man yelled, pausing his poling so he could hear the answer.

"A great wave coming down the river! Get to shore fast as you can!"

Finn doubled his efforts. Freydis kicked all the harder.

"Fast enough now?" asked Paloma.

"I don't think so."

"We've got to go to them."

"We have to!" said Sitsi, clinging to a nearby tree.

A boiling wall of water raged into sight around an upstream meander. Half a heartbeat later the roaring was much louder.

"I'm going," Chogolisa took a pace down the bank.

"No," said Sofi. Her voice was quiet, but it stopped Chogolisa. "They're both better swimmers than any of us."

"We can't just watch it happen!" Sitsi was near to tears.

"You won't help," said Yoki Choppa, all the misery in the world in his voice.

"Where are the Wootah?" asked Sitsi.

"They're running back, but they're not going to get here in time," said Sofi.

Paloma stared at the wave. It stretched the width of the channel, foaming white, tinged pink by the setting sun. Tree branches jabbed from its foaming snout like the spears of charging moose riders.

"Mountain snowmelt," Yoki Choppa informed them miserably.

Finn saw the wave, dropped the pole, snatched up the raft's mooring rope and dived towards the bank. He surfaced with the rope clamped between his teeth and struck towards them overarm, legs kicking up plumes of foam. He was a strong swimmer. The raft jerked after him, faster than before. Still lying on it, Freydis kicked like a toddler in a tantrum.

"They're going to make it," said Sitsi.

"They might," Sofi agreed. "Come on."

The Wootah women leapt down the bank.

Finn and Freydis came closer and closer, but the wall of water was fast. Finn raised his head to take a breath.

"Faster!" Paloma shouted.

He looked at her, wasting precious moments, then wasted even more time by turning to see the raging doom. Finally, he thrust his face back under the surface and wheeled his arms with surprising strength.

He reached the shore. The flash flood was twenty paces away, roaring like a stampede monsters.

Chogolisa plucked Finn out of the water one-handed and tossed him up the bank.

Freydis knelt up on the back of the raft. She looked at the wave, then back at the women. She was like a rabbit frozen in terror, waiting for the coyote to snatch her up and break her neck.

"Freydis!" shouted Chogolisa.

Sofi and Sitsi stepped towards the raft. The wave was ten paces away.

Paloma snatched up the rope "Clear the raft! I'll haul it out."

Sofi and Sitsi jumped back.

Paloma heaved on the rope.

It snapped.

The raft bobbed serenely from the shore. Freydis looked back at them, wide-eyed. She looked sad rather than scared now.

The wave struck.

All was noise. Something whacked into Paloma's head. She flailed and sucked in water. She felt herself rising, drawn backwards. Her feet found solid ground. Her head came clear of the surface. She coughed out water then sucked in air.

Chogolisa had her by the jerkin and was dragging her up and out of the flood. The colossal woman's other hand was clamped around Sofi's wrist. Sitsi was hanging from her neck.

"Get your hand out of my eye, Sitsi!" ordered Chogolisa, pacing sure-footed out of the water. She dropped her fellow Owsla by the trees, where Finn lay on the ground, panting like a dying buffalo.

Erik ran through the trees and stopped, hands on knees, panting like his son.

"What . . . what happened?" he gasped.

"Flash flood," said Sofi. "It took Freydis."

Paloma looked along the river. It was a raging torrent. The head of the flash flood – and surely Freydis with it – was already some two hundred paces away. It was just possible that Freydis wouldn't be crushed by tumbling logs or speared by a swirling branch and might be washed ashore before she drowned. It was even possible that she was still on the raft, carried along on the nose of the wave.

It was also possible that Paloma would have rescued both of them had Sofi told her to strap on her water shoes right at the start, instead of telling her to grab a tree. But Sofi had chosen not to risk her. Did she value Paloma's life more than the two Wootah, especially after losing six of her Owsla? Or had she made the cold but undeniably correct calculation that Paloma was more valuable to the mission than Freydis and Finn? Either way, Paloma wasn't sure she liked it.

"Permission to go after the girl?" she asked Sofi.

"You're bleeding," said Sitsi, pointing to Paloma's head.

Paloma touched a temple then looked at her hand. So she was.

"Go," said Sofi. "Bring the girl back."

Paloma ran, like only she could run.

They watched Paloma go.

Erik felt sick with exhaustion, sick with grief for Freydis but more sick with relief that Finn had been saved.

He hauled Finn to his feet. The boy hugged his father hard and heaved with great, shivering sobs.

*This is my son*, thought Erik. *I made him and I am responsible for him. I was a fool to miss so much of his life. I mustn't miss any more. I must protect him.*

"Let's follow Paloma," said Wulf.

"No," said Sofi. "If Freydis is alive Paloma will bring her back. We should wait. Ottar says we should head south, and—" she looked about. "Where is Ottar?"

Erik unclamped Finn from his chest and looked around.

No Ottar.

"Ottar!" shouted Erik. "Ottar the Moaner! OTTARRR!"

There was no sign of him.

"Everyone quiet," said Sofi.

They watched her strain to listen. Her super-hearing had been a secret that only Erik knew at one time, but he reckoned all the Wootah, with the possible exception of Bodil, had worked it out by now. How she could hear above the noise of the rushing river, Erik didn't know.

"He isn't nearby," she said, turning to the Wootah. "Where did you last see him?"

Erik thought for half a moment, and set off at a run through the trees.

"He's on the hill!" he yelled over his shoulder.

Ottar had been with them when they'd heard Sofi's shout. Erik could picture him throwing stones at a bush. Then everyone had sprinted back to the river. Without Freydis there, and with Gunnhild dead, nobody had been looking out for Ottar.

Erik felt bad about that, but surely the boy would still be pootling about on the hill, harassing a lizard or chasing a butterfly? He just had to get there before a lion or a wolf or anything else that liked to eat guileless little boys found him.

Ottar was not on the hill. Erik shouted and searched, sweat soaking his back. *Where could he be? Surely they hadn't lost both children in a matter of moments?*

They all shouted for Ottar. They searched behind bushes and in a small cave. Erik found himself looking in places he had already looked.

Sofi quietened everyone again.

"He's nowhere nearby," she said. She meant that she couldn't hear his heartbeat. So he might be nearby. But if he were, he was dead.

Wootah and Calnians stood, looking about, shame-faced and confused.

Erik was in a rage. *How had they done it?* They were such fools! How could they have lost both children? They'd come so far, through so many dangers, and in the space of a few moments they'd undone it all with their stupid, selfish negligence. They were idiots, not fit to look after children. His old friends the Lakchans had words for people like them. They were a bunch of fuc—

"I can see him!" shouted Sitsi.

"Oh, thank Fraya!" said Sassa. "Where?"

"It's not good. Can you see something moving on that cliff?"

She pointed to the red cliff, maybe a mile away.

Erik couldn't see anything, but surely Sitsi was wrong. "He can't have got that far away," he said. "He was here when—"

"He's being carried by a squatch," interrupted Sitsi. "It's climbing the cliff with Ottar over its shoulders."

"Is Ottar alive?" asked Wulf.

"I . . . think so. I'm pretty sure he's breathing and I can't see any blood."

"Is the squatch female or male?" asked Sofi. Erik saw what she was driving at. The best possible outcome was that Ottar had been taken by Ayla's sister.

"By its size, it's a male."

"Fucknuts!" Erik kicked a rock. "Both fucking kids! What is *wrong* with us?"

He looked around but nobody would meet his eye.

"We messed up," said Wulf eventually, "but as far as we know both are alive. Freydis is a strong swimmer and—"

"Did you not see that fucking enormous wave? The girl's dead and we deserve to be too. What the fuck were we—"

"That's enough, Erik," said Thyri.

He stared at her.

"As Wulf said, we messed up. What should we do now? Cluck like foul-mouthed hens or get on with rescuing Ottar?"

Erik felt rage swell his chest and his ears burned. *How dare she* . . . he calmed himself. She was right. "Sorry," he said.

"Right," said Wulf. "Most of us will follow the squatch. A couple of us should wait for Paloma and Freydis at the river."

Erik saw Sofi looking from him to Wulf. Was that a wry look in her eye? *This was no time for wry fucking looks! How dare she* . . . he calmed himself again. Planning, not ranting. That was the order of the day. He was worried and he was exhausted. They never included that in the sagas, the bit about everyone on a quest being so very tired the whole time and tetchy because of it. Maybe heroes didn't get tetchy, he mused. Wulf never seemed tetchy. Maybe Wulf was sleeping better than he was . . .

"I'll follow Freydis and Paloma in my canoe," said Keef. "If Freydis ends up on the far bank or an island and Paloma can't reach her, I'll get the girl. Paloma's water shoes won't work on a raging river."

Not a bad point, thought Erik. Although there was simply no way the girl had survived such a weight of water and wood. Keef would simply be retrieving her body.

"Yoki Choppa," Sofi asked, "do you have hair from Paloma or Freydis?"

"Nope. Flood took it."

"Hmm. Probably should have taken some of Paloma's hair before she ran off."

"Probably." Yoki Choppa's face darkened. Erik felt sorry for him. Of all the fuck-ups that evening, his was minor but he clearly felt awful about it.

Sofi nodded and turned to Keef. "If you don't find them," Sofi asked, "will you be able to find us again?"

"I can track a mosquito through a blizzard with my eye shut."

"Keef, you're no tracker," Sassa shook her head. "Finn's

our best. There's room for two in the canoe, isn't there, Keef?
Finn should go with you."

"There is room for Finn. The canoe could take four Finns,
but I'm a far superior tracker to the boy. You've just never
seen me tracking because it's a mundane task best left to
lesser minds than mine."

Erik had wondered about Keef since he'd met him back
in Lakchan territory. Was his pomposity an act? He had
decided that Keef was probably taking the piss all the time,
even in a situation as serious as this one. Below his mock-
heroic posturing, the Berserker was an honourable, brave,
kind and very clever guy, Erik was pretty sure. Pretty sure.
It was also just possible that Keef was actually a total bellend
with his head lodged a good long way up his own arse. Erik
hoped not.

"And," Keef continued, "you might need Finn to read the
mind of the squatch that's taken Ottar. I cannot do that,
because I'm not a freak. But you're right. Someone else should
come with me. Someone not too heavy, who'll be good at
spotting a small girl on the riverbank and seeing Paloma's
tracks without having to stop and look for them."

Everyone turned to Sitsi, who'd been listening in from
the edge of the group.

She coloured. "I'll go," she piped up, eyes as wide as ever.

"You're light enough" muttered Keef, also reddening.

What was going on here, Erik wondered? Keef thought
he was the father of Bodil's baby. He wasn't, of course, Finn
was, but Keef didn't know that and Keef and Bodil were very
much a couple. Or were they? Did Keef know he wasn't the
father? If he was the intelligent man that Erik suspected he
was, then he must know. And now it looked like Keef and
Sitsi had something going on. What was happening?

Erik shook his head. There was no point dwelling on
the nonsense of other people's love lives at the best of times,
and this was far from the best of times.

"All right," said Sofi, as if there was nothing odd afoot. "Keef and Sitsi, follow Freydis and Paloma in Keef's canoe. Yoki Choppa will take some hair from each of you. If you catch up with them so far downriver that coming back is impractical, stay where you are and Yoki Choppa will find you."

Keef pointed at his head. Erik had chopped Keef's hair off to elude the Owsla way back on the other side of the Water Mother. It had grown back to a blond fuzz about half a thumb long.

"I don't have a whole lot of hair," he said.

"Don't need much," said Yoki Choppa, lifting a little flint knife from a pocket in his breechcloth.

The warlock snicked a pinch of hair from both of them, then pressed a small bundle into Sitsi's hand. "Take your power animal with you," he said. "Here is enough to last a few moons for you and Paloma."

"We'll be back much sooner than that," said Sitsi, but she took the bundle.

Erik looked at Yoki Choppa. It shouldn't take them long to get back. Had the warlock foreseen something? And, come to think of it, he'd had the bundle made up already. How had he known that Sitsi was going to head off after Paloma?

"Come on, Sitsi!" cried Keef. "Let's go!"

The two of them ran off to the river. Erik looked at Bodil. She was waiting patiently, apparently unaffected by Keef's departure.

"Why is the river like that?" she asked.

"What do you mean?"

"All rolling and raging and fuller than it was?"

"Because of the flash flood," Erik explained.

"Surely a flash flood comes and goes? Like a *flash*." Bodil pursed her lips as if she'd made a very good point.

Erik squinted at her, missing children forgotten for a moment. Was she being serious? She held his eye. Apparently so.

"No," he said, speaking as clearly as he could, "it's a sudden increase in flow, caused by a storm, or, as in this case, lots of snow melting quickly. The river will stay high for a while. It will probably get even higher as more melted snow flows down."

"And I didn't think flash floods happened in rivers," said Bodil.

"Oh. Where else would they—"

"Come on," Sofi commanded. "We'll collect what's left of our gear and follow the squatch."

"Up the cliff? It'll be dark by the time we get there," said Erik.

"That is the way the squatch went."

"So let's stop pissing around and go!" said Thyri.

It was the first cloudy night for a while and about as dark as it ever got when they reached the base of the cliff. The route there had been more difficult than expected; up ridges, down ridges and over a stream that was probably broad enough to be called a river and definitely broad enough to be an arse to cross.

After leading most of the way with Sofi, Erik strode to the base of the cliff and looked up manfully, hands on hips, trying to force a courage that he really, really didn't feel. The cliff was a black, featureless wall rising hundreds of feet above him. He felt the same dizziness and sharp contraction in his groin that he always got at the top of cliffs.

Fear of heights from below. It was a new one.

They had to rescue Ottar. But did they have to climb a cliff at night? Well, yes they did. A boy's life was at stake. This was no time for cowardice.

Erik readied himself. He'd get to the top, or he'd fall and burst like a dropped egg on the very ground he was standing on. One way or another, it would be over.

"We can't climb this now," said Wulf.

Erik's heart leapt. But surely they had to?

"You're right," agreed Sofi. "The river we crossed flows from the massif. Following its gorge should be less treacherous and probably quicker."

Erik looked at Chogolisa.

"It will probably be much easier," she said.

"Oh, good," said Bodil.

Sassa did not look convinced.

Erik the Angry would never know whether the cliff would have been more treacherous than the canyon, but he reckoned it would have been close. There was a great deal of scary scrambling and plenty of horrible climbing as the gorge narrowed, particularly as they approached the top.

The sky was lightening in the east when Erik finally hauled himself over the last lip and lay on the bare rock, arms agonised and useless, his whole body shaking with exertion. Climbing was a lot more tiring than he'd imagined it could be. When he could finally look up, he saw Yoki Choppa perched on a patch of bare rock between two short, gnarled pinyon pines, hunched over his smoking alchemical bowl.

"He's alive and over there," said the warlock, pointing south-east. "About eight miles away."

"Let's go!" shouted Thyri, heading off.

"Not that way," said Sofi. "We'll follow the cliff top until we get to the point the squatch climbed up, then follow its tracks."

Thyri opened her mouth to protest, then closed it. "I guess that makes sense," she said.

# Chapter 8

## Surfing

Keef the Berserker's canoe bucked and swished on the raging meltwater, surging through the night. He said nothing apart from the odd *hard left!, back-paddle, back-paddle!* and so on. Sitsi Kestrel was silent, scanning the banks and the river itself for Freydis's broken little body.

Dawn came.

The current had eased a little, but they were still speeding along. There was no sign of Freydis nor of her raft, but footprints and broken vegetation showed that Paloma had run westward along the river's southern bank at a Hel of a pace, as the Wootah would have said. She had not returned, at least not by the same route.

Sitsi wasn't exhausted and her knees were not sore from kneeling in the canoe because she was Owsla. As well as her personal power animal, the chuckwalla lizard which gave her amazing eyesight, she ate a small amount of tarantula hawk wasp and caribou daily. The wasp and the caribou gave her extraordinary stamina, strength and resilience. She could have kept going all day and another night before even thinking about becoming uncomfortable.

Keef, however, did not have her alchemical advantages. He'd been crammed into a relatively small space and paddling like a frenzied duck all night with neither rest nor food nor drink. He smelled strongly of stale male sweat with a note of fresh male sweat. Usually such a man-ming would have had Sitsi running for the hills, or at least out of nose-shot. She didn't mind it too much on Keef.

They passed three herons, spaced like guards on the shore. The sun's golden rays struck the water. Keef's paddle rate was slowing to almost nothing then suddenly speeding up, again and again.

"Would you like a rest?" Sitsi asked.

He paddled faster, splashing Sitsi with cold water. "Nope."

"We could stop for a short while and eat something?"

"Are you saying I'm weak?" Keef turned, eyebrow raised over his missing eye.

Sitsi was startled momentarily. "No, no, of course not. It's just that I could do with a rest."

"*You* want a rest? Why didn't you say? *Right paddle!*"

They crunched the nose of the canoe into the shingle bank on the inside of a bend, climbed out and pulled the little boat up after them. The far bank was vertical red rock, but their side was a stony-soiled clearing fringed by scrubby woodland.

By the way he moved, Keef was not far from collapse.

"Forty heartbeats here," he said, "then we're off again."

"I could really do with a quick sleep." Sitsi stretched and yawned.

"Sleep? What about Freydis?" Keef yawned, too. If other people yawning made you yawn, Sitsi had learned, it meant you were a kinder person, more interested in and influenced by others' feelings.

"Paloma will find her. If she comes back this way while we're—"

"If *they* come back this way," Keef corrected.

"Of course. If they come past while we're sleeping they'll see the canoe and know that we're here."

"Good point. You can sleep first. I'll lie here and take the first watch."

Sitsi was pretty sure that Keef was asleep before he'd fully stretched out on the ground.

She slipped her arms under him, lifted the big man and carried him to a less stony patch. She covered him with her Owsla poncho, picked up her bow and quiver and headed off to find breakfast.

At the treeline, she stopped and looked back. Yes, he was far enough from the river to be safe from a surge in the flood and she could see no serious predators nearby. His chest rose and fell and he mumbled something that sounded a lot like *Sitsi*.

Paloma Pronghorn ran through the last light of day. She nearly caught up with the wave's leading edge, then had to divert a few hundred paces from the river to cross a tributary. When the stream was narrow enough to leap she stopped to wash the blood off her face and check the cut on her forehead. A long-tailed lizard with a yellow head and a freakishly blue body watched her. It looked like something a child had painted, badly. Not that she'd ever seen a child paint anything well, despite what their parents always told them.

As she'd expected, the cut wasn't too bad. She'd known that running off with blood running down her face was an impressively tough look, so she'd risked her wound not being bad enough to need Yoki Choppa's attention. And, of course, she had a girl to rescue.

Back at the river, she scanned the banks and the churning brown torrent for Freydis the Annoying. It was getting darker. She saw several dozen pieces of flotsam that could have been the girl, but she couldn't be sure.

She scanned again, looking for movement, then realised she was being naïve. Freydis couldn't have survived the torrent. She was looking for a corpse. She stood for a moment. The sunset in the west was incongruously lovely. She remembered the day her sister died.

Paloma had been too young to go hunting, so she'd stayed

at home exercising, running through the routines devised and enforced by her demanding dad. Her mum had returned alone, her face unbearably heavy with sorrow.

"Your sister's dead," she'd said.

She didn't say how she'd died, and Paloma had never asked. Paloma had cried, but only because her mother looked so sad. She'd been too young to know what death was.

From then on, until Paloma had left for Calnia to join the Owsla, her mother had spoken about reincarnation more than any other subject. Nobody ever died. Their soul occupied a different body. Paloma was to grieve for her sister, and to miss her, but not to be destroyed by grief.

Although Paloma was pretty sure it wasn't what she'd intended, she'd used her mother's words as moral justification for slaughtering an awful lot of people on the commands of Calnia's rulers. She hadn't been *killing* killing. She'd just moved their souls along, probably to a better place where empresses didn't want them dead.

And now Freydis's soul had moved along. Paloma would never hear the little girl's clipped voice again, never hear her sing again, never see her raise her snub nose in defiance of some idiotic adult decree.

She'd liked that girl.

She allowed herself a moment's grief, then accelerated downstream, resolving to get ahead of the wave at the flood's leading edge. If she didn't see Freydis there, she could retrace her steps when the water receded and look for her body. However, given the strength of the torrent, it was going to be a while before the river calmed, maybe even a few days. And, of course, Freydis's little body might be underwater, bundled along then jammed in some hidden nook where it would swell and decay and be eaten by fish, only surfacing bit by bit as rotted, chewed limbs were pulled free by the current and . . . it did not bear thinking about.

It was the last light of day when Paloma reached the head of the flood and looked across the churning wave.

She spotted Freydis immediately because Freydis was waving at her.

It wasn't a *Quick! Save me!* wave, it was more of a *Hello! Look at me!*

Paloma, alchemically toughened warrior and the fastest runner the world had ever known, blinked away tears of joy. The girl was lying on the raft. The wave was propelling it along in a way that reminded Paloma of an old dog of her parents that pushed balls from place to place with its nose. Freydis's perch on the crest seemed fairly stable, but the wave was huge and full of other debris. It was amazing that the raft hadn't been smashed by a trunk, or flipped and swallowed by the great weight of rushing white water. It was just a matter of time before something like that happened.

Somehow, she had to get the girl.

Paloma ran along, racking her mind. She could strap on her water shoes, run along the front of the wave, grab Freydis and run on to the other side. That would mean running much faster than she'd run before in water shoes; much faster, in fact, then the time ever a bit faster than normal and the shoes had fallen apart and she'd sunk. If it was just her, maybe she'd have risked it, but if shoes broke up once she'd grabbed Freydis they'd both drown.

She could get a long way ahead of the wave, make a very long rope, tie it round her waist, tie one end around a tree, put on her water shoes, run up the river, grab Freydis, hold on as the flood washed over them and . . . That was an even worse idea. For starters it would take her three days to make a rope long enough.

Freydis was shouting something. Paloma held a hand to her ear.

"Don't try to get me!" she shouted. "I'm okay!"

Paloma watched for a while. Freydis wasn't just lying on

the raft, she was shifting her weight about to counter the rolls and swells in the wave face. Her movements were calm but deliberate and effective, as if she'd been riding rafts on the business end of flash floods all her life.

"Are you sure?" Paloma shouted.

"You'll drown if you try to get me and I'm okay. I'm enjoying it!"

"Can you get to the bank?"

"No! I've got to go where the wave wants me to go. Here, watch this!"

Freydis pivoted her body towards Paloma. The raft sliced lower on the face of the wave, towards the bank. However, a bulge of water pushed the craft back into the middle.

"See?" Freydis shouted.

"I do!"

"Can you run along and wait until it calms, and I'll get myself over to your bank? If you can't keep up, then I'll walk upstream along the bank until I find you?"

"I can keep up."

"Oh good. Thanks very much for coming after me!"

"Any time!" A safe commitment, thought Paloma. The situation was unlikely to recur. "Are you sure you're okay? It's going to be dark soon."

"Oh, yes, it's really fun. It's a shame you're not out here too! Do be careful running along through the dark. This could take a long time! Sorry!"

# Chapter 9

## The Search for Squatch

"Pole a mole." Sassa Lipchewer stood on the edge of the cliff, morning breeze ruffling her blonde crest of hair.

Immediately in front of her the land dropped hundreds of feet, then shot up again in great towers of red rock. The towers ranged from mountainous mesas to stocky needles. Many of their summits glowed red in the dawn sun like the tips of recently extinguished torches.

At her feet were scuff marks made by the squatch where he'd clambered over the top of the cliff.

The others were preparing to head off. The squatch tracks led south-east along a red soil path between tiny green trees.

There was only one set of footprints.

"The squatch must be carrying Ottar," said Wulf.

*Or he dropped him on the way up the cliff*, thought Sassa, *or ate him*.

Sofi led them through the alien landscape. There were two types of gnarled trees, some with blue berries and others with small brown cones – "juniper trees and pinyon pines!" announced Sitsi – and a whole range of little bushes, grasses and cactuses and weird plants that Sassa had never seen before, including spiky balls with a single long, naked twig poking up like a freaky reverse root. All the vegetation was widely spaced out in the red sand, as if it had been planted for display.

Presently a rabbit hopped out from the roots of a pinyon pine. It looked at Sassa, didn't seem to think much of her and set about munching a plant. More and more of the furry little animals bounded from cover until there were rabbits everywhere, skittering across bare rock, nibbling at shoots or scratching their faces with hind legs.

"If I'm reincarnated as a rabbit," said Erik, "I'm coming here."

"Me too," said Chogolisa. "If I'm reincarnated as a coyote."

Sassa could feel the sun baking her shell-shaved head either side of the crest of hair. It wasn't perhaps the best hairstyle for desert sun. She was thinking about hats and searching unsuccessfully for broad-leaved plants when Sofi halted and turned with a finger to her lips.

"What does . . ." started Bodil.

"Shush." Thyri grabbed Bodil's arm and pressed her finger against the woman's lips. Bodil looked startled, but she got the message.

Sofi nodded at Yoki Choppa.

The warlock mulled herbs and presumably a lock of Ottar's hair in his alchemical bowl. As he worked, Sassa watched a comically fat mouse munch seeds under a nearby tree. There was much more life than she'd expected to find in the desert. Or maybe they just saw more animals because there was no undergrowth to hide in? And the animals were furrier than she'd thought they would be. The fat mouse looked like it would overheat in an instant in that fur coat. Or maybe all that hair was useful for keeping the sun off its skin . . .

The warlock set fire to his mix, sniffed the smoke and looked to the south-east.

"A mile, that way," he said. "Alive."

Sassa almost fell over with relief. It felt like she'd been holding her breath for an hour without realising and had just let it out.

"Don't get too excited," said Sofi. "He's still the captive of at least one squatch."

They followed the tracks along a dry, flat-bottomed valley filled with more weird, lush and sparse plants. The valley sides were steep red rock. A moon ago Sassa would have said those valley sides were high cliffs. Now she wouldn't even call them cliffs.

Rising from the land ahead was a short promontory crowned by a cluster of red rock towers that reached skyward like the fingers of a giant's hand. It looked like a god's stronghold.

Sofi gestured for them to stop, then crouched and beckoned for everyone to gather.

"Ottar and the squatch are in there. There's only one squatch." She pointed up at the great hand of rock. "I think both are asleep. Finn the Deep, Thyri Treelegs and Sassa Lipchewer come with me. The rest of you stay here and gather rocks."

"What size rocks?" asked Erik.

"Hurling at a squatch before it gets in mind-crush range sized rocks."

"Got you," Erik nodded.

Sassa looked at Wulf. He smiled reassuringly.

"Come on," said Sofi.

# Chapter 10

## Rage

Paloma Pronghorn jogged along, trying to keep pace with the meltwater surge that propelled Freydis the Annoying westward through the night. It wasn't the speed that hampered her – of course it wasn't – it was the tributaries, cliffs and other annoyances. She spent more time finding her way back to the head of the flood than running alongside it. It didn't help that it was a particularly dark night, nor that she couldn't stop thinking about Freydis. The poor little girl! Trapped on a rushing cascade that could flip her raft and drown her at any moment.

Paloma felt impotent, which was very unusual for her, and, even odder, she was sick with worry. The last time she'd worried like this about someone else was . . . well, it had been a while.

She ran around spindly bushes, leapt yucca and dodged cactuses. She pounded across rock and powered through sand. Coyotes and other night beasts fled as she passed. Owls and giant moths burst out of the darkness and flapped clear, as startled by her as she was by them.

Normally she'd have loved the run through the new desert environment; the clacking of stones tumbling behind her as she ran up scree slopes, the steady susurration of soft, strength-sapping sand, the grippy rocks that she bounded across like a young bighorn.

But she was too worried about Freydis, racked by the guilt

that she could and should be doing more to help. But the girl had insisted that she was fine. Trapped on the raft in the middle of the raging river, but fine.

The child's bravery made the situation all the more poignant. Whenever Paloma returned to the river, she knew that Freydis was still afloat because she could hear shrill singing over the churning water and clonking flotsam.

As the night morphed from blue-black to blue-grey, and she could see that the rushing flood had slowed, Paloma began to get an inkling that Freydis wasn't in quite as much trouble as she'd made out. She was manoeuvring the raft to avoid islands, logs and other debris, so why not manoeuvre to the bank? Thinking about it, hit by a flash flood, surely it would be impossible *not* to be driven onto the bank, and pretty quickly, too.

In fact, it would be difficult to stay in the centre of the river.

Dawn came, Paloma could see the expression on Freydis's face and she knew. The girl was taking the piss.

The head of the flood had reduced from a roaring white-water monster to a big ripple, barely large enough to carry the raft. And there was Freydis riding the raft in the middle of it, leaning one way and then the other, soaring left and right like a gliding bird. She wasn't trying to avoid debris and keep herself alive. She was manoeuvring to keep the craft on the face of the wave. It would have been easier to steer the raft ashore.

Freydis had made Paloma run and worry all night. She'd left the others fretting, even grieving. And all so that she could enjoy herself riding a wave.

Paloma felt pressure growing in her ears.

"Get over here NOW, Freydis the Annoying!" she shouted, surprised by the violence in her voice.

"I can't!" Freydis cheerily called.

Paloma seethed. They must have come a hundred miles in the night, maybe more. How was she going to get the girl back to the others? She could tow Sofi along, but Sofi was alchemically strengthened. She'd surely break Freydis's arms if she tried to pull her at any speed.

"You will come here right *now* or I will drag you ashore and spank the skin off your arse!" she raged.

Freydis's eyes shot wide and her mouth opened. She leant to her left to bring the raft over to Paloma.

Paloma kept pace, shaking with anger, ready to wrench the girl off the raft by the scruff of her neck and spank her.

The raft crunched to rest on a shingle shoal.

Freydis, lying on it, looked up. Her eyes were red and she was crying a little.

Paloma slumped. The girl was tiny and spindly limbed. She was shivering after her night on the river. She was six years old. And Paloma had been about to hit her.

*Wow*, thought the warrior. Now she was calm, her rage seemed amazing, disproportionate, something she'd never felt before.

"Are you going to spank me?" Freydis asked.

"I should. What were you thinking? Why didn't you come to the bank?"

"I was stuck out there," she lied.

"No, you *weren't*!" Paloma felt the rage rising again. Freydis didn't care. The girl might be small but she'd been a selfish dick. "You could have come to the bank right at the start! Couldn't you?" she was shouting. "I ran all night!" As she yelled it, she realised how ridiculous it sounded. She liked running all night.

Freydis stared back at her, wide-eyed.

"Couldn't you?!"

Still no answer.

"What about Ottar? Do you have any idea how upset he is right now? Do you know how much hurt you've caused?

You were having fun and that was all that mattered to you! Fuck everyone else!"

Freydis covered her head with her hands and sobbed.

"I've never had fun before," she managed through her sobs. "And I might never get the chance again."

Paloma took a deep breath and looked up. The sun was blazing out from behind a bluff, but it hadn't hit their section of the bank yet.

The girl had enjoyed herself without considering the impact on others. It was an attitude that pretty much summed up Paloma's life.

She sighed.

There was a pile of dry, dead wood further up the bank, left by a previous, higher flood.

*There's always a bigger flood,* thought Paloma.

"All right, stop crying. I'm sorry," she said. "Let's build a fire, have some food and you can sleep for a while. Then we'll talk about what we're going to do. Sorry I got so angry."

The girl did stop crying, miraculously quickly. "Don't worry. We all get angry sometimes, Paloma Pronghorn," said the six-year-old. "And don't worry about Ottar. He knows I'm okay."

"How?"

"He does. Come on, that fire's not going to build itself."

Freydis skipped up the shingle bank towards the wood. Why, Paloma wondered, did it suddenly feel like the girl was in charge?

Next to the Red River, a good way upstream, Sitsi Kestrel stood with the warm sun on her back, shifting from foot to foot and wondering whether to wake Keef the Berserker.

On the one hand they ought to get going. Sitsi had found Paloma's tracks heading westward, but no sign of the runner coming back east. It was unlikely that she'd taken a different return route. Paloma was savvy enough to realise that she'd been gone longer than excepted, so someone might have been sent to follow her, so she should take the same path back. She was also wilful and selfish enough to ignore that knowledge and take a different route if it suited her even a little, but Sitsi was hoping her Owsla mate would behave decently for once when a dead child and her grieving tribe mates were concerned.

Maybe not dead.

Sitsi was desperate to catch up and find out what had happened, but the river's current was slowing every moment. Every heartbeat they dawdled here would add two to their journey. Or maybe a heartbeat and a half, decreasing to a heartbeat and a quarter the longer they . . . they had to get going, that was the point.

On the other hand, Keef might be offended if she woke him. Some tribes had strange ideas about manliness and what women could tell men to do. She didn't think the Wootah were like that, but she'd never been in a situation like this with them.

*Screw what the Wootah might think*, said a voice in her mind that sounded a lot like Sofi Tornado, *you're Owsla!*

"Wake up, Keef!" Sitsi shouted.

Keef leapt to his feet, Arse Splitter in his hands. He jumped a full circle and landed facing Sitsi, the long axe's spear-like tip pointing at her bare midriff.

"I'm sorry," he said calmly, lowering the weapon. "I meant to stay on watch while you slept."

"That's okay. I've made breakfast."

"Good. Thanks. We'll eat as we paddle." He lifted a hand above his head, sniffed his armpit and grimaced. "Pwarr! Not good. I'll take a dunk in the river before we go. Do you need one?"

"I think I'm all right," said Sitsi.

He looked at her, expecting, she guessed, that she would

smell her armpit, too. She held his gaze and left her arms by her sides.

He shrugged as if to say "suit yourself" and began to undress. Sitsi went to gather their kit and breakfast. She turned to watch him run into the river. His body was white as a warlock painted for a ceremony, but he was lean-waisted, broad-shouldered and well-muscled. He had the sort of figure Sitsi liked.

Keef dressed and they set off. Sitsi paddled in front, scanning the banks. They ate the rabbit that Sitsi had cooked and the tender young rush stems she'd picked. The sun throbbed off red rocks, baking the air. She couldn't stop yawning, for real this time. Paddling all night and worrying about Freydis had taken more out of her that she'd thought.

"Have a sleep," said Keef.

"No. I've got to keep an eye out for Freydis."

"I've got an eye, and it's Paloma we need to watch out for." He didn't need to add that she'd be carrying Freydis's body back along the bank. They were both thinking it now.

"Paloma's not the most observant. She might run by."

"I'll sing, then she can't miss us."

"I'll never sleep sitting up, especially with you singing."

"So lie back. And my singing could lull a livid lion."

She really was very tired. Keef straightened his legs and she lay between them, her head on his warm and solid thigh.

Keef sang a song about a man called Rig having a three-night-long threesome with a couple called Ai and Edda. The song went into the most lascivious – frankly disgusting – detail, but Keef managed to make the words sound heroic and comic and Sitsi loved it.

As he sang, in far, far too much detail, about the birth of Edda's son, she finally fell asleep.

# Chapter 11

## Ottar and the Squatch

Finn the Deep crept along after Sofi Tornado and Sassa Lipchewer. Thyri Treelegs padded behind him, quiet as a cat on the red sand that passed for soil in this freaky landscape of stupidly small trees, aggressively spikey plants, crazily red bluffs and astonishing numbers of rabbits.

He was no longer the Finnbogi the Boggy. There were serious matters at hand. There was a child to rescue and Finn the Deep was capable enough to be chosen as one of this skilful squad. Sofi hadn't chosen Wulf the Fat. Erik the Angry wasn't with them. Even Sofi's own Chogolisa Earthquake had been left behind. It was Finn the Deep time.

Finnbogi the Boggy would have taken no small measure of lecherous delight to be on his own with a trio of seriously hot women. Finn the Deep was not like that. He'd certainly never fantasise about the three women stopping, rubbing scented oil on each other and telling him that this had all been a ruse to get him on his own and . . .

No. He was Deep. He was not Boggy.

He focused on listening for the squatch's mind. He thought he'd found it, but it turned out to be a bighorn sheep pissed off because humans were walking where it wanted to walk. Finn was glad when he realised it wasn't the squatch; that bighorn was one seriously angry animal. He tried to tell it to get some perspective. They were delaying it only a couple of heartbeats, after all. It told him, he was fairly certain, to lower himself arse-first onto a barrel cactus.

Then he found the squatch.

Unfortunately, the squatch heard his mind too.

Sofi held a clenched fist aloft. They stopped.

"You've woken it up," she said.

"Yes. Sorry."

"Do we need to attack?"

"Hang on."

Finn reached out again but found nothing.

The three women stared at him. They were lovely. No, they weren't. Well, they were, but . . .

"Focus, Finn," said Thyri, "the squatch could be ripping Ottar's legs off right now."

"That's probably not helpful," said Sassa.

"It isn't," Finn confirmed. "Please be quiet."

They were silent. Sassa, Thyri and, for the love of Tor, Captain of the Owsla Sofi Tornado were quiet because he had told them to be. They were relying on him. He was Finn the Deep now and – and he really had to focus. Squatch squatch squatch.

*Hello?* he tried.

*Who's that?* replied a voice similar to Ayla's, if you could call something that you couldn't hear a voice.

*Finn. Finn the Deep.*

*What do you want?*

*You've got Ottar the Moaner?*

*The Moaner?*

*That's his name.*

*What a horrible name to give to a baby.*

*It's a tribe thing. We mock the people we love. Can we come and get him?*

*No.*

*No?*

*You don't deserve him. You left him when he needed you. I*

*found him terrified and upset because his sister was in danger. You left him.*

*I didn't leave him. I was with his sister.*

*So it was you that put his sister in danger?*

*Well, yes, but she made me.*

*You left him on his own. A baby in the middle of nowhere. You don't deserve him. He wanted me to take him.*

Finn sighed. This was not going well.

"What's happening, Finn?" asked Thyri, but both Sofi and Sassa waved at her to be quiet.

*He's not a baby, he's a boy.* He tried. *And the others left him by mistake to try to save his sister. As soon as they realised they'd left him they ran back. When we realised you'd taken him we walked all night – we climbed a cliff – to get him back. Doesn't that prove we deserve him?*

*Did you save his sister?*

*. . . No*

*What happened to her?*

*She was swept downriver by a flash flood.*

*You let her drown?*

*Not on purpose. And she may not have drowned.*

*You don't know if she drowned? No, no, stop talking now. You are not taking him. He's mine and I'll look after him.*

*He will want to come with us.*

*He will not, and even if he does it's because he doesn't know what's good for him. Babies don't.*

*Can we talk about this face to face?*

*Come any closer and I'll kill you all. In fact, go away now.*

*We are Ottar's people. He belongs—*

*That's it! I'm coming to kill you.*

*But we're Ottar's friends! I'm his brother, sort of—*

He was interrupted by a roar; a real-life, bone-shaking, trouser-filling roar.

Finn and the three women looked up at the cluster of pinnacles. The squatch ran out. It was huge, at least as large as the largest squatch from the Shining Mountains.

It looked about and spotted them, a hundred paces away in the valley below. Beating its chest, it roar-screamed, even louder now it wasn't shielded by rock. Then it charged.

Finn looked at the three others in the elite squad and raised his hands apologetically.

"Stop fannying about, start running," said Sofi. And she was off.

Finn had never been a fast runner. He should have been able to go faster, but it was like he was in a dream. Thyri, Sofi and pregnant Sassa tore away, leaving him in their red dust.

The squatch was on him in a moment.

*I am your friend!* he mentally squeaked as a great paw grabbed his head from behind and whisked him into the air.

All he heard from the squatch was rage.

The beast grabbed both his feet with its other paw, held him across its chest and pulled.

Finn felt his neck bones pop.

He pummelled at the beast with his fists and tried to bite the fingers encircling his head, but he might as well have attacked a tree.

*I am Ottar's brother*, he roared in his mind.

Something that felt pretty vital popped in his neck. Tor's fucking balls, he thought. He'd come through all this only to have his head ripped off by something which was meant to be on their side.

Weird clouds bloomed in his mind. He felt another pop in his neck.

Sofi came sprinting back, hand axe in one hand, dagger-tooth knife in the other. She jumped and flew at the squatch, power and beauty combined in the perfect killing animal.

But then she seemed to collapse in mid-air. The squatch

stood aside and Sofi fell past to crumple in a heap on the red sand.

Ayla's sister roared, and pulled. Something snapped in Finn's groin.

Would his legs come off before his head, he wondered, as the agony seized him.

Then he could think no more. He could do nothing other than scream as the squatch continued to tear him in two.

# Chapter 12

## Wasp Men

Freydis the Annoying slept by the fire.

Paloma Pronghorn brained a squirrel with her killing stick, skinned it, spitted it and set the shiny carcass over the flames. While the rodent roasted, she sliced stems from beavertail cactus and rubbed them in sand to remove the spines. She used her knife and her killing stick to carry rocks from the fire to a pool left in a pothole by the receded flood and added the chopped-up cactus stems to the boiling water.

Paloma had cooked plenty of animals before because it was fun, but she'd never cooked a plant. Other people cooked plants. She ate them. But she'd seen it done and thought she'd give it a go, to kill some time while the child slept. That's what she told herself. She knew full well that she was really trying to make amends to the girl for losing her temper. Now that she was calm, she was a little freaked out that she'd become so angry. She had very nearly hit the kid. She'd no idea that she had a temper like that.

It was because she'd been so worried about Freyis all night, obviously, so you could argue that it was an anger born of noble sentiment and affection. But that was a reason, not an excuse.

A red-spotted toad floated to the surface of her cooking pothole, upside down, limbs splayed. Paloma hoiked it out. It slapped wetly onto the rock and lay still. *Sorry*, she thought.

Innowak's tits, she was not doing well. Checking your pool for animals was probably step one of pothole cooking.

She flicked the dead toad into the river.

Was she going to be a dreadful parent who shrieked at their children in public, she wondered? Her father had been one of those. The first emotion Paloma could remember was embarrassment as her father yelled at her and her sister in a purple-faced, vein-throbbing rage because they'd been mucking about in some busy but sombre place.

She fished out a piece of cactus on the point of her knife, blew it, tried it and decided it needed a little longer.

Of course, she'd have to meet someone with whom to have children before she worried about what kind of mother she was going to be. That didn't seem likely at the moment. She was annoyed with herself for snogging Finn. When the group was reunited, she mustn't, she thought, get so drunk that she shagged him. Then again, she'd managed to resist that easily enough last time and she'd been properly shit-faced. There probably, she mused, wasn't enough booze in the world to make her shag Finn.

Freydis woke.

They sat on the beached raft and Freydis ate while Paloma explained their situation. She was outlining it to herself really, laying out the challenges and possible solutions, not expecting help from a six-year-old.

"So I guess the answer," she said at the end, "is to walk back along the river."

"It's not," said Freydis, her voice muffled by a mouthful of squirrel (she'd tried one bite of cactus and gone straight back to squirrel). "We should carry on down the Red River on the raft until we find somewhere nice that we can live for a while."

"Should we?"

"We should. The rest are headed south. You say we came south-west overnight, over a hundred miles?"

"We did."

"So we're here," Freydis drew lines in the sand. "And they're there. We could walk back upriver and then south and hope to catch up, which we probably won't, or we could walk east to try to meet them and get lost, or we could wait for them to come west. So we wait. We can't wait here, though, there's no shelter. We might be found by living versions of that wasp man, or worse, so we need a cave or at least some proper trees."

"How will the others find us?"

"Ottar always knows where I am. As long as you stay with me and he's with them, they'll find us."

She peered into the child's eyes. Freydis stared back at her, chewing squirrel.

Paloma stood. The broad, brown river rushed by. Could she lie on the raft and kick her legs and propel them upstream? For a hundred miles? Maybe. But even if she could they'd still have to track the others, which would be boring and difficult.

So, waiting made some sense, and it also made sense to find somewhere decent to wait. But was she really going to hunker down in a desert that everyone said was full of monsters and disasters and risk never seeing her friends again on the say-so of a six-year-old?

She guessed she was.

"Okay, let's get some provisions together and—"

A scream rang out downriver. Paloma had heard a lot of screams in her time but this was a new one. It was loud and bone-juddering but also melodious, as if a woman was being tortured with her lips sewn around the mouthpiece of a bone flute.

"We should hide," said Freydis.

"Owsla don't hide."

Another scream ripped the air, then another, each louder than the last.

"However," Paloma continued, "we could lie tactically under these bushes until we see what's making that noise. And let's put the fire out. We don't have enough squirrel to spare so we don't want anyone joining us."

"Good idea!"

They scooped sand over the fire then lay together under a low bush. Moments later a large flying creature flapped around the downstream meander. Five more followed.

At first Paloma thought they were large birds flying quite slowly, then she realised it was a trick of perspective and they were very large birds flying at a good clip. Then she realised that they weren't birds at all. She very nearly gawped.

The dead one had been pretty awful, but the wasp men looked a lot more fearsome when they were alive. Shiny insectoid man-sized bodies were carried along on huge, leathery wings. Round black eyes on stalks protruded from acorn-shaped heads. Six crab legs ending in human-like hands sprouted from their thoraxes, and, above those, two sturdier limbs ended in long, thick pincers. Shiny black abdomens hung like armoured pinecones, stings like black, pointy penises protruding from the tips.

"*They're not very nice, are they?*" Freydis whispered.

"Shall we be quiet for now and discuss them when they've passed?" Paloma suggested.

The creatures flapped by. Their wingbeats sounded like soiled blankets slapped against rocks.

Then they started screaming again and Paloma missed the wing-slapping. The screams were directed at something on the far side of the valley. Paloma got up on her elbows. It was a lion, a big one. The creatures flew towards it, screaming and screaming.

The lion stood transfixed, as if frozen by the onslaught of sound. A flying horror flapped down, grabbed the lion's torso with six hands and snipped off its head with a pincer, with as much effort as a man snicking the head off a flower with a knife.

The wasp men landed. Paloma couldn't see past the tightly packed monsters, but it was clear that they were ripping the lion apart and eating it.

"What's happening?" whispered Freydis.

"They're resting for a while."

"Have they seen us?"

"No. Stay where you are."

Much more quickly than one would imagine it took six human-sized animals to eat a large cat, the beasts flapped skyward, dripping blood, leaving nothing but a bloody stain where the lion had been.

Paloma waited a while after the creatures had disappeared around the next upriver meander, then crawled out from their bush.

"What were they doing?" asked Freydis.

"Hunting, by the looks of it, along the river. I hope nobody followed us . . ." she tailed off. Chances were that at least some of their friends had followed them down the Red River.

Sitsi Kestrel stood before the Swan Empress Ayanna on the Mountain of the Sun.

"You are accused of remaining alive while six of the Owsla have been killed. Have you anything to say before we cook you and eat you?"

All the dead Owsla – Morningstar, Talisa White-tail, Luby Zephyr, Sadzi Wolf, Caliska Coyote and Malilla Leaper – stood behind the empress. Sitsi's joy at seeing her friends again made her forget for a moment that she was to be cooked and eaten. But only for a moment.

She didn't want to be eaten!

She turned to run, but the dead Owsla women screamed, chased her down and grabbed her. They tore at her, ripping her clothes. They lifted her above their heads, chanting her name and shaking her.

"Sitsi! Oi, Sitsi!" It was Keef. She was in the canoe. Her head was on his lap and he was shaking her shoulder. She sat up. They weren't in Calnia. They were on the northern bank of the Red River. With the hand that wasn't shaking her, Keef was holding the low rocky bank.

"Get out smartish," said Keef, "and take your bow and arrows please."

Sitsi did as she was bid. She'd been awake for about three heartbeats and Keef hadn't make a joke yet. Something was very wrong.

The Owsla man followed her up onto the rock platform. He reached back down to the river and lifted his boat out, then grabbed Arse Splitter from it.

"What's happened?" asked Sitsi.

"I heard a screech like nothing I've ever heard before, then a couple more, coming closer. I reckon there are monsters approaching."

"Wasp men?"

He shook his head. "Sounded much bigger. Remember that dragon thing that burst into a cloud of wasps when we met Dead Nanda's people?"

"No? What are you talking about?"

Keef raised an eyebrow. "You've forgotten about the dragon?"

Sitsi smiled. "Yup, it's completely slipped my mind. A flying monster that burst into wasps after I shot it isn't a big deal for me."

"Ha! You had me. Good. Anyway, point is, by the noise of them, we've got a few more of The Meadows' monsters flying towards us."

The stood and listened. Nothing.

"I really did hear it," said Keef, sounding as if he was trying to convince himself.

Sitsi stretched and looked around.

The landscape had changed while she'd slept. Upriver, debris-skirted towers and mesas of red rock thrust monument-ally out of the green and red land. Downriver, the channel entered a canyon and took an immediate sharp turn out of sight southwards.

Standing next to her was the one-eared Wootah man peering downriver with his one eye, looking for the monsters he said he'd heard.

She had woken from a really weird dream into a weirder reality.

"What exactly did you hear?" she asked.

A screech echoed out of the downriver canyon. It sounded like the scream of a demon having its nipples twisted off by a bigger demon.

"Something like that," said Keef.

More screeches rang out, closer. Whatever was making them would surely appear at any moment.

"We should hide," said Sitsi.

"You hide. Arse Splitter and I will greet the beasts."

"There's no point only one of us hiding."

"So don't hide."

Sitsi snorted, strung her bow, plucked a dozen arrows from her quiver and placed them on the red rock. Dry ground, space all around and almost no wind. It was a good archer's perch. Excitement thrilled through her limbs. It had been a while since she'd put an arrow in a foe. She just hoped these weren't impervious to arrows . . .

Keef peered downriver, axe in hand. For once, he wasn't leaping about like a fool. Motionless, he radiated a calm, reassuring strength.

The screechers flew into sight. There were six of them — living versions of the dead horror they'd seen upriver, with bodies the size of bears and wings to match.

They weren't insects as someone had said, because they

had eight legs, not six. They were more like flying lobsters. Their human-like hands, six on each beast, opened and closed as they flew, as if ready to grasp their prey. Yuck, thought Sitsi.

Their heads were worse than their hands – black and featureless, other than for a line which was presumably a mouth, and two black balls on stalks which must have been eyes. Those eyes. Sometimes Sitsi regretted having super-eyesight. Their eyes were all black initially, but as she focused in on the leader's, the sheath that encased the eyeball slid back to reveal an interior of shiny, swirling white-orange, with a dark red dot in the centre.

The dot focused on her. He, she or it screamed and changed course towards them. The rest followed, blaring their ear-offending screams.

Keef was saying something. The creatures were coming fast, a hundred paces away now.

"What?" she shouted.

"What?" he shouted back.

She looked at him and gestured that she couldn't hear. He made arrow-shooting gestures.

*Well, obviously*, she thought.

She shot the first one in the head. Its wings folded and tumbled into the Red River with a splash that they couldn't hear above the screaming of the others.

Sitsi breathed out. So they weren't arrow-proof. She paused for a moment to see if slaying the first deterred the others. No. If anything, they screamed louder and flew faster towards them.

She put the next arrow through the beast's abdomen to see what that would do. The arrow cracked through the chitin body in between the pincer arms without too much trouble, but the wasp man flew on, apparently untroubled.

Headshots, then.

She shot four more, then Keef shouted: "Leave the last one to me, please!"

Sitsi skipped clear, keeping an arrow ready on her bowstring.

Seeing that the missile threat was gone, the final attacker slowed. It had a sting the length of a forearm on the end of its abdomen, like a spear tipped with a pearlescent globule which had to be venom.

"Watch that stinger, Keef!" she cried.

Keef nodded, pacing and swinging his long-handled axe from side to side. He probably, thought Sitsi, spent at least half his waking moments practising with that one weapon. He was no Owsla – he didn't have the alchemical advantage – but he was skilled.

That said, he didn't have eight limbs, six hands, giant pincers, a body that could take an arrow through it without harm, or wings.

The beast flapped closer. Keef stood, arms open, Arse Splitter in one hand. It looked like he was inviting the beast to have a go at his chest.

It ignored the offer. It flapped almost lazily upwards until it was fifty paces above, then dipped its head, tucked its wings and fell, pointed end of its closed claws foremost.

Bouncing on his toes, Keef took his axe-spear in two hands and watched it come.

Ten paces up, the beast flipped in mid-air and stopped. It hovered at head height, pointed its sting at Keef and squirted creamy white goo in a wide, heavy spray.

Sitsi gasped.

Keef leapt backwards, landed on his hands and threw himself sideways. He rolled and leapt up as the beast squirted again.

The Wootah man jumped, avoiding the ejaculate.

Where the first salvo had landed, Sitsi saw that the rock

was dissolving in oily bubbles. One did not, she guessed, want that stuff on one's skin. The Owsla outfit left her head, arms, midriff and thighs exposed. She backed away.

"Shall I shoot it?" she called.

"Don't shoot! If it's anything like me . . ." Keef danced, spinning towards the wasp man. It pulsed its thorax to squirt again, but only managed to dribble a cupful of gloop onto the rock below.

The Wootah man swung Arse Splitter, holding the weapon by the end of the shaft, and sliced the attacker's head from its body. The beast fell.

"Ha!" Keef danced a circle. "The creature sought to send the Wootah man to Valhalla, but Arse Splitter showed him to the halls of the headless!"

"You said something about *If it's anything like me?*" Sitsi asked when Keef's victory routine was done.

"Ah, that, yes." His pale face reddened like a shrimp dropped into boiling water.

"Yes?"

"Never mind that. Now, I am a humble man and although—"

"You are a humble man."

"Please don't interrupt when I'm proclaiming."

"I'm sorry."

"Apology accepted. So, I am a humble man and although nobody could have doubted the outcome of my fight with the beast, it would have been more difficult to fight all six. I would still have won, obviously," he looked enquiringly at Sitsi and she nodded, "but I would have needed to exert myself. Had Arse Splitter and I been attacked by a dozen of the fell creatures, maybe even we would have fallen. Your bow, however, could have sent two dozen or more of them back to their foul realm. So, I would like to make a bow like yours and I will allow you to teach me how to use it."

"I'd be glad to," said Sitsi, "but you have to ask."

"I am in your land and happy to adapt to your bizarre Scrayling ways. Please will you teach me to shoot a bow?"

"I will."

"I may also require aid in its design and fabrication."

"So?"

"Please will you help me make it?"

"I will."

They smiled at each other as the wasp man's venom bubbled in puddles of dissolving rock.

# Chapter 13

## Paternal Support

Finn stopped screaming to draw breath and heard *Taanya! Taanya!* in his mind.

Mercifully, the grip on his neck and feet was relaxed, then released. He whumped down onto the red sand. Moments later Sassa and Thyri ran up, skidded to a halt and stood, wary but ready to attack.

*How do you know my name?* asked the squatch.

*I know more than your name*, Erik continued, *I know that you're kind and good. I know you're attacking us because you think we're a threat to Ottar. We are not. We love him. Your sister Ayla would tell you as much.*

Finn's neck and hips were in several sorts of pain. He crawled away from the squatch, over to the prone Sofi.

*Ayla? How do you know Ayla? Have you seen her?*

Sofi was unconscious but breathing.

*She's our friend*, Erik continued. *We helped each other to escape from an evil bastard who had us imprisoned in the Badlands, then she helped us escape from your father Berlaze.*

*Berlaze? Wait, no, tell me first what she was doing in the Badlands.*

*Why don't we all join Ottar and talk about it? We don't want to leave him alone, do we?*

*You'll try to snatch Ottar!*

*And you can kill us with your mind if we do.*

*Good point. Come on then.*

Finn looked up – an apology would have been nice – but the squatch strode away.

"Well done, Finn." Sofi was sitting up and rubbing her head.

"Actually, it was Erik. He got into her mind."

"What did he say?"

"He was nice to her."

Thyri laughed. "Did the big warrior need Daddy to rescue him?"

Finn held her eye. "I suppose he did."

They walked up to Taanya's eyrie. The circle of rock towers, maybe twenty paces high, sprouted imposingly from the promontory. It would have made a wonderful longhouse, Finn thought, or more accurately a tallhouse, for the most vainglorious jarl.

Finn was limping and his neck felt seriously odd, but he wasn't badly damaged. Sofi was physically fine after her mind crush, but she was scowling like a newly caged lion. Not a fan of losing fights, that one.

"How come the gods didn't make any weird rock structures near Hardwork?" Finn asked, not speaking to anyone in particular.

"Are you sure it wasn't a demon?" asked Thyri, walking behind him.

She had a point. The whole world west of the Shining Mountains was far too messed up for any god to have created it, apart from possibly Loakie, but Loakie was no maker of worlds.

The path climbed up the side of the bluff through the pinyon pine, juniper and rabbits, then doubled back on itself along the ridge, towards the spectacular natural fort where Ottar was apparently concealed.

A passage led to a roofless chamber with a packed earth floor. A fire smoked in one corner. In the another, perched on a plinth and looking very pleased with himself, was Ottar the Moaner.

Finn, Erik, Sofi and Wulf sat with Taanya and told her everything that had happened from the Badlands on, and about their quest to go to The Meadows and defeat the force there that was bent on destroying the world.

It was odd conversing in silence, not least because they could hear the others buggering about outside. By the sounds of it, Thyri was sparring with Chogolisa, Ottar was chasing rabbits and Sassa was chasing Ottar. Bodil and Yoki Choppa were gathering herbs and insects.

*Finn*, he heard in his mind after a while. *Finn?* It was Erik.

*Yes?*

*Have you been paying any attention?*

*Not really.*

*Do try to keep up, please. Will you tell Taanya what Ayla told you?*

*She sends her love, and she said that you'd be able to tell us more about what's going on at The Meadows.*

*She also said*, Sofi added, *that you might know how we can defeat the force at The Meadows.*

*Haven't got a clue*, thought Taanya. *I had noticed some strange weather, and there have been a lot of new animals flying around. They've killed quite a lot of predators, but they haven't troubled me and I don't trouble them.*

*So you can't help?* thought Wulf.

*I cannot.*

*Do you know anyone who might be able to?* asked Erik.

*Yes.*

*Who?*

*A man like you, called Ola Wolvinder. He lives two days' walk from here. Probably four days of your short-legged walking. He lives alone because nobody would want to live with him. But he knows everything. Or at least a lot. He's old.*

"Ola Wolvinder?" said Wulf, giving Erik a meaningful look. "Interesting name."

"And he's old . . ." Erik widened his eyes knowingly.

"What?" said Finn. "What are you talking about?"

# Chapter 14

## Separate Ways

Paloma Pronghorn poled the raft to avoid a shoal on the inner curve of a broad meander. It was even hotter than the day before and the landscape had climbed yet another notch in splendid weirdness. It was still made up of red cliffs, skirted mesas and towers, but they were larger and even less likely looking. In some places there was no vegetation at all, just scree and heat-cracked boulders. On the outer edge of the meander, a red and black rock wall without so much as a blade of grass blemishing its precipitous face plunged directly into the water.

The current caught the raft and Paloma sat. There was no wind and the sun blazed, but they'd made comically large reed hats and the odd splash of spray from the river was refreshing. For the first time she could remember, Paloma didn't yearn to run. She was happy listening to the girl's stories.

They'd been a lot quieter when they'd set off, listening out for more of the flying creatures or any other horrors, but none had appeared and they'd relaxed.

Freydis the Annoying spoke without seeming to draw breath; a skill learned from Bodil Gooseface, guessed Paloma. She told legends of gods and heroes from the old world, the story of Olaf Worldfinder crossing Olaf's Salt Sea a hundred years before, travelling inland along rivers and across great lakes and forming the town of Hardwork, how the Goachica had looked after them that first winter and ever more, until the Calnians destroyed their town.

As the raft bobbled over one of the rare stretches of tame rapids, Freydis asked why the Calnians had destroyed their town and killed almost all the Hardworkers.

"Adults," said Paloma, "are dicks."

"Dicks, Paloma Pronghorn?"

"Silly, nasty, selfish people."

"Raskova the Spiteful and Marina the Farter, who were Jarl Brodir the Gorgeous's daughters, were silly and nasty *and* selfish and they were children. And you're an adult and you're nice and kind."

"Some children are dicks and some adults aren't. And I have done some silly, nasty and selfish things."

"Like what?"

"I'll tell you another time."

"I know. Like kissing Finn the Deep."

"How do you know about that?"

"Ottar told me."

"Who told . . . oh, never mind. What was I talking about?"

"Why your people killed all of mine."

*Not all*, thought Paloma, but she didn't say it. Her tribe had killed most of Freydis's tribe, and tried to kill the rest of them, so she wasn't in a position to quibble.

"The point is adults can be as silly and nasty as children, but the difference is that some of them have power, so they can do nasty things for silly reasons and hurt people badly."

"Like kissing someone and hurting them because they like you afterwards but you don't like them in the same way?"

"Yes, that would be one example." *Freydis was meant to be six years old. Could that be right?* "Another, much more serious and important example, would be setting off to massacre another tribe because your empress had a dream about them."

"Why didn't anyone tell the empress it was a silly thing to do?"

"You don't *tell* an empress anything."

And so they chatted, floating down the river, keeping an eye out for somewhere to hole up and wait for the others. But there was no rush. The Meadows was southwest, and that was the direction the Red River was taking them.

"How about you stop paddling," said Keef the Berserker.

"Why?"

"Save your arms in case you need to shoot a whole flock of those insects."

She didn't need to save her arms. She knew that he just wanted to do all the work to look heroic. And who was she to stop him? She tucked her paddle into the canoe beside her, trying to quash the urge to tell him that the wasp men weren't insects. Insects had six legs, not eight.

"You're calling them insects?" she heard herself say. Seems she couldn't quite quash the urge.

"Yup."

She squeezed her lips tight and tried to focus on signs that Paloma had run along this part of the river. Her traces – a bent twig here, some missing leaves there – would have been invisible to most others, but to Sitsi it was like Paloma had run along with paint-soaked brushes attached to her elbows.

Keef broke the silence after a while: "Why does it bug you so much that I think the wasp men are insects?"

"Because they're not?" She was annoyed that he'd realised she was annoyed.

"And you know that. So why does it matter to you if I've got it wrong?"

"Because it's good to be right."

"And you are. Why worry about anybody else?"

"Because . . . Pull to the bank. I've lost Paloma's tracks."

Keef angled the paddle and the boat's nose shifted

shorewards. "Could she have diverted away from the river again?"

"She's only done that when she's needed to before. There's no need here, the bank is flat and clear." Sitsi stood in the prow and looked upriver. "Yes, she stopped back there."

The large-eyed Owsla woman leapt from the canoe, almost too terrified to confirm or deny what she thought she'd seen.

But it was clear. A raft had been dragged up the shingle and pushed out again. There'd been a campfire. And, all around, were large, fresh human footprints and small, fresh human footprints.

"Keef! Freydis is alive!" she shouted, still examining them to be triple certain. "The raft stayed intact. She must have rode it all the way here!"

She spun. Keef was running towards her. He picked her up and held her tight and shouted: "Wooootah!"

Sitsi put her arms round him and squeezed hard. He felt wonderful, he smelt wonderful.

He put her down. She looked up at his pale blue eye. He looked back.

"Right," he said, stepping away.

"Right," she agreed, stepping back herself.

"So where did they go?"

"Downriver, on the raft."

"Why? And why did Freydis stay on the raft for so long? And how?"

"We'll catch them up and ask."

"Could take a while."

"It could."

"Well, at least we'll be in the same boat. Ha ha ha!"

She punched his arm.

Erik the Angry and Chogolisa Earthquake fell back to the rear of the group walking southwards. Taanya was leading the way, carrying Ottar the Moaner. Erik suspected that the squatch still intended to keep Ottar. The best idea might be to kill Taanya in her sleep and find their own way to Ola Wolvinder, but he wasn't sure if he'd be able to do it, nor if he wanted to. She was helping them and she was Ayla's sister.

What was more, the boy seemed to like the squatch. Every now and then they heard a burst of manic laughter and roaring chuckles up ahead as the two of them larked about.

"I'd still rather I was carrying him," said Chogolisa, as if reading Erik's mind.

"Me too," agreed Erik. "And I'd rather Freydis was on my shoulders and not—" he shook his head, not far from tears.

"She'll be fine. She's not the dying type," Chogolisa reassured him.

"Sure. And there are benefits to not carrying them. You can have enough of a child's warm groin pressed against the back of your neck."

"You can."

They walked on under the blue sky and burning sun, past low sandy hummocks backdropped by green hills. Far ahead and southwards were snow-capped mountains. To the west the land dropped away into hot, red haze.

It was getting towards camp-making time when two figures walked towards them from the west.

It was a man and a woman, both maybe ten years older than Erik. They stopped fifty paces away and stared at the Wootah and Calnians.

"Don't worry, we mean no harm!" cried Wulf. "In fact, the opposite. If you need food, or would like to shelter with us for the night, you are more than welcome."

"How do we know you don't mean us any harm?" asked the man. His voice was a smoky drawl, similar to Weeko Fang's, their guide who'd been killed by the squatch.

"By my winning smile?" Wulf asked.

"The last person who robbed us was smiling."

"Do you get robbed a lot?"

"Are you new here?"

"Taanya isn't." Wulf pointed at the squatch. "The rest of us are."

"Go back where you came from." He seemed unimpressed that one of their number was a squatch. "There's nothing here but death. If the monsters or the land don't get you, the people will. The only men and women west of here are the destitute and the bastards preying on them. We've had everything taken bar our lives and that's only because we're too old to eat. They ate everyone else."

"Who did?"

"Monsters ate some, people ate the rest."

"We won't eat you." Wulf laid his hammer on the ground and spread his arms.

"If you're truly decent, walk on."

"You're sure we can't help you?"

"You want to help? Then get out of our way. We mean to head on east. You should do the same. The gods have gone mad in the west."

"Gods?" cried the woman, her voice like a melodramatic mourner at a funeral, "Gods? The gods fled the west a long time ago."

# Chapter 15

## Caught

Paloma Pronghorn and Freydis the Annoying drifted on downstream between red rock banks, chatting and looking for somewhere suitable to hole up and wait for the others.

The Owsla warrior enjoyed the day alone with a child more than she would have guessed. It made her feel like an actual adult for once. Talking to the girl, she remembered when she'd thought and spoke like Freydis. She saw how much she had changed since then, how she had become a woman like her own mother. She felt a burgeoning, warm desire to look after the girl, to encourage her to enjoy and explore the world. She wanted to protect the child from . . . well, everything. She felt a new, keen sense of horror at the danger that surrounded them, not for herself but for Freydis.

It was weird.

Talking to Freydis all day was also, paradoxically, a return to childhood. When they set out on the raft together, Paloma's approach had been didactic: she tried to tell Freydis about the things they were passing and how they worked. However, perhaps because this bizarre land was as new to her as it was to Freydis, Paloma found herself dropping the instructor role and conversing with Freydis as an equal. As well as the strange world around them, they talked about what they'd been through together since they'd met by the Water Mother.

Paloma listened more than she spoke. That was another surprise. Generally, Paloma found herself thinking about other things when people – usually Sitsi – launched a barrage of opinions at her. Freydis, however, was interesting. She had observed a lot. She explained how Sofi controlled Wulf by letting him make all the minor decisions while making all the important ones herself, and gave examples. Paloma nodded – the girl was spot-on – and wondered how it came to be that this spindly limbed, pale-skinned, *six-year-old* was a more astute observer of human behaviour that she herself would ever be.

They drifted along, failing to find an appropriate place for a long-term camp. Time went quickly and soon the first bats of the evening were flitting among bankside cacti and scrub.

Paloma angled the pole in to steer around an islet of tangled flotsam, and told the girl not to worry.

"I'm not worried."

"Maybe you should be." Paloma glanced skyward.

"Why?" Freydis was wide-eyed.

Paloma sighed. She didn't want the child to be afraid, but she did, she realised, want her to appreciate that Paloma was her brave and necessary guardian. What was wrong with her?

"There's no reason to worry. I'm just kidding. We can camp on the bank and carry on tomorrow."

As if to contradict Paloma, they floated around a bend and into a steep, bank-free gorge. Paloma was confident that the land would flatten out on at least one side soon enough. It always had before.

"But what will happen if the monsters come in the night?" asked the girl as the cliffs loomed high on either side.

Paloma looked at Freydis. She had the strangest sense that the child was humouring her.

"I won't let them hurt you."

Freydis nodded, apparently appeased, but Paloma was pretty sure it was her need to be the protector that had been satisfied.

They drifted down the darkening gorge in silence, Paloma looking at the girl. She was the first child Paloma had spent any time with. Maybe all children were like that these days, she thought.

Around the next bend, satisfyingly, there was lowland on both banks.

"Right," said the speedy Owsla woman, picking up the pole, "I'm hungry and it's about time we—"

"Look!" Freydis pointed downriver.

A bridge spanned the channel. It was the longest bridge Paloma had ever seen by some margin and also the most complicated – a mass of criss-crossing timber beams and struts. Back east, streams might be bridged, but a river this wide would be crossed by boat.

Paloma scanned the banks. Bridges meant people, and people, in her experience, meant trouble.

She couldn't see anything amiss, but she didn't like it.

"Let's carry on downriver for a while." She didn't cease her vigil.

"Yes," nodded Freydis.

They drifted on.

A noise on the southern bank startled them. A coyote padded into sight from a clump of bushes and strolled along, eyes forward and tongue lolling as if lost in its thoughts. Freydis coughed, the coyote leapt as if it had been hit on the rump with a sling stone, darted a glance at the girl and the woman on the raft then ran for the rocky hillock some hundred paces from the bank. From where three people were running towards them, fast, leaping bushes and rocks.

Two were lean and one was large. Not Chogolisa large, but big enough. By the pace he was going, he wasn't fat.

All three were, in fact, preternaturally quick, either alchemically enhanced or bolstered by some other magic. Big balls of black curly hair bounced around their faces as they ran. They would have been comical if they hadn't been terrifying.

They headed for the bridge. They were going to reach it before the raft did.

"Pissflaps," said Paloma.

"What does that mean?" asked Freydis.

She pointed.

"Oh no! Are they going to jump on us?"

Paloma dropped the pole and handed Freydis her killing stick.

"Whack them with this if you need to."

"What are you going to—"

Paloma jumped into the water behind the raft, grabbed the backmost log, took a big breath, submerged her face and kicked. It took a few moments to get going, but soon it felt like they were shifting along at a decent clip. Water surged in her ears.

She looked up after a while to take a breath.

"We're going to make it! Keep kicking!" Freydis was shaking her hands, lips pursed.

When she looked up next, Freydis was beaming. "You did it!"

The three runners were staring at them from the bridge, twenty paces back. They were all women, not men as Paloma had guessed by the way they ran. They wore light brown smocks which left bare, muscled arms; very muscled in the case of the large one. They had narrow eyes and cat-arse mouths, framed by manes of curly black hair. Sisters, Paloma guessed. They did not look kind. Despite their run, they weren't panting.

The large one held a big bundle and the other two had spears; the stocky, thrusting type and not the throwing type, thank Innowak. They glowered after the raft.

"Bye!" Paloma shouted. "Sorry we're going to miss the party!"

Freydis giggled.

The women stared hatred.

And then they disappeared.

Paloma blinked.

The trio were still there, but they'd squatted and arranged themselves in the framework of the bridge so they were almost totally invisible. Their cloaks, hair and arms looked like parts of the wooden structure.

"Clever!" Paloma called. "Any other tricks? I have an uncle who can make a rabbit crap gold."

The women remained motionless. It was sinister, but it was a lot better than if they'd followed along the banks. Paloma looked downriver. *Ah, there you go,* she thought.

The river cut into a gorge once again and it would be impossible to follow on foot next to the channel. Although, if you could run as fast as those three, it would be a doddle to sprint to the top of the gorge's cliffs and hurl rocks down on them.

Paloma resumed her kicking. She powered along, enjoying swimming for the first time. Pushing a relatively large raft crewed by a relatively small girl removed all the trying-to-float arse-ache which had so far done its best to elude her.

At her first breath they were nearly at the gorge.

"The women haven't moved," said Freydis.

Paloma nodded, dunked her face again and kicked on. After a while she thought she could hear Freydis shouting through the churn of the water. She stopped.

"—ALOMA PRONGHORN, STOP! Oh, thank goodness, you've stopped. I've been shouting for an age."

"What is it?" She looked back. The gorge had meandered and she could no longer see the bridge.

"A canoe was coming down the river behind us."

"Oh no." Paloma pulled herself onto the raft, snatched up her water shoes and began to strap them on.

"The canoe will be under the bridge by now," said Freydis. "There's no point you running into danger, too."

"Running into danger is what I do," said Paloma, glancing downriver. "Stop on that next island and wait for me."

And she was off, slapping across the water.

"It was them!" Sitsi cried.

"Who?" asked Keef.

"Rabbit Girl and Happycheeks the chipmunk. Who do you think?"

"I can't see anyone."

"They've gone round a corner. Come on, paddle!"

"You've seen the big wooden thing across the water?"

Sitsi gave the bridge a quick scan, then checked the banks and the hills on both sides.

"There's no danger, it's just an old bridge. Come on. There's no way we can go quick enough to catch them by sunset, but—"

The canoe surged as if struck by a fresh flash flood had struck it. Sitsi smiled. You didn't need to understand much about Keef to make him do what you wanted.

She saw the ambush far too late. Sitsi opened her mouth to shout a warning as two people jumped from the bridge holding a net between them.

They splashed into the river either side. Keef and Sitsi were squashed down into their canoe, trapped like livestock. The mesh was tight, heavy and taut. Sitsi couldn't even get at the knife at her waist, let alone grab an arrow to chuck at their attackers.

Head bent uncomfortably, Sitsi could see a woman up on the bridge, very large and hard-faced with curly black hair. She was hauling on a rope which Sitsi guessed was going to pull the net tighter and haul them ashore.

She was right.

The big woman heaved the canoe across the channel and up onto the bank. Sitsi prepared herself to attack the moment the net was released. Arse Splitter's metal head was by her feet. Keef would grab that, so she would leap in the other direction with her bow. Or would her knife be more use?

It was a moot argument, because they didn't release the net. Instead they tied it around the canoe with twine rope. Sitsi was squashed, head between her knees. She couldn't move her arms or legs.

"Can you let us out, please?" Keef tried.

Nobody answered.

"We are great warriors," he continued. Sitsi worried he was about to threaten them, which would not have been clever. "We can help you with whatever catch and rob thing you have going here. I'm sure you're good – you certainly caught us nicely and you look fantastic – but Sitsi here can shoot the eyebrows off a butterfly a mile away and I'm the most skilled axe man outside Valhalla. She's Calnian Owsla, I'm Wootah Hird. We are the best."

"It's not a catch and rob thing," said one of the trimmer women. "It's just a catch thing." She spoke the universal tongue in a sharp accent that rattled in her throat. Like the other two women, she had a large, pointed nose. They were definitely sisters. "We're not going to rob you."

"Oh, good," said Keef.

"We're going to kill you."

"That would be a mistake. We can be useful."

"You are going to be useful." The big one began to haul them away from the river. Her accent was similar, but her voice was shriller. "We're going to eat you."

"Only reason you're not dead yet," said the third, following alongside, "is to keep you fresh."

"We could help you find others to eat," suggested Keef. "You're great warriors, you say?"

"The greatest."

"I see. Thanks for letting us know. Usually we let our food go and have a good old chase. We like that."

"We do," confirmed the other smaller one.

"But we don't want to risk that with the *greatest* warriors. So we'll keep you tied up in your boat and kill you with spears when we're hungry."

"Then I must warn you," Keef said gravely, "that I intend to soil myself."

"Go ahead. You'll crap yourself anyway when we stick a spear in you. You all do. We'll give you a good wash when we gut you."

"I have unusually sticky crap."

"Don't worry. Soap made from human fat works wonders on shit and we've got more of that than we'll ever need."

"Hmmm." Keef was out of arguments.

"Have you heard of the Calnian Owsla?" asked Sitsi.

"Can't say I have, no. Hang on, though . . . is it a bird?"

"We are the finest warriors in the world. The rest of the Owsla will come looking for us. If you mistreat us in any—"

"You're more boring than your friend, even if you do have funny eyes. I don't want to listen to you. Come on, girls, let's go."

"You will listen and—"

"Silence, or I will kill you now." The woman's tone was so matter-of-fact that Sitsi believed her. They weren't going to talk their way out of this one.

The big woman dragged the canoe uphill across the desert, Sitsi and Keef trussed inside. Sitsi could see at first, but soon the canoe twisted upside down and they scraped over rock, sand, spiny-twigged bushes and small cactuses.

Behind her, in between grunts and ooofs, Keef managed to say, "Well, at least we're still in the same boat."

"That wasn't funny the first time," said Sitsi.

"Quiet, you two," said the smaller women who'd done most of the talking, "or I'll put a spear through—"

The canoe turned on its side and Sitsi saw what had interrupted the woman.

Paloma Pronghorn was sprinting up the hill towards them like an avenging whirlwind, brandishing a water shoe in each hand.

Sitsi smiled. Erik had gone to a lot of trouble sharpening and fire-hardening the heavy wood on the shoes' oval heads. It would be nice to see his efforts pay off.

The three curly haired women stepped to meet their attacker.

"What's happening?" asked Keef.

"Paloma's coming."

"She looking mean?"

She wasn't. She was smiling like a loon. Paloma loved a fight.

"Formidable more than mean. You would not want to be in our captors' sandals," Sitsi replied.

"Good."

Ten paces out, Paloma leapt and spun and flew towards the women, legs and arms a blur. It was one of her standard moves from the Plaza of Innowak. The crowd loved it and it worked every time.

The largest captor stepped to meet her. Paloma's water shoe flashed out of the flurry of limbs and cracked into the big woman's forehead. Sitsi didn't see quite what happened next, a cactus was briefly in the way, but a moment later the large woman was holding Paloma's ankle with one hand and swinging her around her head, like a child with a doll. Paloma was not light. This was a Chogolisa-level display of strength.

"Rip her leg off," said one of the slighter sisters.

The large woman grunted assent, gripped the ankle two-handed and swung round all the harder.

Paloma managed to twist and deliver an almighty whack to her spinner's head with a water shoe. The blow would have killed any normal person.

The curly headed giant didn't seem to notice. She spun faster, leaning back and putting all her weight into it.

"Stop!" Sitsi heard herself shout.

Faster and faster the woman danced in her circle. Sitsi thought she could hear the sinews in Paloma's knee and hip snapping.

"No!" she shouted.

Paloma lashed out with the water shoe again. This time she went for her own leg, slamming the hardened wooden blade into the twine which held her leather legging above the knee. The knot popped.

The giant had been gripping Paloma by the legging. When it came loose, she tumbled backwards. Paloma flew in the other direction. She landed hard, but was up in the blink of an eye. The other two enemies charged and Paloma fled up the hill, limping badly.

One of the attackers was faster than the other. She was also faster – Sitsi couldn't believe her big eyes – than Paloma. Her friend was injured, she told herself.

Two hundred paces up the hill, Paloma stopped and ran back at her pursuers, much faster than she'd being going moments before.

*Ha!* thought Sitsi. *She wasn't injured, she'd been drawing them away and spreading them out!*

Paloma smashed her water shoe across one face, then the other, sprinting on before either woman could strike back.

The desert dwellers turned and resumed their chase, as unaffected by the blows as their big sister. There was no way they were going to catch Paloma unless she messed up again, but nor did there seem any way for Paloma to hurt them.

Sitsi slumped with disappointment, which made her

bonds slacken a little. She tried again to get her knife, but it was no use.

The large woman returned to guard the canoe.

Paloma stopped and stood, ten paces away. She looked mean now.

"Come on then, little one," said the big woman in her strangely high voice. "Attack me. I'll rip your pretty leg off and beat you to death with it."

"Her sisters are coming!" Sitsi shouted. It would be only moments before they were on Paloma.

"Shut up!" A kick rolled the canoe and Sitsi could see no more.

Moments later they started shifting along the ground again.

"Was that one of your Owsla?" said the deepest of the throaty voices. "I'm not sure about *greatest* warriors in the world. But they are very good at running away."

It was dark by the time Paloma found Freydis. She'd lit a merry little fire on an island and was roasting a fish on a stick.

"Where are Sitsi Kestrel and Keef the Berserker?" asked Freydis.

"We're going to have to rescue them a different way."

"What happened?"

Paloma told her.

"So you can't hurt them? Like Beaver Man?" Freydis turned the charring fish. She sounded interested more than worried.

"I don't know. I couldn't make a dent in them. Then again, maybe I shouldn't have attacked three enhanced warriors armed only with a pair of shoes."

Freydis held up the obsidian moon blade which had belonged to Luby Zephyr. It glinted darkly in the firelight.

"Do you think this will cut them? Perhaps you could slice their tummies open and pull out their guts?"

Paloma smiled at the sweet voice conjuring up such a messy image. "I don't know." The blade was as sharp as any and Luby had indeed sliced open many tummies with it. She'd stuck the blade's pointed ends into plenty of eyes and necks, too.

But Paloma's hardest blow with hardened wood hadn't even bruised the women. Would the moon blade trouble them?

Paloma Pronghorn tracked the three captors and the dragged boat through the night. Dark mesas, bluffs and spikes of rock loomed. Moths, bats and owls swished through the calm, cool air. Unseen beasts scurried between bushes.

Freydis the Annoying ran behind, insisting that she was fine every time Paloma asked. The girl had stamina.

Paloma had the rope from the raft wound around a shoulder and Luby's obsidian moon blade in her hand. She was ready for the fight, but far from sure that she would win it.

She had to win it, she told herself.

If she lost, they'd get Freydis.

It was madness, of course, to bring the girl on a rescue attempt against three foes who might well be invincible, but it would have also been madness to leave her alone in a land busy with monsters and evil arseholes like the ones who'd captured their friends. In an insane world, one had to choose the least insane path.

The track of a canoe dragged across desert was absurdly easy to follow. Keef and Sitsi's captors knew that, of course. If they'd been the Owsla, they'd have laid the track over open ground. Sitsi would have waited on a rise and shot any foes who followed it.

The trail was crossing open ground now, so Paloma was half expecting an arrow in the chest at any moment. Again, she wasn't worried for herself. She'd always been so lucky that she was pretty sure she couldn't actually be killed.

She tried to keep in between any likely archer perches and Freydis.

The track plunged down a sandy chute into a dry stream bed. The newly risen moon shone through the slim twigs of dead trees and sliced sharp silver shapes onto the sand.

The stream bed was worse than the open ground. With their stout spears, this would be the place for the sour-faced warriors to ambush them.

They didn't, though. The trail emerged from the stream and followed a moderately used path to the head of a canyon, then down into the craggy cleft. There was something weird moving about on the ground, just before the track plunged over the canyon head.

Paloma approached slowly. It was a tarantula killing a mouse. She shuddered.

"Gosh," said Freydis, appearing at her side and peering down. "That's not very nice." She rolled the big spider and its victim over with the toe of her leather boot, but the tarantula kept its hairy legs wrapped round its prey and the mouse stopped struggling.

Paloma looked down the canyon. A cloud passed over the moon and she spotted the glow of a fire reflected on the western canyon wall, half a mile down. It had to be their lair.

The warrior's creeping terror for the child was blown away like autumn leaves in a tornado, replaced by the fizzing in her legs that she always felt before a fight. Her breathing calmed and her shoulders relaxed. She smiled.

Signalling Freydis to follow, she walked swiftly and silently away from the tracks, along the western rim of the canyon.

"What's that smell?" whispered Freydis after a short while. "Is it roasting pig?"

Paloma didn't answer. It wasn't pig.

Soon they could see the sisters' cave.

It was more of a niche than a cave, sliced into the far wall of the canyon three paces above the steam. It was maybe twenty paces wide and three high with a flat floor. Its interior was lit a flickering red-gold by a large fire. Two of the curly headed captors were sitting and staring into the dancing flames. The other sister was standing by the fire, turning a large spit. Impaled on the spit was a human body, its fat bubbling over the crackling flames.

# Chapter 16

## An Old Hardworker

Every time they stopped on the first day of the walk to find Ola Wolvinder, Wulf the Fat asked Yoki Choppa to use hair and his alchemy to divine the whereabouts of Keef the Berserker and Sitsi Kestrel. Finn the Deep could see that it was more often than the warlock considered necessary, but he did it anyway. He might not talk much, but Yoki Choppa was a good guy.

Other than a pause after dawn, the warlock reported that the two of them were heading south-west at an extra-ordinary pace.

"They're going faster than canoes are meant to go," said Chogolisa Earthquake. "They must have left the river and started running."

"A canoe made by Keef with Keef paddling does go a lot faster than canoes are meant to go," said Sassa Lipchewer.

"And the river is still in spate from the snowmelt," added Yoki Choppa in an uncharacteristic blurt of unsolicited information.

That night Keef and Sitsi stopped moving, as one would expect, but then all the next day and the next they stayed in the same place.

"They must have found Paloma and Freydis," said Sassa Lipchewer at the camp three nights after leaving Taanya's home, "but why aren't they coming back?"

"Because they're waiting for us," Wulf answered. "They

know that's the general direction we're planning to head, but don't know where we are. But they do know that we know where they are."

"That does make sense," Sassa nodded uncertainly. "I just hope Freydis is . . . Do you think she's all right, Ottar?"

He barked with laughter then hopped from foot to foot, grinning.

That meant precisely nothing, of course. Ottar was Ottar. But Finn the Deep decided to take the boy's reaction as confirmation that Freydis was alive. It suited his own buoyant mood to do so.

This new mood was entirely the result of Thyri Treelegs' thawing towards him. It seemed the further she was from Paloma, the happier she became; or perhaps the more she liked Finn.

They'd trained all three days of the journey so far. That evening's bout had been almost like the old times, when they'd just left Hardwork and been sharing a sleeping sack. Thyri had smiled several times, and when she whacked him with her sparring staff it wasn't malicious any more. It was more playful, and, dare Finn think it, flirty. He was pretty sure he wasn't imagining it.

He didn't risk suggesting that they share a sleeping sack again; he didn't want to ruin it. And besides, he was Finn the Deep now. If he was to end up with Thyri then he would woo her with words and deeds like a hero of old, rather than getting his jollies rubbing up against her in a sleepsack like Finnbogi the Boggy had.

The following morning the soft brown, folded hills to the east became larger and the green mountains behind were craggier and more looming every time Finn looked.

A little before noon, Taanya, still with Ottar on her shoulders, led them eastwards along a path that penetrated and climbed the sandy hills.

They were lucky to have Taanya, Finn was happy to admit. There were no signs of an actual path, but the squatch confidently avoided the steep gorges and peaks. Lucky to have her, that was, if she wasn't leading them to their deaths. She seemed genuine and helpful and Ottar liked her, but Beaver Man had been charming one-on-one and he'd been a madman who wanted to destroy the world. And, by the way she acted at night and wouldn't let anybody else carry him, it seemed like Taanya still thought Ottar was hers.

They emerged from the sandy hills, crossed a dip jammed with lush foliage and buzzing with bees, then began the slog up the mountain. The path zigzagged steeply. It was hot. The view opened up behind them to the west and they saw more of the Desert You Don't Walk Out Of, so red and smoky that it looked like it was on fire. So far away that they almost looked pretty, three red-black tornados skimmed slowly along the horizon.

Their destination lay across that baking, threatening land. Could humans even survive somewhere that looked that hot? And somewhere out there, hopefully, Freydis was waiting for them with Sassa, Keef and Sitsi. Finn shuddered. How could Freydis have survived? He promised Oaden that he would never perv at another woman – indeed he would never have another inappropriate thought about any woman . . . any of his immediately group, anyway – if Oaden kept Freydis alive.

After several false summits – there were always false summits – the way finally flattened out. Taanya led them back west along a well-used path cresting a spur of land between stunted trees thronged with hordes of sniffing, stretching and scurrying squirrels, chipmunks, mice and other little animals. The air was fresh, cool and floral. After a while, the aroma of stew wafted along on the breeze. It smelled just like the ones Gunnhild used to make back in Hardwork.

Odd, thought Finn, with a pang of sorrow that his aunt was no longer with them.

He caught up with the others at a clearing. They were all standing and staring. As well they might.

There, looking out over the Desert You Don't Walk Out Of, maybe a thousand miles from home, was a mini Hardwork.

At the far side of the clearing was a heavily built wooden longhouse, the same, as far as Finn could see, as the Jarl's longhouse they'd left behind. To their right was a replica of a Hardwork storage hut. To the left was a smaller version of the church where Finn had lived. In front of the church was a life-sized (or death-sized, depending on how you looked at it) carved Krist on a wooden cross, although this one had a much bigger, beardier face than the Hardwork Krist and a great carved mane of hair.

Finn gawped. His fellow Wootah and Calnians were gawping, too, apart from Yoki Choppa and Sofi, obviously, and Wulf and Erik, who were looking at the longhouse with wry twists on their lips and a twinkle in their eyes. Finn reset his face into an expression of manly expectation that better fitted Finn the Deep.

*But what, in the name of Tor's big sweaty balls, was going on?*

"Ola Wolvinder?" Sofi called out.

A man strode out of the longhouse and stood, hands on hips. His eyes skimmed over the men and the squatch, then lingered on the women as if they were a delivery of livestock. Finn couldn't help but let his mouth fall open anew. The man was Erik's height and breadth across the shoulder, but a good deal slimmer in the midriff. Silver and black locks swept majestically back from his temples like metallic waves. His beard jutted from his chin like an aggressively healthy shrub.

He wore a white shirt and faded blue trousers, baggy like

Keef's. His skin was the same colour as the Hardworkers' sun-bronzed complexions. His eyes were large and incongruously bright; they looked wet with tears. And they were blue. Scraylings – everybody in the new world apart from Hardworkers, in other words – had dark eyes.

This man was a Hardworker. He was one of them.

Finn knew he'd seen him before, then realised it had been very recently. He looked at the cross. Yes, Krist's face was a well-carved likeness of the guy standing in front of them.

Wulf strolled forward as if it was all just another day, hand held out and open. "Greetings, I'm Wulf the Fat."

"Salutations travellers! I am Ola Wolvinder." He smiled and shook Wulf's hand warmly. His booming voice suited his hairstyle. Was he a god? Or was he simply a Hardworker who lived a thousand miles from home and thought that carving his own face onto a statue of Krist was a reasonable thing to do?

Finn caught Sassa Lipchewer's eye and lifted his eyebrows to ask *What's going on?* She smiled back at him as if she knew and his mind boggled all the more.

Erik, Thyri, Chogolisa and the rest of them walked forward to shake Ola Wolvinder's hand. He greeted them enthusiastically, then stood back and raised his arms for silence. Finn wasn't sure why he'd held back from greeting the man, but nobody, including Wolvinder, had noticed.

Not for the first time, Finn wished that Gunnhild Kristlover was still around. He would have loved to have heard what she made of a man carving his own face where Krist's was meant to be.

"Now," proclaimed the sonorous stranger, "I'd like you please to rest from the road and ready yourself for a feast! I have been expecting you. You will find that the church and the hut contain everything you need, including the most comfortable beds you've encountered for a long while. When you are ready, come into the longhouse and we will eat! More importantly, we will drink!"

"Sounds like a plan," grinned Wulf.

"Now, Taanya," Olaf addressed the squatch. "You won't fit into the longhouse. I have enough stew for you, but I daresay you'll want to find your own food?"

Taanya plucked Ottar from her shoulders, looked around the rest of them as if to say *you'd better not try anything* and lolloped away.

Ola Wolvinder treated each woman to another salacious once over, then marched magnificently back into the longhouse.

Finn found himself standing next to Bodil Gooseface. "But who is he?" he asked, not expecting an answer.

"Don't you know?" she looked at him pityingly.

"Um, no." *Surely Bodil didn't know?*

"Ola Wolvinder," said Sassa, joining them, her lips twisted in a smile. "What does that sound like?"

"A guy's name?" Finn felt hot. Bodil was looking at Sassa with an eyebrow raised. He was being patronised by Gooseface!

"Why don't you tell him, Bodil?" Sassa suggested. Erik, Chogolisa and Wulf were watching, enjoying Finn's discomfort far too much. Thyri, thank Loakie, was talking to Sofi.

"He's Olaf Worldfinder," explained Bodil. "Founder of Hardwork."

Finn looked from Bodil to the longhouse, gibbered briefly, shook his head, then blushed and looked at Bodil, amazed and suspicious.

Sassa Lipchewer was enjoying Finn's confusion. Wulf had told her his suspicions about the name Ola Wolvinder as soon as they'd left Taanya's home, and she'd told Bodil. So it wasn't entirely fair that Finn was feeling foolish, but she wasn't about to help him out.

Olaf the Worldfinder was meant to be in a burial mound a thousand miles away, but here he was. He must have been a hundred and fifty years old, yet he looked like a sixty-year-old, and a superbly fit one at that.

Sassa wasn't that surprised. They'd been led there by a twelve-foot-tall beast who communicated with her mind. Not long ago she'd seen a giant hurl an empress into the mouth of a monster to save them all. Amazing just wasn't surprising any more.

Wootah and Calnians washed and rested. Everyone seemed too weary to discuss Olaf, but they perked up as they filed into the longhouse at sunset.

Sassa was almost rattled by the interior of the building. As far as she could work out, it was exactly the same as Jarl Brodir's longhouse back in Hardwork. Same size, same furniture, same torches in the same sconces on the same walls, same sleeping alcoves for the Hird. The bowls of stew steaming on the table, the wooden jugs, the birch and horn mugs – it could have been directly transported from their old life on the shores of Olaf's Fresh Sea.

Olaf the Worldfinder had built the Hardwork longhouse, so maybe it wasn't odd that he should build another similar one. The mind-knottingly weird thing was that the carvings that covered every interior surface – walls, chairs, bed alcoves, table legs and so on – looked very similar to the Hardwork version. Most of the ones in Hardwork had been carved long after Olaf's supposed death, many during Sassa's own lifetime. So how could they be here?

She looked for an animal that she had carved herself. It was meant to be a horse, an animal that she knew only from its description in sagas from the old world.

She found it. Sort of. It was in the same place, but it was different, with longer legs and a shorter neck. She was pretty certain that Olaf's carving was a much better representation of a horse than hers.

"Sit down, please, all of you, wherever you like," called Olaf Worldfinder, standing at the head of a rectangular table with room for one at each end and six or seven down each side. "Apart from Sofi Tornado and Wulf the Fat, who I'd like up here on either side of me, please. Oh, and Chogolisa Earthquake, I made a stool for you." He pointed halfway down the table, where a sturdy stool broad enough to accommodate Chogolisa's mightily muscled arse took the place of two chairs.

Olaf watched them take their seats, pouring mead into a birch wood cup from a jug identical to the ones they'd used in Hardwork. By the mild slurring in the old man's voice, Sassa guessed it wasn't his first refill.

She sat next to Wulf and Yoki Choppa sat opposite, next to Sofi. Each place had been set with a steaming bowl of stew and a mug of mead. Olaf sat, took a long draught from his cup and looked up. Everyone was watching him expectantly. At meals with the Jarl, one didn't start eating until he said so, and their Oaden-faced host had a lot more of the Jarl about him than any of the Hardwork Jarls Sassa had known.

He blinked. His pale blue, wet eyes were the only part of him that looked a century and a half old.

"You will all be wondering how I am here, not devoured by worms thirteen hundred miles to the east."

All the Wootah plus Chogolisa nodded. Had they really travelled thirteen hundred miles, Sassa wondered? Olaf did seem like he'd know.

"I'm more interested to hear what you know about The Meadows," said Sofi.

Olaf smiled, his eyes lingering on Sofi long enough to make Sassa a little uncomfortable. "Of course. The tale of my life is extraordinary, but I shall tell you only how I came to be here, as I know you must be keen to eat. After we've eaten, I'll tell you what I know about The Meadows. Does this *satisfy* you, Sofi?"

The way he said *satisfy* made Sassa feel like spiders were running up her arms.

"It does," said Sofi, giving him a look that might have melted rock.

"So," said Olaf, "I'm sure all you Hardworkers—"

"They're called Wootah now," said Chogolisa.

"Wootah? Why? Actually, it can wait." Olaf looked irked that the tribe he'd founded had changed its name, but Sassa suspected he wanted to keep the audience – he seemed more of a talker than a listener.

"You *Wootah* will know the stories of why we left the old world, and how I led your ancestors across the Great Salt Sea, and I'm sure you've told your Calnian friends?"

"We know all about your heroics and adventures!" chimed Bodil.

Olaf looked at Bodil. He seemed surprised, as if noticing her for the first time. Then he smiled like a toad.

"The Goachica were kind to us," he continued. "Had they not fed us that first winter we would have perished and none of you would be here. However, I became tired of the Goachica's geographical limitations, and my fellow *Hardworkers* became boring. Crossing the Great Salt Sea and travelling five hundred miles inland was enough for them. But I had no such limits. I left one night and began nearly a century of travelling. I have been to the frozen north, to the hot wet forests of the south, to islands populated by people and beasts you could never imagine. I have met fascinating men. And many women. Many women. Yet it was near here that I learned the alchemy to keep me alive and –

"Did you fake your death?" interrupted Finn. Bodil scowled at him. Sassa smiled.

Olaf Worldfinder glanced at Finn, then looked at Bodil to deliver the answer. "I colluded with the chief of the Goachica. When a Goachica nearly my size died we passed his corpse off as mine. Not many people, Bodil, have watched their own funeral from a nearby tree. It is an interesting experience."

Bodil nodded as if resolving to give it a go.

Olaf took a long draw from his cup. "You will want to eat now, so I will tell you more of my exploits later."

"Just one more thing," asked Wulf. "How did you know we were coming?"

"Your little magic man told me." He pointed at Ottar. Ottar put his hands over his face. "I became a warlock some ninety years ago so was able to decipher his message."

"How did he send it?" Sassa asked.

"I do not know and I will not pry." His eyes flicked from her eyes to her chest and back. It reminded her of Hrolf the Painter, the man she'd killed. Now she thought of it, wasn't Hrolf a direct descendant of Olaf?

"I do not like prying," Olaf continued. "That is why I live alone. However, I do know that you are on a quest to destroy the force at The Meadows. I admire the effort."

"Can you help?" asked Wulf.

"Let us eat. After that I will tell you everything I know, and what I think you should do next."

They tucked into their stew. It was delicious. For a while the noise of eating and drinking filled the room, only interrupted by the Wootah men refilling their mead mugs. Sassa looked at Sofi. The sucking and squelching of lips and tongues and saliva, she mused, must be pretty disgusting when you have super-hearing.

"So," said Olaf when the eating had slowed. "You've heard that there's a force in The Meadows set on destroying the world and your quest is to stop it. You've seen some of its effects, but you know very little about it."

"That's about right," said Wulf.

"I, too, have seen the impact. I have seen many, many tornados rip through the land to the west. Storms worse than any I've encountered – and I have seen some storms, let me tell you – have threatened to topple even these stout buildings. We are at the edge of a canyon six hundred paces deep. The land shakes often. When it does, more and more of the canyon side crashes into the river below." Olaf paused to drink. "And, of course, there are the monsters. The most common here are screaming, flying beasts with claws that can take a head off and a sting that will kill a man, but I've seen worse and I've heard of much worse. Nearer The Meadows itself are crawling, slithering miscreations that could destroy a tribe simply by sitting on it."

"So what is the force at The Meadows? And why is it trying to kill us all?" asked Erik.

"When I heard that you were on your way I undertook," he paused dramatically, "a vision quest."

"A what?" Bodil asked.

"Of all the great journeys I've taken, my dear – across raging seas and through jungles full of killer serpents – the vision quest is perhaps the most dangerous, although I never left this hill. Or at least I don't think I did. It is hard to be certain."

Olaf took a long pull on his mead mug. Sassa drummed her fingers impatiently.

Olaf winked at her, then looked back to Bodil. "To depart upon a vision quest, one must ingest a concoction of horribly powerful drugs. Stoned off one's mind, it seems, one can view the world as if one were a god. It is a very dangerous thing to do. Only the bravest can take part. In all my travels, I have seen only one other person embark on a vision quest. And he never came back."

"Where did he go?" asked Bodil, wide-eyed. Golden candlelight danced on her tanned skin. The darker skin, pregnancy, or perhaps both, suited her, thought Sassa. No wonder the old goat seemed captivated. Although Sassa suspected that if Bodil hadn't been in the room he'd have been captivated by one of the other women.

"He died, my dear," Olaf said kindly. "Only the very strongest survive a vision quest. So, set on my task, I ventured southwards to the Cloud Town. I was hoping the Mindful Folk there might know what was happening in The Meadows and so negate my need for the vision quest, but unfortunately everyone who has approached The Meadows over the last decade or so has been killed."

"It's been going on a decade?" asked Finn.

"The Mindful Folk did, however, have the poisons one needs for a vision quest," Olaf continued. "They come from a variety of tiny frogs found in the jungles to the south."

He'd totally ignored Finn. Finn bristled.

Olaf shook his head, oblivious to the young man's pique, then drank again. His silver mane remained set in immobile waves. Sassa wondered what he used to keep it so gloriously immobile and whether it would be better for her fin than the stuff Paloma had made for her.

"What did you find?" asked Sofi.

"The force is emanating from a huge triangular building in the centre of The Meadows. It, or rather I should say, she, is set on destroying the world."

"She?" asked Erik. "Who?"

Olaf was not to be rushed. "Five hundred miles west of here is the territory of the united Warlock and Warrior tribe."

"We've seen a statue of them next to the Red River," said Erik.

"Ah yes, I know the one. They are powerful and their influence spreads a long way. Or at least it used to . . . but on with my tale. I thought the Warlock Queen was a myth, a bedtime story for Warlock and Warrior children, but my vision quest informed me otherwise.

"A thousand years ago a warrior woman with a magic bow came from the east. I suspect she came across the Great Salt

Sea because I know she was as beautiful as some of the Hardwork . . . sorry, Wootah women."

He looked at Bodil and smiled. Bodil giggled, apparently delighted. Sassa blinked. She herself had never been a fan of seedy come-ons from older men — much, much older in this case — but everyone was, of course, different.

"Along with the archer was a warlock girl and the archer's young son. The Warrior and Warlock tribe tell wonderful tales of their marvellous adventures, but I know you are keen to hear the relevant part."

"Indeed," said Sofi.

"The warlock girl and the archer's son became lovers — it's the greatest romantic tale — then king and queen of the Warriors and Warlocks. They had a child. She became the greatest warlock the world has known. But she was strange. Some say evil."

Olaf looked around the candle-lit table. The Hardwork carvings stared down from the walls. Sassa had goose pimples.

"The child became the Warlock Queen, chief of the united Warrior and Warlock tribe. She had her own child, a boy. He was killed. It is a tragic tale, but one that would take a week to tell. Suffice to say that the Warlock Queen was destroyed by grief and she killed herself. Or so everyone thought."

Olaf drank, then continued, almost in a whisper. "This very Warlock Queen's spirit — or perhaps her still-living form — is now set upon destroying the world. From what I've seen and heard, she has the means and nobody can stop her."

The hundred-and-fifty-year-old founder of Hardwork sat back, refilled his mug and drank some more.

"Why's she so angry?" asked Chogolisa.

"I've told you all I know. If I know women — and I've known many, many women — it's because of her child's death. Women are crueller than men, but they only become angry enough to destroy a world when a child is involved."

If Sassa knew anything about men, it was that they didn't know much about themselves, let alone women. But she stayed quiet.

"Why wait a thousand years?" asked Wulf.

"That I do not know."

"How do we stop her?" asked Sofi.

"The Warlock Queen's body is entombed at The Meadows. Her tomb is a vast, triangular stone building called The Pyramid. It's clear that you have to go there. But—"

Olaf shook his head.

"But?" prompted Thyri.

"Dozens, maybe hundreds, have been killed trying to reach it."

"How. Do. We. Stop. Her?" Thyri pressed, enunciating each word as if Olaf was a three-year-old who wasn't getting the message.

"That will require another vision quest. However—"

"You mean you don't know," Thyri sneered.

Olaf glared at Thyri in a way that was clearly meant to terrify her. She held his gaze.

"More research is needed," he said eventually.

"Will you undertake another vision quest?" asked Sofi.

"I will not. I was lucky to survive the last one."

"I thought you died when you died?" pressed Thyri.

"You die when you die is old world philosophy," said Olaf. "I left the old world a long time ago."

"Do you have the vision quest drugs here?" asked Sassa. A vision of Bjarni Chickenhead smoking a pipe filled her mind. He'd have gone on the dangerous vision quest for the fun of it. Which was, of course, why he was dead. She must, she told herself, make sure that Wulf didn't go the same way.

"No. You will have to travel to the Cloud Town."

"I'll go on the vision quest!" announced Finn.

"We'll decide that later," said Wulf. Sassa kicked him. "Where is the Cloud Town?"

"South over the mountains, on Bighorn Island. It used to be a lovely five-day stroll, but, with the way the land has been destroyed, and the monsters, it will take you ten days, possibly more, and it will be very dangerous."

"Just like everywhere else then," said Finn.

"The next stage," said Olaf, "will make your journey so far seem like a walk on the beach."

"I got attacked by a giant wasp when I was walking on the beach once," announced Finn.

"But I will give you the provisions you need and prepare you the best I can," said Olaf.

They sat around the table drinking and discussing. Sassa – avoiding alcohol because of her growing baby – had the dubious delight of watching the others get drunk. Finn repeated several times that he would go on the vision quest.

"It won't be you," said Wulf.

"Nor will it be you," Sassa whispered when the others' attention had moved on.

"It is the sort of thing a leader ought to do."

She looked at him and he shrugged. He was right. It probably should be him. But it wasn't going to be.

"We'll see," she said.

When Ottar fell asleep with his head on the table, Sassa said she was tired too and would help him to bed.

She took the boy to pee in the woods, on the edge of the massif, and stood with one hand on his shoulder and the other on her stomach. She could feel the little heart hammering away inside her, she was sure of it.

In front of her and the urinating child – he'd drunk a lot, not mead Sassa hoped – the land plummeted. The sandhills that they'd come through were a small rise, then the rocky tracts carried on silver and endless in the moonlight, fissured with canyons and spiky with mountains. All these details looked tiny from her perch but were no doubt precipitous and fearsome to cross. Somewhere beyond all of it, west of west, were The Meadows, The Pyramid and the insane, dead Warlock Queen. It was so vast, and Sassa was so small, and the mite inside her even smaller.

A twig snapped and she spun, pulling her knife free of its sheath with one hand and shoving Ottar behind her with the other. Taanya was standing five paces away, towering over the squat pines, huge, furry and terrifying. It was a still night. How had the squatch crept up on her like that?

*I'll take the boy to bed*, thought Taanya. She crouched down and held out a paw. Ottar toddled over to her and took it sleepily.

The phrase "choose your battles" occurred to Sassa as she did nothing to stop the boy from going.

*You shouldn't have him so near the edge*, thought Taanya as she scooped Ottar into her huge arms.

Sassa followed them back to Olaf Worldfinder's home. When she was certain Taanya wasn't buggering off with the boy, she returned to the overlook with her bow and a sheaf of practice arrows that were too badly made to be used in action.

She shot one as far as she could westward. With Sitsi gone, Sassa was the only archer in the group. She was determined that she'd be good enough to defend Ottar, Wulf, her unborn child – the lot of them.

She'd intended to shoot only a couple, but she ended up loosing arrow after arrow into the endless west, towards the Warlock Queen. She worried about the journey to come, about how they were going to get Taanya to let Ottar come with them, all the time niggled by the knowledge that any of the arrows she shot had a slim chance of skewering some hapless night-time beast going about its innocent business below.

\* \* \*

Finn opened his eyes, slowly. Light flash-flooded in and washed giddily around his head. He began to sit up, thought better of it and lay back down again.

He remembered Olaf Worldfinder – Olaf Worldfinder! – telling tales of the old world. He remembered sitting next to Thyri and . . .

He sat up.

By Oaden, it was amazing.

He thought through the evening again. Yes, he was right. He actually remembered saying his goodnights and going to bed.

He was more or less certain that he hadn't tried it on with Thyri or made a tit of himself in any way. But he'd drunk so much. Surely he'd done *something* cringeworthy? He tried to remember. Thyri had laughed at his jokes. So had Chogolisa, Erik and Wulf. He'd had a chat with Sofi at one point. Surely he'd said something mortifying to her? No, he was sure he hadn't. Yoki Choppa had joined them and they'd talked about vision quests. Yoki Choppa said that they weren't quite as dangerous as Olaf had made out. Only about one in four people who went on one was killed.

Then he'd gone back to the others and had a big chat, full of laughs.

He hadn't been last to bed. He'd left Sofi, Yoki Choppa, Thyri and Erik talking. Bodil had been chatting away with Olaf; Finn had a vision of her with a hand on his arm, laughing like a braying elk. And Finn had walked out of an evening's heavy drinking earlier than some other people, still capable of rational thought, without having been a dick in any way.

There was a first time, it seemed, for everything.

He looked around. The other cots in Olaf's church were empty.

He dressed, walked out and blinked in the light. It was

cloudy, for once, and relatively cool. Finn thanked Tor for the clouds even though it was unlikely that they were just for him. The thunder god probably had more important things to do than make Finn's hangover more bearable.

Once his eyes had adjusted, he saw everyone else was preparing to leave. Olaf was standing over by the life- or death-sized carving of Krist which had his face. He caught Finn's eye.

"What is that sword on your hip, young man?" he called out.

"It's Foe Slicer." Finn walked over to the very elderly man.

"Well, well, well. You've brought my old sword back to me."

"Well, you left it behind I guess and they buried it, then Brodir had it for a while and—"

"Thank you for carrying it all this way to me."

"Oh. Would you like it back?"

Olaf looked at Finn and Finn returned his gaze. He really was a splendid looking man, priapic beard and sweeping hair much like Oaden's, he reckoned.

"Foe Slicer was my father's sword, and his father's. It is the weapon with which I slew not one but two white bears, saving my fellow adventurers from certain evisceration." Olaf smiled. "She is mine. So, yes, I would like her back."

Finn looked about. Everyone else was busy. He wanted to call for Wulf but he didn't want to look lame.

"However, I can see you like the blade," Olaf said, sounding kind, "and, as I left her behind, you do have some claim to her. I will fight you for her."

"What?" said Finn. "Not again."

Olaf laughed heartily. "I'm joking, my serious young fellow. Do you young not have senses of humour any more? I left Foe Slicer. I have no claim on her. I have lived without her for nearly a hundred years and you'll need her on your coming journey. However, I must say it stirs me to see her again. Perhaps you could bring her to me when the quest is done?"

"I will bring her back," said Finn, thinking that he wouldn't. And he wasn't going to refer to it as "her" ever again either.

Olaf strode away to bother someone else and Finn busied himself bundling his kit together. He looked up when Bodil walked into the wide yard, went over to Olaf and put her hand on his arm. She stood there smiling, making no moves to pack up her stuff.

"What's going on?" he asked Erik.

"Bodil's staying."

"What?"

"Makes sense, for the baby."

Finn looked about. Everyone had been watching him and everyone looked away, apart from Sofi, who held his eye until he looked away.

*The baby. His baby.*

"But . . ."

"Why don't you go and talk to her?" Erik picked up his snow shoes and began to strap them to his pack.

"Do I have to?"

"Yup."

*Squirrelcocks*, thought Finn. He was hungover as Hel and finding the world difficult enough. It wasn't the perfect time to have a deep talk about deserting his unborn child.

He sighed, then walked on over.

"Bodil, can I have a word, please?"

"Sure!" She looked a little surprised. "Go for it."

"In private?"

Bodil looked at Olaf as if she needed his permission and Finn found himself, annoyingly, doing the same.

"Take all the time you need," Olaf waved a magnanimous hand.

They walked behind the longhouse and found a sandy path leading among juniper and pinyon trees to the tip of the promontory.

Finn was going to leave his child. In exactly the same

way that his own father had left him before he was even born.

No, Finn was worse. Erik hadn't known he had a child on the way. Finn was wilfully abandoning his unborn son. Or maybe daughter. He imagined a little girl, a mini Freydis, sunlight in her blonde hair, asking where her daddy was. He blinked back tears.

At the end of the promontory the land dropped six hundred paces into the black canyon below.

There was no time to piss about.

Finn looked Bodil in the eye. "Bodil, I am the father of your baby."

"You're not."

"It's not Keef."

"I know."

"So it must be me."

"No."

"Bodil, the timing. When we—"

"Olaf will be the father of my baby."

"Oh . . . I see." Finn felt massive relief at the same time as a growing ball of guilt threatened to burst his stomach. It was an odd sensation. "But—" he said.

Bodil smiled simply. "I don't want you to be my child's dad."

"Why?"

"I think you're a bad person."

"I'm . . . I'm really not. I . . ."

"After we got together by the river, you stopped talking to me. That wasn't nice."

"Sorry."

"What does sorry mean? I don't need sorry, I needed you to be nice to me then. I was very upset."

"I was embarrassed and I didn't know you were pregnant."

"But then you did know."

Finn looked at his boots.

"And still you ignored me. You let Keef pretend it was his, but you knew it was yours. Why did you do that?"

"I . . . don't know."

"I do. It's because you're a bad person."

He couldn't hold her eye. He felt hot and sick. She was right. He'd been an utter shit. He'd saved them all from the Badlands but that paled into nothingness when you considered how he'd treated Bodil.

"You're right," he said. "I'll change. I'll stay here too and—"

"Please don't. I don't like you. I don't want you here."

"I'll come back."

"Why?"

"To see my—"

"No. Not yours. Mine."

"But I—"

"Just go, Finn. I'm going to stay here. Tell the others farewell."

"But the others—"

"Just go."

# Chapter 17

## Paloma loses a fight

Freydis the Annoying and Paloma Pronghorn looked down at the corpse roasting on the sisters' fire. They didn't need to say it. The blackening body was too small to be Keef the Berserker. It was Sitsi Kestrel-size.

"It isn't Sitsi," said Paloma. "She doesn't have much fat on her. Her flesh wouldn't bubble and pop so much."

"Are you sure?"

*No. Even the skinniest people bubble like that when they're roasted.*

"Yes."

"Are you ready?" Paloma checked the straps on her remaining leather leg piece. She'd been wearing an Owsla outfit every day for the best part of a decade, so she felt a bit naked without the legging that the biggest sister had ripped off.

Freydis nodded and blinked, looking, for once, like a scared six-year-old.

Paloma resisted the urge to hug her. "Good. It might even work, you never know."

She pranced down the side of the gorge with a pace and grace that would have made any bighorn sheep feel a lot less smug about its own cliff-hopping skills.

She paused at the bottom to allow her eyes to adjust to the gloom. The sky was lightening, but the narrow canyon was dark. Full daylight would have suited her better, but every moment was a moment that Keef and Sitsi could be killed. If Sitsi wasn't already dead and roasting.

She stole along the west side of the stream in the dark, expecting a thick spear in the guts at any moment and cursing Yoki Choppa, yet again, for denying her the daily dose of rattlesnake that had made dangerous escapades like these seem enjoyable. The aroma of cooking human flesh did nothing to ease her nerves.

She reached the cave without being killed and stood across the stream from it, gripping the obsidian moon blade in one hand and her killing stick in the other.

The three captors were sitting by the fire in the lofted alcove. The roasted human had been moved from the fire to rest after cooking. It was still impossible to tell whether it was Sitsi. It was someone, though. The three sisters were definitely on the cuntier end of the personality spectrum and that steeled Paloma's rattlesnake-free resolve somewhat.

She headed on down the canyon and found the place to set her trap. She hoped she wouldn't need it, but it was good to have a fallback if everything went to shit. If it all went to shit, of course, chances of her being able to use the fallback were about zero, but it was still reassuring.

She gripped her weapons and walked back. She could put it off no longer.

It was attack time.

From this new approach she could see the canoe on the far side of the cave, but its opening was turned away and she couldn't see if Keef and Sitsi were still trapped in it.

She readied herself.

The canoe rocked.

"I told you!" cried the largest of the captors, standing up. "You move once more, I said, and I'll put a spear through that canoe. So here you go. One of you is about to get a spear in your guts."

*One of you.* So they were both alive and Sitsi wasn't cooked. But she was about to be speared.

*Tits*, thought Paloma, *so much for planning.*

She sprang over the stream and bounced into the cave.

The two smaller women sitting by the fire turned. Paloma slammed the point of Sitsi's moon blade into the nearest one's eye. It sliced in right up to Paloma's gripping hand, which was satisfying. She withdrew and the woman fell forwards into the fire.

The other two looked from their eye-stabbed sibling to Paloma and back again.

Paloma looked at them, blood and aqueous humour dripping from her moon blade.

There was a surprisingly awkward moment.

"Oh dear oh dear," said the slighter women eventually, standing and hefting her stocky stone-headed spear in two hands. "You killed our sister. You'll die slow for that."

The smaller remaining sister advanced around the fire. The large woman came around the other side.

Paloma wouldn't have chosen to fight in the tight cave, but she couldn't risk trying to draw them out in case they paused on the way to spear Keef and Sitsi.

"Stay back, Xamop," said the smaller woman. "I'm going to take this one apart myself."

"Go for it," said Xamop. "But I want the breast meat."

"Done." The spearwoman attacked.

Paloma dodged the first thrust and whacked away the second with her killing stick. She lunged a slice at the woman's midriff, but spear shaft blocked moon blade. The parry was followed by a lightning-fast counter, and the sharp stone spearhead opened a gash in Paloma's thigh.

Paloma jumped back, leg throbbing with hot pain. This was not going to plan. The woman was much faster than she should be, definitely enhanced. The spear's reach was far greater than the moon blade's, so Paloma should have got in close, but that was the opposite of her normal "run in, whack 'em, and run away" style of fighting. Keef's spear Arse Splitter was lying by his canoe, but to get that she'd have to go through both sisters.

Her attacker advanced, thrusting and thrusting. Paloma twisted like an eel, but her opponent seemed to read Paloma's every move.

Three thrusts in a row cut Paloma on her other leg and both arms. Another knocked the killing stick from her hands.

The Owsla had drawn out enough people's deaths as long as possible for the crowd's and their own amusement for Paloma to realise that it was now happening to her. She didn't like it one bit.

Within moments she was pressed against the back of the cave, twisting side to side as the thrusting stone spear flashed sparks off the rock wall. She was in trouble. That was the problem with Owsla powers and training. It was entirely based on fighting unenhanced foes. As soon they met someone nearer their level they didn't know what to do.

Through it all she heard a weird, guttural coughing. She realised it was her attacker, laughing.

"Stop, wait!" she held up a hand.

To her surprise, her attacker stood off but kept the spear point hovering around Paloma's midriff.

"What do you want?"

"Do you know," Paloma asked, "that there are herbs that will soothe that throat of yours? Stop you being so raspy."

"Finish her!" called the large woman from over by the canoe.

Paloma's attacker narrowed her already narrow eyes so that they looked like they were closed. "You think you're beautiful, don't you?" she spat.

"Nope. I *know* I am."

"I love killing people like you," the pinch-faced woman

continued. "People who've had an easy time of it because they've lovely limbs and a face the right shape. Well, let me tell you, your day is over. It's different now. The times when people like you could just swan about and—"

"Do you know you spit when you talk?" Paloma interrupted. "I don't know if you can do anything about it, but you ought to try because if you are worried about your looks, it doesn't help at all."

The narrow-eyed woman's jaw dropped and rose again as her mouth widened into a raging scream of hatred.

The moment when she thought she'd goaded her opponent just enough to make her drop her guard and was about to swing for her neck with the moon blade, Paloma felt a hot, weird thrust in her guts.

She looked down. The spear was in her stomach. Blood pulsed out around the stone head. *Ah*, she thought, *it seems I may have lost a fight*.

She looked back up at the curly headed woman.

"Not so clever now, are you?" Her adversary leant in and spat in her face. "Beautiful ones like you taste better, did you know that?"

"You missed," said Paloma.

"What?"

"You missed my stomach."

Curly Hair looked down. Paloma swung the obsidian blade into her neck.

The woman let go of the spear, her eyes flashing almost wide in surprise.

"Glurk," she coughed blood.

Paloma twisted her blade with one hand and grabbed the spear shaft with the other. She wrenched. The stone head came free with a gouting suck. The pain wasn't too bad – one advantage of being an enhanced Owsla warrior – but she felt blood wash over her hand. Too much blood. She pushed her attacker.

The dying woman staggered back, tripped over her friend in the fire and lay on the rock.

"You've killed my sisters," the large woman hissed, advancing across the cave. Paloma pressed a palm over her wound. Blood seeped around the sides and between her fingers. *Yup*, she thought, *that's far too much blood*. It was probably a life-ending injury. It was also going to make it difficult to rescue her friends.

"You're sisters!" managed Paloma. "Of course. I can see the resemblance now you mention it. How long have you been living here?"

The pain in her gut was increasing towards a debilitating level. She needed to keep this one talking until . . . well, in a perfect world, until Keef and Sitsi freed themselves and rescued her. She wanted to shout at them to get on with it, but the giant was between her and the canoe and could still easily put her spear through it.

"My name is Xamop," she said. "You can use it to beg me for mercy while I kill you slowly. I am going to make you very, very unhappy."

"You won't have to try. I'm already unhappy. I've never actually been happy. I think I was last happy when I was a child. Did you have an enjoyable childhood? I'm guessing not."

"You think this is all a big joke, don't you?"

"And you don't?" She was feeling fainter by the moment. She was going to have to wrap this up one way or another.

"I hate the way you speak. First thing I'm going to do is bite your tongue out."

"*Bite* it out? How will that work?"

"I'll show you." Xamop charged.

Paloma swung her blade, but Xamop was even quicker than her smaller sister. She chopped the edge of her hand into Paloma's wrist. Her whole arm thrilled with pain, her fingers sprang open and the blade fell.

She saw the punch coming but couldn't avoid it. It struck her chest like a charging bison and sent her flying clean out of the cave.

She whumped onto packed earth. She touched her stomach. The wound was wider. She could feel a bit of gut poking out.

*Fuck*, she thought.

She had to get up. She had to run.

She lifted her head and pressed her hands into the ground. Xamop landed on her. She grabbed Paloma's arms, forced them above her head and held them there with one hand. The Owsla woman tried to pull free but it was as if her wrists were encased in rock.

"Time to die, beauty."

Xamop slid her free hand down Paloma's torso, found the gash in her stomach and slid her fingers into it. She smiled at Paloma.

Owsla were almost impervious to pain. Paloma was glad of it because this was seriously painful. Innowak knew what it would have been like had she been unenhanced.

She gasped, trying not to scream.

"Now," said Xamop, her voice softening as Paloma could feel her fingers probing deeper inside her. "What shall we pull out first? Maybe your spine."

She thrust her hand deeper. Paloma could feel fingers touching her backbone. She passed out for half a heartbeat, but managed to force herself back into consciousness.

"I thought you were going to bite my tongue out first?" she managed.

"Oh, that's right, isn't it? Thank you, I'd quite forgotten."

The fingers withdrew from her abdomen. It was such a relief that Paloma almost said thank you.

Xamop rearranged herself to get a better angle at her mouth, sliding her seat from on top of Paloma's hips to her thighs.

Paloma Pronghorn was the fastest runner the world had ever known and she had very strong legs. She put all her might into those alchemically enhanced muscles and thrust upwards.

Xamop bucked but kept hold.

"Oh!" she said as she landed. "There's still strength in—"

She thrust again, harder. Xamop flew a foot into the air. Paloma powered a knee into her groin with everything she had.

Xamop yelled and fell sideways.

The speedy Owsla jumped up and set off down the canyon, through the trees. Blood was flowing from her stomach. She was horribly injured – sure to die, annoyingly – but she could still outrun the big woman. Until the wound got the better of her, anyway.

"Stop!" Xamop yelled behind her. "Come back here and fight me, or I'll go back and kill your friends!"

"How about I . . . stop here . . . and wait for you?" called Paloma. She was trying to sound more incapacitated than she was, but it wasn't much of a stretch. "I can't . . . make it back."

"Oh, you poor thing, I'll come to you then. Never let it be said I'm not kind."

Paloma staggered on to where the stream had carved a shingle clearing between shrubs and trees, where she'd laid the rope. She grabbed one end and ducked behind a tree.

Xamop limped into sight. The knee to the groin had injured her. It was good to know she could be hurt. She stepped into the loop and Paloma flicked and yanked the rope tight around the woman's ankles. She pulled, and Xamop keeled over like a felled oak.

"Now!" Paloma shouted with all the air in her lungs.

There was a rumbling, then a roar. Freydis's job had been to collect a pile of rocks, find a lever and be ready to drop the rocks into the canyon at a moment's notice. It was a big ask for a six-year-old, but Paloma had reckoned that Freydis was equal to it. By the sound of it, she was right.

Xamop sat and grappled at the rope. Paloma yanked again. She felt her stomach wound tear further, but there was no time to worry about that.

The big woman floundered on her back as the first rock plopped into the stream. Paloma ran clear as what sounded like half the canyon side tumbled into the valley.

*How had Freydis made such a large rockfall?*

Paloma dropped the rope and pulled the edges of her gash together. The wound would need washing and sewing up, soon, if there was to be any hope for her. She was feeling very faint. She needed a rest.

The last few pebbles clattered down the side of the gorge, then all was quiet. Paloma walked back, gripping her wound. The clearing was thick with dust.

The down-canyon breeze quickly cleared the air, revealing a pile of broken rocks. The sky was now blue overhead, but it was still quite dark in the shaded canyon. Even in the dim light, however, Paloma expected to see at least a hand or a foot poking out of the rubble.

*Maybe she was completely buried?* she was thinking when the rope loop dropped around her shoulders and tightened.

She tried to pull away, but the towering Xamop grabbed her by the hair, wound the rope round and round her arms, then stood back and looked at the trussed Owsla woman, her chest heaving.

"That hurt," she said.

"I can see why."

One side of Xamop's forehead and an eye were mashed. Her lips were bleeding, her chin was black and misshapen. Innowak knew how many more wounds her clothes were concealing. She was, however, surprisingly chipper.

"Shall we have another go?" she said.

*Oh, not again*, thought Paloma as the giant grabbed her

hair. Paloma kicked the woman's shin as hard as she could, but she might as well have kicked a boulder.

With two strong fingers, Xamop squeezed Paloma's jaw to open her mouth. With her other hand she gripped her tongue and yanked it, hard, so that it felt it might rip out at the root. She pulled it much further from her mouth than Paloma had known it could go. She could *see* it.

This, thought Paloma, is not going well.

Xamop leant in, opening her mouth.

*Dog's cocks, she really is going to bite my tongue off.*

The Owsla woman kicked all the harder, bucked and strained to pull her tongue back into her mouth, but the grip was unshakable.

Xamop's mouth widened. A pointed metal tongue jabbed out of her mouth.

*What kind of monster . . .?* Paloma had time to think before the grip on her hair and tongue was released and she whumped down onto the sandy canyon floor.

"Roll away, please," came Keef the Berserker's voice, "your friend is heavy."

Paloma rolled. Keef was standing behind Xamop, holding Arse Splitter's shaft. The weapon's spear-like metal tip had pierced the back of Xamop's head and protruded from her mouth. He twisted to release the blade and the dead woman fell forward.

Sitsi Kestrel walked into the clearing. "Thanks for rescuing us!" she beamed.

Paloma opened her eyes and tried to smile at her friend. "Door delcome," she managed.

Sitsi Kestrel cleaned, stitched and dressed Paloma Pronghorn's wound, then she and Keef the Berserker dragged the three sisters' bodies down the canyon to the main Red River valley. Freydis the Annoying tied their rope around the cooked torso and hauled that down-canyon, too. The skinny girl was stronger than she looked, thought Sitsi. Paloma came, too, even though Sitsi had told her to rest. Sitsi didn't complain. She could tell Keef was amazed to see someone who'd been speared in the guts get up and walk shortly afterwards, and she'd been concerned that Keef hadn't fully appreciated yet just how amazing the Owsla were.

"Let's eat a bit of each of them," said Paloma, as they watched the women's corpses burn by the Red River's rushing waters.

"Yuk, no!" Freydis jumped up and down. "Why would we do that?"

"To kill their souls," Sitsi answered. "and make sure they don't have another life after this one."

"And to give us better next lives," added Paloma.

"Which bit do we eat?" Keef sounded keen.

"We don't," said Sitsi. "We can't extinguish a soul."

"I agree," said Freydis. "I think that they were evil—"

"Exactly!" Keef interrupted.

"But killing a soul is an evil thing to do, isn't it?" Freydis continued. "So if we do that we're just as evil as them."

Keef looked at the girl for a few moments, opening and closing his mouth, then shook his head, spun on his heel and headed off to destroy a barrel cactus with Arse Splitter. Sitsi smiled.

"And, of course," she said while he was busy, "you only destroy a soul if the fire is started with an Innowak Crystal, and this one wasn't."

"Good point." Paloma nodded.

They left the sisters burning, headed back up the canyon about a mile to the cave and set about making a home where they could wait for the rest of the Wootah.

"Why bother?" asked Paloma. "We'll only have to wait a day or two."

Sitsi looked at her. Paloma was serious. She had no concept

of how fast other people moved, or how often life got in the way of plans. "We left the others a hundred miles away, setting off to rescue Ottar. Who knows how long or how far that will take them? We could be here for a moon or more."

"You make a clever point as usual, Sitsi. And if my injury didn't prevent me from lifting things, I would help you make that camp." Paloma flashed a healthy smile. "I'll look after Freydis. That's much more important work. Children are the future."

Paloma ran off down the canyon. She was out of earshot before Sitsi could reply.

So Sitsi and Keef set about making a home. While they scrubbed and tidied, foraged and stored, repaired and re-made, Paloma and Freydis mucked about.

Sitsi let her get away with it, even though Paloma was putting more strain on the wound playing with Freydis than she would have done building the camp. She didn't mind doing all the work with Keef. He was creative, practical, hardworking and fun. He was the perfect partner. When they took breaks from drudge work, they made arrows and Sitsi taught the Wootah man how to shoot his new bow.

Together they built a low stone and mud wall along the front of the cave. They hung ropes from the top of the canyon down to the cave, so that they might escape a flash flood and set up noise traps all around to alert themselves to anyone approaching.

The stream emerged from a spring not far away at the head of the notched valley, so the water was drinkable. Food was easy enough, too. Sitsi could shoot anything that flew or ran and Keef was improving with the bow. The barrel cactuses were crowned with a tasty yellow fruit which was easy to harvest with a couple of sticks and a modicum of patience, and Paloma proved surprisingly willing and able to prepare and cook the fruit of the beavertail cactus.

By the third day Keef and Sitsi had finished building their home and they had enough food stored in desert willow baskets to last the next winter. The only slight issue was the noise traps going off throughout the night, since large nocturnal creatures used the canyon as a route from higher ground down to the Red River. The first few times they'd sounded, the adults had all run out, weapons ready. Now they were so blasé about the false alarms that one of them went to check while the others went back to sleep.

Paloma and Freydis spent their days haring about in and around the canyon. Keef and Sitsi didn't see them much and when they did they were usually laughing.

There was only so much archery practice one could do, so Keef and Sitsi spent a good deal of their time like the children of an emperor. i.e. in a state of well-fed idleness. Sitsi wasn't used to it at all, but Keef was a good instructor and she soon came to appreciate the joys of what Keef called 'just fucking around'.

At the head of one branch of the canyon was an arch of rock like a high roof over the spring. The arch was split from the cliff behind as if a god had sliced a giant axe through the land. Keef liked to walk across the arch, sparring with imaginary foes. Sitsi hated watching him. She also didn't much like him jumping between the pinnacles of rock at the head of the canyon, either. When she realised that she'd never stop him, she gave it a go herself. It was actually quite fun, and it felt a lot less dangerous than it had looked.

She also worked out that she could stop Keef leaping about and terrifying her by suggesting another session of archery practice. He was happy to shoot a bow until his fingers were sore, although she had to guess when his fingers were sore because he'd never admit it.

He wasn't a bad archer, despite his one-eyed inability to perceive depth.

"I reckon I had two eyes for long enough to know how far things are from each other," he said.

Sitsi's favourite times were when Keef's fingers were sore, when he'd leapt enough chasms and slain enough imaginary foes, and they simply sat and talked.

They could chat for hours, about how to improve their camp, about the desert and its animals, and about their lives before the Calnians had come to kill all the Hardworkers. Keef liked to sit somewhere dramatic for these discussions, like the top of a rock tower, but Sitsi preferred the big round boulder near the cave. It overlooked a deep pool behind a dam built by departed beavers. If they sat still, a chuckwalla would often appear and munch poolside leaves. It pleased Sitsi to see her power animal in its native environment. It was a hefty lizard but it had a gentle docility about it which appealed to Sitsi.

Huge tadpoles held sway in the pool itself, patrolling about with flicks of their tails and munching smaller entities. They were pretty loathsome. Sitsi and Keef spent a good while guessing what the tadpoles might become. Wasp men, Keef had concluded.

Of the wasp men that had attacked them on the river, or any other monsters, there was no sign. Every time she mentioned the monsters to Keef he told her not to worry. They were ever watchful, and he had a bow as well now. So, yes, the monsters might come, and, yes, that was a worry, but, because there was nothing they could do to change that – other than be prepared, which they were – there was no point in worrying about that particular worry.

Sitsi, who couldn't stop worrying at will like Keef apparently could, was also concerned that the others might not find them.

"Yoki Choppa tracked us through a storm and a tornado with that hair trick," Keef said. "There's no reason to think he'll fail now."

"I suppose."

"And, even more than that, Ottar would never leave Freydis behind. Don't you worry. They're coming."

Paloma Pronghorn's new best friend was a six-year-old girl called Freydis the Annoying. She wouldn't have called that one a few moons before, when she'd spent her days raiding enemies and braining captives for the amusement of the crowd.

She knew that Sitsi thought she was pissing about with the child to escape the boring chores, and that was true, but someone had to keep an eye on the girl all of the time – there were monsters around after all, as well as the usual lions, bears and wolves that might kill a child – and she knew that Sitsi would rather be mooning about with Keef.

Paloma also told Sitsi that her stomach wound prevented her helping. They both knew that was bollocks. It did slow her down a bit, but it was more or less healed by the second day. The scar would last a moon perhaps. It was good to be Owsla.

She was also enjoying herself a great deal, and she really was teaching the child a useful thing or two which might benefit them all one day.

"You're not very annoying," Paloma told Freydis on the first full day in the canyon.

"Everyone else says I am."

"Everyone else? Pah. Part of growing up is realising that everyone else is an idiot. You're meant to work it out yourself, but I'll give you that one."

"So if I'm not annoying, do you think I need a new name? You're not *meant* to get one until you're older, like Finn the Deep."

"I think we can bend the rules, given the situation. What would you like to be called?"

"How about Freydis Pronghorn?"

"No. That would be weird."

They tried to think of a name until Freydis got bored and wanted to go on Paloma's shoulders while she ran.

"We'll just call you Freydis for now," Paloma decided.

A few days later, Paloma and Freydis lay looking over the canyon side, spying on Keef and Sitsi who were sitting on the big rock above the pool. Paloma knew that Sitsi knew they were there, but she didn't care and neither did Sitsi, or at least she knew she couldn't do anything about it.

After a while Keef and Sitsi climbed down to the pool, stripped facing away from each other and leapt into the water. They splashed each other for a bit, which was as erotic as their stalkers had ever seen them get, then climbed out chastely on their individual sides to dress, facing away from each other again.

"Are they going to get married?" asked Freydis.

"Not at this rate."

It made Paloma's palms itch. She'd never seen two people so in love. She was determined to sort it out. For a while she planned to shag Keef to spur Sitsi into a jealous rage that would show her true feelings. However, while thinking about it lying on her bedding that night, she realised that the plan was driven almost entirely by her own desire for some action and Keef being the only bloke she was aware of for hundreds of miles. And besides, they didn't have any booze. Not booze for Keef; Paloma was gorgeous and knew that Keef would shag her at the drop of a feather, no matter how much he was in love with Sitsi. The booze was for her.

Her chance to play love warlock came a few days later. Paloma and Freydis were spying on their companions from the top of the canyon, as usual. Sitsi was cooking a special bighorn stew and there was much preparation to do, so Keef ran off up-canyon to spar with imaginary foes.

They followed Keef. Paloma was pleased that Freydis was silent behind her. She'd been teaching the girl how to run faster while making as little noise as possible.

Keef climbed up the head of the valley, sprang onto the rock arch and posed manfully. Paloma was pleased to see that he acted like that even when he didn't know anyone was watching.

"Stay here and stay hidden," she told Freydis.

She leapt onto the other end of the arch, killing stick in one hand. The arch was about eighty paces long and its relatively flat top was around two paces wide. But it was two paces of flaky, crumbling sandstone. Most people would be terrified even crawling across it.

Hird man and Owsla woman strode confidently towards each other. There was no need to say it, they knew what was about to happen.

Keef glanced down the valley. *He was checking that Sitsi wasn't watching.*

"Let's go," he said.

It was a reasonable spar. No, thought Paloma, let's be generous. It was a good spar; the best she'd had with someone who wasn't Owsla.

At the end the two of them sat on the arch, looking down the valley, Keef shining with sweat. The gorge was choked with trees and bushes. Further upslope was red sand dotted with shrubs and cactuses, all overlooked by orange domes of rock. They were a long way from the woods, lakes and fields of Calnia.

"Do you think the giant screaming insects will come back?" asked Paloma.

"I guess," Keef nodded. "They seem to like warning people they're coming, so hopefully it won't be a problem and Sitsi will shoot them out of the sky."

They didn't speak for a while. Paloma guessed they were thinking about the same thing. She wanted to be talking about it, but couldn't think of a subtle, tactful way of bringing it up.

"Why don't you get it on with Sitsi Kestrel?" she said in the end.

Keef looked at the sky.

There was a long pause

Eventually, Keef sighed and said, "They're not insects, you know."

"What?"

"The wasp men. They've got eight legs. Insects have six. So the wasp men aren't insects."

"You're spending too much time with Sitsi. Which brings me back to my question."

"I can't get it on with her."

"Because of Bodil Gooseface?"

"Because of Bodil Gooseface."

Paloma shook her head. "You're an adult. You have no duty to Bodil."

"I have."

Paloma took a deep breath. *The things she did for others.* "You know it's not your baby, don't you?"

Keef fixed her with his one eye. "Just how dumb do you think I am?"

"I had wondered."

Keef breathed a little laugh through his nose. "Yeah, I do know that it takes more than a couple of days after a shag for a woman to know she's pregnant. And I know when she and Finnbogi . . ."

"You mean Finn?"

"He was Finnbogi when he shagged her."

"Fair enough. Point is you know the baby's his."

"Yup."

"So what's the problem?"

"When we got together in the Black Mountains, Bodil

asked me to be the father. She wanted someone strong to help her look after the child."

"Okay, I understand why that wouldn't be Finn, but what about Wulf and Sassa and the rest of you lot? Can't you all muck in?"

Keef hurled a stone off the arch. They watched it sail down and hit a barrel cactus.

"A child is best brought up by a united man and woman. It's why we have marriage."

"There are loads of tribes where the whole village rears a child. They reckon the best parenting comes from every adult the kid knows."

"Yeah? Well, first I think that's bollocks, and second we don't have a whole village. This kid will need a dad. A good dad."

"Some of the best people I know are orphans."

Keef nodded. "Yup, me too. So a child doesn't need a father, but it helps a lot, both the child and the mother. That's double, triple, a hundred times the case out here or wherever the Hel we're going to be when it's born."

"Let me get this straight. You like Sitsi, she likes you, but you're not going to do anything about it because of a promise to a woman who you slept with once when she was pregnant with another man's baby."

"I didn't promise. She asked and I said I would."

"And that's the same as a promise for you?"

Keef shrugged. "I suppose so."

"Couldn't you hook up with Sitsi and look after Bodil's baby as well?"

"Would that work?"

Paloma picked a slice of rock loose from the arch and tossed it off the edge. It slapped down on the mud surrounding the spring below.

"No."

"No."

"Are you in love with Sitsi Kestrel?"

Keef looked at his knees.

Paloma grinned. One of the things she liked about the Wootah was the way their skin changed colour so much. Keef had become the colour of a boiled pig.

They sat in silence for a while, throwing stones off the arch.

"You are a good man, Keef," Paloma said eventually.

"The best," he agreed. "Which reminds me. I better be getting back down to the cave. Sitsi wanted some things for her stew."

"Okay," she said as they stood to go. "So you're not going to get together with Sitsi. But if you do fancy something casual while we're here, I am up for it. We could go for a hunt, quick bang, nobody need ever know and you won't owe me anything. Come on, it'd be fun. We can do it now if you want? You won't take long and the herbs can wait."

Keef looked her in the eye, presumably to see if she was serious. She held his gaze.

The Wootah man shook his head and smiled, turned away and walked off along the arch.

Paloma watched him go. She was in Owsla uniform with exposed arms and midriff, one naked thigh and one leg completely bare. Keef hadn't even glanced at her figure when she'd offered to shag him with no strings attached.

So he was gay. That explained a lot.

# Chapter 18

## Massacre

S assa Lipchewer and the rest of them descended from the range of hills where Olaf Worldfinder and now Bodil Gooseface lived. They passed through a zone of grassy woodland that was just like the forest behind Hardwork. Apart, of course, from the colossal view across a sun-shattered plain towards snowy mountains.

As they reached the flat land they saw six more hobbling refugees hunched. They hurried away from the Wootah and Calnians, glancing over their shoulders.

"We are friendly!" Wulf yelled, but the refugees only sped up.

They headed on southwards, led by Taanya the squatch, towards Bighorn Island and Cloud Town. The land that had looked flat from the hills was in fact undulating and craggy. There were far fewer animals here, and those they saw bolted at their approach. It was hot and the going was hard.

Olaf had said the journey would take ten days. It was going to be a long ten days.

As they trudged along the gravel bed of a dry gulch lined with dead trees, Sassa thought she might shed a tear or two about Bodil staying behind with Olaf Worldfinder. She pictured Bodil's face and thought about all they'd done together. She couldn't cry, though. She realised something and stopped dead. She was glad her friend was gone.

"What's up?" asked Wulf.

"Just thinking about Bodil."

"We'll see her again."

She nodded and carried on. She tried to convince herself that she was pleased because Bodil's baby would be well looked after, and should be safe. But that wasn't true. If she'd really thought a baby was going to be that much safer with Olaf, she would have stayed there herself.

She and Bodil had hung out together since she could remember, but only because they were girls the same age who'd been put together by their parents. Sassa thought about the times she'd spent with Bodil and realised, with a thrill of guilty pleasure bordering on the unacceptable, that she didn't actually like her.

It wasn't because Bodil was so thick. It was because she was so uninterested. She never asked a question, never seemed to notice anything around her. She'd gone through the whole awful Badlands experience – their whole journey so far – as if she were watching it happen to someone else who she didn't care about.

Bodil spoke the whole time, but she never said anything insightful, useful or fun. She'd been spouting the same boring crap since she was about ten. No, Sassa was not going to miss Bodil. She was glad to see the back of her best friend and couldn't muster the slightest remorse at the idea of never seeing her again. *Screw a shrew!* What kind of person did that make her?

"*We never know how much we love someone until they are lost,*" said the ghost of Gunnhild in her mind.

*Very true*, Sassa agreed.

"Wulf," she asked, "are you going to miss Bodil?"

"Bodil?" he replied. "Sure. It's like losing a limb. Wow! Look at that spikey lizard!"

They caught up to Finn the Deep who was walking dejectedly on his own. Sassa saw that he was crying. "What's up, Finn?" she asked.

"I am a bad person." He sniffed snottily.

"Bodil and her baby," said Wulf, "are going to be a lot happier with Olaf. It is a real shame that you couldn't stay with them, but fact is we need you."

"They don't need me. And you don't need me. I'm the second worst fighter. The worst one is Ottar. You need him for the prophecy. If we had a vote for who gets killed next, everyone would vote for me. I'd definitely vote for me."

"Tell me," said Wulf. "How many times has Sofi Tornado saved all of us?"

"She fought Beaver Man by the lake . . ."

"And Sitsi shot him and Chogolisa drowned him. She herself has not saved us all once. And neither have I."

"You led us from the Owsla and—"

"Sure, and Sassa, Erik, Thyri, Keef, Bjarni, Gunnhild – Freydis and Ottar, too – have all done useful things. But you're the only one who's saved all of us, Finn. And you've done it twice."

"But I—"

"If you hadn't controlled the pigeons, we'd all have died, for sure. If you hadn't beaten the squatch, we'd have had no head start up the mountains, and we would have definitely been killed."

"I suppose."

"You're wrong about that vote, Finn. In fact, if I had to vote for one person to stay with us, I'd vote for you."

"Really?"

"Really really."

"But . . . You know what I did to Bodil."

"You were a shit," said Sassa.

Wulf put a hand on her arm.

"He was," she persisted. "You asked my advice, Finn. I said you should talk to her after you shagged her. And you didn't. You let her be miserable."

Finn sobbed.

"No," Sassa shook her head. "Stop crying. You shouldn't be feeling sorry for yourself."

"It's Bodil I'm feeling sorry for," Finn sniffed, "and the baby."

"Bollocks," said Sassa. Wulf touched her arm again and she shook her head. "No, Wulf, I'm not going to let him off. You've been a shit, Finn. I'm glad you know it now, but that doesn't change what happened."

She sped up. She was too angry to talk any more.

"Did you see that spiny lizard back there?" she heard Wulf ask as she accelerated out of earshot.

They came upon the massacre around noon the following day.

Sassa was up at the front with Sofi and Wulf. The first thing they found was a severed foot, lying on the path. Sofi kicked it into the scrub.

"Weird," said Wulf as they reached the top of a gentle rise. "I wonder what happened to its—"

He was cut short as the land opened up in front of them and there were dead people – more specifically parts of dead people – everywhere.

Sassa couldn't tell how many had been killed because they'd been ripped to pieces and their body parts strewn around. The sandy soil was stained black. The sparse desert scrub was painted black with blood.

Were there a hundred people here? A few corpses were more or less intact. Many of these were swollen and grotesquely purple, eyes bulging yellow. Others had melted faces. There were insects, rodents, birds and a couple of coyotes feasting on the bodies, but not as many as one might have expected. Perhaps there was a lot of food here and only so many carnivorous animals in the miles around, Sassa found herself crazily musing.

"Erik," said Sofi, after jogging back to the others, "there's a gristly scene over the rise. Please can you grab Ottar, distract him and carry him through?"

"Sure," said Erik, walking over to Ottar.

*Leave the boy alone,* thought Taanya, loping up from where she'd been shambling along at the back of the group. *I'll take him.*

*Okay*, thought Erik, glancing at Sofi.

Taanya scooped up Ottar into her arms and ran. She leapt daintily past the chunks of dismembered humans and disappeared over the next rise. To be fair, thought Sassa, she got Ottar out of there a lot quicker than Erik would have done. But would she stop? She didn't trust Taanya with the boy. Judging by the way Sofi watched her go, she felt the same.

"Yoki Choppa, Chogolisa and any willing Wootah, will you help me see if there's anyone alive?" asked Sofi.

They looked for survivors. It was a grim job, and there were none. Sassa found she could look at all the body parts impassively, as if it was just so much meat. That worked until she saw a child's doll lying still gripped by a small arm. Then she cried.

"What happened here?" Sassa asked nobody in particular when she'd recovered.

Sofi straightened up from where she'd been examining a burned patch of rock next to a severed leg. Her eyes were hard and dark as fire-tempered wood.

"There were about ninety people, heading east," she said. "They were attacked by flying creatures yesterday, around this time of day. The creatures had claws, hands like humans and an acidic venom. Living versions, I suspect, of the dead wasp man we saw. None escaped, and none of the creatures were killed."

Sassa looked about. "Where are the wasp men now?"

"I can't tell. They flew in and flew away."

Sassa scanned the sky. Erik and Finn, who'd overheard Sofi, were doing the same.

"Listen, everyone!" Sofi called out. "These people were killed by flying beasts, possibly wasp men. Most of them were unarmed and they were not warriors. With our weapons we will be able to defend ourselves. However, we must keep close and all be ready to fight. Sassa, you have the only bow. You and I will take the lead with Wulf, if Wulf agrees?"

Wulf nodded.

"Chogolisa, Thyri and Erik will take the rear. There will be no more than fifteen paces between Chogolisa and me at any time. If one needs to stop, we all stop. We're also going to increase the pace."

They found Taanya and Ottar waiting just over the rise. *Taanya, could you stay in the group and carry Ottar from now on please?* Sofi asked.

The squatch lifted an eyebrow. *I'll protect him.*

Finn the Deep didn't mind that Sofi hadn't selected him for the lead or the rear guard, even if it was just him and Yoki Choppa who were the presumably incapable middle of the march. It just didn't matter. Things were more serious now. The sight of the dead had left him nauseous and shaken, but also determined to do his bit to keep his companions alive.

For the rest of the day he walked with the reliably unchatty warlock, one hand on Foe Slicer's hilt, ready.

That night he trained as hard as he ever had with Thyri, perhaps harder. He didn't look at her legs once, nor did he try to deconstruct everything she said to search for hints of affection.

Nearby, Sassa pumped arrow after arrow into trees, retrieved them, and started again.

They went to sleep with no fire, beneath a canopy of trees on the bank of a stream.

Finn took first watch with Chogolisa and Sassa and afterwards fell asleep to dream of being chased by giant disapproving babies who wanted to rip him apart with their claws. He was woken by a ruckus.

There was no light in the east, so it was still a good way from dawn.

"What's going on?" he asked.

"Ottar and Taanya are gone," said Sassa.

"Cocks," said Finn, hoping it hadn't happened on his watch, then telling himself off. Concern for Ottar should have been his priority.

"Get ready to go," said Wulf. "We'll all head back and—"

"No," said Sofi. "Chogolisa and I will be quicker on our own. The rest of you wait here, under the trees."

"Do you want my bow?" asked Sassa. "If you get in range of her mind crush—"

"No, you'll need it here in case our flying friends appear."

The Wootah and Yoki Choppa waited in the dark. Finn slept. He felt a bit guilty lying down and closing his eyes with Ottar in such danger, but there was nothing else to do and it really would be better for everyone if he was fresh in the morning.

He woke after dawn. Wulf was where he'd been when Finn had fallen asleep, standing at the edge of the gully, looking back over their path.

Finn climbed up to join him.

Wulf greeted him then nodded northwards, hard-faced.

There were two figures maybe a mile away, one much larger than the other, jogging towards them. No sign of Ottar the Moaner.

Wulf set off to meet them. Finn followed, pounding along the stony ground.

"Where's the boy?" called Wulf when they neared.

Chogolisa twisted to show them her back, where Ottar was curled in a woollen papoose, asleep.

"And Taanya?" asked Wulf.

"Don't worry about her," said Sofi.

Immediately afterwards, Finn questioned what he'd seen. But . . . he was pretty sure that Chogolisa had shaken her head, as if in disapproval.

They headed back, Sofi striding ahead. When they'd woken in the night, Finn had thought it was pretty reckless that they'd let Taanya get away with Ottar. But now the problem was dealt with. Taanya was presumably dead, Ottar was back with them and he wasn't going to be kidnapped again. Had Sofi pushed Taanya into running away with him by talking up the dangers ahead and giving her the task of protecting the boy?

Taanya had helped them. She might have tried to rip Finn in half, but she'd done that to protect Ottar. And without Taanya's sister Ayla they'd probably be dead in the Badlands. Sure, killing Taanya was the most efficient way of dealing with her designs on Ottar. But was it the right way? If Sofi was so ready to kill, were any of them safe? What if one of them hurt their leg and was slowing the group?

"Great. So who's going to guide us now?" said Thyri when they reached the others.

"We follow the path south," said Sofi, "and look out for a mesa with a town on it."

"And Ottar knows the way, don't you, Ottar?" said Erik.

Ottar nodded. The look on his face reminded Finn of the time back in Hardwork when they'd played hide and seek and Ottar had been unable to find anybody.

"Taanya?" said the boy.

Erik and Finn looked at Chogolisa. "He slept through all of it," she said.

"All of what?" asked Finn.

Chogolisa shook her head and strode away.

"Taanya's gone back to her home," said Erik.

"Why?" asked Ottar.

"She has to look after the rabbits," said Finn.

"Oh." Ottar pouted and looked at the ground and began to cry silently.

"It's okay, Ottar," Erik squatted next to him. "The rabbits need her and she's happy with them."

Ottar sniffed.

"How about you go on my shoulders?" said Erik. "I'll be a thunder lizard and you can be Beaver Man."

A hint of a smile played on Ottar's lips as he raised his arms up to the big bearded man.

They'd been going a short while when Sofi called out, "To the trees! Fast as you can."

Finn and the rest of them ran full tilt towards the fir woodland a few hundred paces up the valley side.

He was still running when he heard a noise like nothing else he could imagine, apart, possibly, from a large herd of pigs with breathing problems screaming as they were slowly mashed in a gigantic butter churner.

The screaming grew louder and louder. Finn looked about, sure that whatever was coming must be upon them.

"Get down. Stay silent," whispered Sofi.

Finn lay in the scrub on the edge of the trees next to Thyri and tried to pant noiselessly.

By the loudness of the screams he expected to see the beasts immediately, but it was a good thirty heartbeats before they came flying up the valley.

It was a flock of wasp men, dozens of them, and one much larger animal – a giant, six-winged, spike-legged beast with a disgustingly bulbous bladder-like body, like the one that Sitsi and Sassa had shot down on the far side of the Shining Mountains. The cacophony was so awful that he pressed his hands tight over his ears.

Finn understood why there'd been no dead creatures among the dead people the day before. The noise was so terrible that it must have been near impossible to fight back.

Suddenly they stopped shrieking. They hovered in the valley, over the spot that the Owsla and Calnians had fled from. They'd see their tracks into the trees. They had to. Any idiot could have found and followed their trail through the grass.

The monsters hung in the sky. Finn could hear the low, loud thrum made by the slapping of leathery wings. Each of the man-sized wasp men had six human-like hands. Among the giant stings, the claws and the huge grey sac body on the giant flier, it was those hands that freaked him out the most. He imagined one of the creatures pinning his arms with one pair of hands, strangling him with another and tearing at his genitals with the other. And then it might use its claws . . .

He was very close to leaping up and sprinting deeper into the trees. Very close. Then the screaming resumed and the monsters flew on.

"Fowl an owl," breathed Sassa when they'd disappeared.

"Good of them to warn us they were coming," said Wulf.

"Yes," said Sofi.

"Moss," said Erik. "Come on, Finn, help me find moss. We can use it for earplugs if they catch us in the open."

The monsters didn't catch them in the open. They didn't hear them again, or see any other monsters all the way to Bighorn Island. It was a slog, but the going was easier than Olaf had said it would be. The mountains they had to cross were snow-capped, but they were only above the snowline for a morning. It would have been longer, but for Erik's snow shoes. There had been landslides, leaving loose debris of rock, earth and broken trees in parts, but they tied a rope between themselves and clambered across.

On the morning of the sixth day of travelling, a great, flat-topped mass rose out of the south-east.

"Is that Bighorn Island?" Thyri called up to Ottar, who was high on Chogolisa's shoulders.

"Yop!" said Ottar.

As if to prove him right, a woman appeared on the track ahead, walking towards them.

"Stop," said Sofi. "Weapons ready."

# Chapter 19

## Cloud Town

The woman was about Finn's age – short, with long hair teased into a cascading mass. Her white dress was decorated with pink, blue and yellow shells arranged in animal shapes, and her sandals were adorned with black shells. Bright eyes sparkled in a way that reminded Finn of Olaf Worldfinder's and her smile was literally disarming. As she walked towards them, beaming away like a happy mother trying to reassure a worried two-year-old, Finn found himself sliding Foe Slicer back into its scabbard. All the others lowered their weapons and relaxed.

"Welcome, Wootah and Calnians!" she chimed. Her voice was as comforting as her smile, even though it was a bit freaky that she knew who they were. "Chief Meesa Verdy would have come himself, but he had unavoidable business elsewhere and sent me in his stead. I am his daughter, Moolba. On behalf of Meesa Verdy and the rest of the Cloud Tribe, welcome to Bighorn Island."

She gestured at the steep-sided plateau soaring out of the ground to the south-west.

"Not an island then," said Thyri.

"It's an island of cool and calm in the desert," smiled Moolba.

"How did you know we were coming?" asked Erik.

"Ola Wolvinder told us."

"How?" asked Thyri.

"Oh, we're always talking to Ola. Now, follow me, please. You've come a long way, but I'm afraid that it's still something of a hike to Cloud Town."

And so it was.

They ascended a winding path up the long scarp that led to a high plateau. The world opened around them as they climbed and again Finn could see miles of baking red desert punctured by jagged mountains to the west.

It became greener and greener as they climbed. Soon there were signs of civilisation. They passed fields sewn with neat rows of plants and turkeys strutting about in vast rope pens.

Finn found himself walking in the lead, next to Moolba and Sofi.

"Where are all the bighorns?" he asked the chief's daughter, hoping to point out how silly it was that there were no bighorn sheep in a place called Bighorn Island.

"There are plenty around," she smiled, "although probably not as many as when the land was named."

"Ah," said Finn, disarmed yet again.

They approached half a dozen field workers. The men and women looked up, then went back to their business without any apparent interest in the newcomers.

Finn felt slightly insulted. Erik and Wulf were both huge compared to your average Scrayling; Sofi, Sassa and Thyri were gorgeous. And Chogolisa was a giant.

"Not that interested in the outside world, your lot?" he asked Moolba.

"They see a lot of refugees."

"We're not refugees," said Sofi.

"I did not say that you were. I'm taking you to Cloud Town. We don't take refugees to Cloud Town. If you were refugees, you'd be allowed to stay one night. You are all welcome for as long as you like."

"What do you do to the refugees after one night?" asked Sofi.

"Hundreds come," said Moolba. "We can feed them for one night. I wish we could do more, but we don't have the stores."

"How do you make them go?"

"We tell them that they can stay for one night only. Most accept that."

"And those that don't?"

Finn could tell that Sofi was embarrassing their host. "What's that design on the tree over there?" he asked. He pointed at a dead pinyon pine. There was a line with three triangles above it carved into the trunk. "I saw it on the turkey pens, too."

Sofi gave Finn a stink eye and dropped back. Moolba put a hand on Finn's arm and smiled. "Thanks for asking. The triangles represent the three branches of the Cloud Tribe. The Mindful, the Landfolk and the Dead."

"I see."

"Hundreds of years ago our ancestors branched off from the Warrior and Warlock tribes. We had no need for a standing army, so the Warriors became the Landfolk, who tend to the land, and live on the mesa top. The Warlocks became the Mindful. We all live in Cloud Town and similar places. The Dead are . . . well, they're dead."

"Got it," said Finn, glancing back at the men and women working the field. "But why aren't the Landfolk interested in us? Some of us have blond hair and Chogolisa's a giant."

"The Landfolk are not interested in much, but they farm well and they are capable warriors. Have you come across any dangerous creatures on your way here?"

"Only a huge flock of flying bastards with claws that could take a buffalo's head off."

"We've encountered those as well. All the Landfolk that you see working out here are no more than a few paces from a bow and supply of arrows. Should any monsters come, they will see them off."

"We saw a flock of wasp men a hundred-strong," said Finn.

"That's a worry," said Moolba, as if it wasn't a particular worry. "If they do attack in numbers, the Landfolk will retreat to a village."

She pointed ahead at what Finn had taken to be a rocky outcrop, but which he could now see was a huge, blocky building.

Closer, he could see that it was built from pale, flat stones, regularly sized as if each had been hewn into shape, then painted red, yellow and white. The design of three triangles with a line under it was daubed all over the walls.

*What a pain in the arse it must have been to make this*, thought Finn, *but what a result!*

It was as if benevolent giants had constructed dozens of square, stone-built huts then fitted them together up to three levels high, to create a squashed up, on-top-of-itself village. Children chased under drying laundry and between the wooden sheds that had been erected on some of the roofs. Men and women were dotted all about the roofs and around the edges, hanging laundry, hammering, weaving and generally being industrious. The children bounced balls. *How did those balls get so bouncy?* Finn wondered. There were ladders, notched poles and walkways between the building's many blocky rooms, but, as far as Finn could see, there was no way in from the outside.

He was about to question Moolba about it, but his father jogged up and asked:

"How do they get into their homes?"

"The doors are on the top of each dwelling. They climb ladders which they can pull onto the roofs."

"To protect them from attack?"

"Exactly. They are more fortified than you can see from here. Within the walls are underground chambers whose only access is a small hole. A child with a spear in his underground house can hold out against an army."

"Unless the army filled it with water," suggested Erik.

"Well, yes," admitted Moolba, glancing to her left. Finn followed her gaze and saw a circular pond, forty paces across, clearly man-made by the brick wall that surrounded it. They'd been busy up here.

"Or poured a bucket of angry rattlesnakes through the hole," suggested Finn.

"Okay, a child can hold out against any army that isn't carrying around vast quantities of water or bucketloads of angry rattlesnakes."

"Were they built to protect you from the monsters?" Erik asked.

"No. These villages predate the monster attacks by hundreds of years. They were built to defend against the Warrior and Warlock tribe after the split. The Warriors and Warlocks are still by far the larger tribe and rule the land west of here. Or at least they did before it all fell apart."

"Did the Warriors and Warlocks attack you?"

The chief's daughter shook her head. "No. Their leaders are invited here every few years, shown hospitably and given a tour of our impregnable defences."

"I see."

"Good." She smiled and Finn was very much on her side against the Warriors and Warlocks.

"Have the wasp men and the huge flying monsters visited you here?" asked Erik.

"We've seen wasp men, but so far the only casualties have been animals. But from what refugees tell us, much worse creatures than the wasp men will come."

"So you've been taking in refugees?" Erik looked about him. "Where are they all?"

"They can stay for one night," said Finn, "they don't have the supplies to keep them for longer."

"And then?" asked Erik.

"And they go," said Moolba. She sped on ahead, out of conversation range.

"She's a princess," said Chogolisa, catching up to Erik and Finn.

"She certainly is," agreed Erik.

"No, I mean a real princess. You saw those shells on her dress and sandals?"

"Um . . . yes?"

"You didn't notice them, did you?"

"Well, no, but I believe you."

"Wow, men are unobservant."

"I saw them," Finn piped up.

They both looked at him, then Chogolisa continued: "It's the sort of thing Empress Ayanna would wear in Calnia. The shells are from the sea. We're a long way from the ocean, so those shells are immensely valuable."

"What can they do?" Erik asked.

"They can't *do* anything."

"Why are they valuable?"

"Because it took a lot of effort to get them here. Even more – much more – than it took to get seashells to Calnia. So it shows that the person wearing them is important enough to merit that effort."

"It takes more than well-travelled shells to impress me," said Erik.

They walked along a broad, well-trodden path between the juniper and pinyon pines. Bighorn Island was much larger than Finn had thought. It was late afternoon by the time Moolba stopped.

She was standing on a cliff edge. Finn joined her, looked down and gasped. They'd walked along a promontory of the plateau and were looking back at the main massif. A hundred paces below the top of the cliff, hewn into the rock, was a gaping alcove a couple of hundred paces long and fifty high.

They couldn't see how deep it was because, crammed into it like an overindulged child's toy collection, were towers, courtyards and other buildings, combining to create a town far larger than any Finn had seen anywhere before, let along squashed into a cleft in a cliff.

There were tall towers with straight walls, towers with curved walls and a host of terraced, circular platforms. Like the village they were painted red, yellow and white, and the line with three triangles design adorned most of the walls.

Linking the buildings were heavy wooden ladders, notched poles and walkways, all teeming with two distinct groups of humans. People dressed in white swanned around sedately, sat in groups and walked in and out of the buildings. Others, dressed in uncoloured leather, swarmed about carrying things, sweeping with brooms and generally doing the kind of drudge work that Gunnhild had forced Finn to do back in Hardwork. It wasn't a great stretch to distinguish the Landfolk from the Mindful.

Above and below the town in the cliff were Landfolk climbing and descending the vertical rock on a network of foot- and handholds.

The whole thing – the town in the cliff, the swarming people, the death-defying climbers – was like something from a dream.

"Welcome to Cloud Town," announced Moolba.

Finn gulped. All of them, even Yoki Choppa and Sofi, stood and stared. Finn thought of how much Gunnhild and Bjarni would have loved it. He thought that one day he'd love to show something like this to his own children. Like the child that he'd left behind with Olaf and Bodil who would never know him . . . He blinked back tears. Luckily everyone was too busy staring at Cloud Town to notice.

"Wow," said Erik.

"Does this impress you more than well-travelled shells?" Moolba asked him.

Erik coloured. "When I said the shells don't impress me—"

"I wasn't meant to hear. You should know that sound travels more clearly up here than in the lands below. You should also know that I would prefer a plain dress, but I dress as the daughter of the chief is expected to. I believe that one should choose one's wars and I don't believe that the war of what I wear is worth waging. Do you agree?"

"I do. Sorry."

"Don't be sorry, that's the point."

"I see. Sorry."

"Okay, apology accepted. Please don't apologise again."

"Are we going down there?" Erik pointed to the town.

"We are."

"Can I wait here? I'm not a great climber and—"

"Don't worry," Moolba smiled. "We'll be going down in baskets."

"Baskets?" Erik balked.

They followed Moolba to four sturdy wooden frames built on the edge of their promontory. Four taut, thick hawsers and a load of thinner, droopier cords ran up from the cliff town to the frames. Squads of the plainly dressed people were pulling at the cords, drawing four baskets jerkily from the town. It was several hundred paces' drop from the baskets to the woodland that fringed the mesa below.

"Some of us climb the cliffs for amusement or if we're in a hurry," said Moolba, "but generally we prefer to be carried up and down."

"But there are loads of people climbing," said Thyri, watching the baskets' jolting progress towards them. Finn guessed that she'd rather climb down. He wasn't sure which he'd rather do. Both options looked simply awful.

"The climbers are Landfolk. Mindful travel in the baskets, Landfolk climb. All guests are given Mindful status, unless they prove they don't deserve it."

"And how would they do that?" Thyri asked.

"By being rude."

"I see," said Thyri.

"Good!" Moolba smiled at her. "Let's sort ourselves into baskets. There are nine of you and one of me, so you four . . ."

Finn was put into a group with Yoki Choppa, Sassa and Moolba.

The Landfolk hauled the baskets to the top. They were wicker-made, perhaps a pace square, with sides that came up to Finn's navel. Moolba untied a couple of leather cords and opened a door in one side. The door's hinges were six more leather cords.

If Finn had been designing something to transport people over a chasm, he would have made something sturdier. A lot sturdier.

"In we go then!" said Moolba. "Don't hold onto the rope above."

*Well, obviously,* thought Finn.

Sassa gestured for him to go in first. She didn't look much happier than he felt.

Erik was paired with Ottar and Thyri, both of whom were already in the basket. Ottar was bouncing on the wicker to some happy tune only he could hear. Thyri was staring into the middle distance, jaw set. A few hairs had escaped from her ponytail and were blowing lightly about her rosy cheeks.

Finn's father was standing next to the basket, wide-legged, hands griping the wicker side, looking from basket to chasm and back again and blowing hard.

*Let others' terror lend bravery to the fearful,* said Gunnhild in his mind.

*Thanks, dead Aunt Gunnhild!* he thought back. His father's panicked funk did make him feel a lot better. He stepped into the basket. Thick wicker creaked and shifted and creaked some more. The sides came up as far as his hip bones.

The wobbly, wicker sides. It was bad enough making people

travel in creaky baskets. *But surely they could have build the sides a bit higher!* It was like they wanted to fall out.

There was a stomach-churning lurch as Landfolk swung the basket out over the fearful drop. Finn considered vomiting in horror. Before he could even cough, however, they were zooming down towards the town, much faster – and more smoothly, thank Oaden – than the baskets had ascended.

He gripped the low sides. He bent his knees and stuck his bottom out, where it bumped into Sassa. They turned to look at each other, wicker creaking underneath. Sassa's mouth was in more of a twist than usual, her neck sinews were tightly exposed and her eyes were wide.

"*Shag a stag*," she whispered.

Yoki Choppa and Moolba were standing in the basket as if they were in the middle of a grassland admiring the view. They weren't even holding the sides, for the love of Loakie.

"Woooo-tah!" yelled Wulf from somewhere.

Finn tried to look for him, but the world whirled crazily so he closed his eyes, gripped the sides all the harder and squatted all the lower.

His Aunt Gunnhild had once told him that he was scared when people like Wulf weren't not because he was more of a coward, but because he had a better imagination and so was more able to imagine what could go wrong. Basically, because he was cleverer. He liked that take on things.

The basket lurched sickeningly. Finn thought, *this is it! We're falling!* But they bumped onto something solid. Finn opened his eyes. The cliff top was four hundred paces away and a hundred paces above. They were on the edge of the notch town.

Yoki Choppa, Moolba and Sassa were already out of the basket. A toothy young man offered Finn a hand, but he raised his own to indicate that he didn't need help.

"Not many people enjoy their first go!" chirped the man. "But you look even paler than most!"

"This," announced Finn, "is my natural skin tone."

"Oh, sorry." The man backed away looking seriously abashed. "I didn't mean to offend."

Finn felt bad.

He stepped from wicker onto stone. It was a welcome transition, but he was already dreading the return journey.

They were on a broad landing platform on the edge of the town, at its lowest level. The amazing settlement looked even larger from here, with buildings towering four, five, even six levels above them.

The Landfolk cleared away and a couple of dozen white-clad Mindful approached.

They said you couldn't judge people by their appearance, but Finn had always disagreed with them. By looking at Jarl Brodir and Garth Anvilchin, for example, you could tell that they were, respectively, an oily shit and a thug. By that token, these Mindful were an intelligent but haughty bunch. Even the children had an air of *oh dear, who are these dreadful outsiders?* about them.

It seemed that he was right. The Mindful looked at the newcomers, one of them had a quick word with Moolba, and then they walked away as if the whole thing was just a bit embarrassing.

Finn chose to ignore them and gawp at the town instead.

The whole place was under a roof of yellow-white rock. If you'd looked over the top of the mesa directly above, you wouldn't have known there was a large town tucked into the cliff a hundred paces below. The rock roof was stained black in several places, presumably by fires. Right at the top of the town – it was strange to think of a town as a vertical thing, but this one was – were a set of square stone rooms jammed against the rock roof, overlooking it all. That was where Finn would like to live, he decided.

"Those are storage chambers," said Moolba, appearing next to him and following his gaze, "full of supplies in case we get stuck in here."

"Have you ever needed them?" asked Finn.

"Not yet. However, if you consider the things we've seen recently and the stories coming from the west, I have a feeling it may not be long before the Mindful are stuck down here for a long while."

"What about the Landfolk?" Finn asked.

Moolba looked around her. "There are those," she said quietly, "who say that they will be safe in their stone villages. Others think we should invite them down here until the emergency has passed."

"Which side are you on?"

Moolba smiled. "I hope it won't come to taking sides."

"Moolba?"

It was Sofi, calling her from the other side of the landing stage.

Moolba strolled off. A squawk made Finn jump. It was a large, crazily red bird with red and blue wings and a vicious looking beak, staring at him. He backed away.

"Don't worry," said Chogolisa, ambling up. "It's only a macaw. They're from the southern jungles. Loads of people in Calnia had them as pets. They only bite if you goad them."

"Is Chief Meesa Verdy here?" Sofi asked, although she knew the answer, because she'd heard one of the white-dressed people whisper to Moolba when they'd arrived.

"He isn't. He's gone to deal with an irrigation problem on the western island. He won't be back for a while, so I'm standing in for him. What can I do for you?"

"We need the ingredients for a vision quest. Olaf said you have them."

"Olaf?"

"Olaf Worldfinder is the Wootah tribe's name for Ola Wolvinder. He—"

"—led their ancestors across the Great Salt Sea a hundred years ago?" Moolba interrupted.

Sofi raised an eyebrow.

"I've spent a while listening to Ola's stories," Moolba explained. "And by their yellow hair and blue eyes . . . it wasn't a great leap."

"No," agreed Sofi, nearly smiling.

"Why don't you come with me and tell me how you ended up crossing the world with them?" asked Moolba.

"And the vision quest ingredients?"

"You can have them in return for your story."

"Your warlock will agree?" In Sofi's experience, warlocks didn't like giving away their precious materials to anyone, let alone strangers.

"We're all warlocks here."

Sofi looked into Moolba's sparkling eyes. Despite being black rather than blue, they reminded her of Olaf World-finder's. The other Mindful had similar eyes. Wet and shining, like the eyes of much older people.

Moolba watched Sofi work it out and nodded in possibly patronising congratulation.

"Fine," said Sofi, "I'll tell you our story in return for the herbs."

"Done. As long as the person who takes them knows there is about a one in four chance that they will die."

Sofi nodded.

"It will be you, won't it?" Moolba asked.

"It will."

"You've never taken an hallucinogenic drug in your life, have you?" she said.

Sofi hadn't. Why would you? People had told her she should try everything. She'd asked those people if they'd like to try having a barbed fishing spear rammed up their arses.

Moolba looked past her to the others. "You're their leader," she said quietly. "They will be lost without you. They will try to persuade you that one of them should take the quest."

"Do I look persuadable?" Sofi asked.

"I like you," said Moolba. "Come with me."

The chief's daughter led Sofi across the town, along a complicated route of ladders and walkways, then down into a circular underground chamber. Sofi's eyes adjusted in time to see Moolba crawling through a small opening in one wall. Sofi sighed, and followed her.

The tight tunnel emerged ten paces later inside a narrow, windowless tower, dimly lit by a square hole in the roof. A ladder on one wall led up and through the hole. Sofi climbed the ladder and emerged into a circular room, where she found Moolba. She walked over to the small window and saw the Wootah and Calnians milling about below.

"This is my room, and it's deemed important," explained Moolba. "All the important rooms have complicated routes leading to them. They say it's to confuse invaders. Although I've never seen the point. If invaders are wandering about our town then we've already lost, and it's a pain when you forget something and have to nip back for it."

The room contained two plain chairs, a table, a low cot with a thick mattress, a few barrel cactus-carved storage pots and some wooden boxes. Other than the ladder emerging on one side of the room, the small window was the only opening. Sofi wondered how they'd got the mattress in there.

"Please, sit down," Moolba gestured to one of the chairs. She took the other. "Food and drink will come. Please tell me all about your journey with the Wootah, and then we can discuss the vision quest."

Sofi began with the day she'd been summoned to the Mountain of the Sun and ordered by Ayanna to complete the massacre of the Goachica and the Mushroom Men.

Presently, a boy arrived with deer and squash stew and a delicious cactus syrup drink. Sofi talked as she ate.

Moolba listened, interrupting only now and then to ask Sofi to clarify a point.

Sofi had never spoken for so long before, nor revealed so many of her thoughts. She told Moolba how Malilla Leaper's mutiny had upset her. She told her that the other women had lost their love of killing after Yoki Choppa removed the rattlesnake from the Owsla's diet, but that her own love of killing had been reduced only a little, if at all. She probably hadn't needed to kill Taanya the squatch to get Ottar back. She'd told herself it was the easiest and quickest way, but the fact was she'd wanted to kill the annoying beast and she'd enjoyed doing it.

She noticed it was dark outside and she was still talking. She wondered if she'd been drugged. She didn't mind. It was a wonderful relief to talk. She told Moolba about the Badlands, the Green tribe and the Shining Mountains. She told her about the loss of Luby Zephyr. She explained how guilty she'd felt when Freydis the Annoying had been swept away, and how ridiculous she'd felt praying to Innowak to keep the girl alive, particularly because she was still planning to slaughter the Wootah after the quest was done. Or at least she was considering it. Yoki Choppa's theory that there were millions more Mushroom Men over the Great Salt Sea was convincing, but it was just a theory. Empress Ayanna had seen that the Wootah would destroy the world. What if she was right? Surely there was enough risk that it made sense to kill this handful of people?

On the other hand, she was beginning to feel real affection for the Wootah, particularly the idiot Finn, whom she'd loathed initially but now regarded like a brother. Like an annoying little brother who would have benefited from regular beatings, sure, but a brother all the same.

As she talked about killing the Wootah, the room began

to swirl and her eyes felt like they were being sucked backwards into her head. She recognised the feeling. She'd fainted many times in the early days of Owsla training, before alchemical warping had hardened her.

She closed her eyes and opened them to find Moolba standing over her.

"I—" she began.

"Shush," said Moolba, placing her cool hands around Sofi's neck.

Sofi tried to lift her own hands but she couldn't.

Moolba smiled, and tightened her fingers.

Sofi couldn't move at all. Her brain clouded.

"Why?" she managed.

The skin on Moolba's face greyed and slackened and she became an impossibly ancient, ravaged crone.

*But her eyes are the same* was Sofi's final thought.

# Chapter 20

## Breaking the Rules

Sitsi Kestrel had decreed that none of them should venture more than a couple of hundred paces from the canyon.

"It's not just the wasp men, other monsters, flash floods and tornados," she'd instructed Paloma finger-waggingly. "The Red River runs along the southern border of Wormsland. I don't know exactly how far we've come, but by my estimates Wormsland is directly across the river."

"So?" Paloma had asked.

"Don't you remember what the Popeyes said?" Sitsi had replied.

"The Popeyes?"

"Those people with bulging eyes who were on the Plains Strider with us."

"Oh yeah, I think I remember them. What did they say?" Paloma remembered them very well and knew exactly what they'd said, but she enjoyed goading Sitsi.

"They came from Wormsland! Don't you pay any attention to anything? They said a murderous tribe had pushed them out of their territory."

"And we need to hide in case the nasty people frighten us, too?"

"I think we need to avoid recklessness leading to the death of a small girl."

"Hmmm."

"Go on, answer. Would it make sense to avoid encounters

with any monsters or monstrous people until the rest of the group get here, for the sake of Freydis's safety?"

"I suppose."

"So, do you promise you won't take Freydis more than a hundred paces from our canyon?"

"Can I think about it?"

"Paloma!"

"Okay, fine, we'll stay near the canyon."

Several days after that conversation, Paloma was tired of spying on two should-be lovers who were never going to do anything beyond endless archery practice. She was itching for adventure. She'd also never been great with rules. Here there was only one and she wanted to break it. She needed to break it.

Freydis looked bored, too. Surely it was bad for a child to be stifled like this? If children have no risk in their lives, how can they learn to avoid it?

So, about half a moon after they had arrived in the canyon, Paloma told Freydis she believed that it was important for the group's safety to know what lay in the vicinity of their canyon. The girl nodded agreement and smiled in complicit naughtiness.

The following dawn they dressed silently and prepared to leave.

"And where do you think you're going?" asked Sitsi from her bedding on the opposite side of the cave from Keef's.

"To the canyon mouth," said Paloma, "to throw stones into the Red River."

"Have fun!" yelled Keef.

"Be careful," said Sitsi.

Paloma strode down the canyon with Freydis skipping along behind her, humming a cheery little tune. It was, of course, mused Paloma, Freydis's wilfulness in staying on the raft that had caused Paloma to be speared in the stomach, tongue-stretched by an ogre and stuck here with the world's most frustrating non-lovers. But this was different. They weren't going to get into trouble this time.

"Which way?" asked Freydis when they emerged from the narrow opening of their gulch into the wide Red River canyon. They could have climbed the crumbling red rock cliff on the far side, but if Sitsi was right then that would take them into Wormsland, the area populated by the tribe who'd forced the Popeye people from their land and into extinction. It was probably, on balance, not the best idea to take Freydis up there.

"We came from upriver. Let's try downriver," she said.

Since they'd arrived, the current had reduced from sprayful charging to a sluggish brown roll. Perfect for water-running. Would it work with a child on her back? Only one way to find out. She unstrung her water shoes from her little backpack.

"Will I go on your shoulders?" Freydis was bouncing on her toes.

"You can swim, right?

"I'm a good swimmer."

"Excellent. You can rescue me if it doesn't work. Let's go!"

It did work. Paloma slapped along the river like a giant duck on an extended take-off run, with Freydis whooping on her shoulders. They meandered between high red and black cliffs, then burst out into a wide, lush area of lower land. Paloma slowed and ran onto a shingle beach, pleased that she managed it without falling. If she had, Freydis would have flown face-first into the stones. The less cut and bruised the girl was when they returned, the less Sitsi would be able to complain.

"Aw," said Freydis as Paloma swung the girl down from her shoulders.

"We can be seen for miles running down the river here," said Paloma. "If anything or anybody means us harm, I want to see them first." She might not be overly cautious like Sitsi, but she wasn't an idiot.

They picked their way along the boulder-strewn bank. It was hard going for Freydis until they discovered a path a dozen paces from the river. They walked along in the shade of whispering trees and long-fronded bushes. Chipmunks sniffed at them and ran for cover. A long-limbed lizard on a nearby rock looked them in the eye as it pumped its forelegs up and down in a motion that looked exactly like press-ups.

"Hey, look at me, girls!'" said Paloma, pointing at the lizard. Freydis giggled.

"We should have done this days ago," said Paloma. "There's no dang—"

An angry, guttural roar sounded from somewhere nearby.

"—ger" finished Paloma, widening her eyes at Freydis.

They stopped. The hair-raising roar rang out again. It was coming from a little way downstream, on the far side of the river.

"That's a squatch," said Paloma.

They crept up a low scarp of rock that protruded over the channel.

On the far side, on stony ground busy with low bushes, were three men, a woman and a one-armed squatch. Two of the men and the woman were holding ropes tied around the squatch's neck, pulling in opposite directions, presumably to keep the beast out of mind-crush range.

The squatch had one arrow sticking out of its remaining bicep, and another in its back. The archer shot a third into its thigh. The squatch roared again, sounding more angry than hurt.

"You have to rescue him, Paloma Pronghorn," said Freydis.

"Do I? The squatch tried to kill us."

"The Badlanders tried to kill us, too. Are all humans bad?"

"Hmmm." Paloma had killed enough people herself, and did think that most adult humans were inherently bad, but the girl sort of had a point.

The three men were dressed in leather breechcloths, the woman wore the same with a jerkin. They were young and strong, and the woman was very tall, but they didn't move like they'd been alchemically enhanced. Unless she was missing something, it should be a doddle to put an end to the torment. But then what?

They had the squatch at rope's length for a reason. If she rescued it, it would probably get close enough to crush her mind. And who knew what the creature had done? Maybe it deserved a bit of torture.

"He's only got one arm!" said Freydis. "Please, Paloma Pronghorn?"

"Shoot it in the head!" shouted one of the rope-holding men.

"Let's not hurry," said the woman.

The other rope-holder laughed. "Yeah! Kill the fucker slowly."

That did it. Paloma did not like people swearing near Freydis.

"Stay here, Freydis. Stay low. Scream if anything attacks you."

The fastest person in the world zipped back down to the river, strapped her water shoes to her feet, ran across, unstrapped her shoes, leapt up the bank and landed with her killing stick in her hand.

"Hi," she said brightly.

The archer swung his aim from the squatch to Paloma and back. The other two looked from Paloma to the tall woman, mouths open. So she was the boss. She had straight, unadorned black hair, round, plump cheeks and exposed upper teeth. She looked quite a lot like a prairie dog.

"Who are you and what do you want?" asked prairie dog.

"Why are you tormenting the squatch?"

"I asked first."

She had asked first. There was no need to be overly antagonistic. "I'm Paloma Pronghorn. I'd like you to convince me that this squatch deserves what you're doing to—" she glanced at the squatch, it looked like a male, "—him. Or free him."

"And if I don't?"

"Then I'll free him. You and your men will probably be hurt, but I'll try not to kill you. Unless you really annoy me."

"Shoot her."

The archer switched his aim, drew the bowstring and loosed.

Paloma stepped aside, flashed out a hand and caught the arrow.

*Phew*, she thought. She only managed that trick about one out of three times and she would have looked like an idiot if it had gone through her hand – which had happened before.

She twirled the arrow in her fingers. "Let him go and run away."

*And you*, she thought at the squatch, *don't chase them.*

*I'll do as you ask.*

The tall woman regarded Paloma calmly. "All right," she said. "Let's go, you three."

"But, Chief Tarker, she's just one woman and we—"

"Can you catch an arrow?"

"Not one that's been shot from a bow, no, certainly not at that range, but—"

"But nothing. She's not just one woman, she's something else. Keep an arrow on the beast as we leave."

"But, Chief Tarker . . ."

"If she really wants the squatch she's welcome to it. Drop the ropes and run on three. One, two, three."

They dropped the ropes and ran off to the north. The archer left last, jogging backwards, arrow trained on the squatch.

The beast sat and pried the nooses from its neck with a claw, one eye on Paloma. She waited for thoughts of gratitude but none came.

*What do you know of the land west of here?* she asked in the end.

*I'm the only survivor from a squad of twelve. You wouldn't last a heartbeat.*

When she'd first seen them, Paloma had thought all squatch looked alike. However, after a few hours as their captive, she'd seen that their faces were as varied as human faces, and their voices, although internal, just as diverse. This one had the sort of pinched expression you might find on a bitter human and a whiney tone to match. She began to regret freeing him.

*You're one of the squad sent by Berlaze.*

The creature's face twisted in satisfying puzzlement.

*Yes. Berlaze sent us to find out what was happening at The Meadows and to stop it.*

*What did you find?*

*Why should I tell you?*

*Because I saved your life.*

The squatch grunted.

*Two of us were burned to death by spinning columns of fire that travelled faster than we can run. More were killed by creatures that I'd never before seen nor heard of. There were flying, screaming beasts, scorpions the size of hills that sprayed geysers of venom from their tails and crushed buffalo with their claws, and more — each more bizarre and dangerous than the next.*

The squatch loosed the final rope and tossed it aside.

*Five of us saw the pyramid in the centre of The Meadows. It is where the evil comes from. We waited for dark and tried to approach, but it is encircled by monsters for miles around. All my fellows were killed. I lost my arm to the claws of one of the smaller creatures and fled. I have been running east ever since, avoiding humans who would kill me. The humans who remain in the west are as aggressive as the monsters, although rather easier to kill. These ones who would have murdered me waited like cowards until I was asleep, then trapped me.*

Paloma picked up one of the discarded ropes. It was good and would come in handy so she began coiling it, walking towards the squatch.

*You're lucky I happened along*, she thought.

*Yes, I am. But are you?*

She stopped and looked at the sitting squatch. That was definitely a smile, and not a nice one. She tensed to run but her head was filled with the most dreadful pain.

She dropped to her knees as the squatch stood.

He raised his arm, claws out.

"No!" shouted Freydis from across the river, "she saved you!"

*The only good human*, thought the squatch, *is a dead human.*

He pulled his arm back to strike. There was a soft *zip* followed by a *thwunk* as an arrow pierced his eye. He crumpled.

Paloma closed her eyes. The pain in her mind was hateful, but it was ebbing. She swayed and shook her hands as if she was shaking water from them. It seemed to help.

She opened her eyes to see Sitsi pulling her arrow from the squatch's eye. The archer glanced at her, then returned to her task.

"I'm sorry," said Paloma.

"I'm disappointed," said Sitsi. "You promised—"

There was a rumbling and the ground began to shake. Paloma ran back to the river intending to return to Freydis, but saw Keef halfway across the Red River in his canoe with Freydis kneeling up in the prow. Keef was paddling to stay in the centre of the channel, which was as good a place as any during an earthquake.

The rumbling and shaking stopped, but they heard the long, loud roar of a rockslide further south and all around them smaller stones were still skittering down slopes.

Sitsi appeared at Paloma's shoulder. "Shall we go back to our canyon?" she asked.

# Chapter 21

## Whitecap

S ofi Tornado flew high over dark green forests and light green clearings. The land looked like the jungles of her youth, but the air was fresher, hotter and dryer, tinged with a floral scent rather than reeking of decay. It felt like she'd been flying high above the land all her life, yet she knew that Moolba had murdered her only moments before.

She stretched her arms to slice satisfyingly through the whooshing air, then righted her course. A glance left and right confirmed what she'd known. Her arms were wings.

She felt the familiar desire to hurt and kill. The end of her long, brown wings ended in splayed, individual feathers. So she'd died and returned to life as a whitecap eagle. She could have been a slug or a rabbit or a toad, so eagle was more than acceptable. Hard to beat, in fact.

It was odd that she'd joined the eagle mid-life, though. Souls were meant to enter bodies at birth.

Even more at odds with the Calnian conception of after-life was that she could remember Moolba killing her, and everything before that, as if she'd gone to sleep and woken as an eagle. Animals were not meant to remember their previous human lives. It was clear that they didn't, otherwise everybody would be hassled by animals the whole time. Sofi pictured a racoon scrabbling up to a hut window and barking *I'm your mum*.

Her thoughts were interrupted by voices far, far below.

Her alchemically enhanced hearing still worked, then. Or maybe eagles had great ears too.

"We shouldn't be doing this. We'll get caught," said the first voice. His whining tone reminded her of Finnbogi the Boggy when they'd first met him.

"Can you stop ruining the mood?" said a more confident sounding man. "This is an adventure. Try to be more of an adventurer."

"It's all right for you, you're used to being in danger," replied the whinger.

"That's the point! We're not in *danger*. We're having an *adventure*. Look at it that way and you'll start enjoying yourself. And you'll be much less of a drag to others. And we're not in danger, anyway. Even if we were, you're not going to help by complaining the whole time. All that's going to do is ruin my fine mood. So stop, please."

"Nobody's allowed in The Meadows!"

"Exactly! So who's going to catch us?"

"Not who. What."

"You mean the Warlock Queen?"

"*Don't say her name!*"

"She has been dead for centuries."

"Spirits don't die."

"We've got this far, haven't we?"

"She's luring us in."

"Oh, for the love of all that's good, I wish I hadn't brought you."

"I'll wait here then."

The adventurer sighed. "I'm sorry. It is a bit scary perhaps. But do try to buck up. I need your help and you really will be a lot happier if you try to enjoy it. And so will I."

"Well, try being nicer."

"Oh, by my uncle's shiny helmet . . . I'll be nice if you stop whining. Deal?"

"But we're in terrible danger!"

"We are not. Let's just climb in silence, okay?"

"Okay."

Sofi flicked the end of her wings and swooped. Swooping was good. Light flickered off the back of a fish in a pool a long way below. She felt an urge to dive and kill it but resisted. So she still had her hearing, and now she had eyesight like Sitsi Kestrel, which made some sense for an eagle. But was she actually dead? She didn't think so any more. She was pretty certain she knew what was going on, and she was happy to go along with it.

She glided over a broad clearing busy with enormous, long-horned buffalo and other oversized and strangely horned grazers.

Up ahead, protruding from the lush land and rapidly growing bigger, there was a smooth-sided, black pyramid. Sofi's suspicions were confirmed. She was flying over The Meadows, towards The Pyramid, tomb of the Warlock Queen. She'd thought that The Meadows was an ironic name, or at least an exaggeration for a patch of green next to an oasis in the desert. It seemed, if anything, "The Meadows" was underplaying it. "The Jungles" would have been more apt.

Two men were climbing the sides of The Pyramid. One was bulky and shaggy maned, wearing tattered leathers. The other had short hair and was dressed in freshly laundered cotton.

The men disappeared into an entrance three-quarters of the way up the black, new-made mountain.

*I'll follow them in*, Sofi thought, diving down. Fifty paces off she found herself backing her wings. She didn't want to go inside The Pyramid. She felt very strongly about it. It was not a good place.

*No matter*, she thought. *I'll wait.*

She returned to the pool with the fish, caught it and ate it, then amused herself by diving at the enormous mammals and making them stampede.

"I told you it was dangerous," she eventually heard.

She flew up to see the two men emerge from The Pyramid, carrying a wooden box.

"Yeah, sorry. It was a bit tougher than I thought," said the shaggy haired one. He'd lost his leather shirt and was bleeding from several cuts.

His companion was more badly injured. He was limping and his white cotton shirt and trousers were stained almost completely red.

"We'll never make it to Wormsland!" cried Short Hair. "The Warlock Queen will—"

"We have to. Buck up. Once we get the coffin there and unleash its magic, nobody will be able to hurt us."

"She's coming. She'll catch us and—"

"Will you please try to look on the bright side for once?" asked Shaggy Hair as they set off carefully down The Pyramid's side, carrying the coffin between them. "The coffin's lighter than we thought it would be. And we're alive."

"Bright side!" wailed Short Hair. "Bright side! Do you know how much blood I've lost?"

"No."

"Well, neither do I. But it's a lot! I could die any moment and the Warlock Queen—"

"Will you shut up about the Warlock Queen? Those were ancient traps that attacked us in there, nothing more. If the Warlock Queen was up and active and could have stopped us, she would have done way back, when we walked into The Meadows. She died hundreds of years ago. She has no power now."

"But her dead child does?"

"You are such a downer. We need to get the coffin to Wormsland and combine the magic—"

"So you say but how do you know if—?"

He was interrupted by a low rumble.

The two men stopped, looked all around and then at each other. They were halfway down The Pyramid.

It was shaking.

Shaggy Hair hefted the coffin onto one shoulder and the two of them sprinted headlong down the steep side. Short Hair tripped almost immediately and bounced the rest of the way down in a flailing, limb-snapping tumble. Shaggy Hair somehow kept his feet.

Short Hair crumped to earth and lay in a dead looking pile. Shaggy slowed his run, looked back at his probably dead companion, then ran off westward into the trees, coffin on his shoulder.

The great black pyramid continued to rumble. For a while Shaggy was hidden by trees, but soon he came out into a clearing, now jogging. The giant grazers scattered as he pounded between them. At the end of the clearing he slowed to a walk, turning to see if he was being pursued. The Pyramid had calmed and nobody was following.

It took him several hours to reach the edge of The Meadows, scale a shoulder between two mountains and head eastward into the arid desert that surrounded the lush jungle.

Sofi, flying high above, had seen and heard what she needed. Shaggy had stolen the dead Warlock Queen's child and taken it to Wormsland. So, annoyingly, Olaf World-finder had been right about a child being involved. Surely their quest was now to retrieve the child and take him home?

She flew around wondering why Moolba had strangled her, and how she was going to get back.

She tried spooking the large herbivores again, but the fun had gone out of it. Now she knew what it was, she wanted to return to her human body and get on with the quest.

When Shaggy and the coffin were a speck on the horizon and Sofi was contemplating catching another fish just for something to do, The Pyramid began to rumble again, this time much more loudly. The dreadful sound swelled from a rumbling to a scream. She flew back to investigate.

She was perhaps a mile away when the world to the west suddenly blazed blinding white. She recovered her eyesight in time to see the jungle and grasslands evaporating in a wall of shimmering light that was heading towards her at tremendous speed. She backed her wings.

Too late.

A blast of searing heat struck her and sent her tumbling. She fell and fell, then hit something with a shocking crunch. She'd landed on the branch of a tree. She grabbled the trunk with her talons.

She lay, breathing hard, eyes screwed shut against the heat and the agony, unable to move. She'd never known pain could be like this.

She opened an eye.

She was folded over a branch on the only tree left standing for miles around. She tried to use her wings to rearrange herself but that didn't work, because one of them was now just a bloody shard of bone.

Somehow, knowing that increased the pain.

Travelling north to Calnia as a child, Sofi's captors had stopped with a tribe that ate no animal flesh. They maintained that animals could feel pain, so it was wrong to hurt them. Sofi had wondered about it for a while afterwards, then reached Calnia where the point was moot. The Calnians were so keen on causing pain to humans that nobody considered giving a crap about animal suffering, but every now and then Sofi had wondered if animals did indeed feel pain.

And now she knew. She nearly passed out – she wanted to pass out – but she willed herself to remain conscious because a woman was walking towards her from The Pyramid. She had Mushroom Man features – her skin was pale, her hair blonde and her eyes blue – but she was dressed in the white cotton shirt and trousers of a desert dweller.

The Warlock Queen – it had to be her – raised her hands. Around her, the earth and felled trees rolled and shifted, then erupted and coalesced into twisted creatures. Most fell back to the ground, flailing. Some crawled on. A six-legged, hairless dog leaking green goo from every orifice, ran ahead westward, past Sofi's tree and on. Presumably, it was pursuing Shaggy. It didn't get far before it, too, collapsed.

The Warlock Queen reached Sofi's tree and looked up. The mad pain in those eyes made Sofi forget her own for a moment. She saw a vision of a boy. A little boy, maybe six years old, with tousled brown hair and bright blue eyes like his mother's. The Warlock Queen had been woken when the men had taken him and she yearned to have him back. More than that. She wanted him alive again. For that to happen, she would need her child's corpse and a live boy. A live boy who looked just like hers, six years old with wavy brown hair and bright blue eyes.

Finally, Sofi understood why Ottar the Moaner was vital. First, they had to retrieve the coffin. Then they had to take it, with Ottar, to the tomb of the Warlock Queen, where she would take Ottar's body for the soul of her dead son. Did Yoki Choppa know? Did Ottar himself know that he was going west of west to die?

# Part Two

## Desert

# Chapter 1

## Lizard Netting

Sofi woke with a shout.

Moolba was sitting on the cot, watching her. It was early morning. She touched her neck. The chief's daughter stood. Sofi readied herself.

"Drink this," said Moolba. She held out a cup.

Sofi didn't take it. "What happened?" she asked.

"The vision quest drugs were in the stew. You fell unconscious soon after finishing it, then murmured for the rest of the day and into the night. You shouted at first light. You paled and your pulse weakened so much I was about to intervene, but then it strengthened. You've been muttering and jerking about ever since."

"I see."

"What did you find?"

"I have to get back to the others." Sofi stood. The room swayed.

"They're fine," said Moolba. "You need to sleep. Everybody sleeps after a vision quest. And you should drink."

Sofi took the proffered cup and sniffed it. It smelled like water. She downed it.

"Take my bed," said Moolba, pointing to the cot. "I'll find somewhere else. I've been awake all night watching you." She headed for the window that served as a door, then turned. "Unless . . .?"

Moolba looked at the cot, then at Sofi.

Sofi felt the corner of her mouth rise in half a smile.

The smaller woman walked back and looked up at the captain of the Owsla. Her sad eyes sparkled and her lips were plump.

*Oh, why not*, thought Sofi.

Sassa Lipchewer was playing a game of catch with Ottar, Chogolisa and Thyri. She wasn't enjoying it. She'd rather have been sitting down. However, Ottar was laughing and shrieking as if the game was the greatest thing that had ever happened to anyone, so she soldiered on.

Cloud Town's construction and cliff cleft situation were amazing, wonderful and magnificent, and the elegant Mindful and teeming Landfolk were a fascinating spectacle. Then, once you'd got over all that, Cloud Town reminded her of when she'd been snowed in for three moons with only her parents and her brother Vifil the Individual for company (Vifil, of course, had spent the whole time doing his own thing).

She couldn't practise archery in such a populated place; the Mindful were all too busy to have a conversation and the Landfolk wouldn't talk to her. It would have been too much of an imposition to ask them to run her up to the mesa top in a basket so she could fire a few arrows and, besides, she didn't want to be too far from where Sofi was having her vision quest. If that's what she was doing. They'd guessed that it must be. Wulf was a little piqued that Sofi had gone on the quest without giving him the chance. Sassa was very glad she had.

She hoped that Sofi Tornado was all right and asked Tor to protect her. But she was glad it wasn't Wulf.

At lunchtime the subservient Landfolk brought them food. Sassa was spooning the final mouthful of their excellent ragout when Moolba appeared, followed by Sofi.

Both women looked tired, happy and flushed, as if they'd

just woken up. Actually, they looked like they'd just had sex, but Sassa put that down to the vision quest.

"Did you find what we're looking for?" asked Chogolisa.

"Yes," said Sofi. "We leave tomorrow."

"Where to?" asked Erik.

"Wormsland."

"That doesn't sound so great," said Thyri.

"Actually, it's an amazing place," Moolba reassured her. "It's named for a large number of rock formations shaped like worms with their backs raised. Arches, in other words. It's striking and beautiful."

Thyri raised a nostril that seemed to say she'd seen plenty of striking and beautiful, thanks, and was not impressed.

"The Popeye tribe came from Wormsland," said Wulf. "They were kicked out by invaders. Those invaders probably aren't the most affable people. Why are we going there?"

"To get a wooden box," said Sofi. "We'll tell them why we want it, and hopefully they'll give it to us. If not . . ." Sofi shrugged.

Sassa guessed the shrug meant *I'll kill them all*. She and Sofi really were very different people.

"What's in the box?" asked Wulf.

"A long-dead child," Sofi said, matter-of-factly.

"Right."

"It's the child of the Warlock Queen. She wants it back."

"I see." Wulf nodded as if it was what he'd expected. "How far is Wormsland?"

"About ten days' walk to the north-east."

"Yoki Choppa," asked Wulf, "where are Sitsi and Keef?"

"About ten days' walk to the north-east," said the Warlock.

They spent the evening with the Mindful again. Finn the Deep found it all quite hard work, again. He wanted to talk about their quest, playing up the others' roles, then to be asked questions that would force him to describe his own heroic deeds. However, the Mindful only wanted to talk about themselves and their town in the cliff.

It might have been easier — let's face it, would have been easier — if they'd had booze. But they didn't. The evening before, Erik had asked if they had any mead or wine and they'd looked at him as if he'd suggested a group wank.

"We do not see the point of drinking a poison that decreases our intelligence," explained one white-clad bellend.

Even worse than the absence of alcohol, for the second evening in a row, Thyri was getting on very well with a fellow who looked like a Scrayling version of Garth Anvilchin. Finn hoped he'd seen the last of Garth when Sassa had shot him through the face to stop him throwing Finn off a cliff, but apart from the darker skin, hair and eyes, this guy was pretty much him.

Finn had spoken to Scrayling Garth the previous evening, before he'd noticed how much he looked like the big-chinned twat. Annoyingly, he was a kind, happy, clever fellow. So, character-wise, he wasn't a bit like Garth. That was even more of a worry.

Finn had long ago decided that Thyri's attraction to Garth must have been physical. Anvilchin had been *such* a tool that it couldn't have been anything else. And now she'd met someone who looked like him and was also a decent human being. Were they going to lose Thyri like they'd lost Bodil? If would be just Finn's shitty luck if they did.

Moolba the chief's daughter came to sit next to him. She handed him a cup of the sweet drink that the Cloud Tribe thought was a substitute for booze.

"What's up?" she asked.

He told her. Why the Hel not? They were off in the morning, and Moolba was sober, so chances were she was capable of keeping a confidence.

When he'd poured out his troubled history of adoring

Thyri, Moolba asked: "Do you know the most important trait in a lover?"

*Big tits* was the first thing that sprang into Finn's mind, although he wasn't that into tits and it certainly wasn't what he really thought. It was his Loakie side, trying to get him into trouble. He was trying to be a bit more Tor these days. But Tor would probably say "big tits" too then laugh his manly god laugh. So what would Oaden say?

"A keen sense of smell?" he asked. *Where did that come from?*

Moolba gave him the look he deserved, but she didn't get up and run away. "That's not the top of the list, no," she said carefully, as if talking to someone unhinged. "The most important thing about whoever you fall in love with, above all else, is that they like you, too. Love you, preferably."

*Well, yeah*, thought Finn. He was being patronised by a woman who couldn't be much older than he was, if at all.

"It may seem obvious," the lecture continued, "but it is possible to spend a lot of one's life obsessing over people who will never like you. I don't expect you to take this in – every generation of humans excels at making the same mistakes as the previous one – but please, for your own sake, accept the notion that if someone doesn't like you, they are not the right person for you. For your own sanity, and everyone's happiness, quench your feelings and move on."

"So what should I do?" asked Finn. "Be myself and see who likes me, then go for them?"

"Oh, *no*. No, no no." Moolba shook her head as if saying no four times wasn't enough. "Being yourself is the last thing you want to do. Every culture I've ever come across teaches every child not to be themselves from the moment they can listen, and there's a reason for that. Don't be yourself. Be the best you can be. Then see who likes you."

Finn looked into Moolba's bright eyes, surrounded by that buoyant mane of healthily bouffant hair. They were very strange eyes. Strange and appealing.

"I don't suppose you're one of the people who likes me?" he dared, thinking at the same moment that he didn't need alcohol to make a tit of himself.

She snorted a little burst of laugher. Not exactly the response he was looking for. "No," she said. "Sorry. You're a great guy, Finn, but you're very much not my type."

"Oh. I guess you prefer the more muscle-bound warrior sort, like him." Finn nodded at the Garth lookalike who was laughing like a god at something Thyri had said.

"Not quite," said Moolba. "I prefer the more female type."

"Oh!" *Well, that was different.* Finn grinned and looked around. Nobody was in earshot. He leant towards Moolba. "Which of our lot do you fancy most, then?"

The following morning Erik the Angry approached Yoki Choppa as he packed up his alchemical kit.

"Have they moved?" he asked. He was pretty sure the warlock shook his head in reply. "But they are alive?"

A tiny nod.

"Do you think they're captives of the tribe that invaded Wormsland?"

"Do you?" asked Yoki Choppa

Erik shook his head. "No. They knew we were heading west, and they know we can find them, so the safest thing to do is to wait."

"But?"

"But what?"

"Would Sitsi and Keef take the safest option?"

Erik though for a moment. "No, probably not."

"So why might they wait?

Erik looked at the warlock, pleased and a little flattered to be having such a long conversation with him, but also frustrated that he was clearly missing something obvious.

"Because they've got someone fragile with them," said Chogolisa, who'd walked up behind him.

"Freydis!" Erik slapped his head. "She's alive! They're staying put because they've found Freydis. So it means Freydis is alive, doesn't it, Yoki Choppa?"

The warlock inclined his head in a way that could have meant anything and went back to tidying his things.

The Wootah and Calnians left Cloud Town.

Neither the Landfolk nor the Mindful attempted anything approaching a meaningful goodbye. Erik reckoned that the former were too timid and the latter too haughty to make any real contact with the Wootah or Calnians. Yes, some of them had seemed interested – the chief's daughter Moolba had had a good chat with Finn and Thyri had hit it off with a young man – but neither Moolba nor Thyri's young man were there to bid them farewell.

The jerky basket ride back up to the mesa top was horrific – there were a couple of serious lurches – but the notion that Freydis was alive had lifted Erik a good deal and he made it without passing out in terror or yielding to the niggling but powerful urge to leap to his death.

Moolba had assigned Nether Barr, an ancient looking lady, to show them the way to Wormsland. Her bare feet were dark, cracked and curled as dried bark. She wore cotton trousers, a small backpack and, despite the hot sun, a thick woollen jumper like the Wootah wore in winter. She held a long-handled net in one hand and swung an empty bag in the other. Erik couldn't help thinking she had a face like a coyote chewing a bee.

He wanted to ask her about Wormsland but, before all the Wootah had even climbed out of their baskets, Nether Barr scuttled away across the mesa top without a word. The Calnians and Wootah looked at each other, shrugged, then followed.

Erik expected the elderly Nether Barr to flag after her rapid start, but whatever the opposite of flagging was, she did that. Whenever they lost sight of her – behind a clump of trees or rocky crag – she always reappeared further ahead than she'd been before. It was as if she was sprinting when they couldn't see her.

Erik was both embarrassed and overjoyed that the little old woman whom he'd thought would be useless had to stop and wait for them, even though she regularly darted off the path to net a lizard and stash it in her bag.

Not long after they'd set off on the second day's walking from Bighorn Island, the earth shook. It disturbed the more easily disturbed and made a few pebbles roll down slopes. Wulf the Fat, Sofi Tornado, Yoki Choppa and Nether Barr walked on as if nothing was amiss. It didn't last long and the others soon forgot it.

For four days the going was generally downhill and easy, either over partially wooded grassland or stony soil crowded with small-leaved, thorny bushes taller than Chogolisa. If you hadn't known the path, the bushes would have been impenetrable, or at least a serious pain in the arse to penetrate, but Nether Barr led them unerringly along dry stream beds and through leafy passages.

In the evenings they ate cactus and Nether Barr's lizards. Grilled to a crisp, the reptiles were tasty. The old lady helped Ottar make his own net and the boy delighted in failing to catch lizards. When he finally did trap a little striped one with a long tail, he studied it carefully then let it go.

They passed several stone-built stores of dried seeds and plants, but Nether Barr said they were not to raid them. That surprised Erik, because up to that point he had thought that she couldn't speak.

There was no sign of the wasp men, wasp dragons or any other dangerous animals other than the odd lion, but Erik noticed that Nether Barr never led them far from a stand of trees, an overhang or somewhere else they might shelter if they heard the wasp men coming.

The landscape changed on the fifth day. The flat, dry valleys were choked with tall, willowy plants, but the valley sides and higher land were bare rock. The rock was mostly red, but also yellow, white, green, black and purple, and often clumped into rippled hills and columns, or hewn by ancient and mighty gods into towering angular spires.

"Slickrock," said Nether Barr, surprising Erik by dropping back to walk alongside him and Chogolisa.

"Slickrock?" repeated Chogolisa.

"The bare rock is called slickrock. It's a bad name, because it's not slick. It's very grippy. Walk with confidence and, if you can, grace. If we meet anyone I know, I don't want them thinking that I'm leading a bunch of dolts." She sped off again. Ottar followed along happily behind her.

"He always likes the weird ones," said Erik.

Chogolisa looked down at him, one eyebrow raised. "Which of us would you say was normal? And, talking of normal, have you noticed how Ottar doesn't need to be carried when he's enjoying himself?"

"You mean he could have walked—"

"For all the miles that we carried him, yes."

"The little bugger!"

"On the bright side, it has made me appreciate walking without a child on my shoulders a lot more."

"There is that."

Nether Barr was short of neither confidence nor grace. She scaled vertical faces and tripped down precipitous drops like a bighorn. As on the easier ground, it looked like she was moving slowly, but she was always miles ahead. Somehow Ottar kept up with her, skipping happily across clefts and bounding blithely down cliffs that had Erik sweating with terror.

Indeed, for the first days across the slickrock, he was terrified almost all of the time. As soon as he started thinking *I'm getting used to it now, it's not so bad*, they'd have to pick their way down a dizzying drop or traverse a crazily narrow ledge three paces above the rock below. Three paces might not have been that high, but anything high enough to hurt you if you'd fallen gave Erik the willies. The narrow ledges a hundred paces above rocky doom made him giggle with pure terror.

Gradually, he became more comfortable. The slickrock was much grippier than it looked. One could actually manage what had seemed like frighteningly steep slopes without too much bother. You just had to believe you could. Moreover, because of the way the rock lay in differently eroded bands, there were always shaded overhangs to shelter from the sun during the rare breaks that Nether Barr allowed.

By the third day on the slickrock, they were all leaping and climbing, if not quite as well as Nether Barr, then certainly like her willing and capable students. Erik became so confident that he tried to find his own route a couple of times. He always ended up backtracking after he came to a terrifying ledge or a vertical face.

*How does Nether Barr know the way so well?* he wondered.

# Chapter 2

## Age

The third day on the slickrock, it was hot.

Erik was sweaty as a cheese in the sun on a summer's day and didn't smell much better. Nether Barr forbade him from bathing in the black pools hidden in rock pockets or washing in the brave little springs that glugged out of rock in dry valleys then sank into the sand a few paces later. He was very glad she knew the whereabouts of regular water sources in the arid land, because he was even more thirsty than he was smelly.

Erik was feeling parched again towards the middle of the day when he noticed that they were more exposed than usual. Red slickrock stretched in every direction, with not a bush, overhang nor any other hiding place to be seen. In the distance were towers, pinnacles, snow-capped peaks and great masses of dark red, scree-skirted bluffs.

He slowed down to wait for Sofi and warn her of the potential danger of being so exposed, but she held up a finger for silence.

"Wasp men!" she shouted.

Erik's breakfast somersaulted in his stomach. Nether Barr shut off like a wasp-stung jackrabbit.

"Follow her!" shouted Sofi. "Moss in!"

Wootah and Calnians sprinted across the baking slickrock, stuffing the moss that Erik had gathered for them into their ears as they went.

All too soon, Erik could hear the screaming of the wasp men. There was still no shelter in sight, and it was far too hot to be running so fast.

Chogolisa steamed past him, Ottar whooping on her shoulders. Finn and Thyri ran by. Soon everyone was ahead of him bar Sofi, who jogged at his shoulder. She always waited for the slowest. With Gunnhild gone, that was Erik. It was depressing. He lowered his head and ran harder. He was buggered if he was going to be slowest. Putting all his effort into running, partially blinded by sweat, he didn't see the lip of rock that tripped him. He slapped down hard on knees and palms.

Sofi heaved him up by the elbow, as if he was some old man who'd fallen. Which, he realised with resigned misery, he kind of was.

They ran on, further and further behind the others.

"Erik, there's a drop ahead!" Sofi called over the dread screaming of the wasp men, her voice muffled through the moss in his ears.

He looked up. The others had disappeared, presumably over the upcoming drop.

The wasp men's wailing intensified. He turned. Two dozen of the creatures were zipping towards them, low over the slickrock, black mouths agape, great wings flapping hard, pincers open and ready. They were a lot closer than Erik would have liked.

"We have to speed up," said Sofi.

Erik paused for half a heartbeat at the drop. Below them was a flat expanse of bush-choked dry valley. The far side was a rocky bluff like the one he and Sofi were standing on. Nether Barr had almost reached the bluff already. Wulf, Sassa, Finn, Thyri and Yoki Choppa were keeping pace with her, Chogolisa and Ottar not far behind. How had they got so far ahead? How could Yoki Choppa run so fast? Surely he was older than Erik?

Sofi took his hand and half helped, half pulled him down the slope. He wanted to say he could do it on his own, but the strong young woman's support and encouragement did make the descent a lot easier.

They followed the others' footprints in the red sand. Halfway across the valley, he dared take a look over his shoulder. Wasp men looked back with glowing orange eyes. Most of the airborne monsters were flapping up higher, presumably to gain a better view of the humans fleeing through the bushes. But a pair of them were headed directly for Sofi and Erik.

"Fight?" Erik asked, hefting his club Turkey Friend in his hand.

"Fight," confirmed Sofi.

The two wasp men flew at them, mouths open and screaming, pincers waving. Their eyes glowed like hot coals.

One went for Sofi, the other for Erik. It sliced a claw at his neck, but he was already swinging Turkey Friend. The weighty club smashed through insectoid arm and burst the creature's head in a surprisingly liquid explosion. The creature crashed down.

He jumped round to help Sofi, but her attacker was already dead, decapitated by her dagger-tooth knife.

Erik forgot his exhaustion. A thrilling rush nor far off lust fizzed through his limbs. He did like a fight.

The remaining wasp men flew higher and screamed at Sofi and Erik.

"Here they come!" He was itching to kill more.

But they didn't come. They hovered, heads cocked as if they were studying the humans.

"They saw how easily we dealt with their friends," said Erik.

Sofi took the moss from one ear. "Or they're waiting for the others."

"The others?"

"There are a couple of hundred more a mile away, closing fast."

"A couple of hundred?"

"Give or take half a dozen."

"That's probably too many."

"Which I guess is why these ones are waiting. Not as dumb as they—" Sofi jumped round, axe raised.

Someone or something was charging through the bushes towards them.

Finn ran out into their clearing. "What are you doing – wow." He looked at the dead wasp men, then up at the rest of them flapping in the sky. "Sorry, I didn't know you were so far behind."

"I tripped," explained Erik.

"Oh. Sorry. But don't hang around here. There's shelter this way."

Finn led them through the bushes. The wasp men kept their distance. The humans reached a stream and ran along it to where it flowed under bushes at the base of the bluff. Thyri was waiting. She pushed a bush aside.

"Follow the channel," she said.

They splashed along. The steam flowed parallel to the bluff, then under a ledge, sheltered on the open side by thick bushes. Erik thought this looked like a pretty good hiding place, but it was fatally flawed by the fact that the wasp men had seen them go in there.

"Keep going!" called Thyri behind them.

The stream cut into the bluff itself. Erik ducked as they splashed into a passage hewn through the rock. A dozen paces in they came to a torch-lit chamber. All their group was there, plus Nether Barr and two other Scraylings.

"Hello," said the new Scraylings.

"I'm Amba Yull," said one, a rotund and cheery looking woman.

"And I'm Chartris," said the other in a sensible voice. She

was a toothy woman with high cheekbones. Both Amber Yull and Chartris were around Finn's age.

"Hello," said Sofi and Erik.

The politeness was a little surreal, backdropped by the screaming of the wasp men reverberating along the passage and welling ever louder.

"Don't worry, you are safe in here," Chartris reassured them. "They're simple creatures and won't tarry when they can't find us." Her tone was efficient and a little bossy. She reminded Erik of a woman who'd looked after the smaller children back with the Lakchan tribe.

"Are you the Pothole tribe?" asked Sofi.

"Yes, we are. You are a bright one, aren't you?" Chartris looked younger than Sofi, but she spoke to the Owsla captain as if she were a praise-needy child. Erik couldn't decide if that amused or irritated him. Or scared him because of how Sofi might react. "We are called the Pothole tribe in the universal tongue, although in our own language we're called *the people*."

"A lot of tribes are called *the people* in their own language," said Sofi.

"Yes, that's true. Well done," said Chartris.

"Why Pothole people?" asked Finn.

"There are a lot of potholes around our village, and we cook food in them. Sometimes the names given to tribes in the universal tongue are not very imaginative."

"Although, arguably, more imaginative than *the people*," Erik opined.

Chartris gave him a look.

# Chapter 3

## Sofi's Dance

The wasp men dispersed quickly, which pleased Sassa Lipchewer. She didn't like being stuck in the cave. She walked next to Amba Yull as they headed for the Pothole village.

"How do you know Nether Barr?" she asked.

"Nether Barr's my great-aunt. She's Pothole."

"I see! She certainly knows her way across the desert."

"Where's she taking you?"

"To Wormsland."

"From Bighorn Island?"

"Yes."

"Oh, deary me, she's taken a bit of a detour."

"Has she?"

"You'd be almost there by now if she'd taken a direct route."

"Oh." Without thinking, Sassa put a hand on her stomach. "Why do you think she came this way?"

"She might know something I don't about the route between Bighorn Island and Wormsland. Knowing Nether Barr, though, it's more likely she wanted to drop in on her family. She's a great woman but she does tend to pursue her own agenda."

Sassa couldn't blame her. She'd have given her right ear to see her family again. "It's good of her to take us at all, and I suppose we'll get there in the end."

"So when is the baby due?" asked Amba Yull.

Sassa looked about herself. There was nobody in earshot, apart from Sofi Tornado, of course, but she was always in earshot and she already knew.

"I think in about a hundred and sixty days. How did you know?"

"The way you put your hand to your stomach just now. I've got two children myself and I used to do that. And, now that I know, your face does look a little puffy."

"Thanks!" Sassa laughed.

"How are you feeling?"

"Well, puffy faced for one, and my fingers feel fat. My back hurts, my thighs ache and there's a line growing from my belly button downwards."

"I got all of that, too," said Amba Yull. "The thighs were the worst for me."

"Thighs aren't great, but I think walking all day helps. It's my back where I'm really feeling it. I'd give an awful lot to sit down for a moon or two."

"Why don't you? Can't this lot leave you with us and pick you up on the way back?"

Sassa looked at the happy Potholer. She hadn't realised it, but she'd been aching to talk to somebody who'd already had a baby. She wanted to be reassured by a woman who'd experienced childbirth, not just by a super-powered warrior and a supportive husband. She'd been speaking to Amba Yull for only a short while, but she already felt closer to her than any of the women in her group, especially with Sitsi Kestrel and Paloma Pronghorn elsewhere. Chogolisa Earthquake was sweet, but only interested in Erik and the children, and Sofi Tornado was not a chatter.

"Would your tribe let me stay?" asked Sassa.

"Of course! Unless you've got any filthy habits we don't know about yet?"

"Oh, I've got loads."

Both women laughed, then walked on across the red desert.

It was dark by the time they approached the Pothole people's village. Chartris' idea of a short walk was longer than Sassa's. If you had to stop for a meal during a walk, Sassa reckoned, it was not a short walk. When they had paused to eat, their guide Nether Barr had carried on ahead to tell the Pothole villagers that visitors were on the way.

They could see the settlement from a long way off, lit up by torches. It was based around a cluster of huge boulders perched on a low dome of rock.

At each end were two poles topped with cages. Sassa could make out a hunched figure in the nearest pole-top cage.

*Rear a deer*, she thought, *what weirdness is this?* She was seriously considering staying behind with the Potholers, but not if they had caged dwarfs on poles.

"Those are watchtowers," said Chartris, as if reading her mind.

"Oh. Who's watching from them?"

"There's a horned owl in each one. They know the wasp men are coming before we do."

"How do they tell you?"

"Hopefully you won't find out, but you'll know if they do."

"Have you been attacked by the wasp men much?" Sassa asked Chartris, thinking how much small talk had changed since she'd left Hardwork a little over three moons before.

"Not here. We've seen them from the village, but they've always kept their distance. We think the torches frighten them at night, and that all the activity during the day keeps them away. But we're seeing more and more, so it's possible that they are waiting until they have the numbers to mount a big attack."

"Are they that calculating? They look like insects."

"According to Erik, when they held back from attacking him and Sofi earlier, they were waiting for reinforcements. He said there were hundreds more coming, which is far more than we've seen before. If a flock that large finds the village we might be in trouble."

"Aren't you worried they'll follow us back?"

Chartris pursed her lips. "In a way, I hope they have. We've put a lot of work into preparing for a big attack, so, maybe perversely and I'll probably regret saying it, I'd like to see the new defences tested. Other tribes have fled. We've chosen to stay. I'd like to know if that was the right decision."

Sassa thought she could feel the horned owl watching her as they walked up the gentle slope to the torch-lit village. She'd seen plenty of the animals on their travels but never felt a malevolence like this from any of them. Perhaps it didn't much like being stuck in a cage.

She could see now that there was a wooden walkway running all the way around the perimeter of the boulder cluster, a little over Chogolisa's head height. There were sheds built on it every couple of dozen paces. If the walkway and sheds were the new defences Chartris had mentioned, she couldn't really see how it could help, other than to make them easier targets for the wasp men.

"Most people will be on their beds by now," said Chartris, "So if you don't mind—"

"Wasp men coming!" shouted Sofi.

"You're mistaken," Chartris yelled back. "The owls would—"

A dread shrieking burst from the nearest cage, then the other three started up.

"Everyone who can fight, onto the platform!" yelled Chartris over the noise of the owls. "The rest of you follow Amba Yull."

"How many?" she shouted to Sofi over the noise of the owls.

"A lot. Hundreds."

Sofi ran on and Sassa stood. It felt like her stomach was trying to rise up and out of her mouth. She was going to be sick.

*No*, she told herself. There's work to be done. Baby-saving work. She swallowed and ran after Sofi.

Up at the village, dark figures were scaling ladders onto the platform. Teams of three headed for each of the little sheds.

Yoki Choppa and Freydis were running with Amba Yull to the northern end of the rock cluster. Other adults were mustering gaggles of jogging children in the same direction.

"You all right?" Wulf asked, taking her hand. His big blue eyes weren't taking the piss for once. He looked almost ready to cry with concern for her.

"Never better."

"You know you shouldn't fight, don't you?"

"I'm an archer, Wulf, and these buggers fly."

He nodded. "I know. You'll be more use than any of us. Just be careful, please."

"When am I ever not careful?"

"Marrying me was a risk."

"We all make mistakes!" She hugged him, pressing her head into his hard, warm chest. "You be careful, too," she said.

"I will," he said, prising her arms away. "Let's go. Those monsters aren't going to shoot themselves out of the sky."

They ran towards the village. Potholers sprinted about holding burning brands and pressing them against torches on short poles. By the time Sassa and Wulf reached the base of the ladder the whole place was lit up like a weird orange day. They dropped their backpacks and headed up onto the platform. Sofi and Erik were climbing the next ladder along. Sassa glanced over her shoulder.

A darkly shimmering mass which had to be the flock of wasp men was blocking out the stars to the east. It was very large – maybe larger than the millions-strong flock of crowd pigeons that had pulled the Plains Strider – and it was growing by every heartbeat. They were coming fast.

The screaming started. The creatures must have been a mile or more away, but still the sound made her wince.

"Can you use a bow?" a man on the platform asked Wulf. He was a gentle looking fellow, his tone more like someone asking Wulf if he would like a drink, while hoping that he wasn't intruding.

"Sure." Wulf took the proffered weapon.

"Great. Try to hit them in the head, if you don't mind. That's the only shot that will stop them in one go. Grab a spot in between the seated bows. You'll find quivers of arrows there. There are also spears, in case they get close and shields in case they spray venom. You'll also need this moss to put in your ears."

"Got moss, thanks," said Wulf.

Sassa thought with half a smile that Erik would be disappointed that the Pothole people had also come up with the moss in ears idea.

The sides had been removed from the constructions that Sassa had thought were sheds to reveal sturdy tripods, each supporting a chair and a giant bow. Three people operated each. One was seated – it looked like he or she would do the aiming and loosing the bow – and the other two were pulling back rope-like bowstrings and nocking projectiles that were more spear than arrow.

The wasp men closed, their screams louder and louder. She could still hear the owls on their watch posts, however, shrieking as if determined that they would be the loudest animals in the desert that night. They didn't have a hope.

Sassa stood with Wulf on one side and Chartris on the other. There were quivers of arrows on wooden tripods all around. Along the front edge of the platform were troughs filled with light, stone-headed spears.

They were near the centre of the long side of the wooden oval that crowned the cluster of boulders on the dome of rock. There were perhaps two hundred defenders in total, all with bows. Chogolisa was easy to spot about twenty people along. Erik and Finn were next to her. She couldn't see Sofi.

Seeing her own people among the defenders filled Sassa with pride. The Wootah stood there strong and ready to die for a town they'd stopped in on their way to defeat the mythic force in The Meadows. It was like something from the sagas.

The wasp men screamed louder. Much louder. A head-crushing wall of sound hit them. Some staggered, some crouched, some put hands over their ears; none were unaffected, despite the moss. Sassa fought to stop her sense of pride and resolve dissolving into gibbering terror.

The wasp men were close enough now that the defenders could see individual animals zooming towards them on leathery wings. The Pothole people recovered quickly from the noise. The chair bows loosed their giant arrows. Moments later half a dozen wasp men fell out of the sky, but it wasn't much of a dent in the hard-skinned horde speeding towards the vulnerable village.

Sassa pulled, aimed and loosed.

"Wait until they're closer!" yelled Chartris.

Sassa nodded to where the wasp man she'd skewered through the face was tumbling groundwards from the swarming mass of monsters.

"Oh! Carry on then!"

She did. She'd brought down five before the other small bows started shooting. Wasp men fell like heavy rain but still they came, hundreds and hundreds.

Wulf piled a couple of arrow-stuffed quivers at Sassa's

feet. "Chartris!" he yelled. "When they get here, we'll use spears and shields to defend Sassa. Sassa, keep shooting from behind us."

"Got it!" yelled Chartris.

"Right!" shouted Sassa. Her arm was already tired from pulling the string again and again. But she'd keep going while there were wasp men to kill. She'd keep going for Wulf and her growing baby, for Ottar, for the rest of the Wootah. For the Calnians, even if they had killed her mum and dad. And Chartris. She was sure the woman was less spikey once you got to know her.

The wasp men swarmed down. Sassa loosed arrow after arrow. The attackers slowed and began to dodge, making it harder to hit their heads. She tried a couple of body shots but they had no obvious effect. On the upside, slowing down like that was a seriously dumb move, because if they'd kept coming at the same speed they would have overwhelmed the defenders. So they might be bright enough to attack en masse and even to dodge arrows, but they clearly weren't *that* bright. Or perhaps they were clever enough to be cowardly. Sassa didn't think that she'd be that happy charging a barrage of near-certain death, even if it would help her fellows behind her win the day.

Off to her left, a wasp man hovered above the nearest owl on its pole, leant back and stuck out its half-pace-long-sting, preparing to spray. Sassa shot the beast and smiled when it fell and the owl shrieked on. She liked owls.

Dozens of the wasp men landed on the bare rock expanse running up to the boulders and marched towards the supposedly safe place where Amba Yull had taken Ottar and the other children. Three pairs of hands swung purposefully on each attacker. Wings were folded on their backs and claws held high.

Sassa shot one of the walking wasp men, but the beasts

in the sky were closing dangerously, and much faster, so she returned her attention to those. Surely the children were hidden away somewhere secure?

Wulf tossed his bow aside and snatched up a spear. "Behind me, Sassa!" he yelled above the screaming.

She glanced back to the wasp men advancing on the ground. There were far fewer now, and others were falling. Was someone shooting them? No, it was Sofi Tornado! She was dancing among the enemy, axe in one hand, short spear in the other, braining them with the axe and jabbing her spear into heads. Yoki Choppa was down there, too, blowpipe pressed against his lips and spear in one hand, but Sassa's eyes returned to Sofi. The other Owsla women had always said that Sofi was the best warrior, but Sassa had never seen why. Surely Paloma with her speed or Chogolisa with her strength were more effective in a fight, she'd thought.

But now she got it.

Sofi was running, twisting, leaping and striking so quickly and perfectly that the wasp men couldn't begin to defend themselves. Sassa's jaw dropped. The Owsla captain was so fast, so fluid and so constant; almost a blur as she killed wasp man after wasp man with the regularity of a drummer marking out a fast beat. *Jab it in a rabbit*, thought Sassa. She had never seen . . . she refocused. This was no time for spectating.

The airborne wasp men flapped their wings to slow themselves further and hover outside spear range. As if they'd practised it – and maybe they had, who knew what creatures like this got up to in their free time – they angled their abdomens forward to point stings at the defenders, clearly intending to douse them in venom. Fingers on their vile, human-like hands twitched. Claws open and closed. Orange eyes stared hotly. Dangling below their chests, their segmented, pendulous abdomens shone wetly and disgustingly. Sassa shuddered.

"Shields!" someone shouted. Sassa hopped back and kept shooting as Chartris took up a shield. Wulf hurled spears, taking out several creatures. They weren't outside *his* spear range. They killed so many wasp men so quickly that none had a chance to spray. There were a couple of screams from defenders further along, but most of the line was dealing with the beasts as effectively as Sassa's section.

Hundreds of wasp men had been killed by the well-prepared Pothole tribe. The surviving creatures, maybe half of them, fled. The sudden silence and calm felt almost as deafening as the attackers' screams.

*Was it over?* Sassa dared to hope.

But the flock of wasp men turned and hovered outside even the range of the giant seated bows, watching silently with glowing eyes.

Then, just when Sassa was wondering whether they were going to hover there all night, the wasp men turned and flapped away.

Everybody held their breaths for a few heartbeats.

"They may come back!" someone shouted. "Everybody hold!"

The defenders stood, weapons in hand, peering into the darkness around their illuminated hill.

Sassa Lipchewer massaged her right bicep and forearm. She'd never shot so many arrows so quickly. She would, she resolved, practise more with –

"They're coming! Fast from on high!" yelled Sofi from the rock platform below them.

"Where are they?" called Chartris.

Sassa looked up. "They're diving at us!"

The creatures were dropping like hawks onto mice. They were silent this time, but Sassa fancied she could hear the whistle of wind over their wings. She loosed an arrow at them. She may have hit one. There wasn't time to string another.

The wasp men slowed at the last moment, swung round and landed among the defenders, lower pair of hands acting as feet. They resumed their screaming, slashing and snapping at the defenders with long claws.

Wulf set about them with Thunderbolt, smashing head after head. The monsters were focusing on the chair bows, fighting off the string-pullers and slaying the strapped in and helpless shooters. Wulf headed for the nearest, where at least one of the Pothole tribe was already slain. Sassa dropped her bow, ducked behind him and reached for a spear.

As she stood, she saw Chartris struggling to free her spear from a screaming monster's chest. The speared wasp man grabbed the weapon's shaft with two hands, seized Chartris' shoulders with two more, placed its claw almost gently around her neck and squeezed.

Chartris' eyes widened, blood gushing over the claw. Their young and patronising guide's head tumbled from her body. Blood spurted from her severed neck and her arms flapped in a macabre dance.

Sassa yelled and ran at the beast. It released Chartris' twitching body and swung a claw. Sassa ducked and jabbed her spear at its face. She missed.

The creature grabbed her arms. She struggled but it was impossibly strong. It raised a claw, clamped it over her face and squeezed. *You stink of rotting meat*, she thought as the beast began to crush her face.

The claw wrenched away and spiralled skywards. Her vile would-be killer's grip loosened and Sassa pushed it away.

Finn decapitated the beast with Foe Slicer, ducked another wasp man's attack then cleaved it crown to neck.

He looked about for more to kill, as did Sassa.

Their section of the defences was clear. Twenty paces along the platform, the fighting was thick. Erik the Angry was swinging Turkey Friend, dispatching plenty, but there were too many. One of the beasts grabbed his bicep with a claw.

Erik roared and dropped his club. The beast raised its other claw.

Sassa looked about for her bow, but she couldn't see it. Wulf and Finn set off at a run.

Erik punched the monster and he swung back for another, but it grabbed his hand. Its claw closed around his neck.

Launching out of the darkness of the rock platform below, like a great leaping fish, came Chogolisa. She landed, clasped the wasp man's head in a mighty fist and squeezed.

The head exploded. The claws released. The giant woman grabbed the monster by the torso and hurled it off the platform.

Erik smiled, looked at her, then down at the blood pulsing from the horrible gash in his arm, and collapsed.

Sassa found her bow. There were a few wasp men still attacking the southern end of the walkway, but Pothole people were running in and these were swiftly dealt with. Wulf was walking towards her, wiping wasp goo off his hammer.

"Erik's hurt," he said. "He's lost a lot of blood and—" his expression changed to shock. "Your face! What happened?"

She touched her cheek. It was wet. Blood, she guessed.

She turned to Finn. He was panting and scanning the sky, Foe Slicer in one hand, looking, if you didn't know him, pretty heroic.

"One of them got in close," she told Wulf, "but Finn dealt with it."

"Well done, Finn," said Wulf.

"Do you think they're gone for good?" Sassa asked him.

"I hope so," he said.

\*    \*    \*

Finn reached to stroke hair from his father's brow. The brown strands were pasted on with sweat, so it turned into more of a yucky wipe than the sensitive brush he'd intended.

Erik's eyes were closed and his breathing shallow. He was white-faced and he looked old.

"Is he going to be okay?" Finn asked Chogolisa, who was also squatting next to him, hand clamped around the wound on his arm in an attempt to stop the bleeding.

"Get Yoki Choppa," she replied. "Quick as you can."

Finn leapt up, much more worried. Could you die from a cut arm?

"Yoki Choppa!" he shouted, climbing down the ladder. "Yoki Choppa!"

He found Thyri Treelegs first, walking about and stabbing her sax blade into the faces of any wasp men that still had faces.

"How many did you get, Boggy?" she asked, grinning as she spiked another head.

"Erik's hurt. Where's Yoki Choppa?"

"Tor's cock, sorry! He's over this way, follow me!"

They found Yoki Choppa and all three climbed back up to the platform. Erik's eyes were open. Finn let out a breath he didn't know he'd been holding. But then he noticed the lake of blood. Surely that hadn't all come out of Erik's arm?

"Will everyone stop fussing? It's only a scratch," said Erik, propping himself up on his good elbow. "I . . . oh, hang on," he fell back and muttered, "quite a deep scratch" as he passed out again.

Yoki Choppa pressed herbs into the wound, bound it tightly and told Chogolisa where to find a bed for him.

"I'll sit with him," said Finn.

"Is there any point in Finn staying with him?" Thyri asked the warlock.

"From Erik's point of view, no. He'll either die from loss of blood or he won't."

"In that case, Finn, come with me," said Thyri. "There's work to be done. There always is after a battle, but they don't put that bit in the sagas."

*Why does she think she knows more about battles than me?* thought Finn. *I've been in every battle that she's been in!*

But he followed her.

They toiled long into the night, dragging the surprisingly light but still awkward wasp men corpses south of the village and hurling them into a pit. It wasn't just the awkwardness of the eight-limbed, two-winged horrors that was problematic. They also had to avoid the smoking puddles of venom that spilled from the horrible creatures.

Finn the Deep considered pointing out that they'd been walking all day, and in a way it wasn't the Wootah and Calnians' mess, and hadn't the visitors done plenty to help the Potholers already, so could they perhaps turn in?

But he didn't.

Along with the other Wootah and the Calnians, he helped to clear the bodies. His only break was every now and then going to the cool chamber where his father was lying. Erik was very still. Every time he visited, Finn placed a hand on his chest to check that he was breathing.

Talking to the Pothole people as he worked, Finn learned that three defenders, including Chartris, had been killed. Five more were badly burned by the wasp men's venom and many more were cut and bruised. All the injured were expected to recover, apart from, Finn worked out by their embarrassed pauses and pained looks, his father. He went to find Yoki Choppa.

"Erik's going to live, isn't he?"

"Most people would die from that wound," answered the warlock. "I suspect he is tougher than most people."

"What can we do?"

"Let him sleep. His body is creating new blood. Either it will make enough or it won't."

The sun had risen by the time they finished their nasty work. Finn was finally allowed to slump down onto a really very decent mattress in an excellently cool and clean cave carved into one of the gigantic boulders that formed the Pothole village.

He'd intended to sleep on the floor of Erik's chamber, but Yoki Choppa caught him and told him not to go in. Somehow he ended up sharing a mattress with Sofi Tornado, but he was too worried about his father and too exhausted to even get the faintest of horns about it.

Five heartbeats later, it seemed, Wulf was waking Finn. There was no sign of Sofi.

"Time to get up," said Wulf.

"Erik?" asked Finn.

"Is eating breakfast. Go and join him."

# Chapter 4

## Vertigo

"This is the best gear for the desert," said Amba Yull, dumping a pile of clothes onto the slickrock where they were preparing to leave. "To thank you for your help." She stood back, looking like she was trying to look happy.

Erik walked over and inspected the pile. There were cotton trousers and shirts plus tough, light bighorn kid leather hats in a variety of sizes.

The Wootah found their sizes and thanked Amba Yull. Chogolisa, Sofi and Yoki Choppa politely declined the gifts, as they'd done with the Green tribe's wonderful boots.

Erik loved the new hat particularly. He felt surprisingly bouncy after apparently nearly dying the day before. He hadn't when he'd woken – he'd felt like crap – but Yoki Choppa had made him eat raw minced buffalo meat for breakfast and given him a tea which contained Rabbit Girl knew what, but which left him feeling inappropriately giggly.

"You sure you're all right to walk?" asked Chogolisa.

"Fine as wine! Geed as mead!"

"What?" She looked a little appalled.

"Sorry, it's the tea Yoki Choppa gave me."

"Fine, but try to sound a little less euphoric." She nodded towards the Pothole people going about their mornings with lowered heads. "These people are grieving."

"Ah."

"Will you be able to walk all day?"

"I could dance all day."

"Erik!"

"Sorry. I'll be fine as long as we don't go too fast. Or get attacked."

Hopefully they wouldn't be attacked, or at least not by the same lot. Yoki Choppa had taken matter from the severed limbs of several wasp men who'd fled, so he could use alchemy to track them. The flock was dozens of miles to the south and heading further away. Wormsland was north and a little east.

They set off across the slickrock, under the already baking sun.

Nether Barr led with Ottar trotting along beside her. Next was Sofi, striding like a lioness: the battle seemed to have put new vim in her step. The Wootah swished along behind her in their new gear. Erik walked at the rear with Yoki Choppa and Chogolisa. He looked up at the pretty woman walking next to him. She smiled back. He stifled a happy giggle.

The going was easy for about fifty heartbeats, then they headed up a narrow path with a rock wall on one side and an increasingly hair-curling drop on the other. Erik didn't mind too much. Perhaps, he mused, he was no longer scared of heights?

The path led up to a plateau, which steadily became an ever-narrowing massif with huge drops to either side.

Erik felt his terror of heights returning. He put it down to loss of blood. The peninsula was narrower and narrower, though, and the drops to either side were verging on the crazily huge.

Long-eared jackrabbits, instead of watching them pass as usual, spooked and zoomed back the way the Wootah and Calnians had come. Erik wondered what the panic was for.

He found out and wished he hadn't.

The promontory came to an end a long, long way above

a river snaking along the base of an insanely deep canyon. Was it a mile deep? On the river's far bank was a high, scree-skirted cliff, rising vertically and vertiginously to the same dizzy height as the headland Erik was gawping out from.

Spanning the chasm, stretching from their promontory to the cliff opposite, was the most frightening thing Erik had ever encountered. And he'd fought thunder lizards. It was a stupidly long, stupidly spindly rope bridge.

The bridge was attached at both ends to what looked like sturdy wooden structures dug into the rock itself and weighted with more rocks. The bridge must have been two hundred paces long, a mile above the ground. Well, maybe not a mile. But certainly sickeningly, insanely high. The lower part of the bridge, which you were meant to walk on, Erik guessed, was made of two ropes each as thick as his calves. The other two ropes, strung higher and presumably intended as hand-holds, were as thick as his wrist. And that was it. Four ropes.

*Surely we're not meant to cross that fucking thing?*

"I think that's the Red River," said Sofi, standing on the edge of the abyss. Right on the edge, like a madwoman. "The same one we rafted down out of the Shining Mountains."

"Are we nearer Keef and Sitsi then?" Erik asked, thinking *Tor's sweaty balls, if it broke when you were halfway, you'd be falling for ever.*

"A couple of days' walk away," Sofi answered.

"You, you and you," said Nether Barr, pointing at Erik, Wulf and Chogolisa, "wait over there. You're crossing last."

*In case it breaks under our weight*, thought Erik, *because it's built for Scraylings and both Wulf and I are twice as heavy as the heaviest Scrayling and Chogolisa is at least as heavy as both of us put together. And everything decays eventually, so it's not a case of* if *these ropes will snap, it's* when, *and –*

"We're the Heavies!" cried Wulf, slapping Chogolisa and Erik on the shoulders, apparently delighted by the turn of events. "Or should we call ourselves the Big Ones?"

"How about the Bridge Breakers?" offered Chogolisa.

"Please be quiet," said Erik.

Nether Barr announced that Finn and Thyri would go first, then Yoki Choppa and Ottar, then Sofi, Sassa and the elderly guide herself.

"You heavy lot come afterwards, one by one."

"If it's going to take that long," suggested Erik, "perhaps it would be quicker if we heavy three climbed down the cliff and up the other side?"

"That would take much longer," smiled Wulf, "and I can't see a bridge down there. That river doesn't look swimmable, either."

"I'm a good swimmer," Erik muttered.

Nether Barr explained how the first two should walk out of step with each other to reduce strain on the rope, and then it was time to go.

Erik felt faint.

Finn and Thyri set off cheerily counting "One, one, two, two" as they paced along the ropes. Erik was slightly annoyed that Finn seemed to have forgotten his own fear of heights, or at least was good at faking bravery. It made him ill seeing his son so high off the ground, so he tried looking over the edge of the cliff and contemplating the rock strata and soaring birds. That made it worse. He walked over to Sofi.

"How would you fight a man armed like me?" he asked, hefting Turkey Friend.

"Are you taking me on?"

Was there a smile in her eyes? Possibly.

"No, no. No. Just in case we come across anybody trying to kill us who's armed with a hand axe and a dagger, I want to know how they might attack me."

She showed him how she'd kill him in half a heartbeat

without him being able to do a thing about it, which was a little unnerving. Then they discussed possible counter-moves that could work against unenhanced warriors with hand axes.

As they sparred and talked, Yoki Choppa and Ottar followed Finn and Thyri. The boy sang as he went, his warbling, nonsense words echoing up from the impossible depths, fainter and fainter until it was Sofi's turn to cross with Nether Barr and Sassa.

Finn, Thyri, Ottar and the warlock were tiny figures on the far side. Erik wished that he was over there.

He asked Chogolisa and Wulf to play a game in which everyone concealed one, two, three or no stones in their hands and each had to guess the total amount of stones. The winner would cross first. Erik was desperate to be first, but he knew he would lose. And he was right. Chogolisa won the first game and Wulf won against Erik.

"See you on the other side!" called Chogolisa. If she was scared, it wasn't showing. She gripped the runners and placed a big bare foot on one of the lower ropes.

For her first couple of paces the rope was on the rock, then she stepped out, over the abyss.

The ropes thrummed tight. The heavy struts of the wooden support groaned. Erik gasped.

Everything held. Chogolisa loped confidently across the divide. The bridge sagged much more than with the others, so Erik had to stand nearer the edge than he would have liked to see her.

She was about a third of the way across when there was a *swish* like a loosed bowstring behind him. There was another *swish*, then another.

Erik and Wulf spun round. A foot rope was springing apart where it was attached to the wooded support struc-ture. Another strand went, then another. In a couple of heartbeats, cords were unravelling like intertwined worms which had suddenly decided they hated touching each other.

"Help me!" Erik called to Wulf, squatting and grabbing the rope, thinking as he did so that their strength was nothing compared to the rope's anchor. It wasn't just Chogolisa's weight they'd need to hold, but the weight of the rope itself.

"Chogolisa-lisa-lisa-lisa!" Erik's shout echoed across the deep canyon. "Get off the left foot rope! It's coming apart!"

"My left or your left?" Chogolisa shouted.

The rope snapped and yanked Erik off his feet. Surprised to be flying a foot off the ground, it took him a moment to let go.

He hit the ground with an *ooof*! He scraped along, rolled, made a grab at a stunted bush, missed, and bounced over the edge of the cliff.

He fell. One leg jerked and he swung into rock. He gripped onto it, eyes tight shut.

"You're going to have to help a bit," grunted Wulf's voice.

Erik opened his eyes. He was upside down, several hundred paces above the red skirt of scree and the valley floor. Stones were falling around him.

He wasn't plummeting to his death because Wulf had hold of his foot.

"You're too heavy to pull up, man!" his rescuer sounded strained. "Can you use your hands?"

Erik could use his hands. He could have done an awful lot at that moment to stop himself from falling.

He jammed his fingers into clefts and walked them in a backwards, upwards crawl as Wulf hauled on his foot. A few sweaty heartbeats later, he was lying on his stomach, looking out over the drop.

Chogolisa was watching him from the bridge, balancing on the remaining foot rope. The severed rope lay against the far cliff. It didn't reach the bottom, not nearly. They were a long way up.

*How did they get the ropes across when they built the thing?*
Erik found himself thinking. *And why the Hel did they build
it? Did they not consider that shit like this was bound to happen?*
Then he yelled: "Come back, Chogolisa! Slowly!"

"No, don't!" shouted Wulf. "Keep going! You're halfway!
No point coming back!"

Chogolisa nodded, turned and carried on, walking carefully
along the single rope, hands tight on the two support cords.
Erik checked the join between the cables and the support
structure. All seemed to be holding.

Chogolisa made it across without further incident, if one
considered Erik almost crapping himself every time she took
a step as no incident. When she reached the far side, he was
both relieved and horror-struck because now it was his turn.

"Let's go!" Wulf grinned at the big man's discomfort. "Shall
I do big bounces or small jiggly bounces on the way across?"

"We cannot go together."

"Why not? We definitely weigh less than . . . I mean to
say it's a strong rope. Take your boots off for a better grip
and you'll be fine. Hang them round your neck. Come on,
let's—" He looked up from unlacing his boots and saw Erik's
face. "All right, all right. Do you want to go first or second?"

"First. No, second. Oh, cunt-faced pigfuckers, I don't know.
Big bears' cocks. Squirrel-fucking, salmon-buggering—"

"Erik?"

"Sorry. You won the game, you go first." *And then I might
just stay over here for the rest of my life*, he thought.

Sofi Tornado watched Wulf the Fat striding confidently
across the broken bridge, smiling like a teen on his way to
meet a girl who's promised him a kiss. Sassa Lipchewer was
standing next to her. Her heartbeat wasn't much slower than
her growing baby's.

"The rope will hold," said Sofi.

"Will it?"

"It will." *It might not*. The other rope had snapped so this one could. In fact it was more likely because it was now doing the job of both ropes. But the Wootah woman believed her and her heartbeat calmed.

When he was about twenty paces away she could hear Wulf's heartbeat, too. It was hammering away faster than usual, even taking the exertion into consideration. Wulf knew the rope could go and he was more scared than she'd ever known him, but you really could not tell by looking at his happy face. Sofi found herself smiling back at him. It was impossible not to.

Wulf arrived, and, far away on the other side, Erik set off. Unhappiness was etched deep on his face. Next to her, Sassa and Wulf's heartbeats were slowing, but Chogolisa's was accelerating. So she really did like the man. Sofi wasn't quite sure what to do about it. Owsla were allowed lovers, but not romantic relationships. However, they were a long way from Calnia and, chances were, Calnia wasn't there any more. More importantly, if Erik survived to the end of the quest, it would complicate matters when Sofi slaughtered the Wootah. If indeed she was going to. It was not an easy decision.

She couldn't help vaguely hoping that the rope would snap and solve her problem for her.

Or Erik might, she mused, die of fear. He was breathing shallow and fast through his open mouth like a rabbit with an arrow in its gut, and his eyes were wide as an owl's.

Fact was, though, he was a good deal lighter than Chogolisa and she'd made it across. The chances of the second rope snapping while he was on it were slim.

Then she heard a rumble. *Ah,* she thought, *unless this happens*.

There wasn't time to shout a warning. The ground lurched so hard and suddenly that she was almost thrown off her feet.

The world buckled. Rocks were tumbling. The Wootah and Calnians who'd crossed the bridge were crouching. She heard a *poing!* from the far side of the canyon as the second foot rope snapped.

When the bucking had reduced a little, Sofi half stood and looked back across the chasm. The second foot rope was gone. The two hand ropes had held, Innowak knew how, but they were whipping about in rippling waves. Fifty paces out with a hand rope under each armpit, Erik was bouncing on the ropes like a child's toy.

"Fucknuts!" he shouted. "Catpussies!"

The earthquake calmed. Stones tumbled down the canyon walls, and there were some major rockslides still falling up and down stream, but the land around them was still. The group climbed to their feet, walked to the edge and looked at Erik, hanging on the hand ropes above the canyon. The wooden support on the other side had fallen askew. That was something of a worry, but Sofi guessed that if it had survived this far it wasn't likely to fall now. The question was whether Erik could pull himself fifty paces to safety.

"Badgers' balls!" he hollered.

"You're fine!" Wulf yelled. "The ropes will hold. Pull yourself along."

Erik hauled himself half a pace with one arm, then rested, dangling unhappily. He used the same arm to pull himself again but managed only a quarter of a pace before stopping and panting.

"One arm is a lot weaker after the wasp man cut," said Chogolisa.

He didn't have a hope. Sofi reckoned he might make another five paces. Probably not even that. He had fifty to go. *Looks like the Chogolisa and Erik problem is solved*, she thought.

"Take your time, Erik! You'll be fine!" Thyri shouted.

"I'll go out there and get him," said Wulf.

"No, you won't," said Sassa.

"I'll go," offered Finn, sounding, to Sofi's surprise, like he actually meant it.

"None of you will go," said Chogolisa. "The extra weight will probably snap the ropes. If it doesn't, how could you help him?"

Erik pulled himself along, but managed hardly a finger's breadth before slumping and yelling with the pain it caused his injured arm.

He hung by the armpits, panting and defeated. It was just a matter of time.

Sofi turned, wondering whether to suggest they set off rather than watch him fall to his death, and found Yoki Choppa standing behind her, looking at her.

"What?" she said.

He held her gaze. One of his eyebrows raised very slightly.

She looked back at Erik, hanging like a doll. He could probably stay like that for a while, and it looked like the ropes were going to hold.

She knew what Yoki Choppa wanted her to do.

She sighed. She wasn't going to do it. It was too risky. She didn't particularly mind dying, but their mission was to get Ottar and the body of a dead Warlock Queen's child to The Meadows. They could do that without Erik. Without Sofi, they'd struggle.

She opened her mouth, about to tell everyone they had to leave him. Sassa, Finn, Chogolisa, Thyri and Wulf were staring at Erik in naked despair.

Out in the canyon, Erik tried to pull himself along again with his good arm, but made no progress.

Finn stood looking at his father and weeping quietly. Chogolisa was sobbing.

"Fucknuts!" Erik shouted.

"Fucknuts indeed," said Sofi, shaking her head.

Before she could change her mind, she ran and leapt onto

the half-pace-apart hand ropes, one foot gripping each of the rough cords. She pressed with her feet to judge the ropes' strength and pliability. Yup, they were good. She could do it as long as the ropes held. And there wasn't another earthquake. Or any aftershocks, which there always were.

She ran out along the ropes, over the edge of the cliff.

"*Put your fat in a cat,*" said Sassa Lipchewer. Her mouth was hanging open but she didn't care.

Sofi Tornado was several hundred paces above the canyon, running along the hand ropes towards Erik. The slender ropes were bouncing and stretching, but the Owsla captain sped along like a squirrel on a branch.

Sofi reached Erik and stretched over him, placing her hands on the rope behind his head. They stayed like that for a while. Sassa could hear Sofi's voice, but not what she was saying. What was she going to do? What could she do?

After what seemed like far too long, still holding the rope with her hands, Sofi lowered herself gracefully and circled her legs around Erik's midriff. Sassa couldn't see but she guessed she'd linked her feet behind his back.

Somehow Sofi persuaded Erik to let go of the rope. She lowered herself slowly, so she was bearing their combined weight, dangling from the rope by her hands. Her legs were wrapped around the hefty Wootah man, facing away from the watching Wootah and Calnians.

Slowly and deliberately, the Owsla captain squeezed both ropes together, then shifted her hand one over the other, twisted her body and let the ropes spring apart again. She was left holding two ropes in different hands, facing them.

Erik dangled, big woolly head pressed against her chest.

Sofi slid one hand along the rope, then the other, again and again, swinging towards them. The hand ropes strained and thrummed.

Sassa shook her head. Sofi hadn't looked for a moment like she wasn't going to make it. Her precision, her strength, her confidence, her intelligence all combined to produce the most extraordinary feat Sassa had ever seen. There was no point comparing yourself to such a person. All you could do was watch in awe.

A *crack!* ran out. The support structure on the far side toppled, fell forwards and . . . stopped. The bridge held.

Sofi kept coming.

Chogolisa squatted at the edge of the cliff.

They were maybe five paces out when the rightmost rope snapped.

Sofi didn't blink. She kept coming hand over hand along the remaining rope. Chogolisa grabbed Sofi's wrists and stood, pulling rescuer and rescued up and out of the canyon. She plonked Erik onto the rock. Sofi unwrapped her legs and Chogolisa swung her onto her feet like a graceful dancer.

Sassa closed her mouth. She could not believe what she had just seen.

Erik shook, not unlike a wet dog, then looked at his rescuer.

"Um . . . Thanks."

"You're welcome," said Sofi. "Try not to do it again."

Nether Barr looked from Sofi to Erik. If she was impressed, it didn't show. She touched the remaining rope over the canyon with a snarl, said something in her own language, then sped away across the desert.

"Anybody know what she said?" asked Finn.

"I don't know," said Wulf, "but I guess it was something along the lines of *you broke our fucking bridge.*"

# Chapter 5

## Canyon Invaders

"Ottar's over there," said Freydis the Annoying, walking back from the target cactus with an armful of arrows and nodding westwards.

Sitsi looked across the canyon and over rocky scrubland. With her enhanced sight she could see Paloma watching Keef trying to sneak up on a jackrabbit with Arse Splitter. But no small boys.

"A long way over there," said Freydis.

"That's west," said Sitsi Kestrel.

"Yes."

"But he should be coming from the south-east."

"He's coming from the west."

"You're sure?"

"I am."

"How far?"

Freydis frowned and peered westwards. "Don't know."

She could be right. It had been long enough that they could have circled around.

"Is Bodil Gooseface with him?" Sitsi blurted.

"Why Bodil Gooseface?"

"I mean all of them. Are they all okay? I just said Bodil because I think she's the most likely to come to harm." Sitsi twirled an arrow and tried to look nonchalant.

Freydis gave her a strange look. "I don't know. I just know Ottar's over there and he's coming here. He might get here today, he might get here in ten days. Please can we shoot some more arrows?"

"Go for it. I'll watch."

It was nine days since she and Keef had rescued Paloma from the squatch. Sitsi had been going just a little insane spending all her time with Keef, so she suggested that Paloma and the Wootah man hunt while she taught Freydis how to make bows and arrows and how to use them. It wasn't because she didn't like Keef. Quite the opposite.

She tried to tell herself she loved him like a brother. He was so funny looking with his little head, one eye, one ear and pale skin, how could it be otherwise? But she knew she was lying to herself.

She was sure he felt the same. She was aching to tell him that Bodil's baby wasn't his. But it would be the wrong thing to do, plus she wanted the beginning of their love to be romantic.

*How did you two get together?* she sometimes fantasised that people in years to come would ask. *Well, it's a funny story,* she'd answer in her fantasies. *He shagged someone else who was already pregnant with another man's baby. I told him that it wasn't his baby, and he ran into my arms. What about the mother? Oh, we ruined her life and the baby died.*

That would not do.

She wished she could have talked to someone about it, but there was only Keef himself, Freydis and Paloma. Paloma would tease her and be coarse.

She looked at Freydis, standing and holding the bow and pulling the string exactly as she'd shown her. She couldn't bring herself to discuss her love live with a six-year-old, even such a precocious one.

Her policy was to keep trying to convince herself that Keef was just a great friend. When the others got here and they carried on west, he'd be hanging out with Bodil more than with her, because they were lovers who were going to share a child. But Sitsi could still enjoy friendly moments with him. That was all she needed, wasn't it?

She sighed and looked around again. Still no sign of the Wormsland people whom Paloma had attacked.

She hadn't been angry with Paloma at the time. She'd been ready for her to break the rules and head out of the canyon, so she and Keef had been ready to follow. It had been no great surprise that Paloma had managed to pick a fight with some warriors who Sitsi was certain were from the nearby Wormsland tribe, and very nearly get herself killed by a squatch.

Sitsi didn't mind all that, but she had become more and more frustrated with Paloma. She'd apologised but she hadn't meant it. She'd put them all in danger – worst of all she'd put Freydis in danger – and Sitsi just knew that silly, selfish Paloma was perfectly capable of doing it all again.

The following day, Sitsi decided to risk Paloma running off with Freydis again, and spend what little time they had left in the canyon with Keef. They sat and chatted by the tadpole pool while Paloma and Freydis hared around up-canyon.

They did talk about things other than tadpoles as they sat there, but at that moment Sitsi did happen to be talking about how creatures could change from one thing into another. She was trying to bring the conversation around to the human reproductive cycle – specifically how long it was between becoming pregnant and knowing that one was pregnant – when one of Keef's trip alarms sounded.

They slipped off the rock and headed down-canyon, along the sandy path and into the narrow, wooded section where their cave was. Keef went first with Arse Splitter and Sitsi followed, arrow strung.

"Stop," she whispered, as they reached a stream crossing. "Someone's coming."

They melted back into the trees.

A sour-faced old lady carrying a long-handled net appeared

on the other side of the stream. Not what Sitsi had been expecting. The woman stopped and sniffed the air.

She held up a hand.

"It's Sitsi Kestrel and Keef the Berserker," said Sofi Tornado, appearing beside the old lady. "They're hiding in the trees." She pointed at them.

"Hello, Sofi," said Sitsi, sauntering from cover. She could act cool, too. "Is . . . everyone with you?"

"Not everyone." Cold dread seized Sitsi. *Who'd died?* "But nobody's dead, or badly hurt," continued Sofi, and Sitsi started to breathe again. "Now tell me, are Freydis and Pronghorn with you?"

"They are. They're running about somewhere nearby. Paloma and her—"

"Freydis is alive!' yelled Sofi. "They're all here!"

*That's right*, thought Sitsi, *tell the others that everyone's fine but leave me wondering who's not with you. Is it Bodil?*

Cheers and whoops from her old friends and a "WHOOOOO-tah!" from Wulf rang out from the cover of the trees down the canyon.

"WHOOOOO-tah!" Keef yelled in reply.

The Wootah's pure joy made feel her bad about her pettish thoughts. She tried not to be too excited that she couldn't hear Bodil Gooseface. No Yoki Choppa either, but he wasn't the cheering type. Surely Bodil would have been whooping loudest if she'd been with the rest of them?

"Can you keep going at the front? I'm stooped under a branch here," came Chogolisa's voice from the trees.

"Follow me back to our camp!" Sitsi shouted so all the people still hidden by the trees could hear. "There's room for everyone there."

"Tell me quickly, Sofi," said Sitsi as they followed Keef up the canyon, "who's not with you? If it's Ottar I don't know what Freydis will—"

"Ottar's here," said Sofi.

"Then who is missing?"

"Let's wait until we've got everybody together."

*It is Bodil*, Sitsi thought. *Sofi knew about her and Keef — Sofi knew everything — and she was enjoying the torment. But what could have happened?* Sitsi prayed to Innowak that Bodil was all right. Or at least not too badly hurt.

Keef was walking ahead of them, in earshot. He didn't turn, but the back of his neck was a brighter red than usual. Was he terrified that the missing person might be Bodil? Or elated?

Finn the Deep stopped to adjust Foe Slicer's baldric and let Ottar, Erik, Chogolisa, Sassa, Wulf, Thyri and Yoki Choppa overtake.

He didn't want to see Paloma Pronghorn.

He was desperate to see Paloma Pronghorn.

He felt sick. As the others headed up along the path chatting away, he stood on his own. He'd been pondering Moolba's words about the self-destructive stupidity of buffalo-headedly pursuing someone who wasn't interested, and had more or less persuaded himself that he was no longer in love with Thyri.

But now he was going to see Paloma. She wasn't interested, was she? But she'd kissed him! While they'd been apart, it had been all too easy to forget the slights, to enjoy the memory — and to lavishly embellish the memory — of their evening in the Black Mountains, and believe that maybe, just maybe, Pronghorn found him as attractive as he found her. Or at least attractive enough to kiss him again.

But now he was going to see her, and he'd have to deal with the reality that, since they'd kissed, she'd hardly looked at him, and, when she had, she'd looked like a frightened and slightly disgusted deer.

She was a decade older than him. She was beautiful, clever,

funny, one of the best warriors in the world and cool as a
badger's bollocks in a blizzard. But he was Finn the Deep!
He'd carried them from the Badlands, he'd defeated Krusha
the squatch and . . . who was he kidding? He knew who he
was. No matter his deeds, he was still Finnbogi the Boggy.
He'd just been lucky a couple of times. What was more, who
was the one person in the group who he hadn't really saved?
The only one able enough to escape anything on her own?
Paloma Pronghorn. And Sofi probably. And possibly Sitsi
and Chogolisa. But that wasn't the point. Paloma had no
reason to be impressed by his heroics and no reason to be
grateful. Nobody did. He'd done what he'd done to save
himself as much as anyone else. Nobody owed him anything.

If anything, he deserved the opposite of gratitude from
Paloma, whatever the opposite of gratitude was, because he
had abandoned his child. How dare he think he deserved
anyone's love? Who was to say he wouldn't do it again?
Maybe Paloma would fall for him, he'd get her pregnant,
and then leave again! That was the type of man he was! He
shook his head, ill with self-loathing.

He would go back afterwards, that's what he'd do. When
the Warlock Queen had her baby back, he'd return to his.
He wasn't such a bad guy. He was a man on a quest.

He reckoned he had one chance with Paloma. Before they'd
kissed, Finn hadn't shown any romantic interest in her – you
couldn't count ogling her – because he was certain she'd
never go for him. But she had! She'd kissed him! So, he told
himself, if he acted in the same way again, surely she'd kiss
him again. It was foolproof. He wasn't going to ignore her.
He was going to be civil and calm.

*Don't be yourself. Be the best you can be. Then see who likes
you.* That's what Moolba had said. It would definitely work.

*Only fools are certain*, said dead Gunnhild in his mind.

It might not work, he admitted.

The others were far ahead and it was quiet in the canyon.

Finn was alone for the first time in a long while. He looked up at the high red cliffs on both sides. Any number of monsters could have been watching, about to jump down on him. It was *so dangerous* and their quest had hardly begun. It had two parts – collect the coffin of the Warlock Queen's child and take it to the Warlock Queen. And they hadn't done either of those things yet. Suddenly Finn realised that he was going to die in this terrifying land. He'd been lucky so far. Surely the next monster that attacked or the next rope bridge that snapped was going to kill him.

He hurried along the path to catch up with the others.

They were all waiting for him in a clearing, as if proceedings couldn't begin before he got there. Well, that was nice.

He beamed at Sitsi, waved manically at Freydis, nodded manfully at Keef then smiled in a manly rather than manful way at Pronghorn. She smiled back at him, looking a little embarrassed.

An excellent start.

Sitsi bounced on her toes next to Sofi and Nether Barr and watched the others arrive in the clearing by the cave.

Happy little Ottar came first, bouncing and grinning. Keef crouched with his arms wide and the boy ran to him, giggling. Erik and Chogolisa came next, just as Paloma and Freydis came sprinting from up-canyon. Chogolisa picked up Sitsi and hugged her. Over Chogolisa's shoulder she saw Freydis walk up to Ottar. Ottar hid his face in his hands, then opened them to reveal a big grin.

The children both opened their arms, stepped forward and hugged. It was like watching two pieces of a well-carved puzzle slot together. The tears that Sitsi had been holding back burst from her eyes. Would she ever love as much as these two children loved each other? Would she ever be loved that much?

Sitsi wiped her tears and nose as Sassa and Wulf bounded

from the trees, holding hands and happy, and headed for the embracing children. She'd suspected that Sassa was pregnant before, now she knew. Her bump wasn't the only change. Her crest of hair was a thumb's breadth longer, the rest of her head freshly shaved. She also looked several notches tougher and more seasoned as did Wulf.

Chogolisa headed for Paloma, who was hugging Sofi (wow, thought Sitsi). Thyri Treelegs appeared next, looking happy for once, as well as stronger and leaner, her big legs thrumming with muscle. In another world she might have made good Owsla. She spotted Keef and skipped over to hug him.

Then came Yoki Choppa, half a smile on even his face.

There was a gap then Finn the Deep appeared, attempting a cool saunter and trying to look everywhere other than at Paloma, while glancing at Paloma every other heartbeat. Sitsi went to give him a hug. He looked like he needed one.

"The adventures we've had!" he said. He looked markedly fitter, too – broader of shoulder, trimmer of waist and clearer of eye. The Wootah were toughening up.

"I have made much mead!" said Keef, striding up.

"But it's not even lunchtime yet," said Sitsi.

"There is much to tell," explained Keef. "We will drink while we prepare food, drink while we eat and tell our tales, then drink and talk some more! You can begin with the tale of how I rescued Paloma from the giant. I will help you with the details."

He was looking around as he spoke. Sitsi was, too.

"Where's Bodil Gooseface?" asked Freydis.

Sitsi watched as everyone avoided looking at Keef, apart from Paloma, who was looking from Sitsi to Keef and grinning naughtily. *That woman!*

"She's fine," said Wulf. "She's happy and well."

"But?" said Paloma.

"Well." Wulf turned to Keef. "We met Olaf Worldfinder."

"Did you tell him he's got the same name as the bloke who founded Hardwork?" Keef asked.

"It's the same guy," said Finn.

"*The* Olaf Worldfinder?" Keef raised an eyebrow.

"Yep." Wulf nodded.

"Weird," said Keef, as if that was that and he didn't need to know any more.

This was one of the reasons Sitsi loved Keef. Some people might feign nonchalance at hearing that the man who'd founded their tribe a hundred years before was still alive. Keef was genuinely unfazed.

"I'll tell you all about it later," said Wulf, smiling. "We met him shortly after we last saw you, maybe twenty days ago. He'd got a strong, safe homestead high up above the desert. There's a lot of game there and it's untouched by the monsters and disasters."

"And?" Keef asked. Sitsi could guess what was coming. She tried not to smile.

"And Bodil decided, for the sake of her baby, to stay there."

"With Olaf Worldfinder."

"Yup."

"Bodil and her baby will live with Olaf Worldfinder," Keef confirmed."

"You've got it," said Wulf. "He will raise the child as his own."

Keef turned to Finn, raising the eyebrow above his missing eye. Finn had the good grace to turn dark red and look at his feet.

Then Keef turned to Sitsi.

"Sitsi Kestrel," he said. "Would you mind coming with me to fetch the mead?"

"Before you go," said Wulf, "Sofi discovered what we need to defeat the force at The Meadows."

Looking Sitsi in the eye, Keef said: "Stories are better with mead. I can wait."

"Me, too," said Sitsi.

They jogged out of the clearing before anybody else could say anything.

Thirty paces up the path, hidden by trees, they stopped.

"This will come as a surprise," Keef said sombrely, "because I'm sure you think I am good at everything. But I'm not very good at this sort of thing. So." Keef looked to one side, then back at her. "Bodil's baby is not mine."

"I know. Everyone knows. Why didn't you make Finn take responsibility?"

"He'd have been a shit father."

"And you think you'd have been a better one?"

"I don't think, I know."

"Especially if you and Bodil had been a couple."

"Two united parents are good for a kid. I wish I'd known my dad."

"So you've supressed your love for me for the sake of an unborn baby who isn't yours?"

"What makes you think I love you?"

Sitsi smiled. "I don't think, Keef the Berserker, I know."

She leapt onto Keef, wrapped her legs around his waist, grabbed his head with both hands and clamped her mouth onto his.

# Chapter 6

## Great Worm

Sofi Tornado and Paloma Pronghorn strode behind Nether Barr up into Wormsland the following morning. Freydis followed next to Paloma, with the rest of the group behind. Reunited, Sofi felt renewed vigour in the group, a bolstered sense of purpose. Having half of the remaining Owsla back was part of it, for sure – Paloma's speed and Sitsi's shooting would be a blessing when they were next attacked – but she couldn't deny that she was pleased to see funny Keef and precocious Freydis again. It was particularly interesting to see how close Paloma had become to the girl. Sofi wouldn't have picked that one.

"Tell me more about Chief Tarker," she asked Paloma.

"She's tall, cruel, and pragmatic. With a face like a prairie dog."

"And you thought it was a good idea to pick a fight with the tribe we have to negotiate with."

"She was tormenting a squatch."

"Which tried to kill you when you freed it, so she had reason to torment it."

"They were enjoying it too much."

"Do you remember what we used to do?"

Paloma sighed. "Yeah, but we're all lovey-dovey now, aren't we? You'd have rescued the squatch, too."

She wouldn't have done. "Tell me more about Tarker," she said.

"I think she's rational enough to talk to us. Her men wanted to fight me, but she saw that I was enhanced and saved them from a beating. When she hears what we want and why, I think she'll give it to us."

"Good." Sofi wouldn't mind killing Tarker and any number of her people to get what she needed, but she didn't want to risk the others.

"And just so I'm straight," Paloma asked, "we want a dead baby in a coffin?"

"More a child than a baby, I think."

"And you saw this after taking a huge dose of a horrible drug and hallucinating?" Paloma sounded sceptical.

"It's called a vision quest. I saw two men raid the Warlock Queen's tomb and steal her young son's coffin. They planned to take it to Wormsland. There was an earthquake. One man died, the other fled with the box on his shoulder. He was pursued by the Warlock Queen but she was too late to stop him."

"So we take this kid's body back to The Meadows, the queen will stop freaking out and we can go home?"

"That is the idea."

"And when you saw all this you were an eagle?" Paloma grinned.

"Yes."

"Right."

"*How* did you become an eagle?" asked Freydis. Sofi had forgotten she was tagging along and listening. The child walked freakishly quietly, much more so than before.

"It's really easy," said Paloma. "Have you never tried it? Just stick your nose out and flap your arms."

Freydis did so and laughed. Paloma laughed along. Sofi didn't.

Paloma was enjoying this far too much. She was actually mocking her captain. Four moons ago Sofi would have beaten the crap out of her to remind her of the pecking order. Now?

Now she was tempted to think *fuck it, she's my friend and friends mock each other. If you can't take being mocked, you'll never have friends.*

And she wanted friends.

She stopped. She really did. For the first time in her life she actually wanted friends. She even wanted the child's approval.

"Are you all right?" asked Paloma.

"Fine. Thought I saw something on the ground."

The track evened out then descended through a wide, cliff-sided red rock canyon. Topping the cliffs on both sides were huge slabs of rock, standing on their ends as if arranged by giants to watch people passing below. Hidden high up in the shadowed lee of one of the slabs Sofi could hear two people watching them and talking in a language she didn't understand.

Sitsi skipped up to join them. "There's a man and a woman crouching in the shadow of the triangular chunk of rock to the east," she said without looking up.

"Does the woman look like a prairie dog?" asked Paloma.

"A bit." Sitsi nodded

"That's the chief, Sofi Tornado!" said Freydis, "the one who Paloma Pronghorn scared away when Sitsi Kestel had to save her from the squatch!"

"Thanks, Freydis." Paloma gave the girl a gentle whop to the head.

The path rose out of the monumentally sided valley and into a red, sparely vegetated desert. Several more great slabs of rock soared out of the parched land like the weather-chapped fins of gigantic sea beasts. Sofi remembered Beaver Man saying that the Badlands had once been covered by oceans and showing them a fossilised turtle shell. Perhaps these fins of rock had once belonged to sea monsters? Relatively, it wasn't an outlandish idea.

As they walked, half a dozen people shadowed them to the west, making no effort no hide, nor to approach.

Near the middle of the day the Wootah and Calnians came to two red rock towers. One was a slender pyramid with a huge boulder balanced on top, the other stout and phallic even to Sofi's eyes.

"How the Tor's hairy nuts did that boulder get up there?" asked Wulf.

"It could be one of Tor's balls," suggested Sassa, "the hair sheared off by wind and rain through the eons."

"You're right. Nice to see a bollock making a stand for itself for once. I'm getting a bit bored of rocks that look like cocks."

"You wouldn't think that, the amount you go on about them," smiled Sassa.

"I only point out the good ones – like that one." He pointed at the stout tower.

"It's that kind of thoughtful discernment that makes me love you."

Sofi might have been changing – might have been becoming softer – but she was certain she would never get used to the Wootah's capacity for talking shit. She held up a hand for silence.

Waiting for them below what Sofi now, annoyingly, thought of as the god's bollock, were a couple of dozen dark-skinned men and women. The men wore breechcloths, the women breechcloths and jerkins. All were armed with bows or spears.

A woman strode out to meet them. She was tall and lissom, with bulging cheeks as Paloma had described.

"Stay here everyone," said Sofi, choosing to forget for a moment that it was meant to be a joint captaincy. This was a time to look commanding.

"Chief Tarker," she said.

"And you are?" The woman stopped five paces distant.

"I'm Sofi Tornado of Calnia. We are Calnians and Wootah, from east of the Shining Mountains. You've met Paloma Pronghorn." She looked back at Paloma, who waved. So much for looking commanding.

"I've heard of Calnians. You're an aggressive tribe who've caused much pain to many people. I take it the pale ones with dyed hair are the Wootah?"

"They are the Wootah. Their hair is not dyed. Their ancestors come from the far side of the Great Salt Sea."

"I see." Tarker didn't look impressed. "Why have you invaded my territory?"

"Is Wormsland *your* territory?" Sofi knew that Tarker's tribe had taken the land from the Popeye tribe a year before.

"Yes." Chief Tarker held her gaze.

"We're not invading." Sofi wasn't going to push the who-owns-the-territory point, unless she needed to. "We're passing through. We are on a quest. You've probably been troubled by monsters and big weather recently."

Tarker's face hardened. "We've lost more than you can imagine."

Sofi nodded. She could imagine a lot but, again, it wasn't a useful fight to pick. "We are heading west to put an end to the monsters and the freak weather."

"How?"

"We need something you have. The coffin of a boy."

Tarker raised her eyebrows. "What will you give me for it?"

"You get to keep your life."

Tarker's men and women lowered their spears and took a step forward. Sofi held up a hand for the Wootah and Calnians to stay put.

"Are you threatening me?" asked Tarker.

"The coffin contains the child of the Warlock Queen. She will continue killing until her child is returned to her, or until there are no people left to kill."

"You intend to take the coffin to The Meadows?"

"Yes."

"Have you any idea what's happening west of here?"

"Some."

"You won't get halfway to The Meadows."

"We will try."

Chief Tarker looked at Sofi. Sofi looked back. She liked this woman.

"All right," said the chief eventually. "The box you seek is here. It was brought here by a man a decade ago, when another people had this land."

"The Popeye."

"Indeed."

"We met some. They are dead now," said Sofi.

"I'm not surprised, they were a weedy lot. So, the man who brought the box died. Collapsed on arrival and never woke, apparently. The Popeyes decided he'd been killed by dark magic coming from the box itself – ("Great!" said Paloma behind Sofi) – so they kept it somewhere where nobody would stumble on it by mistake."

"Where?" Sofi asked.

"It's lashed to the middle of an arch of rock called the Great Worm. You can have it if you can take it."

"What's the difficulty?"

"Gaven?" called Chief Tarker.

An elderly man stepped forward. He was bald, with a skull so flat that Sofi guessed he'd had a board strapped to it throughout childhood.

"Tell Sofi the problem with the Great Worm."

"The presence of the coffin has soured the land around like a corpse rotting in a grain store." His sing-song voice did not tally well with his grim news. "I told people to never go there. Four people didn't listen to me. They died."

"How?" asked Sofi.

"I don't know. I found them. There were torn apart and

their limbs strewn around the base of the Great Worm. I don't know what beast or beasts killed them. Theirs were the only remains I found."

"Were there tracks?" asked Sofi.

"I'm afraid I fled before I thought to look, and nobody's been there since."

"Sounds like our kind of place!" chimed in Wulf. "Let's go!"

Chief Tarker shrugged, then nodded. "You'll be doing us a favour taking the thing away. Follow me."

She turned and walked northwards.

Sofi gestured to the others to follow, then caught up with Tarker.

"Tell me," the chief asked as Sofi fell into step, "did your woman have fun with the squatch she rescued from us?"

Wormsland tribespeople headed off to the east, leaving Chief Tarker striding ahead with Sofi, and their warlock Gaven, who was talking to Yoki Choppa.

Sassa Lipchewer was surprised and slightly miffed to discover Yoki Choppa was capable of conversation. And she actually heard Sofi laugh. Did the two most reticent of the Calnians get along only with their own kind? Were the Wootah really so different? She was grateful to Sofi for telling her about her baby's heartbeat, and she'd risked herself to rescue Erik, but Sofi's orders from Empress Ayanna had been to kill all the Wootah. They'd all assumed that this order was redundant now that they were all friends and Ayanna was dead and the Calnian empire she'd ruled over was no more. But Sofi had never mentioned the order, or, more importantly, never said that she planned to ignore it.

Did Sofi keep her distance, wondered Sassa, because she still intended to kill all the Wootah when the quest was done? Sassa could pretend that Wulf, Keef and Erik would protect them, but she'd seen Sofi fight the wasp men. The Wootah wouldn't last a heartbeat. She pictured them placing a small coffin at the base of The Pyramid, and Sofi turning, axe in one hand, knife in the other –

Giggles from Freydis and Ottar wrenched her from morbid fantasising. Ottar had found a tortoise. The tortoises were much larger here than they'd been back at Hardwork. Sassa touched Wulf's arm and they stopped to watch. The children marvelled at the armoured creature. Freydis told Ottar not to touch it. The boy dodged her restraining arm and stroked its back while the reptile blinked uncomplainingly and Freydis tutted.

It was such a joy to see those two together again. Sure, it was great that Keef had been freed from his false obligation to Bodil and got it on with Sitsi, but the greatest happiness of the reunion by far was Ottar and Freydis's innocent delight.

One day, Sassa hoped, she and Wulf would watch their own children play and bicker and discover. She could not wait. She knew there were terrible dangers ahead, but they'd survived so many that she was beginning to believe that they might get through it. She didn't want to jinx it, but she really did feel that both her and Wulf's days of death were a long way off.

Wulf nudged her arm. He gestured back with his head. Nether Barr had dropped twenty paces behind, and was dragging her net along the ground, with her head down. Given her usual sprightly, lizard-chasing ways, it seemed something was wrong.

Sassa touched Wulf's arm, nodding for him to go on, then stopped to wait for the old lady.

"Hello!" she said.

Nether Barr looked up, then looked down again.

"What's up?" asked Sassa.

"Nothing."

"Go on," said Sassa, "a problem shared—"

"Is a problem burdened on other people," interrupted Nether Barr, before carrying on anyway. "It's seeing those lovely children having such a wonderful time," she said, "and you with one on the way. Makes me wish I'd had my own."

"I'm sure life's a lot easier without them," Sassa suggested.

"I could have had them," Nether Barr continued. "I should have done, but I had to adventure, didn't I? I could have settled down with Croxton or Roccker, I was a beauty and I could have had any of them, but no, I wanted to see the world. I was the great traveller. By the time I realised I wanted children it was too late."

"Where did you go?" They were walking past a large arch of rock, the biggest they'd seen yet.

"Where didn't I go?" Nether Barr quickened her pace as she spoke excitedly. "I went all over the Desert You Don't Walk Out Of. North, south, east, west, you name it, I went there."

"And beyond the desert?" Sassa asked.

Nether Barr eyed her suspiciously. "No. Why would I want to leave the desert?"

"Why indeed?" Sassa replied, trying not to be smug about the fact that she'd seen more of the world than the great traveller without even trying. "Have you been to The Meadows?"

"I have seen The Meadows, which is as much as anyone's done for a few hundred years, other than the man who stole the coffin, of course."

"What was it like?"

"The most beautiful place I have ever seen. Green and lovely. Parrots everywhere. Apparently there are more amazing animals, but I never saw them."

"Do you think the Warlock Queen is behind all these monsters and disasters?"

"Oh, yes. If you saw the paradise she'd made in the middle of the dry desert, you'd believe she could do anything."

They chatted on, Nether Barr telling Sassa about all the places she's seen in the Desert You Don't Walk Out Of, and Sassa realising that maybe Nether Barr had seen more of the world than her. The Desert You Don't Walk Out Of, it seemed, was seriously big.

"I don't mean to be rude," said Sassa when Nether Barr paused, "but you've hardly been chatty on this journey. Why not?"

"Nobody's spoken to me."

"Surely they have."

"No. Only Ottar has shown me any attention."

It was true. But then again Nether Barr had always been off ahead . . .

"You're a clique, you see," the old lady continued. "People in a clique don't need to talk to outsiders."

"I'm sorry," said Sassa.

"Oh, don't be. I know it isn't malicious. It's nice to be part of a clique. I was in one once. It was north-west of here, near the Salt Lake. There were seven of us—"

Nether Barr carried on, hardly drawing a breath, as if making up for all the time she hadn't spoken. Sassa didn't mind. It was interesting stuff and it was a shame when they arrived at the mouth of the shadowed canyon that led to the Great Worm and Sofi asked her to be quiet.

Who knew what Sofi and Yoki Choppa had talked to the Wormslanders about, but they seemed to have made good impressions, because both their warlock Gaven and Chief Tarker announced that they'd come with the Wootah and Calnians into the dangerous place.

The narrow canyon opened into a wider, red desert valley. Ahead was a forest of rock towers. Green bushes and cactuses were bright against the red rocks, which lay in crazily shaped clumps and mounds all around. It was another rabbit paradise. The appealing little animals hopped everywhere, leaving trails in the red sand. Friendly looking crows watched from red ridges. Butterflies busied themselves between flowers.

It didn't look or feel evil. Sassa heard stifled giggles from Wulf and Finn. Many of the rock columns had bulbous ends.

Sofi was standing on a rock to the right of the path, a hand on one hip, the other holding her axe. The others gathered around and waited for Sassa and Nether Barr.

"Right," said Sofi (which Sassa translated as *you should have walked here more quickly, Sassa Lipchewer and Nether Barr*). "The Great Worm is half a mile ahead. Do you mind if I give orders to the Wootah, Wulf?"

"Go for it."

"Tarker, may I include you and Gaven in the plan?"

"Sure," replied Tarker, looking amused.

"Sassa, Tarker and Keef," Sofi continued, "you're in front with your bows. Sitsi and Freydis, take the rear."

The serious look on Freydis's face as she headed to the rear, bow in hand, was adorable and heartbreaking. Sassa was also, she realised, piqued that Keef had learned to use a bow. Sassa was the Wootah's archer. She chided herself for her childishness. Keef wouldn't be as good as her after half a moon's practice, anyway.

"The rest of you protect the archers and Ottar. Paloma, range nearby. If we're attacked, run around and kill as many as you can."

Paloma ran ahead, killing stick in hand.

Weapons ready, they marched across the rabbit-busy land. The rocks narrowed. A thousand monsters could have been hiding behind the fins and towers of rock. Sassa felt like she had spiders crawling all over her skin. Terror, she realised.

It was a long half-mile. Then they saw the Great Worm.

"Fuck a woodchuck," said Sassa. Arching across the sky, seventy paces above the ground and a hundred paces long, was a slender arch of red rock. What mad god could have made such a thing? How did it stay up? It looked like a good gust of wind would do for it.

She saw the coffin, lashed to the centre of the rock bridge. A wave of foreboding made her feel sick and faint. Was it some evil magic flowing from the dead boy in the box? Or was it being pregnant and walking a long way in the heat? Either way, she had to take Wulf's arm.

"Everyone, wait here," said Sofi.

"No," said Wulf. "I'll get the kid."

Sassa turned to him. "You will not."

"I'll go," said Paloma. "The Great Worm doesn't look too strong. If it breaks, I'll be fine. Whereas you, Wulf, will be killed."

"The Worm has stood for thousands of years," said Sofi. "Wulf can go."

Sassa got it, she really did. Sofi had been on the vision quest. Paloma had rescued Freydis. Sofi had saved Erik's life on the bridge. Finn had saved Sassa from the wasp man. Sofi was doing Wulf a favour. It was time for him to do something dangerous to help them all.

But not this. Paloma would have the box down in a trice. If anything attacked Sofi or Paloma up on the arch they'd be able kill it without a bother, or leap down to escape. They were enhanced warriors. Wulf was not. If Wulf fell from the arch, he would die.

"My love," she said, "this is one for the Owsla."

"Sorry, Sassa. It's Wootah time," he grinned.

"Paloma and Sofi live for this sort of thing. You saw Sofi rescue Erik. You're a great warrior, Wulf, but your skills lie elsewhere. If the box on the arch were soup, Paloma is a spoon and you're a fork."

"You can eat soup with a fork."

"If you had a bowl of soup, and a fork and a spoon on a table in front of you, would you use the fork?"

"For the larger lumps, yes. Can I borrow your knife, please, Erik?"

Erik handed Wulf his obsidian blade and before Sassa could argue any more, Wulf ran towards the southern end of the arch.

They watched as he clambered up the steep slope and ran – ran, the idiot – across the narrow span. Sassa looked at Sofi. She was watching calmly. So she couldn't hear any trouble coming. Sassa unclenched her fists, toes and buttocks and tried to calm her breathing.

Wulf dropped to his knees by the box. His elbow rose and fell as he sawed away. The rope sprang apart and tumbled down to the desert – a long way below. Wulf picked up the box and held it above his head.

"WOOOOOOOOT—"

The ground shook.

The Great Worm shook.

Wulf dropped to his knees, clutching the box.

Sassa spread her hands for balance, looking up at the arch. Surely such a spindly bridge couldn't survive such a violent quake?

Then the ground all around erupted. Bushes, trees, rocks, even rabbits, launched into the air with a crunching whoosh and stayed aloft, swirling and howling in mini tornados.

Sassa could only just make out the people around her, let alone her husband.

"Somebody help Wulf!" she shouted, but she couldn't hear her own cry. She stumbled in the direction of the arch. All around her, swirling rocks, plants and animals were smashing together and coalescing into new, weird forms. They were becoming animals. Monsters.

Sassa strung an arrow.

A sharp-beaked thing twice the height of a man emerged from the maelstrom and towered over her. It raised a serrated claw, lowered its face, opened its beak and screamed. Sassa shot into its open mouth and jumped clear as it fell.

A horrific sound, like the bark of a tortured dog, rang out behind her. She turned. A beast the size of a buffalo with multiple short legs and a huge round head was charging her. She tried to string an arrow and fumbled. The monster leapt, gaping mouth full of black teeth.

Sassa screamed and raised her arms.

Chogolisa steamed in, ramming the beast with a shoulder. Sassa stared open-mouthed as the huge woman jumped onto the animal, gripped it with her great thighs and punched it into bloody stillness.

The air cleared for a moment and she saw Wulf. He was still standing! But he was far from safe. Sliming towards him from the arch's northern end was a giant slug with a multitude of arms waggling from its fat body. Rushing at him for the other end was what looked like a mob of badgers.

"Sitsi!" she shouted as she shot an arrow into the slug thing, "Help Wulf!" Sitsi spun and shot arrow after arrow. Badger creatures flew off the arch, six of them in three heartbeats. But there were plenty more.

Then Sassa had her own problems again. More creatures were forming out of the debris storm. There were misshapen beasts with long legs, short legs, bulbous bodies, great mouths, no mouths, crab claws, scorpion stings, serrated pincer jaws and all manner of mutations.

A crowd of them came at her. Too many to shoot. She loosed an arrow at the nearest, jumped down into a sandy floored gully and ran towards the arch. She had to get to Wulf!

Something that looked like a bald, eight-legged fox with a baby's head burst from the sand and screamed at her. She hesitated for a heartbeat, then kicked its baby face as hard as she could.

She bounded up a slope. A dome of rock blocked her view of the Great Worm and Wulf. She looked around.

Erik, with Freydis on his shoulders, was whacking his club at a cluster of giant beetles with one hand and holding Ottar's hand with the other. Ottar, brave little boy, was stamping on huge spiders. Freydis shot a shiny winged flying horror which shrieked and tumbled.

Keef had a massive, multi-limbed monstrosity speared on the end of Arse Splitter while Finn dodged the creature's flailing arms and chopped at it with Foe Slicer. Thyri slashed the legs out from a man-shaped thing with what looked like a bag full of bees for a face. Nether Barr threw a writhing, two-headed snake at a hairy, long-armed animal that was bouncing on two legs and howling at her. Yoki Choppa was dashing about blowing darts into creatures.

If the others were doing well, the Owsla were amazing.

Sofi was dancing her dance of death, axe in one hand, dagger-tooth knife in the other, dispatching a foe every heartbeat. Paloma was haring about in a blur of limbs, slaughtering even more. She brained the beast that was threatening Nether Barr without stopping and had killed two more before Nether Barr had realised that her attacker was dead. Chogolisa was holding a great boulder two-handed and pummelling the brains out of a colossal lizard. Sitsi was pumping arrow after arrow into the ranks of attackers.

But she couldn't see Wulf. She ran to get a clear line of sight. She saw for a moment that he was still up on the arch, swinging at some lumpen thing – possibly the slug beast that she'd shot – with his hammer, then something whumped into her and knocked her flat.

Sassa rolled onto her back. A monster was looming over her. It looked like it was made of water. Its head and hands were featureless, shimmering lumps. It toppled. She rolled, but too slowly. It landed on her with its full weight like a bucket of fish. She gasped and sucked in horrible goo. She choked and clawed the stuff out of her mouth. She sat. She was covered greasy sludge. The monster had gone.

She clawed the ooze out of her eyes and spat. The slime tasted of cactus and clay.

She looked about again for someone to come with her to help Wulf.

Sofi, Paloma and Chogolisa were battling a flabby thing the size of a small hill. She could see Chief Tarker and the warlock Gaven now, whacking away with clubs at a host of yapping animals with huge teeth.

She ran, and was finally able to see Wulf.

He was still standing! He saw her and waved. Sassa sighed with relief. Then she saw the snake. The giant reptile, thicker than Chogolisa's torso, was slithering up and along the arch, winding around it like some climbing weed. It was very long, it was very black and its head was larger that a buffalo's.

"Someone help Wulf!" she shouted again, but everyone was busy.

She reached for her dropped bow, but it slipped from goo-coated fingers.

By the time she managed to grasp her bow, Wulf had seen the snake. He was bouncing from foot to foot, hammer ready.

The snake was huge. And Sassa's fucking fingers were too slippery to grip an arrow.

She wiped them on her cotton trousers, looking about for help.

The snake writhed closer, the front of its body on top of the Great Worm, the rest wrapped around it. Wulf raised Thunderbolt.

And Sassa relaxed.

She was wrong to be worried about him. It was even insulting to be so desperate to get help to him. She thought of her *help Wulf!* cries and was embarrassed.

He was a great warrior. He'd fought who knew how many of the vile creations, all the while balancing on that arch, and prevailed. While she'd been busy getting covered in monster yuck, he'd probably dispatched more serious opponents than a snake.

Still, it was very big.

It reared its head and flicked dozens of forked tongues.

Wulf smashed Thunderbolt into its jaw.

It screamed – such a scream that she could hear it above all the other monster yells – and recoiled.

Wulf stepped in to finish it.

The snake reared again, flicking multiple tongues.

The tongues leapt out of its mouth.

The tongues latched onto Wulf's arms, legs and neck. They weren't tongues. They were two-headed snakes, like the one Nether Barr had thrown at an attacker.

Wulf prised a snake from his neck and threw it away. He gripped one that had latched onto his arm, but he didn't have the strength to wrench it off.

His arms fell to his side, hammer dangling. He turned, shoulders slumping, and looked at Sassa.

He held her eye for a moment, smiled, mouthed something that looked like "Wootah" and toppled forwards off the arch.

Sassa ran, dodging creatures that snapped and slashed.

She found the coffin first, lying on slickrock, still intact. *Tough box,* she found herself thinking, ridiculously.

Wulf was nearby, lying on red sand. *Could the sand have cushioned his fall?*

His skin was grey and his eyes were closed. The snakes were gone, but there were small circles of blood on his new white trousers and shirt.

"No!" Sassa yelled.

She tossed her bow aside and leapt onto him, not caring that there were creatures bent on killing her all around. She felt his neck. Nothing. She put her ear to his open lips. No sound, no motion. She grabbed his shirt and shook him.

"Sassa."

It was Yoki Choppa. He put his blowpipe to his lips, shot what looked like a giant, inside-out caterpillar that was slithering towards them, then crouched next to her and Wulf.

"Please make him live," she sobbed.

Yoki Choppa poked a finger into Wulf's mouth and held still. Then he shook his head. "I'm sorry."

"No!" shouted Sassa.

She saw through tears that the others had arrived and were standing uselessly, watching her.

"You!" she pointed at the Wormsland warlock. She'd forgotten his name. "Do something!"

He shook his head.

"Sofi?" she implored.

The best warrior in the world shook her head, too. *She was only good for killing!* Sassa's rage swelled and then dissolved.

More of the group arrived, staring at her in sorrow and pity. She fell onto Wulf's unmoving chest and sobbed.

# Chapter 7

## Magnificent Worm

Sassa must have fallen asleep – Fraya knew how. She woke to Wulf's smell and had a moment's bliss before she remembered he was dead.

She sat. Wulf looked grey and dead. It was nearly dark. Wulf's last day alive was coming to an end. She touched her husband's cheek. It was cold.

Sofi should have gone for the box. Or Paloma. But it wasn't their fault that Wulf had insisted. Sassa should have stopped him herself. That's what wives were for – that's certainly what Wulf's wife was for. He always leapt before he looked. Her duty was to look for him and to hold him back when necessary.

She'd failed.

"*You die when you die,*" she said, out loud. Hardworkers did not mourn their dead.

It seemed the Wootah did, though, thought Sassa, as a huge sob welled up from her stomach.

Wulf wouldn't see his baby! Wulf would have loved his baby. She pictured a tiny human hand clasped round Wulf's finger while he beamed down, eyes shining with joy. She sobbed all the more.

After she didn't know how long, she looked up.

She started. Finn was sitting on a rock five paces away.

"How dare you!" she raged.

"We've taken it in turns—" he stuttered.

"Spunk on a fucking skunk. You've been spying!"

"No . . . no. I'm guarding you and . . . Wulf. It's dangerous here."

She saw now that his sword was unsheathed and across his lap.

"Sorry." She shook her head. "Are there more monsters?"

"No. The ones we didn't kill died, then most of them melted into the ground. A few of the bigger ones left bodies behind."

"I see." She looked down at Wulf. He'd been killed by a monster made out of the land. She wondered what he'd have said about that.

"Shall we go back to the others?" Finn asked.

The rest of them, plus the warlock Gaven and Chief Tarker, looked up as she climbed down the gully side into the sandy clearing.

There was meat roasting on the fire.

Life went on.

Erik nodded to Sassa. He picked up a sturdily constructed wooden frame, about the right size for carrying a body, then headed off up the hill. Chogolisa and Finn followed.

Sassa realised she was standing there like an idiot and everyone was trying not to stare. All apart from Ottar, that is. He was sitting on the sand and apparently finding out how many stones he could cram into his mouth in one go. Sassa envied his obliviousness.

She caught Paloma Pronghorn's eye and the speedy Owsla woman patted the rock next to her. Sassa walked across and sat, thinking that she'd never before seen Paloma sitting down during the day.

"It may not be the end for Wulf," said Paloma.

Sassa looked at her. What kind of fresh nonsense was this?

Paloma nodded to where Nether Barr was standing on the edge of the group. The hardy lady's weathered face looked a little less angry in the soft evening light.

Nether Barr gestured with her head. Sassa got up and went over.

"Follow me," said Nether Barr. "And eat this. You'll need strength." She handed her a crispy little lizard.

"What about the rest? And Wulf?"

"They'll follow and bring him." The elderly lady set off.

Sassa looked at Paloma, who winked. The rest of the group nodded encouragement, apart from Sofi who wouldn't meet her eye.

"What's going on?" asked Sassa, ducking to avoid a cactus hanging from a rock.

"I lived here with the Popeye tribe for a while. I had a Popeye lover."

"Did you?" Sassa asked, wondering what the fuck this had to do with anything, and why she was having a chat when she could have been spending her last moments with Wulf's body.

Nether Barr continued, very much as if Sassa's husband hadn't just been killed. "I met a Popeye man called Sealter at a gathering in the Pothole village when I was a little younger than you. He loved me, so I thought. But he was also attracted to younger women. Girls. Maybe he did love me, but he couldn't help what he was."

"Oh?" said Sassa, still wondering why she was listening to this, as well as taking issue with the idea that people couldn't help what they were. Surely helping what you were was pretty much what life was all about?

"I became pregnant. Before I could tell Sealter, a man accused him of sleeping with his daughter. Others came forward. It was soon clear that Sealter had had various degrees of contact with more or less everybody's daughters. He was good-looking and charming, so most of the girls, if not all, had been willing. But they were too young to know their minds. As a general rule, one shouldn't shag children."

"No, indeed," said Sassa, while her brain screamed, *Why am I listening to this now?*

"Sealter was remorseful. However, the chief said he had to die. Most agreed. I certainly did. The warlock suggested an alternative."

The red sandy path crested a rise and Sassa looked back. Owsla and Calnians were a hundred paces behind. Wulf was on the litter, borne by Keef and Erik, his hammer strapped to his chest. The men were struggling. Wulf would find that funny, thought Sassa, and he'd be touched that they were making the effort.

"An alternative?" Sassa asked.

"The morning that the chief made his pronouncement," continued Nether Barr, "a girl called Hampsee whom Sealter had abused was bitten by a rattlesnake."

"This is a fascinating story," said Sassa, "but I'd really like to—"

"Bear with me. You will see the point. The girl died. The Popeye warlock, whose name I forget – age does that to you – had heard things about the Magnificent Worm from the previous warlock."

"Is the Magnificent Worm better than the Great Worm?" Sassa asked, despite herself.

"It's different. Not as long but more spectacular. I thought you were keen to get to the point?"

"I am. Sorry."

"The Magnificent Worm, so the idea goes, pulls magic from deep in the earth, like a magic sponge. Sealter, the warlock said, should lie that night with the corpse of the dead girl in the hollow next to the Magnificent Worm. If he slit his own throat with rock chipped from the arch, so the theory went, his life would be transferred to the girl by morning."

"What?" Sassa blinked.

"He'd die. She'd come back to life."

"Oh."

"Sealter agreed to do it." Nether Barr looked ahead as if peering into the past. "Possibly he wanted to make amends. Possibly he didn't want to be pinned out on the desert floor to be eaten alive by animals, which was the alternative.

"The girl's father took some persuading to let Sealter lie next to his daughter again. There was even a fight between the father and the mother's brother, which the father lost when the brother kicked him in the balls. These were not the Popeyes' most glorious days.

"Now I think about it, they were an unpleasant people all round. I thought I'd picked the best of them and he turned out to be a child molester. I didn't shed a tear when I heard they'd been driven from their land. Given the amount of help that the Potholers and Cloud Tribe sent when Tarker and her lot invaded – which was none – it seems nobody liked them much."

"So what happened? Did Hampsee come back to life?"

"I'm getting there. By nightfall everyone was persuaded. Hampsee was laid in the hollow. Sealter chipped a shard from the Magnificent Worm and lay next to her. Her mother sat by the arch and waited. The Popeye warlock – what *was* his name? – said whoever loved the deceased most should be the only person up there. He said it was part of the legend. I suspect he wanted the mother and her bow up there to make sure Sealter didn't flee, while preventing the father from keeping vigil. The father was an idiot and would have mucked it up."

Nether Barr started as something large leapt from the bushes ahead. It was a lion, a large male. Sassa reached for her bow, but the big cat took a languorous look at the women then padded off in the same direction they were headed, huge paws silent on the soft sand.

"Now, where was I?" said Nether Barr, following after the lion. Sassa kept and arrow strung, but the animal didn't seem interested in them.

"You were about to tell me if it worked."

"It did. Hampsee and her mother came walking down the hill at dawn the next day."

"And was Hampsee the same?"

"As far as I know. I went back to Bighorn Island that morning. But I did return maybe fifteen years later and Hampsee had children of her own and seemed normal. Or at least as normal as anybody is. I guess she lived until she died with the rest of the Popeye, but I don't know."

They walked on in silence for a while. The sounds and smells of the desert night grew louder and stronger, but the moon was bright. Both women were wary. They couldn't see the lion any more, but there were plenty of other nocturnal desert creatures that could kill them. There were plenty of diurnal creatures that could kill you, too, but it was easier to see those coming.

"So we're heading to the Magnificent Worm now to try to revive Wulf," said Sassa eventually.

"They build them bright where you're from," smiled Nether Barr.

"Do you really think it could work?"

"Hampsee was dead. I saw her. Then she was alive. So yes, it could work."

Sassa felt a flash of hope. However – and it was a very big, plan-buggering however – one vital ingredient was missing.

Did Nether Barr and the others expect Sassa to sacrifice herself?

She would have done it in a shot if she hadn't been pregnant (or *at least you can say you would have*, said the most cynical recess of her mind). But, no, she couldn't kill the growing baby in exchange for Wulf, especially when the only suggestion that it might work came from this potentially badger-shit crazy old woman.

If not Sassa, then who? None of the Calnians. Why would they? Finn? Keef? Thyri? No, no and no. Even if someone did volunteer, Sassa couldn't allow it. Wulf wouldn't have allowed it. He'd rather have stayed dead.

"You are now wondering," said Nether Barr, "who will kill themselves so Wulf can live?"

"They breed them bright where you're from, too."

Nether Barr sucked her teeth. "The Popeye tribe aren't all dead. Tarker's tribe kept some for slave labour. They do all the hardest, dirtiest work. Tarker has offered one of these in exchange for Wulf."

"No." Sassa shook her head.

"Wulf will live. The victim will be freed from—"

"Sorry to be crude, but no fucking way." Tears came to her eyes again. To have hopes raised and dashed was almost unbearable. "Wulf would never forgive me. I'd never forgive myself," she managed.

"Please don't cry," said Nether Barr. "Wulf is coming back. There are no Popeye slaves. I made them up. I wanted to see what kind of person you are."

"Oh."

"I will die for Wulf," said Nether Barr.

Sassa stopped and rubbed her eyes. Nether Barr was still walking. Sassa jogged to catch up. "You can't," she said.

"I don't need your permission. The other Wootah agreed while you slept."

"It's not up to them, Wulf is—" She stopped. Wulf wasn't hers. He was as much theirs. "Why?" she asked. "I'm asking because I'm interested to know. There's still no way you can do it."

"I had you right, Sassa Lipchewer. The rest of your tribe agreed much more readily. I guess I'm just a useless old woman to them, so near death that it doesn't matter."

"I'm sure that's wrong. It must have been because they love Wulf so much and don't know you so well."

"And now you're defending them," Nether Barr smiled. "You're good."

"I'm not. I have killed people."

"You've defended yourself."

"No, I've murdered two men. With one of them – Garth Anvilchin – it was his life or another's. But the other . . ." She thought of Hrolf the Painter. She remembered watching his expression change as she'd pushed her knife into his neck. "I killed the other guy because I didn't like the way he looked at my tits."

"Do you regret it?"

*Good question*, thought Sassa. She mused for a moment.

"No," she decided.

"Good!" Hearing that Sassa was a murderer seemed to have tickled Nether Barr. "And now I mean to die, and I have good reasons."

"You cannot do it."

"Hear me out. There are three reasons I'm giving myself for Wulf. The first is that my mother died aged ninety, her mother aged eighty-nine, her mother aged eighty. I am eighty-eight. So I don't have long left. Wulf will hopefully have many more years than me."

"But won't he just get the years you have left?" Sassa heard herself saying. *Was she really considering this?*

"No, I remember the Popeye warlock whatshisname explaining. The life force itself transfers. The amount of years left are entirely down to the ageing and decay of the revived person's body."

"You can't know you'll die at the same age as your mother."

"True. That's the weakest reason. The next is that I love children. I want you to have a child like I didn't, and I want that child to have a father, like mine wouldn't have done. Did I mention that I was pregnant when Sealter was forced to kill himself?"

"You did."

"I killed that baby before it was born. I've carried that weight all of my life. Now I can do something to make amends before I die. That's my third reason. It trumps both the others and wins the argument."

"But—" Sassa managed.

"But nothing. If it makes it easier for you, I'll give you a condition. You must call the child Nether Barr."

"Of course," said Sassa. If Nether Barr really was set on this . . .

"Good. It's not just your child I want to save. You will face more monsters, disasters and hardships before you complete this quest. I want you to succeed because I want you to save all the children, not just your own. I'm not an outwardly sentimental person, Sassa, but it makes me cry to think how many children that evil Warlock Queen has killed already, and how many more will die if she is not stopped."

They turned off the main path. "We're a little over halfway there," said Nether Barr. "Wulf the Fat, the hero with his mighty hammer, will be a much greater help in achieving that quest than I will."

"He's already managed to die once," said Sassa.

"He'll be more careful next time."

*Next time*, thought Sassa. Was this really going to happen?

"There's a fourth reason," said Nether Barr. "I should have stopped Sealter from hurting those poor girls."

"Did you . . . know?" asked Sassa.

"There were signs. He was always so keen to be with girls. He built canoes for them and took them off downriver. He taught them foraging and hunting by taking them on long trips into . . ." she shook her head. "I should have seen what he was doing. I am partly responsible."

"You are not," said Sassa. "Not in the slightest."

"I've always felt guilty. But maybe you're right. It's moot anyway. I killed my baby. It is a weight I can no longer bear. That's why I'm doing this."

The sandy path led to a long slickrock slope.

"Up here, round a corner, and we're there," said Nether
Barr. "It's about a mile. Funny to be walking to one's death.
I've walked so many miles, but this will be my last. Most odd."

"Nether Barr, you can't do it." Sassa shook her head. "You
die when you die, not when you choose to."

"No more protest. I am doing it. I have no close family,
nobody to remember me. Will you remember me always,
Sassa Lipchewer?"

"Of course."

"Tell you what, I'll raise my barter. Not only will the
child, boy or girl, be called Nether Barr, but you will tell
the child why they have that name and you and they will
remember me for ever. Will you do that?"

"No, because it's not going to happen."

"Say for the sake of argument that it is going to happen,
would you name your child after me, tell them about me,
and remember me for ever?"

"Of course."

"Good. That's settled. Now tell me about the man you
killed – Hrolf the Painter."

"It's not settled."

"Hrolf the Painter, please."

Sassa shook her head. They were halfway up the slickrock
slope. She couldn't let Nether Barr die for Wulf.

But she was still walking.

"Hrolf was attacked by a bear, shortly after we all left our
village, Hardwork," she said.

"What was Hrolf like?"

Sassa shuddered. "He was the most lecherous man alive.
When he looked at you, you could feel his eyes creeping up
under your clothes like worms."

"I know the type."

"I'm sorry to hear it. So, the bear ran away, leaving Hrolf
horribly injured. But not dead, not dead at all. Nobody was
nearby and I suddenly had the idea to kill him."

"Gosh."

"Yes. So I took my knife –"

Sassa continued the tale as the two women walked side by side up the hill, Calnians and Wootah following behind with Wulf's body.

The final section of track was narrow, high enough above bare rock to kill any normal person who fell. As Sassa finished telling Nether Barr about Hrolf, she realised she had hardly noticed a drop which would have given her the willies a moon before.

The Magnificent Worm soared skyward from the side of the hill. All the other arches Sassa had seen, and she'd seen a few, looked like they were part of the landscape, the remnants of a block of rock that had mostly fallen away. This one stood alone, sprouting ridiculously from the rock; a twenty-pace-high stone bridge of shouldn't-be-there.

A wind-smoothed arena lay before the Magnificent Worm, as if carved for spectators to sit and admire it. To the right was a basin, dark in its depths.

Finn and Thyri carried Wulf's body down into the hollow while Nether Barr used Thunderbolt to smash a shard of rock from the base of the Magnificent Worm.

Sassa went over to join everyone else. Sofi wasn't with them. Sassa wondered why.

"I can't let her do it," she said to Sitsi.

"Ayanna died to save us from the thunder lizard. Sometimes sacrifice is necessary."

It sounded to Sassa like Sitsi was trying to convince herself. "That was one for many who weren't already dead," she said. "This is very different. It probably won't work anyway."

"Yoki Choppa?" Sitsi turned to the warlock.

"I've heard Sealter and Hampsee's story before, from a

warlock who was convinced it was true. Nether Barr believes she saw it happen."

"So you don't die when you die!" Keef grinned.

"Not the time, Keef," scolded Sitsi.

Sassa looked from person to person. This was all a little surreal. Was it a dream?

"Right you lot," said Nether Barr, returning with a wicked looking triangle of rock in her hand. "Off you bugger. Leave Sassa, me and the dead fellow."

"Nether Barr," said Sitsi. "Are you certain?"

"Yup. Now go."

Nether Barr took Sassa's hand. They walked down into the basin.

The declivity was oval, with concentric red rings in the rock walls decreasing in size down to its base where Wulf lay alone, a silhouette in the moon shadow. They'd taken him off his litter and stripped him. It shouldn't have been a surprise, she guessed he needed to be touching the magical rock – but she didn't like it. Despite his size, he looked vulnerable.

There was a dark pile nearby. Wulf's clothes. Finn and Thyri had left them for when he woke up.

Sassa bent to hug Nether Barr. The old woman felt hollow and smelled of dried leaves.

"Are you sure?" she said.

There were tears in Nether Barr's eyes. She looked up at the moon, then at Sassa.

"I'm scared now," she said, "but I want to do this. For me, for my baby. Maybe I'll see him. Maybe he'll forgive me."

Sassa nodded.

"Go now," said Nether Barr.

Sassa gripped the old lady's hands one last time then walked away.

Keef the Berserker was standing by the arch of the Magnificent Worm with a bundle in his arms. The rest of them had gone.

"I hope this works," he said.

"Me, too," said Sassa. She wasn't sure that she meant it. She'd felt the magic of the place as soon as they'd arrived – or some kind of force anyway. It wasn't just the Magnificent Worm. The slickrock around thrummed with something she'd never felt before – something powerful and good. She'd begun to believe that it might actually work. But what, exactly, would come back to life? Would it be Wulf? Or a stumbling husk of a man? Or would he be half Nether Barr – stroppy, solitary and obsessed with the pursuit of lizards?

"It'll get cold. You should take this." Keef held out a blanket, which Sassa recognised as Chogolisa's massive Owsla poncho.

"Chogolisa will need that."

"Tarker's village is nearby and they have spare tents, apparently. And besides, I think Chogolisa is too big to feel the cold."

"I don't need it, but thanks." Sassa wanted to be cold. Nether Barr was probably stabbing a rock shard into her neck at that very moment. The least Sassa could do was be uncomfortable in sympathy.

"I'll put it over here," said Keef. "I'll come back up here first thing, but if Wulf wakes up before that and you need to get to the village, go down the bare rock slope we walked up, then turn east along the path we came on."

"Thanks, Keef."

The one-eyed man nodded, smiling reassuringly, and began to walk away.

"Let's hope," he said, turning, "that you don't die when you die."

Sassa sat under the arch. She drew her knees up to her chest. It was quite cold. After a couple of hundred heartbeats, she got the blanket. It would be bad for the growing baby if she caught a chill. Nether Barr wouldn't mind.

She heard a cry from the basin. She wanted to rush down there. But no, Nether Barr had been clear. She must wait under the arch.

She sat.

Shamefully, she slept. She dreamed about the Warlock Queen standing atop her triangular tomb, commanding armies of half-dead Wulfs to spread over the world and kill every living thing. She saw the Wulf-beasts slaughtering animals by the million, burning the trees, clogging rivers with their stinking waste, killing all the Scraylings with disease and violence.

Half aware she was in a nightmare, she forced herself awake. Clouds had blown over. It was very dark.

There was a figure halfway across the sweep of rock that led to the arch. Sassa gasped, then realised it was too small to be Wulf.

"Freydis!"

"Sorry, Sassa Lipchewer!" The girl jogged up to her, waggling her hands. "I was down in the village and I was worried – we saw a big lion on the way down the hill – and I came back to protect you." She pointed a thumb at the bow on her back. "I'm sorry, I know it was just meant to be one of you up here and—"

"Shush. Nether Barr thought that part of the story was nonsense. I'm glad you're here."

"Oh good. Have you been down—" she jinked her head towards the dark bowl "—there?"

"No. I think if he comes back—" the idea that Wulf was going to be revived seemed ridiculous now "—it will be at dawn." She looked to the dark east. "We've got a while."

"Shall I go?"

"No, stay with me. I don't want you walking down to the village on your own."

"I have my bow!"

"Even with your bow."

\*   \*   \*

Sassa woke again as the sky was lightening. The chill was in her bones, despite Chogolisa's large blanket.

Freydis had gone. She worried about the girl for a moment, then decided that she was probably fine. There wasn't much she could do if she wasn't.

Wulf hadn't come to her. But, technically, it wasn't dawn. The sky was light but the sun wasn't up yet.

It was cold. Sassa felt like she was being watched and wondered if Freydis was spying from somewhere.

She watched the rim of the basin, willing Wulf's shaggy head to appear.

It didn't.

The sky brightened, the air warmed. Blazing sunlight stuck the tops of the bare rock hills around and raced downwards as if it were setting the red rock alight.

Wulf didn't come. Of course it hadn't worked. There were tales of gods bringing people back to life, but they weren't gods.

She blinked away tears.

She'd wait until the sun's rays reached her, she told herself.

Light descended the arch, far too fast. She closed her eyes but all too soon felt the unwelcome warmth on her face.

The sun was undeniably up. It was time to check, time to find out, time to know it hadn't worked. She stood.

"Come out, Freydis!" she called, "I know you're there!"

Nobody appeared.

She walked down into the basin. Maybe she'd find Nether Barr asleep.

Wulf lay there still – of course he did – naked and cold. Nether Barr lay next to him. Dark blood stained the rock around, but she looked calm.

The old lady's cotton trousers and woollen top were neatly folded and placed on the bare rock a couple of paces away. Her last act had been to fold her clothes, leaving them tidy.

Sassa tried to blink back tears but couldn't. Two wonderful people had died for nothing.

She put her face in her hands and sobbed.

She was startled by a growl. The lion! She jumped and looked around her. No animals. No Freydis or anyone else.

She heard the noise again and turned.

Wulf's chest rose. As it fell, she heard the growl again. She watched, open-mouthed. Another growl.

There could be no doubt about it.

Wulf the Fat was snoring.

Tears burst from her and she choked back a sob. She dropped to her knees, grabbed her husband by the skin of his hairless chest and shook him, noticing as she did so the bruises and double pricks of blood where the snakes had bitten him.

"What the Hel? Ow! Sassa!"

She stopped. Wulf blinked. "Ooof!" he rubbed his chest. "Wow that hurt. What the . . ." he looked around at the basin, at the arch towering above, at Nether Barr lying dead next to him.

He raised a quizzical eyebrow.

"You died," she said. "Nether Barr gave her life to bring you back."

"Okay. Sure. What?"

It took a good while for Sassa to recover and to explain to Wulf what had happened. She stressed how adamant Nether Barr had been, and explained her reasons. Wulf handled it much better than Sassa did. Soon he was comforting her and apologising for dying.

"Let's go and find the others," said Wulf eventually.

He dressed, then they dressed Nether Barr. Glad as she was about Wulf, Sassa was achingly, guiltily distraught about the woman's death.

"Right," said Wulf, scooping up the dead, light lady into his arms. "Shall we?"

Sassa stared at Nether Barr's body, shaking her head.

"She chose this," said Wulf. "She would have wanted us to grieve and we will. We will call our child Nether Barr as she asked, and we will think of her every time we say that name. But we will not be consumed by guilt. She would not want that, and it will tear us apart if we are."

"But—"

"Guilt is self-destructive and pointless, Sassa. Nether Barr gave me my life back," he grinned his wolfish, naughty grin, the one Sassa had fallen in love with. "And I intend to make the most of it. Not to mope. It's what she'd want."

Sassa nodded, feeling far from comforted.

She walked down the slickrock hill next to Wulf, who carried Nether Barr. She felt otherworldly, as if Wulf's death had been a dream. No, it was more like she was dreaming now. She pinched her arm, expecting to wake in the cold night with Wulf dead in the hollow.

But no, they walked on, through the increasingly hot day – the first day of the rest of Wulf's second life.

"What was Valhalla like?" she asked.

"Tor told me not to tell you."

"You have to keep it a secret from the living?"

"No, just you."

"Seriously, what did you see or . . . was there anything?"

"I didn't know I was dead until you told me. I remember fighting the big snake. Next thing, you were trying to pull the skin off my chest."

"No Valhalla?"

"No anything."

"Nail a quail."

"But I don't think I was properly dead. You die when you die. I didn't."

"I suppose so."

\*    \*    \*

The rest of the Wootah and Calnians appeared from the valley, heading uphill towards them. They were all there, including Freydis.

Wulf raised his arms. "Wooooooo-tah!" he shouted.

"Wootah!" shouted everyone, apart from Sofi and Yoki Choppa.

All the shouters began to run up the hill. Paloma Pronghorn arrived a couple of heartbeat later, towing Freydis. Sassa wondered how Freydis had gained the strength to hold on like that, and to move her legs so fast. Also why she'd gone all the way back to the village alone, when she'd said that she was protecting Sassa. What had the girl been doing up there?

Paloma hugged Wulf, then held him at arm's length, looking him up and down. "Death suits you," she said. "I think you've lost some weight. You diet when you die."

Freydis smiled up at Sassa. "I'm glad it worked," she said.

# Chapter 8

## Red River Ruined

They said goodbye to Chief Tarker and Gaven the warlock the following morning. It was an odd one for Finn the Deep. Sassa and Wulf hugged Tarker and Sofi held the chief's eye in a meaningful but tough way, as if they'd all been through a major trial together. Which they had. But Finn hadn't spoken to Tarker or Gaven the whole time, so he had to fake his "aren't we close now, what a shame to be parting" goodbye. Tarker, Gaven and, of course, Thyri all gave him odd looks as if he'd done the wrong thing.

It was unsettling, but he soon forgot about it because he couldn't stop staring at Wulf. The Wootah chief was striding along with the same easy half-smile on his face as ever. He looked exactly the same.

But was he the same? He'd died, for the love of Loakie! Were there invisible demons on his shoulders? Was he a demon?

Meanwhile, Ottar dashed about, pulling at everyone's clothes and then looking around with his arms outstretched and palms upward. Everyone knew he was asking where his new friend Nether Barr was, but everyone was pretending they had no idea what Ottar wanted. Or at least that was Finn's take on it. Maybe everyone else didn't understand him and it was just Finn who was being the cowardly shit and not explaining what had happened.

In the end Freydis told Ottar that Nether Barr had gone

back to where she came from. That stopped him crying, but
he was still miserable. Inadvertently, thought Finn, the girl
had been very profound.

The Wootah breakfasted with the Wormslanders, then
they put Nether Barr on a pyre and set light to her. Luckily
Ottar was too busy netting lizards and letting them go to
notice the funeral activity. He was getting much better at
catching lizards, but Finn didn't see the point if he was going
to let them all go.

While they stood in respectful silence around the roaring
pyre, Finn looked at Paloma Pronghorn. She was beautiful
and lithe as the lion they'd seen the night before. She hadn't
spoken more than a couple of words to him since they'd all
got back together, so it wasn't clear if his policy of being
cool with her was working or not.

Afterwards, Chief Tarker gathered the Wootah and Calnians.

"The Meadows are almost five hundred miles to the
south-west," she said. Finn groaned. "The Red River runs
near to The Meadows," she continued, "so I suggest building
rafts and taking that route."

Finn almost choked. Raft travel on the Red River was a
doddle! They could just sit down and fish for a few days
and they'd be at The Meadows. Finally, the end was in sight.

At the news that they'd be heading along the river, Ottar
leapt about and shook his head. He gabbled something at
Freydis.

"Ottar says the Red River has gone bad," Freydis explained
matter-of-factly.

"Tell him we'll try, and if it seems dangerous we'll come
off it," said Wulf.

Freydis did, but Ottar was having none of it.

"You can ride with me in my awesome canoe," announced
Keef.

Ottar shook his head all the more.

"Isn't my canoe awesome, Sitsi?"

"It is awesome," Sitsi confirmed.

"How about we go and have a good look at the river, Ottar, then decide?" asked Wulf.

Ottar shook his head all the more, but Wulf announced that they'd go and look at the river.

Wulf shouldn't have asked a question when he'd already decided the answer, thought Finn. It was maybe a little unlike him, but not quite a sign that he'd become a demon from Hel. More likely he was tired.

They collected the child's coffin. They'd left it on the route back to the Red River, at what Gaven the warlock had told them was a safe distance from the Great Worm.

Finn wasn't sure. The coffin felt wrong. He reckoned that the evil, malevolence or whatever it was that had turned rock and plants into monsters came from the coffin.

And by the way everyone stood and stared at the box, they felt the same.

It was plain, dark wood banded with rusted iron. Finn had never seen iron worked like that by any of the Scrayling tribes they'd visited. It looked like something from the old world. Which was odd.

"Shall we open it?" he asked nobody in particular. No one bothered to answer. He hated it when that happened.

"Is it safe?" asked Keef. "I'll be fine if monsters burst out of the ground again, and Arse Splitter will love it, but some of you might have trouble and it would be a shame if Wulf got killed again. It slows us up."

Everyone looked at Yoki Choppa.

He shrugged.

"I brought it from the Great Worm," said Chogolisa, "and it didn't do anything to me. I'm happy to carry it on my shoulder again."

"All right for now," said Sofi. "When we get to the river we'll lash it to its own raft."

\* \* \*

Paloma Pronghorn ran and ran, towing Freydis. They went under arches, through arches, up onto fins of rock, then back to the arches. She liked this landscape, particularly the arches, and she didn't like being near the coffin, so she kept running.

They arrived on a high bank over the Red River. It smelled bad. She felt her skin tingling in the same way as it did when she was near the coffin. Or possibly she was being paranoid and the stink was a rotting buffalo corpse stuck under the bank below.

"It's the river," said Freydis.

"Smelly water?"

"Smelly poison."

Paloma walked up the low, rock riverbank a couple of hundred paces, Freydis jogging alongside. The smell was the same. It did seem to be coming from the water itself.

They waited for the others.

Ottar pulled Sofi back from the river and hopped about, yelling "Way! Way!"

"Stay away from the river," translated Freydis.

"Wash! Wash!" he cried.

"Watch?" asked Sofi.

The girl nodded.

The boy took Erik's hand and pointed at a thick stand of small-leaved plants.

"He wants you to cut a long stem from one of those tall bushes," said his sister.

Erik took his obsidian blade from his belt and did as he was asked.

"In ribba! In ribba!" said Ottar.

"Now dip—"

"I get it," said Erik.

He lay on his front on the rock riverside. Paloma and the others craned to watch. The brown water churned a pace and a half below. The water looked odd. It had a shine that reminded Paloma of Beaver Man's skin.

Erik dipped the frond. The water bubbled, fizzed and smoked. Erik pulled out the branch. A pace's length of leafy twigs had become a finger-length, burned point.

Everyone took a step back.

"My canoe!" moaned Keef. He'd left it tied up in the water downstream.

"Have you seen this before?" Sofi asked Yoki Choppa.

"No."

"Could it just be this part of the river?" she asked.

The warlock pouted back at her, dipping his head a little from side to side to indicate that he didn't know.

"Woll! Woll!" Ottar tugged at her breechcloth.

Sofi crouched and took his hands.

"All the way to The Meadows?" she asked.

Ottar nodded. "An mar."

"And more?"

The boy nodded again.

"Thank you, Ottar." Sofi stood. "I guess we're walking."

Paloma liked adventuring across the land more than most, but so much further on foot did not appeal. "It's five hundred miles!" she said.

"We'd better get started then." Sofi's tone was flat. "Chief Tarker said there's a bridge north of here."

Paloma ran to the bridge and amused herself waiting for the others by tossing pads of prickly pear into the water. They fizzled into a foamy piles of green bubbles then dispersed. Warlocks made liquids which melted matter, but an entire river?

The poisoning of the Red River was the worst of the Warlock Queen's depredations. If this spread – to the Water Mother, for example – it would kill far more people than any number of wasp men. If all streams and rivers became undrinkable, that was pretty much it for all life, human and animal.

Paloma had never considered the seriousness of their quest before. She had never considered the seriousness of anything much. Now she realised how important it was that they reached The Meadows with the coffin. But five hundred miles on foot across an increasingly dangerous land? They'd never make it.

She was amazed that more of the Wootah hadn't been killed in the attack at the Great Worm. They'd been lucky, then beyond lucky that Nether Barr had given herself for Wulf. Paloma didn't like that much. She liked Wulf, would have shagged him in a trice if he'd been unattached or she was sure they'd get away with it, but she wasn't sure about the old lady giving her life for him. He'd died. A second chance was unfair. Luby Zephyr and the rest of the dead Owsla women were still dead. Her sister was still dead.

The others arrived. Freydis skipped ahead and took Paloma's hand.

"Shall we cross first, Paloma Pronghorn?" she said.

The little girl looked up at her, chin jutting and brow knitted in seriousness, messy blonde hair shining in the sun. Paloma didn't like serious people as a rule. However, this small person, most sensible of the Wootah, had become about her favourite person in the world.

With Nether Barr gone, Ottar was their guide again.

He led them north-west. They were going this way to avoid deep chasms, he explained with gestures, and they would turn south-west before the day was out. Paloma understood him before Freydis translated. Not every word, but she got the gist.

The day was hot. Their caribou power animal – the only one that Yoki Choppa was also conditioned to – meant that it didn't affect the Calnians too much, but Paloma could see the Wootah were struggling. They didn't have much water because they'd been planning to drink from the Red River. Maybe, she mused, the Wootah would all die even sooner than she'd thought.

There were mountains in the distance where there would surely be water. Paloma could have run there and back with water skins, but it would probably have taken a day and she couldn't carry enough to make a huge difference.

She looked back. Keef was talking to Sitsi. Erik was walking with Chogolisa, the coffin on his shoulder now. By the look on his face, Erik felt the same about the coffin as Paloma did.

Wulf and Sassa seemed unaffected by the casket, and Wulf seemed unaffected by his resurrection. Sassa was affected by it, though. She was grinning like a loon.

All these couples.

Paloma looked at Finn, trudging along.

He wasn't repulsive, and maybe if he'd been nearer her age she might have considered him. Not that she put a barrier on age. Some nineteen-year-olds were more grown up that Paloma would ever be. And Finn had changed a lot since the day they'd met them on the edge of the Ocean of Grass – improved a lot – but he was still half-baked, more boy than man. So were Wulf and Keef, when you thought about it, but they carried it better. They were the fun, generous-spirited kind of childish, not sulky and solipsistic. So sure, Finn wasn't that bad any more, but there was no way she was getting together with him.

Behind Finn came Thyri Treelegs, striding along with a scowl on her face and her blade in her hand. She was two years younger than Finn, apparently, but character-wise she was years ahead. She was self-obsessed, too, but in a confident, sexy way. Push came to shove, thought Paloma, she'd kiss Thyri before she kissed Finn again.

\* \* \*

Finn the Deep thought he'd been thirsty before. He hadn't. Approaching sunset, his throat was scratchy and his lips puckered like a cat's bumhole. He felt sick and light-headed and, perhaps worst of all, his last piss had been viscous orange goo.

The Owsla were fine. Of course they were. Super-warriors didn't need something so mundane as water.

After they'd eaten, Yoki Choppa handed each of the Wootah a small stone wrapped in leaves. "Suck this," he said. "It'll ease the thirst."

"These stones really work," Finn said to Thyri a little while later, only because she happened to be the nearest person to him.

"Come with me," she said, standing.

"We cannot possibly train tonight."

"Just come."

He followed her. He had enough energy to think that he should be thinking lascivious thoughts, walking behind her swinging bottom and springy thighs, but not enough to actually think them.

She led him around a dome of rock and between a few clumps of high desert bushes. A coyote skedaddled. It was the first large animal Finn had seen all day, which was somewhat reassuring. First, there was life out here. Second, it didn't attack them so it wasn't starving.

"The Owsla have taken against us again," whispered Thyri, her voice harsh.

"You're wrong. They wouldn't. Sitsi's with Keef, Chogolisa is really into Erik and Paloma . . . well Paloma is lovely."

Thyri gave him a look that would have soured a sea of buffalo milk. Finn could have done with a sea of milk right then, now he thought about it. Soured would have been fine.

"They'll do what Sofi tells them to do and I think she still means to kill us. Maybe when the quest is completed but probably before."

"Why?"

"The empress ordered them to. Sofi isn't the sort to ignore an order."

"No way. We've come so far together."

"She is the sort to use someone until she doesn't need them any more."

"You really think she needs us?"

"The Warlock Queen needs Ottar, Fraya knows why, and we're tied in with that."

"I think you're wrong. We're pretty much the same tribe as the Owsla now."

"Don't kid yourself. Be on guard."

"And how do you guard against women that make Valkyries look like chumps?"

"We have to watch for the signs. We know they can die. We'll have to get them first. Maybe in their sleep, maybe another way."

"You're wrong, Thyri."

"You're blinded by lust."

"Come on, let's go back."

It was, Finn mused as he lay on his sleeping bag later, the first time ever that he, rather than Thyri, had ended a period of time alone together. He definitely wasn't in love with her any more. It was like part of his childhood had gone. Maybe his childhood was over. Finn the kid was gone. He supposed he should be glad, but it felt like someone had died.

# Chapter 9

## Goblins

Low on water, they set off in the dark to cover some ground before the heat of the day.

Dawn came like a furnace door opening. Soon it was the hottest day they'd encountered on their journey – the hottest Sitsi Kestrel had ever known. It *would* be the day they'd run low on water, she thought. It was the sort of thing the Wootah god Loakie would have engineered.

She was uncomfortably thirsty with a headache starting behind her eyes, so Innowak knew how the unenhanced Wootah must have been suffering.

She looked back to where Chogolisa was pulling the coffin on a sled. Erik had made the sled the night before, so that nobody had to carry the seemingly tainted coffin next to their heads.

"How are you feeling?" she asked Keef.

"Fine," he croaked.

The other Wootah wore the light leather hats given to them by the Pothole people, apart from Freydis who wore a huge bonnet made of reeds and Keef, who refused to cover his head. True warriors, he said, considered the head to be the least important part of the body and unworthy of protection.

A couple of moons of exposure to the sun had decreased his pastiness, which had been an improvement, but now it looked like his head had been baked. Add the effects of

dehydration, and he didn't look entirely unlike the mummi-
fied corpses that the warlocks had used for practice and
education back in Calnia.

The day wore on and heat flowed across the cracked, red
land like a liquid.

Chogolisa and Paloma were carrying the children while
Erik took a stint towing the coffin. Sitsi worried about pregnant Sassa. She was pink and struggling.

Finn and Thyri were shuffling along unhappily, and Wulf
and Keef didn't seem too much better. Erik was worst of all.
The big bearded Wootah was in trouble, stumbling every
few steps.

Sitsi skipped back to him.

"My turn with the coffin," she said.

"You sure?" he gasped.

"I'd like to." He handed her the ropes. She wouldn't be
as ready with her bow if trouble came, but she was worried
Erik might die if he towed it any further.

Their path joined a broader, relatively well-used track,
which took them up a short but steep slope to the edge of
a broad basin surrounded by a low cliff.

Sitsi thought for a flash that the basin was filled with
people, varying in size from Ottar height to taller than
Chogolisa, but the figures were towers of red-brown rock.
Even with her eyesight, she couldn't immediately tell if
they were natural features or long-weathered statues. They
were definitely made of rock – soft, muddy Badlands rock
mixed with the harder Wormsland rock by the looks of
things – but many of them had distinct facial features –
eyes, tongues, even teeth. Some looked like they were
wearing hats. Others perched in coagulated rows, lumpen
bodies topped with two, three or four faces on pointed
heads.

"Goblins," claimed Erik.

"Wartar," said Ottar, pointing. In the centre of the

statue-strewn declivity, next to a little mesa, was a low, regular circular wall around a small pond.

"A crowd of stone goblins with an unlikely pool in the middle," said Paloma. "There's no way this is a trap."

"Sitsi?" asked Sofi.

"Some of the towers are lifelike, but they are rock."

"There's no way, given what we've come across recently," said Paloma, "that they're going to turn into creatures that want to kill us."

"I hope they do," rasped Keef. "I like a fight before a drink."

"Ottar," Sofi asked, "do you think it's safe?"

The boy looked at the stone goblins but didn't say anything.

"Freydis?" asked Sofi.

"He doesn't know."

"Everyone quiet." The Owsla captain listened for a moment. "Paloma, run around the pond and back."

"So it's definitely safe for me?"

"Go."

Pronghorn returned heartbeats later. "All fine. The ground's weirdly soft, a bit like it was in the Badlands, but there's nothing dangerous down there."

Sofi nodded, "Okay. Don't rush to the water. I'll try it first. If it's all right, do not drink too quickly. Have only a few mouthfuls at first. You'll want to gulp a few skins' worth in one go. Don't."

The advice was good, thought Sitsi, but given brusquely. Sofi was definitely pissed off with the Wootah. Was it because Nether Barr had died for Wulf? Of all of them, Sofi was the only one who'd emphatically disagreed when Nether Barr had announced her plan, and she'd made herself scarce when it was carried out. She noticed Thyri glaring at Sofi — the animosity was not all one way. Sitsi didn't like the tension.

They walked down the track into the goblin world. There wasn't a plant to be seen, nor a blade of grass, nor any animal. The ground was pliant underfoot but there were no footprints. There were weird snake-like trails, and thousands of pock marks, as if someone had gone around jabbing the ground with forks.

Up close, the rocks were even more bizarre. They looked exactly like limbless, pustule-coated goblins. In places it was like mud creatures had stood on each other's shoulders and congealed into high walls of grimacing and grinning figures. Sitsi couldn't help but expect them to come to life and attack. How they'd attack without limbs, she didn't know. She didn't want to find out.

They made it to the low walled tank.

"Everybody wait," said Sofi.

She dipped her hand axe's head into the water and inspected it, then her little finger. She touched her finger to her lips, then scooped water with her hand and took a big sip.

"It's good," she announced.

Sitsi waited while the Wootah drank.

Sofi filled her skin then stood off to one side, listening and drinking. "Fill your skins before you drink much more," she said, "in case we need to run."

Sitsi could feel it, too. There was a presence. She found a space at the wall and filled her skin, all the while looking about herself.

She saw something move at the edge of the hollow.

"Sofi, movement two hundred paces north," she said.

"I heard it. Paloma, scout north and—"

There was a soft rumble followed by the patter of falling stones as a nearby rock demon crumbed.

*Oh no*, Sitsi strung an arrow. The rock fell away to reveal a writhing knot of black snakes. They were segmented, short and fat – the length and width of a big man's forearm – and headless. They weren't snakes. They were huge maggots, or worms. They tumbled to the mud ground, slithered over each other for a couple of heartbeats, then seemed to find purpose. They headed for the horrified humans. Mouths opened to reveal circles of slender white teeth.

"Fuck a duck," muttered Sassa.

Another goblin crumbled open. Then another, and another. More worms fell from some but different creatures tumbled from others. These second beasts were the size and colour of large green iguanas, but each had a snapping claw in place of a head, and eight multi-kneed, spider-like legs.

All the creatures, black worms and green spider-lizards, headed for the group by the pond. They made no sound other than their slithering and scuttling. It was sound enough.

Sitsi shot one of the spider-lizards. It flew back, skewered. So they were easy enough to kill, but it was pointless. There were hundreds of them. Thousands.

Calnians and Wootah struck at the advancing beasts, but had to dance backwards before the seething tide. More and more rock goblins cracked open, more and more creatures tumbled out. There were more than thousands, there were tens of thousands, all with jaws that looked like they'd give a vicious bite. Perhaps they were venomous.

There were so many now that new arrivals fell onto the already advancing surge and there was a sea of creatures several animals deep flowing towards them. The rock goblins were cracking open all over the basin. They were surrounded.

"Up here!" called Wulf. He was standing on the little mesa next to the pond with Sassa and Freydis. Sitsi and everyone else scrambled up to join him.

Their perch was maybe five paces across and two paces high. The sea of black and green monsters flowed against its base. A couple of the spider-lizards climbed its sides, but Finn and Thyri whacked them back with their blades. Sitsi unstrung her bow. It would be more useful as a staff. She held it up to Sassa, who nodded and copied her.

Only Keef's Arse Splitter could reach the beasts below and he was spearing them like a madman, but he wasn't even denting their numbers.

They were in trouble.

Yoki Choppa was sitting cross-legged, nursing a smoking concoction to life in his alchemical bowl. Sitsi hoped he was cooking up something amazing. Nobody else seemed to have any answers.

More goblin towers were crumbling. The sea of creatures was deeper and deeper. By the way both spider-lizards and worms were driving towards them and snapping at them, some urge was compelling them to attack the humans. There were so many that it wouldn't be long before the writhing sea reached the top of their mesa. Then, as far as Sitsi could see, they would die.

Chogolisa leapt backwards as the edge of their little mesa fell away, spilling a new mass of worms. Their very refuge was made out of a cluster of the creature's nests. Surely it wouldn't be long before the rest of it fell away and plunged them into the writhing mass of monsters.

The black and green snapping horde lapped at them in waves, higher and higher.

Then Yoki Choppa stood and flung the contents of his bowl down onto their attackers. Weird screams rang out as perhaps fifty animals convulsed then fell away. The gap they left was filled in a couple of heartbeats.

The warlock shrugged.

Not great, thought Sitsi.

"Paloma, could you run across them carrying Ottar?" asked Sofi.

"I don't want to."

"In theory?"

"I don't think so. They're too small to get purchase. And if I was carrying the boy I—"

She was interrupted by a rumbling roar.

The cliff to the east, the one that looked like a wall of melted goblins, burst outwards in a cloud of red sand. A giant, red-black crab emerged from the dust, broken rock cascading from its humongous carapace. It was ten paces high and twice that across. Black eyes on stalks were the size of bighorns and pincers were bigger than buffalos. Clacking those great grippers above its head, it charged.

"Eyes, Sitsi," said Sofi.

Sitsi restrung her bow, aimed and loosed in a trice. The arrow flew true, hit the crab's eye – and glanced off it. The crab did not appear to notice. She tried the other eye with the same result.

Meanwhile, the sea of spider-lizards and worms was rising around them. It was a toss-up as to whether the crab would get to them first or whether they'd sink under the tide of biting creatures.

"Paloma," said Sofi. "Pick up Ottar. Chogolisa, pick them both up and throw them as far as you can. Then throw the coffin after them."

"Really?" asked Paloma.

"Got anything else?"

"Ride the crab?"

They all looked at the giant beast. It had covered half the ground between the cliff and their perch. As if it had heard their plans, it lowered its claws towards the Calnians and Wootah and snapped them all the faster.

"Nope," said Sofi.

Sofi's plan was desperate and Sitsi didn't see how it could work, but she had no other suggestions.

"All right then," Paloma agreed. "Just don't hit me with the coffin, Chogolisa. Come here, Ottar."

"Nah!" Ottar shook his head and backed away.

"Sorry, kid, we've got to go."

Sofi strode around Finn, who was curled in a ball on the ground, hands clamped over his ears (*that kind of cowardice is unacceptable*, thought Sitsi) and made a grab for the boy.

Ottar dodged. The edge of the little mesa below him crumbled. He fell backwards into the mass of monsters.

Sofi dropped onto her chest and stretched her hand axe out to the boy. He got fingers to it, but the creatures shifted and he sank. Sofi leant further, but Ottar disappeared into the teeming mass.

Sofi tensed to leap after him, but Yoki Choppa crossed the mesa in two strides, shoved her back and flung himself off, arms stretched out like a cliff diver.

He brought his hands together, plunged into the monsters and disappeared.

Sitsi held her breath. There was no sign that anything was happening below the pulsing, teeming sea of monsters.

She nocked an arrow and drew, then loosened the string. She hated this impotence! She wanted to jump in after him, but what could she do?

Suddenly Yoki Choppa surfaced, gripping Ottar by the armpits. There was a black worm clamped to the warlock's cheek, blood pouring. A spider-lizard had its teeth in his neck.

He hurled Ottar towards the mesa. Sofi grabbed the boy's hand, yanked him out of immediate danger and plonked him onto the rock.

Yoki Choppa tried to leap, too, but the worms and spider-lizards surged, pushing him out and away, further from their sanctuary.

The Calnian warlock, co-creator of the Owsla, gave one final shrug, then vanished under the turbulent sea of beasts.

Sitsi very nearly jumped in after him. But it would have been suicide.

Sofi Tornado didn't think so.

She tied a rope around her waist in the blink of an eye, handed the end to Chogolisa and leapt. She disappeared, too, but sprang up immediately in a fountain of creatures.

Hand axe swinging and knife slashing faster than even Sitsi's eyes could follow, Sofi worked her way towards Yoki Choppa.

Freydis ran to leap after her, but Erik plucked her back. "Sofi's better at this sort of thing than you are," he said as she whacked at his arm.

Out in the lake of creatures Yoki Choppa resurfaced. He was much further away now, his face a mask of blood.

"Go back, Sofi!" he called. "Take Ottar to The Meadows."

Sofi was having none of it. She grunted and waded on, but there were half a dozen spider-lizards and black worms hanging by their teeth from each arm now. She could hardly move. Other beasts seemed to sense their chance and surged towards her like waves converging towards a stricken boat in a black sea.

Sofi went under. Sitsi expected her to spring back up, but she didn't.

Chogolisa heaved on the rope.

Way out in the sea of monsters now, bloodied Yoki Choppa regarded them serenely. He lifted his head, shouted "Wootah!" then fell under the tide.

Chogolisa heaved on the rope. Suddenly she fell back, the frayed end of the rope flying up into the air.

Sitsi and several other gasped. Then Sofi emerged from the pile of beasts with a scream of rage. Paloma and Sitsi dived in, grabbed a hand each and pulled her to safety. Sofi stood while Sitsi and Paloma plucked the worms and spider-lizards from her blood-slickened limbs and torso, crushing the beasts in their strong hands and throwing them back into the maelstrom. Despite all the cuts and blood Sofi didn't seem badly injured, but Sitsi had never seen such a look of pain on her captain's face as she stared out to where Yoki Choppa had gone down.

A scream rang out. Sitsi spun round to see Thyri beheading a spider-lizard whose teeth were clamped onto her calf.

Now more and more of the spider-lizards were clambering onto their ever-shrinking perch. The sea of creatures would soon be level with their refuge and the biting worms would follow. The giant crab advanced.

Sitsi whacked away with her unstrung bow, then jumped back as more of the little mesa crumbled under her. She almost fell over the balled-up Finn, then turned and kicked him. This was no time for him to lose his nerve. He stayed in his cowardly crouch and she kicked him again.

"Leave him!" shouted Erik. Neither was it the time for a father to be protective of useless offspring, but Sitsi desisted from kicking Finn and got back to whacking beasts.

She leapt back again as more rock crumbled. The worms were clambering onto the mesa now. She kicked five of them away but fifty more filled their places. She glanced left and saw Freydis shooting arrows uselessly into the mass.

The crab was five paces away.

"Paloma, grab Ottar. Chogolisa, throw them. Now!" Sofi shouted.

"Wait!" shouted Erik.

"What for?!" shouted Chogolisa.

The crab raised a giant claw, blocking the sun, ready to slam it down and crush them all. Sitsi had an almost over-whelming urge to dive out of the way, but the only place to dive was into the sea of worms and spider-lizards.

She closed her eyes, readying herself.

Nothing happened.

She opened her eyes.

The gigantic crab was beating itself with its mighty pincer. No, it wasn't beating itself, she realised. There were spider-lizards all over it, climbing through the gaps in its armour, through the plates that covered its mouth and into its maw.

The huge crustacean snapped at its own front legs, then collapsed sideways. The spider-lizards flowed over it.

Sitsi returned her attention to the immediate attackers and jabbed her bow at a spider-lizard, but it squeaked and fell back before she struck it. Two worms were clamped onto its back. More and more squeaks rang out all around. Beasts began to fall from the mesa. The lake of animals stirred and writhed, now more like choppy waters than the swell that had been rolling towards them.

The worms were attacking the spider-lizards.

The spider-lizards struck back, biting into black bodies and shaking their heads to sever the creatures.

"They're falling back!" shouted Wulf, sweeping Thunderbolt, scattering worms and spider-lizards.

The slithering sea of beasts ebbed as the creatures destroyed each other. The spider-lizards were the more powerful animals, but the worms outnumbered them fifty to one.

Wootah and Calnians watched the battle, apart from Finn, balled up and shaking on the ground. Paloma and Erik squatted next to him, each with a hand on his back. Sitsi finally understood. Finn hadn't been cowering in terror, he'd been trying to control the animals. And he'd succeeded.

"That's enough now, Finn," said Erik. "That's enough."

"Has it worked? Did I stop them?" Finn lifted his head. Before anybody could reply he coughed and heaved. Paloma and Erik hurried him to the side of the mesa, where he jetted watery vomit onto the dead creatures piled below.

*Do not drink too quickly*, thought Sitsi. The young Wootah man who'd just saved all their lives was puking because he hadn't listened to Sofi. Hero to idiot in a couple of heartbeats. He was good at that.

Sofi Tornado leapt off the mesa and ran to where they'd last seen Yoki Choppa, tossing aside creatures, living and dead. The others jumped down and helped her, apart from Erik who stayed with Finn and Sitsi who grabbed Freydis and Ottar and stopped them leaving the safety of the mesa – because nobody else had thought of the children.

The others cleared a space all around where Yoki Choppa had fallen. Not a hair, nor a scrap of his breechcloth was left – just a blood-dark stain on the soft rock.

The screaming of the beasts fell away. All the spider-lizards were dead. Some surviving worms wriggled to the crumbled goblin towers and burrowed into the earth.

The desert all around was a morass of green and black corpses, with a giant dead crab rising out of it.

Picking their way through the dead animals was gritty work, but soon they were walking south-west again with full water skins. There was nothing else to do. There was nothing left of Yoki Choppa for them to burn.

Sitsi fell in with Keef, bringing up the rear, scanning the scrubby desert for danger.

"I'm sorry about Yoki Choppa," he said.

"Me, too."

# Chapter 10

## Stung

Sofi Tornado walked ahead. Already, just a few dozen paces from the valley of the goblins where Yoki Choppa had died, the desert looked normal: low scrub, cactuses, jackrabbits and lizards. She could hear a coyote skulking in a nearby gulch.

Yet just behind them was a scene of carnage, where a giant crab lay dead amidst the corpses of thousands, maybe millions, of creatures unlike any she'd heard of before.

That was life. The banal shoulder-to-shoulder with the terrifying, freakish and tragic. Get on with your mundane life, experience shocking tragedy and horror, then return to your mundane life. So she walked on, back to the task of saving the world. Nothing was going to get in her way. She would take Ottar the Moaner to the Warlock Queen. He was their sacrifice. Sacrifices were necessary.

Yoki Choppa, along with the warlock Pakanda, had made the Owsla. While Pakanda had been like an abusive father, Yoki Choppa had been like a protective mother. After Pakanda's exile, Yoki Choppa had been both parents to the growing girls of the Owsla. He was restricted – certain things were expected of the Owsla and it would have been impossible to refuse them – but he'd protected them as much as possible.

When he'd finally got the Owsla away from Calnia, he'd removed rattlesnake from their diets and they'd regained much of the character that alchemical twisting had stripped away. He was the only person who'd ever cared for the Owsla, who hadn't used them for his own ends. In short, he was the only one who'd ever loved them.

And now he was dead because Ottar the Moaner was an idiot.

That was unfair. She'd frightened the boy and he'd reacted. Then she'd intended to go after Ottar but she'd hesitated when Yoki Choppa hadn't.

The warlock had flung himself so quickly down into the mass of deadly beasts, it was like he'd been waiting for the opportunity to die. She remembered his last moments. Had he tried to save himself at all? She pictured him as he'd gone under. Had that been a look of grim satisfaction on his face or was her memory playing tricks on her?

The Owsla that Yoki Choppa had helped to create had caused so much misery. They'd killed hundreds in battle and probably more for the titillation of the crowds in the Calnian arena. If this were a legend, the Calnian Owsla would not be the heroes, unless you started the tale the day after they met the Wootah.

She liked to blame the Wootah for their uselessness, for the deaths of their own – Bjarni Chickenhead and Gunnhild Kristlover – as well as hers – Talisa White-tail, Morningstar, Luby Zephyr, Ayanna and now Yoki Choppa. She was fairly sure she intended to kill them when the quest was done because Empress Ayanna had ordered it. But maybe the Wootah were the Owsla's atonement? She couldn't blame her women for their victims. They'd been conditioned mentally and physically from a young age to kill. They'd had no choice. Sofi, however, *could* blame herself. She'd been their captain, but it was more than that. She hadn't needed the alchemy to make her a killer. She'd killed animals often and enthusiastically before she'd even heard of Calnia. She still felt an urge to kill, while Paloma, Sitsi and Chogolisa all seemed to have lost their love of it.

Maybe Yoki Choppa had been destroyed by his guilt? He could have walked away. The moment Zaltan had announced he was gathering attractive girls to form an alchemically powered magic squad, Yoki Choppa could have packed up and made his life elsewhere.

Had he been looking for a chance to sacrifice himself?

And was she looking for the same thing?

It wasn't just the guilt for the past. Only she knew that they were taking the boy, the lovely little boy, to his death. And then she was meant to kill the rest of them. *Oh, how she envied Yoki Choppa.*

She spotted a rattlesnake skin lying on the ground. The snake had wriggled free of its skin and carried on.

She sighed. Perhaps the reason she hadn't killed herself already was the possibility that life continued after death. Not a great state of mind, she realised.

She stopped next to a heat-shattered red boulder.

"Wulf, can I talk to you?" she asked when he caught up.

They waited while the others came past. Last were Chogolisa and Erik, pulling the coffin on the sled.

Sofi shuddered as it passed. "Make sure everyone else gets a turn pulling the box," she called after them.

"It's not a bother," said Chogolisa.

"Oh, yes it is," Erik countered. "You know we don't like it. It's a great idea to get someone else to tow if for a while. PALOMA!"

"Shush! We don't need to burden others. If you don't like it, walk ahead."

"Well, I'm sorry I want to help, but you told me yesterday . . ."

When they could no longer hear Chogolisa and Erik's bickering, Sofi turned to Wulf. "What happened when you were dead?"

Wulf nodded as if he'd been expecting the question. "It was like being asleep but not as interesting. One moment I was standing on a rock bridge. The next Sassa was waking me up next to Nether Barr's dead body."

"Nothing else?"

Wulf looked up and sighed melodiously through his nose.

"There was more. But you don't want to know."

"Wulf, much as I'd like to be, I'm not afraid of anything in this world. If there's something in the next that's going to scare me I'd like to hear about it."

"That's the problem," Wulf shook his head, "I don't think it was in the next world. It was in this one. And we're heading for it."

"Tell me."

"I was a bird, flying above The Meadows."

"How did you know it was The Meadows?"

"Big black pyramid, shitloads of monsters stretching for miles in every direction around it. Some of them were huge, much larger than our crab friend back there. So many that I couldn't see the ground for miles in every direction around The Pyramid."

"And beyond that?"

"Brown and red mountains surrounding the basin."

Sofi nodded. It tallied with her vision.

"I could feel the minds of the monsters," Wulf continued, "as if they shared one mind. Strongest of all was the urge to kill, but there was more. They were waiting until there were even more of them, then they were going to head out and kill everything they found."

"And you think this is real?"

"I don't mean to sound like a dick, Sofi, but I *know* it was real. Or at least I think I'm certain. I could be wrong."

"Were there paths leading to The Pyramid? Any route in?"

"Nothing but a mess of monsters. The Pyramid was like

that chunk of rock we took refuge on back there, and the monsters were the worms and spider-lizards, but, like I said, a whole lot bigger."

"Anything else?" Sofi asked.

"There's one more thing. I felt the Warlock Queen's mind. I felt what you said, that she was mourning her missing child and raging, but there was more. I felt that . . . I . . ." Wulf wiped his eyes. *Was he crying?* "Sorry. I understood something that I didn't before."

"What?"

He set his jaw and looked ahead. "I know why we're taking Ottar to The Meadows."

Sofi nodded and they walked on in silence until Wulf asked, "Is there another way?"

"I mean to find one." Sofi realised that she meant it. She didn't want the child to die.

"Perhaps we could—"

Wulf stopped because Freydis and Ottar were waiting for them.

Sofi liked to think she was hard-hearted – she knew she was – but she couldn't look little Ottar in the eye.

"There are two routes we can take ahead, according to Ottar," said Freydis without preamble. She pointed. "It depends which side of that rise we go. One way is in the open, the other is along canyons. Some of them are narrow."

"Shall we put it to a vote?" asked Wulf as they approached the split in the path.

"Canyons," said Sofi.

"Me, too."

"Canyons it is then."

"I meant everybody could vote."

"No, let's not do that." Sofi felt strongly about voting. Some tribes made important decisions by asking the opinion of every adult: the children, too, in the really dumb tribes.

That was fine for decisions like what to have for breakfast, when everyone's view was as valid as everyone else's and the answer didn't matter. When the options demanded insight, experience and knowledge, however, asking people who didn't have insight, experience and knowledge was insanity. You'd do just as well throwing stones to pick at random. Better, in fact, since the majority of people were jealous, self-centred and mean and would always choose the path that best suited them and best fucked over people they didn't like.

"If we ask everyone's opinion," said Wulf, "then it's their fault when it goes wrong."

Sofi smiled. "There is that, but then we also have to endure their smugness if they're right. Let's go into the canyons. Either choice might kill us, but the canyons will be cooler." She could hear by their breathing and heartbeats that the Wootah were struggling with the day's extraordinary heat.

"All right," Wulf nodded.

The children turned to follow the others. Sofi made to follow them but Wulf took her arm.

She waited.

"Yoki Choppa knew, too," said Wulf. "It's why he gave his life for the boy."

Sofi looked Wulf in the eye. He held her gaze. He was not as dumb as he looked, this golden-maned hunk. "All right," she said.

"And please understand that I'm grateful to Nether Barr," said Wulf. "Beyond grateful. If I'd had the choice I'd never have taken her life for mine. But it's happened. We will call our child Nether Barr, we will think of her every day, and I will do the best I can with the years she's given me."

"Or days."

"We've come this far, Sofi. We're going to finish this."

Sofi sighed. "Not all of us."

\* \* \*

A short while later the path forked and they took the north-ernmost trail.

The stony-floored valley narrowed into a sandy slot canyon. It was cooler, but hard, stone walls loomed above. *The canyons were probably the wrong choice*, thought Sofi, *especially given the recent run of earthquakes*. She was still walking next to Wulf, but now they were leading the group.

"The creatures were made of plants and minerals and water," Sitsi was explaining to Freydis behind them. "Plants eat earth and water, and animals, including us, eat plants and other animals. We are made out of what we eat, so we are made of earth and water. The spirit of the Warlock Queen – or whatever it is at The Meadows – can make her own creatures out of earth and water, it seems, skipping the stages that normal animals need to exist."

"But why were they so horrible?" asked Freydis.

"Because she is horrible, I presume."

"Why the spider-lizards?"

"Perhaps she's amalgamating animals she remembers, or perhaps they're creatures from her nightmares. Perhaps she has no direct control over what's created."

"Why were they trying to kill us?"

"It isn't personal, Freydis. They're trying to kill everyone."

The gully opened into a sun-bright bowl, busy with green-leaved trees, bushes and butterflies. Several birds of prey wheeled overhead and Sofi could hear dozens of scurrying mammals and lizards. She was just thinking that this place was more full of life than anywhere they'd seen for a while when she spotted the corpses.

It was a family: a man, a woman and two children no older than ten, lying in a heap half in the bushes on the edge of the path. By the tracks, they'd fled from the direction in which the Owsla and Wootah were headed, where the canyon narrowed into a dark corridor again.

She leant closer. The corpses were covered in dozens of dark welts.

"Stung to death," said Sitsi.

Sofi strained to listen. She could hear buzzing, but only the bees, flies and the few wasps that one might expect in the pocket of vegetation. Leaving Sitsi to organise the burning of the bodies and Sassa and Paloma distracting the children, Sofi walked ahead.

Fifty paces into the slot canyon it curved and she was out of sight of the others. She pressed a palm against the cool canyon wall.

What a joy it was to be alone.

She followed the tracks of the fleeing family deeper into the canyon. They'd started sprinting next to an overhang which sheltered damp mud from the last time water had flowed. Sofi heard something moving and she squatted to look. A couple of red-spotted toads stared back at her from their shaded nook.

The doomed family had begun to jog twenty paces further along. So they'd heard or seen the wasps here, jogged for twenty paces, realised they were in serious trouble and sprinted another two hundred paces out into the open where they'd died. By the way they'd been lying, the children had fallen first and the adults had tried to shield them with their bodies.

Waves of sorrow and pity made Sofi almost weep as she imagined their terror and desperation. She bit her lip. This new sentimentality was a pain in the arse.

She closed her eyes and listened. Nothing unusual. The walls of the cliff were pocked with holes like a sponge. She guessed that the wasps had come out of these, but there was no evidence to support that theory.

It was a long slot canyon, a couple of hundred paces from the clearing and who knew how much further to the end. She jogged on. A hundred paces along, the canyon widened a little and there was a natural ramp in the rock on the north side. It led up to a cave. Sofi wasn't the first to find it. On the ledge outside the cave were a multitude of footprints and the traces of several fires. In a cleft beyond the cave was a tank of dark, cool water. Sofi tasted it. It was good.

She heard the pyre whooshing into flame in the clearing. She ran back.

"So we could go back and take the open route," she told Wulf after reporting her findings, "or keep on through the canyon."

"And there's no sign of the wasps?"

"If they're there, they're not moving."

"And there could be worse things in the open."

"Sure."

"Stick to the canyon, I reckon."

"Let's go, everyone!" she called. "Silently, please. Whatever stung these people to death may be dormant in the canyon walls."

"And," she added more quietly to Wulf, "we don't want them to be woken by grown men giggling at rock formations."

Finn the Deep walked between Thyri and Paloma at the back of the group heading into the slot canyon. He was feeling heroic.

He'd saved them all. Again. It had been easy. Or at least the concept had been simple. The animals attacking them had one desire – to kill humans. All he'd had to do was change that to kill a giant crab. He'd then encountered a difficulty. He couldn't tell the minds of the worms and the spider-lizards apart, so his idea to get one of them to attack the other was foiled. But then he'd told them to attack anything different from themselves, and that had worked.

Simple but, arguably, ingenious.

He could get used to saving people's lives. It made him feel, finally, like he was worthy of being in this group of superb people. He could walk along with Thyri and Paloma without craving their attention. He already had their attention. And, he thought, he was no longer so desperate for Paloma to—

"Run!" shouted Sofi. "Follow me!"

*Cocks!* thought Finn. *Was there never any rest?*

Thyri, Paloma and Finn paused for a moment as, ahead of them, Chogolisa handed the ropes for pulling the coffin to Erik, then scooped up Freydis and Ottar. Finn saw something moving on the canyon walls.

Wasps the size of small birds were crawling from the holes in the rock. They were black-bodied with red wings, exactly like the wasp that had attacked him on the beach in Hardwork, shortly before this had all begun.

One unfurled its wings, took flight and made a beeline directly for him.

"Run!" he shouted. He flapped an arm, but the wasp dodged it and stung his neck. It was exactly where Gunnhild had been stung before she'd died. He grabbed the beast, crushed it and flung it away. The pain was excruciating. He screamed.

Another stung his buttocks, another his leg.

Ahead, Erik yelled as he too was stung.

Finn was stung again on the shoulder, then on his back. The light clothing of the Pothole people was great protection from the sun. Not so good against wasps. *One sting*, he remembered, *one sting on the neck had killed Gunnhild.*

By the time they reached the rock ramp, Finn was whimpering. *His ear! One of them stung him on the fucking ear!* He slapped a hand onto the side of his head and crunched the huge insect against his skull. The pain was staggering. His whole body screamed at him. He screamed back. He'd been stung at least twenty times. He was going to die.

He stumbled. His ear was ablaze and he felt like he'd been stabbed all over with red-hot knives. He was struggling to breathe.

He stumbled again, nearly tripping, but strong hands gripped his arms and held him. He had no idea whose. He couldn't see any more, he could only scream in agony. He felt his bowels empty. *Least of my worries*, he managed to think as a wasp stung him on *his other fucking ear! For fuck's sake!*

Then he passed out.

He woke up Loakie knew how much later. His head was on Thyri's lap and her hand was on his head. He'd know that musky maple scent anywhere. Also sitting in the gloom, with her legs underneath his, hand resting on his shin, was Paloma. If his head hadn't felt like a thousand rats were devouring it from the inside, he would have thought he'd died and gone to a very indulgent god's hall.

They were in a cave. There were sleep sacks and ponchos draped across its opening, hence the gloom. There was a loud, angry buzzing behind the barrier.

He blinked. Apart from the pounding in his head, he felt more or less okay.

"Is everyone here?" he asked.

"No," said Paloma, "we're the only ones that made it."

"What? Really?" Tragedy flooded his mind, along with the realisation that it was just him, Thyri Treelegs and Paloma Pronghorn now . . .

"No, not really. Everyone's fine," said Paloma brightly. "Apart from you. We tried, but we couldn't save your arm."

Finn lifted his hands. They were both there. "*What is wrong with you?!*"

"I get bored cooped up like this."

"Thyri, please can you tell me what's going on?"

"Everyone's fine. You were stung more than everybody else. We're guessing the wasps are attracted to people who wash less. And it seems that Owsla skin is too tough for the wasp stings to penetrate."

Finn touched his neck.

"The sting on your neck did swell up a bit," Thyri touched the spot where he'd been stung. Her fingers were cool. "And Freydis wanted to cut your windpipe and put a pipe in there – Yoki Choppa showed her how apparently and she was keen to try – but we stopped her and slapped on a standard poultice and the swelling reduced."

"Was anyone else stung?"

"I got a couple, Ottar and Freydis were stung once each, Wulf took a couple, Sassa and Keef didn't get stung at all and Erik got five, I think."

"Six," came Erik's voice from deeper in the cave.

"You're the only one who made any fuss," said Paloma.

"But I got stung about fifty times!"

"Ten," said Thyri, "if that." There was a smile in her voice. And his head was on her thigh and she was stroking his hair.

"And are we stuck in here now?" he asked.

"We are," Sassa answered. "We're waiting for the wasps to die or go away. Drink a good bit of water then sleep again."

"But remember to wake up," said Thyri.

"Like Gunnhild didn't?" Finn shivered.

"Exactly like that," smiled Paloma.

# Chapter 11

## Snownado

Finn the Deep woke. It was bright and cold. Thyri's thigh had been replaced by a stone. He sat up. He was alone in the cave, the door covers were gone and there was snow on the ground outside.

Snow? He'd been stung by the wasps on the hottest day ever. *He must be dead! He was in the afterlife! Nowhere near a god's hall! Alone!*

He touched his neck. There was a slight bump, and now he thought about it, his ears and the other places he'd been stung felt a little fizzy. Surely one wouldn't carry wasp stings into the next world?

He walked out of the cave and found Paloma sitting on a rock, watching him with an amused little smile on her lips. The speedy Owsla woman was in her scanty Owsla gear, unaffected by the chill. It could still be the afterlife, he thought.

He looked up and down the canyon. There was a light dusting of snow, and footprints and the drag marks of a sled headed west.

"The rest of them have gone on," said Paloma. "Get yourself together and we'll catch up."

"Um?" he said when he got back, shivering a little. It was very cold.

"You're wondering why everybody buggered off even though you'd been stung multiple times and might have died?"

"I am."

"People on the brink of death don't snore quite so deeply nor dream quite so much."

"How do you know what I was dreaming?"

"You were smiling like a happy cat and calling out names."

Finn reddened. *Fucknuts!* he thought. Could the gods not allow him to look cool for more than half a day?

"Aren't we worried about the wasps?" he asked.

"The temperature dropped in the night and they flew off. We think that the Warlock Queen's creations can't stand the cold and go to ground, like insects and lizards in winter."

"Do you mean Sitsi thinks that?"

"Well, obviously. Put this on." She held out her poncho. "Gather your crap and let's go."

The canyon joined a wider valley. The snow was deeper and Finn wondered if they'd need to don their snow shoes, but they followed the others' trail to the side of a small river where the snow lay thinner.

The effort of jogging after Paloma kept him warm. She was always ten paces ahead, which meant he couldn't talk to her, but he wasn't sure he had the breath to chat anyway.

To their right was a cliff set in a series of enormous rock waves that looked about to break and crush them. Two moons ago Finn could have stared at it all morning. Now he only gave it a glance then went back to watching where he was putting his feet.

They found the others raiding a cluster of half-destroyed skin tents.

"We just can't get rid of you, can we, Boggy?" called Keef the Berserker, walking towards them with a new fur over his shoulders. "Come and look at this."

Down by the river was a dead, hairless dog-like animal bigger than a buffalo. Its stomach was opened, its innards gone and there were great chunks missing from its limbs. Finn guessed those wounds had been the work of scavengers. The cause of death looked to be the four spears stuck in its neck.

"There are a couple more over there," Keef pointed. "But no human bodies. It looks like a tribe here beat the dogs, then headed off."

"Without any of them being killed!" said Finn. It was a cheering thought in this land of misery.

"Unless they burned their dead before leaving," said Paloma. "Which they would have done."

Sassa Lipchewer had found a fur for Finn in the tents. She handed it to him, said how good it was to see him back on his feet and they headed off, towards a snowy shoulder of mountains.

"Shouldn't we go round the mountains?" Finn asked Sitsi Kestrel. Away from the river, they were in snow shoes, winding between boulders and bushes. It was hard going.

"It will be colder for longer up high," said Sitsi.

"Well, exactly."

"So we're less likely to encounter any beasts."

"Oh. Good point."

"Have I told you how I think the beasts are made?"

"Out of the land and plants."

"Well, yes, that's part of it, but now I think there's more to it. You see—"

Finn half listened to Sitsi as they tramped up and up. It was a different climb from the previous mountains they'd ascended – not so steep but very long. Desert bushes and cactuses gave way to trees as they ascended, and soon they were in proper woods for the first time since the Shining Mountains. The snow was less thick on the ground here and they were able to remove their snow shoes.

Just when Finn was beginning to relax and enjoy the

scenery, they caught up with Paloma standing next to another giant hairless dog corpse.

Sitsi walked around it. "This one's been killed by spears, too," she said, "but the spears are gone. Which makes me wonder why the last lot left their spears in the beasts that they killed. Maybe the people in the village *were* all killed, and the dogs they didn't kill ate them, bones and all."

"That's horrible!" said Freydis.

"Yeah, Sitsi," said Paloma.

"And not necessarily true," said Wulf. "This one is miles away from any settlements. The people who killed it would have only had one spear each, which they would have taken with them. Down in the village they'd have a huge pile of spears, so they didn't need to take them out of the dead dogs."

"That sounds much more likely," said Freydis.

Sitsi rolled her eyes. "So why didn't we find a pile of spears in the village," she muttered.

At the summit − or what seemed like the summit but probably wasn't if Finn's experience of walking uphill was anything to go by − was a huge view of red, rocky desert, mesas and mountains to the west, towards where The Meadows was meant to be. Far off were great storm clouds. Finn kept an eye on them. They were very black and swirling weirdly. At this distance they looked like a child's toy clouds, but as he watched a tornado spiralled down.

"Look everyone!" he called, pointing westwards.

Even though they couldn't hear it from this great distance, they could see its awesome power. Finn shuddered, remembering the tornado that had tried to kill him on the far side of the Water Mother. That one had been dark. This one was white.

"Snownado," said Wulf.

"How far away is it?" asked Erik.

"A day's walk," said Sofi.

"That far? But that would make it . . ."

"It's big," finished Sitsi.

Darkness rose through the spinning storm, turning it from white to grey to black as it thickened and thickened. Soon the twister was as wide as it was high, and blacker than the storm clouds. They could hear it now, a quiet yet somehow still huge, all-encompassing rumble.

"Frog a dog," said Sassa. "Ottar, is that the way we're headed?"

Ottar, staring wide-eyed at the vortex, nodded.

"Tornados are rare," said Thyri. "If there's one today, chances are—"

Sofi put a hand on her shoulder and pointed to where another spike of cloud was twisting down out of the black sky. Its point struck the ground and whitened, sucking up snow. It headed north following the path of the first, blackening and thickening. It wasn't as huge as the first one, but it was plenty big enough.

"You were saying, Thyri?" asked Keef.

The descent was their easiest walking for a long while. Sitsi Kestrel might have felt jaunty had it not been for the land of tornado storms that they were walking into and the threat of the huge hairless dogs.

There was no snow on the ground this side of the mountain, and the animals − standard woodland animals, thank Innowak − were back in abundance. Squirrels and chipmunks chased about, a couple of badgers foraged and tubby little birds sang happily from the branches of fir trees.

Keef jumped about waving Arse Splitter and battling imaginary foes. He hadn't done that for a while, Sitsi realised. He was a great man but he was kind of animalistic. When rodents and songbirds thought that there were no predators around, they would dance and sing. It seemed Keef was governed by the same principles.

They came to a large boulder. Paloma was already scouting

ahead and around, but Sitsi thought it wouldn't do any harm to climb up the boulder and see what she could espy.

A couple of miles down the hill, walking purposefully towards them, were twelve warriors. They wore leather trousers, leather jerkins and leather caps. Ten of them carried short spears with oversized stone heads. Two carried ridiculously thick bows and had quivers of thick-stemmed arrows on their backs.

"I think we're about to meet the Warrior and Warlock tribe!" she called down to the others. "The Warrior bit of it, anyway!"

# Chapter 12

## Warriors and Warlocks

Paloma Pronghorn strolled from the trees and joined the path a couple of hundred paces upslope from the large strangers. The trail led through a well-grazed meadow so the dozen people heading up the hill could see her as plainly as she could see them. They were strolling easily, neither aggressive nor defensive. All were men. An impressive looking lot. Their spears had stout wooden shafts and enormous stone heads – more club than spear. The two archers' bows were thicker than her killing stick.

If they were alchemically enhanced and they attacked, she'd be in trouble. Even if they weren't, Paloma might struggle to beat them all. She'd be able to run away, though.

"Hi," said Paloma, cracking her best "I have hidden powers and you should be scared of me" smile.

"Wait here, friends." The oldest looking of the strangers held up a hand and strode forward heavily. He was Erik's height – they all were – with an even broader chest. Although he looked strong and fit, he might have been sixty years old.

"Hello, woman warrior!" he called. His smile was warm, but the word "woman" could have been replaced by the word "little" with no change in tone or intention. No matter. Men who thought of the Owsla as just little women were the most fun to kill. "I'm Janny," he said. "What's your name and where are the rest of you?"

"How do you know it's not just me?"

"Warlocks!" Janny raised his eyebrows. "They have their uses. One of our warlocks saw the twelve of you coming. He said that you were friendly, but he's been wrong before. He also said that you are vital in the battle against the Warlock Queen."

"We *are* friendly and vital," Paloma resisted the urged to step back. The man was large and too close and his bonhomie was false. *Could be his character – plenty of old fuckers were false – or he could be about to attack.*

"Great news!" He clapped a meaty hand onto Paloma's shoulder. "We're friendly, too! Let's wait for the others and we'll take you down to the village. You can rest and spend the night with us."

She slipped her shoulder out from under his hand and he didn't seem to mind. *Phew,* she thought, *he's just touchy-feely and fake then.* She wasn't exactly a fan of patronising, chauvinistic old men, but it was better than another spear to the guts.

Without much to talk about as they waited, Paloma told them about the retrieval of the boy's coffin and their intention to take it to The Meadows, and then stopped, wondering whether she'd already told the strangers too much.

She didn't like the way they all smiled at her one little bit.

Sitsi Kestrel saw Paloma sitting with the Warriors, seemingly at ease, and told Sofi that it looked all right to approach.

The oldest looking of the Warriors – a burly fellow named Janny – greeted them effusively and said that they must spend the evening in their village. He was avuncular and jolly. Sitsi liked him immediately.

She walked down the hill next to Janny, ahead of the others. He told her that he was the leader of a small group split from the Warrior and Warlock tribe, settled in the village they were headed towards.

Many of his tribe, he said, had been killed, many had fled. The couple of thousand who'd survived had found a new base in the Valley of the Gods, just over a day's walk to the west. Many more had been killed since.

"But the Valley of the Gods is a beautiful place, a glory!" Janny raised his arms in praise as the valley broadened and flattened. Up ahead, smoke from village cook fires snaked up into a clear blue sky. "In its way, the Valley of the Gods is even more glorious than The Meadows used to be, but, like everywhere else, it has been hit by the Warlock Queen's disasters and it has suffered. A huge flash flood struck just a moon ago."

"Is the Valley of the Gods close to The Meadows?" Sitsi asked.

"You can canoe to the edge of The Meadows downstream in a few days. Coming back takes longer."

"Have you seen The Meadows?"

"We've launched a series of attacks on the Warlock Queen. The warlocks say that her power is flowing from her tomb, The Pyramid, and if we could get into to that tomb we might be able to stop it. So far we've failed. We haven't even got close. I've been on two raids and both were disasters." Janny shook his head.

"What happened?" asked Sitsi.

Janny walked on, looking grim. "The Meadows is a vast area of relatively flat land surrounded by mountains," he said eventually. "The Pyramid is a huge, triangular man-made mountain more or less in the centre. I take it you've encountered some monsters on the way here?"

"A couple."

"The monsters filling The Meadows are worse. The plain is filled with crawling, striding and slithering beasts. They slaughter and eat each other but they are constantly replaced, growing from the ground itself. That first raid, I thought I'd seen the greatest horrors. Two moons later, about two moons ago, the monsters were larger, more disgusting and much more numerous. I hate to think what they are like now."

"How did you attack?"

"First raid we tried the warrior way. We ran at the tomb with spears in hand. We got a couple of hundred paces before retreating. Of the fifty who'd attacked, ten made it out." Janny stroked his moustache. "The second raid was a warlock-planned affair on a moonless, cloudy night. Only a dozen died on that one, but it got us nowhere. People have tried a few other schemes, but all plans have failed and almost all have ended in death."

"Have any got close?" asked Sitsi.

"Nobody has been within two, maybe three miles of The Pyramid since the disasters started, and now it is impossible to get that close. Impossible." Janny shook his head.

"Why?"

"The monsters. There is no break in them for miles around The Pyramid. It would take an army of men to defeat even one of the larger creatures and they don't appear to sleep. The warlocks say they will spill out soon and we'll all be killed."

"So why are you here? Are you . . ." Sitsi wanted to say *giving up and fleeing* but that didn't seem polite.

"Are we chickening out, do you mean?"

"No! I just . . ."

Janny chuckled. "It's all right. I had a bit of a disagreement with the Warrior and Warlock leaders. Along with a few others," he indicated the people around him, "we don't see the sense in staying in the Valley of the Gods and sending people to die in The Meadows. We want to look for a solution elsewhere."

"What have you found?"

"Nothing!" he laughed. "As you advance in years, Sitsi, you'll realise that people are lazy and flawed. I certainly am! We hadn't come far when we found a deserted but

well-fortified village. We decided to bide in the village, to
see if the others manage to stop the horrors spewing out of
The Meadows. We have supplies and we're safe. Even if a
tornado struck there are underground chambers for shelter."

"But, surely, if an army of the Warlock Queen's creations
is about to surge from The Meadows . . .?"

"Have you noticed the monsters don't like cold weather?
If we're still alive and the Warlock Queen is still undefeated
come winter, we'll head on."

"Sure, they don't like the cold," said Sitsi. "But it also seems
that the Warlock Queen can control the weather."

"You," beamed Janny, "are perhaps the brightest woman
I've ever met."

Sitsi nodded, trying not to smile.

"Now, that large box that your big friend is towing,"
Janny asked. "Is it really the Warlock Queen's son?"

"So we hope."

"Fascinating. Tell me more."

So, as they marched down the hill at the head of the
parade of Warriors, Calnians and Wootah, Sitsi told Janny
everything. He was a very good listener.

The village did look resilient. It was stone-built and squat,
a series of boxes crammed together like the village on Bighorn
Island, but all on one level, three sides of a solid square.
Some of the dwellings had heavy wooden doors and others
had ladders poking up from their roofs.

Sitsi expected to see children and animals in a place like
this, but there were none. The smell of deer and corn cooking
on buffalo-dung fires was very welcoming, however.

Janny shouted a greeting and people emerged. Several tall
women of varying ages ducked under door frames which
had been made for shorter people. They stared at the
newcomers. They wore plain, long cotton dresses with no
adornment; no jewellery, no feathers, nothing. It was weird.

They eyed the Owsla women and Thyri, ignored the rest of them, curled their lips like surly wolves and went back into the dwellings.

Stepping from the ladders onto several of the roofs were shorter men. *Warlocks*, thought Sitsi to herself. Yoki Choppa had been unusual as a warlock in that his dress was unaffected. Nothing about his breechcloth or anything else about his attire said "I am a warlock".

The outfits on this lot, however, screamed warlock. They wore white leather moccasins, purple bandages on their left legs only, red cotton shorts, peaked caps and, most demonstrably and – to Sitsi, most annoyingly – bulky jerkins made of parrot feathers.

Sitsi didn't hate fashion. If people wanted to look silly it was up to them. What riled her were *fashionable* clothes that hampered the user. Some of the children in Calnia, for example, had taken to wearing their breechcloths below their arses rather than around their waists. It was a display against authority – an announcement that they'd make their own rules. Sitsi understood. It was nice for children to feel that they were different from their parents for a while before they matured into conformity. What annoyed her was that breechclothes worn around the arse were such a handicap. They had to be hoisted up the whole time. Running was impossible. A gang of children wearing low-slung breechcloths had been attacked by a bear on one of Calnia's outlying farms. Three had been killed when their breechcloths had fallen around their feet and tripped them.

The parrot jackets were like that. Bulky and fragile, wearing them would restrict movement and you'd waste a lot of time mending them. People who wore fashions like that, as far as Sitsi was concerned, might as well have just walked around repeating the words *I am an idiot*.

The warlocks were all men, like the warriors. She'd come across tribes with strictly defined gender roles before. Again, people could do what they wanted, but, really, preventing half the population from contributing to the most important roles – or the least important for that matter – was even dumber than wearing your breechcloth below your arse.

"Welcome to our village!" called Janny. "These flamboyant fellows are the Warlocks." Sitsi could tell by the way he said *flamboyant* that Janny thought the same as she did about their outfits.

The two groups greeted each other. There was a little wariness, but Sitsi thought that was normal with any two groups of strangers coming together. You could tell a group by its leader, she thought, and Janny was a decent chap. It was odd that the women kept their distance, but the other men were friendly.

They ate an evening meal of deer and cake. The women never reappeared, but after the way they'd snarled at the Owsla, Sitsi wasn't exactly desperate to engage with them. She ended up listening to the life story of a warlock called Pook.

She asked him about the feather jerkins.

"Only warlocks are allowed them," he told her. "When you've passed a range of tests and survived the Initiation, there's a big ceremony and you're presented with the jerkin."

"Are they handed down through the generations?"

"The feathers are, because they're quite hard to get hold of, but you have to make your own jerkin. Then you have to make it again at least once a year. They fall apart really easily."

Sitsi nodded. "Do they now."

The others turned in, leaving Sitsi Kestrel and Thyri Treelegs on watch, despite Janny's insistence that they didn't need a watch.

The two women sat on the roof of the large dwelling allocated to most of the Calnians and Wootah. Paloma and

Sofi had taken their own stone box, since they were on second watch. The roof wasn't actually a great spot to watch from, since torches lit the yard that was three-quarters enclosed by the three-sided building. That meant their night vision was spoiled and it lit up the watchers nicely for any attackers. However, Janny had said it was the best spot and Sitsi's night vision was so good that it wasn't much of a problem.

Warriors and warlocks prepared the settlement for the night then turned in. Muted conversations of Wootah and Calnians below became snores. They watched the stars pan across the sky and the flying creatures of the night flap and flitter by. It was chilly, and they both had blankets. Owsla didn't feel the cold as much as normal people, so Sitsi asked Thyri if she needed a second blanket.

"No thanks," said the girl. That was the sum of their conversation. It wasn't awkward; they simply had nothing to say to one another.

Not long after Erik's snores had begun to reverberate through the roof, Thyri touched Sitsi's arm, then her own ear, then pointed along the roofs. There was someone climbing up a ladder a few dwellings down.

It was Pook, the warlock Sitsi had been talking to. He crossed the roof in a crouch and squatted next to the women.

"Sitsi, you are the most beautiful woman I have ever seen." Pook seemed earnest.

"Oh. Thanks."

"So I have to tell you. Janny is not the good man he seems. We are not good people. We fled the Valley of the Gods to save ourselves. This village wasn't deserted. We killed everyone. We . . . we ate them. We still have some of their meat stored."

"Oh, for the love of Tor," said Thyri. "Did we—"

"We ate deer," said Sitsi. She knew the taste of human flesh all too well.

"Janny plans to kill and eat you, too," Pook continued. "He wants to take the body of the child and use its magic to escape this land."

"When?" asked Thyri.

"And how?" asked Sitsi.

"The warlocks say they'll be able to—"

Sitsi put a hand on his arm for silence. Two people were stealing towards them through the night, just outside the torchlight. It was the two warriors with bows. She would have seen them earlier had Pook not distracted her.

"What is it?" Thyri whispered, peering blindly into the night.

"Prepare to drop off the roof when I say," Sitsi whispered, silently bending and stringing her bow on her lap, "and—"

There were two other figures out there in the night, following the archers. Sofi and Paloma. Sofi had her dagger-tooth knife in one hand and Paloma had borrowed Luby's obsidian moon blade from Freydis.

Paloma stepped on a twig.

The archers turned. Sofi leapt and slit both their throats, but not before one of them managed to yell.

More shouts rang out. Hatches banged open. Warriors and warlocks emerged into the darkness, the former armed with spears, the latter with blowpipes. Armed so quickly after the alarm, they must have been watching and waiting for the archers to kill Sitsi and Thyri.

"Warlocks first, Sitsi!" shouted Sofi. "Paloma, indoors. Kill them all."

"Hold Pook, Thyri," Sitsi commanded, stringing her bow and slotting an arrow as she leapt to her feet.

Sitsi shot and she shot, two arrows every heartbeat, into hearts and necks. As she aimed and loosed, she saw Sofi in her peripheral vision, leaping about the courtyard slaying warriors and warlocks. The sound of killing stick on skull and cut-off yelps came from inside the stone buildings.

By the time Chogolisa emerged from a roof hole to see what the commotion was about, followed by the Wootah, it was over.

All the warriors and warlocks were dead or dying, save Pook, held by Thyri with her sax blade to his throat, and Janny. The leader was kneeling in the village square. Sofi stood behind him holding his short hair, her dagger-tooth knife pressed into his throat.

"What the—" said Wulf, standing on the roof. "Sofi, what is this?"

Sitsi blinked. There were maybe two dozen dead lying about the village square. Blood and brains glinted in the torchlight.

It did look a little shocking. This was the Owsla's first massacre since they'd stopped eating rattlesnake and gained consciences. Sitsi had reacted to Sofi's command instinctively, but now she felt a little sick.

"Janny and his people killed and ate the original inhabitants of this village," said Sofi. "They planned to do the same to us."

"How do you know?" Wulf asked.

"I heard them plotting. I waited until they attacked to be sure. It's clear-cut, Wulf."

"Did you have to kill them all?"

"I haven't killed Janny yet." Sofi tilted the hapless headman's head back.

"Don't, Sofi."

"It was Janny's idea to murder us. They planned to eat us."

"I don't know what black sorcery you used," spat Janny, "but you—"

Sofi punched him hard in the side of the head.

"Don't kill him," said Wulf.

"All right." Sofi drove a knee between Janny's shoulder blades. The Warrior flew forward and fell to lie like a dropped doll, arms and legs immobile, head rolling around, mouth and eyes silently screaming.

Wulf stared. "You've broken his back. It would have been better to have killed him."

"As you wish." Sofi walked over, lifted her bare foot and stamped. Janny's skull burst like an egg hit with a hammer. "Now for the one on the roof. Hand him over, Thyri."

"Pook came to warn us," said Thyri.

Sofi looked up at the busy roof. Keef, Erik, Finn and Sassa had climbed up the ladder and were standing behind Sitsi.

"He's complicit in murder and cannibalism and his warning was too late," said Sofi. "He has to die."

"No," said Thyri. "To kill Pook, you come through me."

"And me," said Erik the Angry.

"And me," said Sassa Lipchewer.

"And me," said Wulf the Fat.

"And me," said Finn the Deep, sounding less than convinced.

"I'm okay with it," said Keef the Berserker. "I'll do it for you if you want."

"Please don't kill me!" whined Pook. "I didn't kill the villagers. The warriors did it."

"The warlocks didn't intercede and they reaped the rewards of murder." Sitsi hadn't heard Sofi sound like this since before they'd met the Wootah.

"It's true!" wailed Pook. "I deserve to die! But I *did* warn you."

"You warned us too late," said Sitsi. "In fact you distracted me so I didn't see the attackers." Sofi was right. If they hadn't been alchemically enhanced, they'd have been killed despite his warning. He had done less than nothing to help them.

"I will make amends! I will travel the land and do what I can to help people who have been attacked by the weather and the monsters."

"You won't last a day," said Wulf.

"It's a chance I'll take. *Please* let me live. I'll atone for everything I did – for everything Janny and the others did, too!"

"Did you eat the flesh of the villagers?" asked Sofi.

Pook looked at his feet.

"Did you?"

"Yes," said Pook quietly.

There was only one thing to do, and the sooner it was done the better. Sitsi pulled her bowstring halfway so the arrow wouldn't go through and hit anybody else, then shot Pook in the back of the head. He fell forward off the roof and whumped onto the packed earth of the courtyard.

"Sitsi!" shouted Wulf. Everyone else gasped and took a step back.

She bent her bow to remove the string, then leapt down into the yard to retrieve her arrow.

She could feel the eyes of the Wootah burning into her back as she worked.

# Chapter 13

## Firenado

Wulf insisted that they burn the bodies and not eat them. Erik was relieved when Sofi agreed.

"That was merciful of Sofi," he whispered to Chogolisa when they finally lay down together.

"If you want to destroy a soul," said Chogolisa, "you need to do it by cooking them on a fire lit by an Innowak crystal. Yoki Choppa had ours and it disappeared with him."

"So Janny and his gang didn't destroy the villagers' souls?"

"Not unless they had an Innowak crystal."

"But Sitsi still killed Pook."

"They still ate people. That's one of the unforgivables. As is murdering people so you can take their shelter and supplies."

"Hmmm."

"Unless an empress tells you to do it, of course,"

Erik felt yet again that this younger woman had seen an awful lot more than he had.

By dawn the pyre was dying down.

"Where are all the warlocks and warriors?" asked Freydis. She and Ottar hadn't woken in the night.

"On a mission," said Erik, "and we're leaving any moment, too. It's breakfast on the hoof this morning."

"And what's that fire? And that smell? What are they cooking?"

"They've left buffalo cooking for when they get back."

"It doesn't smell like buffalo. It's like the smell in the canyon. It's a person!"

"Buffalo smells different over here, and they have different cooking methods."

Freydis shook her head. "What happened, Erik?"

Erik couldn't hold her gaze and found himself instead looking over to where Sofi, Paloma and Sitsi were waiting. They held his gaze, too.

"Come here, Freydis. I'll explain," said Paloma.

The girl skipped away.

Erik shuddered, his mind going back to the far side of the Water Mother when the Owsla had been hunting them. He'd more or less forgotten that the women were bred, trained and warped by alchemy to kill. He thought they had forgotten it too, but the women seemed somehow larger, healthier and stronger this morning. The night of slaying had done them a power of good.

It was still cold, with a few snowflakes drifting down from a grey sky. They wrapped up in leathers and furs and headed off towards the Valley of the Gods, where Janny had said they would find the rest of the Warrior and Warlock tribe. Sitsi Kestrel led the way, following Janny and the others' trail back to where they'd come from a couple of moons before.

They were, Erik couldn't help but realise, walking towards where they'd seen the tornados the day before. Danger behind them, danger ahead of them, and, it seemed, danger in their ranks.

He shuddered. Sofi was right, but it was the *way* she'd done it. She'd enjoyed it. So had sassy Paloma and sweet Sitsi. Then Chogolisa had humped the dead bodies onto the fire as if it was an everyday chore. He knew there was a time when it had been.

Each of the Owsla was two people. A fascinating, capable woman and a murder-loving magic-powered monster. He looked up at the beautiful girl walking next to him, pulling the heavy sled and coffin uphill as if it weighed nothing.

What would happen if they had a serious disagreement? What if he wanted to leave her? Would she kill him?

They crunched along on gravel in dry valleys, along the foot of layered red cliffs, then headed up over slickrock, past yellow-pink domes of rock.

Erik tried to tell himself that the slayings had been reassuring. The Owsla was still tough and ruthless as Hel. Their approach would be vital as they moved towards The Meadows. But the way Sofi had paralysed the man even as Wulf asked for clemency . . . Was she on their side?

"I have a bad feeling about this," said Chogolisa after a while, shaking Erik from his musings.

The sky ahead looked like it was mustering for a once-in-a-century tantrum. Clouds the size of mountains whirled magnificently in a churn of blues, purples and blacks. The sky above and below was dark as the depths of a cave.

The odd seemingly lost snowflake drifted by as they climbed a high ridge then plunged down into a canyon, to a path worn into the rock alongside a churning river.

They crossed the river over a long-deserted, precarious beaver dam and headed uphill again.

Then the weather hit.

One moment there were snowflakes the size of bumblebees, the next a blast of blizzard nearly knocked Erik off his feet. Wind whistled around bluffs and slammed into his face.

"Erik!" shouted Paloma over the storm.

He looked up. She was waiting for him in the shelter of a tree, holding Freydis's hand.

"I've got to scout. Can you take her?"

Erik nodded and picked her up.

He headed on, Freydis's legs wrapped around his waist, her face buried in his chest. He tramped behind Chogolisa, who was carrying the coffin-sled on one shoulder.

His exposed, blizzard-blasted right ear was agony, then it was numb. He should have worn a hat, or at least wound something around his head, but carrying Freydis meant he couldn't use his arms. He was glad for the boots the Green tribe had given them. It was too windy for the snow to settle so there was no need for snow shoes, but the boots kept his feet dry and gripped the slippy surface. Chogolisa was barefoot, as were the rest of the Owsla.

Not that he could see them. Every time he lifted his face, he was rewarded with an eyeful of ice shards.

Oaden knew how long he'd been tramping blind when the weather, already as shitty as he'd thought weather could be, got a good deal worse.

Lightning flashed, thunder rumbled then boomed above their heads as if it were trying to blast them off the slickrock. The wind strengthened into such a gale that walking was near impossible.

Erik jumped when a loud crack rang out, followed by a loud sizzle.

He managed to lift his head to see that a stand of scrubby pines was blazing fiercely.

Sofi appeared, a rope in her hand. "I'm going to run this through your belt!" she shouted into his ear.

"Why?" he shouted back, looking up and seeing that the rope led from Chogolisa ahead of him. He felt foolish; it was obvious what the rope was for.

"Stop you escaping!" shouted Sofi as she rammed the rope through his belt. She was still wearing Owsla gear – breech-cloth, jerkin and leggings to the knee – and nothing else, apart from moss in her ears, presumably as protection against the thunder. She was warm; the snowflakes were melting as they hit her.

Murderer or not, Erik really was very glad that she was on his side.

They carried on, through the torturous cold, wet and wind. Holding the rope, Erik could close his eyes and simply trudge. It would be over, he told himself. Just keep walking, and you'll be through it. Every few heartbeats thunder rang out. No matter how much he tried not to, he jumped like a rabbit every time.

"Don't worry, Erik the Angry!" shouted Freydis into his ear. "It's just the gods farting!" She giggled. It was unlike her to be crude. The girl had spent too much time with Paloma.

But she was right, it was just noise and the cold was just discomfort. It wasn't so bad –

"Run!" he thought he heard someone shout. There was a tug on the rope. "Run!" he heard again – Chogolisa's voice.

"You've got to run, Erik!" yelled Freydis.

*Big dogs' cocks! What now?*

When Owsla told him to run it usually meant "or die", so he ran. He looked up. He could just make out Chogolisa running ahead. The woman, the squat pine trees and the slickrock ahead were lit up a flickering orange. Almost as if . . .

He turned.

The was a column of fire chasing them. A raging, twisting, motherfucking column of fire. Steam burst in geysers as it charged across the rock. Great blazing stars swirled around its flaming trunk, up and up. They were full-grown trees, Erik realised, uprooted by the awesome wind, set alight and hurled skyward.

He'd been wondering what a firenado looked like.

He ran.

He could feel the heat pressing. They crested a rise and accelerated downhill. He widened his steps, desperate not to fall, one hand clutching Freydis to his chest, the other gripping the rope. All the land around was orange, like the most glorious sunset and heating up like a baker's oven. The snow became warm rain. The hair on the back of his head was curling, his neck was starting to burn.

*Were they running in front of it?* he asked himself. *Surely the trick with a tornado was to run at right angles, out of its path.* He hoped that whoever was leading their flight grasped that.

Mercifully, they turned ninety degrees, off the slickrock dome and into a gully. They crashed through trees. A sapling, trodden down by Chogolisa, whipped back and whacked him in the bollocks. He roared but ran on.

"Watch out!" he heard Sofi shout. "There's a drop."

*A drop!* he thought. *Always a drop.* He was carrying an increasingly heavy girl, running for his life and not far off exhausted. So of course there had to be a drop.

Then Sofi was there, her face lit up bright orange. The firenado must be right on them.

"Give me the girl!" she shouted.

He handed Freydis to Sofi and she leapt over the lip of rock.

Erik bent his knees to follow, but something made him turn.

It was right on him.

And there was a fiery face, lunging out of the spinning column. It was grinning, no, leering and laughing it seemed, with the love of murder.

It was the Warlock Queen.

*Well, at least I got to see her face*, he thought, *even if it is the last face I ever see.*

He turned and jumped.

He ran. He fell for far too long and landed with a whump. His legs absorbed most of the fall, but he slammed down hard onto his side. He lay panting, sucking in breath and sure his heart would burst. His breath was hot and suddenly all was bright and burning and roaring.

"Paloma, help!" he heard Sofi yell.

Both his arms yanked – almost out of their sockets, it seemed – and he was flying backwards across the ground as if his hands were roped to half a dozen stampeding buffalo.

He felt his jerkin being stripped away, then he was falling back, panting and spent, so tired that spinning up into the sky as a burning ball of bubbling blubber didn't seem such a terrible option.

The heat pressed. He could see bright light through his tightly shut eyelids, he could hear the crackling roar of the Warlock Queen. He tried to suck in air but there was only heat.

Then, suddenly, it was cooler. He could breathe. He opened his eyes.

They were in a wet cave, lit bright by the flickering light of burning woodland.

"Are you all right?" It was Finn.

"I think so. What . . .?"

"You came in with your back on fire. Sofi and Paloma stripped the fur off you." He pointed to a sad, smouldering lump on the stony ground outside the cave.

He turned to Sofi and Paloma.

"Thanks!" he said.

The women nodded.

They followed the blackened and burning trail of the fire-nado. They avoided burning trees and bushes, but had to cross smouldering, orange-hot soil a few times. Erik was glad of his boots, and marvelled that the Owsla walked uncomplainingly on bare feet.

They headed uphill. Ahead, the sky had settled into a sullen grey. Somewhere under that sky was the Warlock and

Warrior tribe in the Valley of the Gods. Beyond them was The Meadows and the Warlock Queen.

Erik walked on with the Calnians and the Wootah, west and west some more.

# Part Three

The Meadows

# Chapter 1

## Stone Trees

The clouds dispersed and the sun blazed, first twinkling off the snow then melting it aggressively. They walked through a forest of low pines, bright green against red cliffs. Water dripped like rain from branches, gurgled along innumerable rills and splashed down bouncing streams. A few sudden "whumps!" made Sassa Lipchewer jump, but it was just clumps of snow falling from trees.

She was walking on her own because Wulf had dropped back to tow the coffin. Other than Freydis and Ottar, Sassa was the only one who hadn't taken a stint hauling the Warlock Queen's dead son. She felt a bit bad about that, but only a bit. She didn't like the box being near her growing baby. She was prepared to appear unhelpful for the sake of her child. Being as close to the casket as she was made her miserable.

Maybe it wasn't the coffin that depressed her, Sassa thought. Maybe it was the massacre of Janny and his people. Maybe it was seeing her husband dying. Maybe it was the likelihood of seeing him die again.

How were they going to get through a sea of monsters to The Meadows? Did anybody have a plan? She knew Wulf didn't, and she herself couldn't begin to think of one.

That night they made shelters by the side of a lake, directed by Erik. They leant brush against what Sassa had thought were large tree trunks but were actually cold, hard stone in the shape of tree trunks and patterned on the outside just like bark.

The shelter construction was the same method Erik had used to get them out of the rain on the day he'd rescued them from the Lakchans. It was amazing, Sassa considered, to think that she hadn't known him back then, and that Sitsi, Paloma, Chogolisa and her hero Sofi had all been terrifying monsters, trying to catch them and kill them.

The Owsla hadn't changed, of course. They were still monsters. They'd shown that. They were like the lycanthropes of legend – normal people in the day, monsters at night. Except the Owsla didn't need to wait until night.

She walked a little way along the lakeside with Thyri, Finn, Freydis and Ottar, looking for stone trees that were still standing. Freydis said Ottar wanted to see if they had stone leaves and stone fruit.

The following day was very strange. It wasn't too hot, there were no tornadoes or earthquakes, nobody was killed by a bear or stung by a wasp man and they didn't see any dead people or twisted beasts that looked like they'd escaped from the nightmares of a madman.

"This is boring!" announced Freydis after the lunch stop. *Good*, thought Sassa. She liked boring. And, besides, she thought the ever-changing landscape of blue bushes, green trees and assorted multicoloured rock formations was breathtakingly lovely and far from boring. It took her mind off the inevitable horrors ahead.

If by some freak chance they made it through, she had no desire to return to Hardwork. She wanted to walk even more of the land with the Wootah and Owsla, to see what other marvels they could find, even after what the Owsla had done to Janny and his gang. Even more so, in fact. She reaslied something surprising. Wulf had been horrified by the slayings, but Sassa had been impressed, even excited. She took a deep breath, looked left and right then admitted it to herself as she let the breath out of her nose – when the Owsla had killed the warriors and warlocks and tortured Janny before murdering him too, it had turned her on.

She'd never looked at another woman like that – she really was Wulf's and Wulf's only – but, by Fraya and Tor, the Owsla were smokingly attractive. Sofi and Paloma particularly. And Sitsi, all sweet and clever, had plugged that guy in the back of the head like he was nothing to her.

Remembering it made Sassa smile and sent a flush of heat through her. She realised she was looking forward to killing again herself.

*Is that so wrong?* she wondered.

*Yes*, answered a voice in her mind that sounded like Gunnhild, *it's about as wrong as it gets.*


As the sun began to think about setting they wandered into a land of ridges, spikes and fins of rock that reminded Sassa of the Badlands. They found a good camping spot next to a low cliff. Sprouting from the cliff was a tower of red rock maybe twenty paces high, with a bulbous, white top.

Sassa looked at Wulf, then up at the tower, then back at him.

He raised his eyebrows at her, eyes twinkling and she had to run over and hug him.


They left early the following day. It was colder again. Snow that had fallen in the night had settled and was showing no signs of melting any time soon.

It started snowing lightly again as they climbed up into possibly the most bizarre landscape so far. Thousands of columns of rock were all around, ranging from the height of a human to twenty paces tall, some alone but mainly clustered in groups, ranging in colour from yellowy-white to deep red. Growing from the orange soil were tall trees but no grass or bushes.

A good path led up through this garden of weird rocks and tall trees, skirting around the clusters. Sassa and Wulf led the way with Sofi and Sitsi behind.

The easy trail passed through one short tunnel, then another.

"Someone made these tunnels," said Sassa.

"They did," confirmed Sitsi Kestrel. "We must be in Bella's Wood. Bella was one of the first humans. She was being pursued by the Mud People, who were here before humans. She changed herself into a fox to escape. That didn't work, so she turned her pursuers to stone." Sitsi gestured to the rock towers all around.

"Did she build the path as well?" asked Wulf.

"No, no. Bella's Wood is – or was – a popular pilgrimage site. So much so it seems that they've built this path and cut through the rock here to ease people's trek around it."

Sassa could see why visitors might flock to Bella's wood. It was delightful. It renewed Sassa's hope that they might all come out of this alive and bolstered her idea that she wanted to spend her life travelling the world.

The following two days' walking was almost as wonderful. The snow melted but the weather stayed mild. Streams gurgled, birds sang, animals ran about and the sun shone off green trees.

Sassa relaxed so much that it was something of a surprise two days later when Sitsi yelled, "Hold!"

They stopped. They were crossing slickrock. Huge domes of swirling patterned rock and great, white, flat-topped peaks loomed ahead.

"We're coming into the Valley of the Gods," Sitsi told Sofi.

"Because of these amazing rocks?" Sassa asked.

"That, and the twenty-three warriors and warlocks watching us from that hill ahead."

# Chapter 2

## The Valley of the Gods

They walked with leather-clad warlocks and feather-jacketed warriors across white, yellow and red slickrock. They looked a lot like Janny and his gang, but this lot were women as well as men. Finn wanted to talk to them, but they didn't seem interested in him and he was no good at striking up conversations.

The path headed for a cliff and Finn the Deep thought it had to end, but it continued crazily along a ledge not much wider than his foot. It was very high; by some way the most precipitous ledge Finn had shuffled along so far.

It was horrible and he was terrified, but it was a refreshing sort of terror, like the cold in winter after walking out of an overheated home. Of all the fears he regularly experienced those days, Finn mused, fear of heights was his favourite. You knew where you were with fear of heights. It was a simple case of thinking *Oh Oaden this is high, I hate it and I wish it was over* and being careful not to fall, and then it was over. It was a nice reliable terror with no surprises. Plus, it distracted him from his two other major fears, namely fear of embarrassment and fear of monsters. His swiftly developing fear of monsters was the worst. He had no idea what would attack them next. He was becoming used to embarrassment.

Ottar and Freydis were behind him, singing a weird duet in which Ottar made frog noises in the chorus. That helped his terror. If the children weren't scared – his foot slipped.

He gripped rock with his fingers and managed not to fall. He carried on feeling a bit sick and surprised he hadn't shat himself. Actually, the children singing didn't help much. They were idiots who should have been scared.

Finally, mercifully, they reached a wide track that wound at a sensible angle down the side of a broad, magnificent valley.

Finn could see why they called it the Valley of the Gods. Lately, when he'd been unable to sleep at night, he'd tried to take his mind off monsters and embarrassment by amalgamating all the astonishing sights they'd seen and trying to design the perfect landscape, where he would live with Paloma and Thyri; along with Erik, Wulf and the others when he was feeling generous.

He'd made up some pretty smashing places, but nothing he'd thought of came close to the beauty of the Valley of the Gods.

Red cliff-sided mountains soared majestically from a wooded valley floor. Patches of snow nestled tastefully in niches around flat-topped, tree-fringed, white-rock summits. Eagles and condors glided on high. Fat songbirds chirruped with brazen happiness. Rodents hopped, stopped and twitched their noses at him. Bighorn sheep stood imperiously on outcrops as if they knew they looked good.

"It's lovely here," he said to a female warlock who'd fallen back to walk with them.

"Yes," she said. She was about Erik's age and she walked in a flat-footed clumping sort of way, as if she'd done an awful lot of walking and had had just about enough of it. "The Valley of the Gods. Or at least it was before the Warlock Queen killed them all."

"If she killed all the gods, does that make her a god, too? God of gods perhaps?"

"I suppose. She'd be the most powerful god since the landmakers. Maybe more powerful."

"Is she really that mighty?" Finn asked.

The warlock shook her head. "We thought this valley's gods would protect us. But the Warlock Queen got us, even if she did strike indirectly."

"Indirectly?"

"Four days ago there was a colossal storm to the north. A flash flood came roaring down the canyon shortly after sunrise. It was a big one. We reckon a landslide must have emptied a lake. Luckily, most people were up, we heard it coming and everyone got clear. It destroyed our village and most of our crops, though. Our new little town, which we'd put a lot of effort into over the last few moons, was buried under mud and rock."

"I'm sorry."

"Don't be. Nobody died and we're building a new place to live higher up the valley side. We live on and, hopefully, we will do so until the Warlock Queen is defeated. Which brings us to you. Maya – she's our chief– sent us to meet you. A couple of the Warlocks said you were going to help against the Warlock Queen."

"That's why we're here."

"There aren't very many of you."

Finn looked at the Wootah and Calnians ahead and behind. It looked like Ottar had eaten something he shouldn't have done because there were green smears either side of his mouth and Freydis was telling him off.

"I suppose there aren't," he said, "but we're more effective than we look."

"How did you come to be saving the world?"

Finn looked at her. She wasn't mocking him. "I was minding my own business and it just kind of happened."

"Tell me all."

"How about I tell you some? It would take weeks to tell you all."

"Go for it. I'm Ollia, by the way."

"Finn the Deep."

He told their tale as they walked down into the wonderful valley, leaving out irrelevant parts and incidents that showed him in a bad light.

The valley flattened out and they followed a narrow, uneven and muddy path above the flash flood's devastation.

"It was all woodland and pasture before," said Ollia. "Lovely and teeming with life."

"Wow," said Finn. It wasn't lovely now.

A gigantic tongue of jagged boulders, smashed stone and red mud filled the valley floor. Finn saw a rattlesnake winding its way between boulders, but no other animals.

"The Virgin River's still flowing below that lot," said Ollia.

"It will carry it all away, too, given time," said Erik, who'd joined them.

Finn realised he'd seen the place before, in a dream. Or had he? The moment he thought he had, he questioned himself.

The path turned back up the valley side after a while. After a short climb they arrived at the new home of the Warriors and Warlock tribe.

Sofi Tornado guessed the woman watching them climb the slope was the chief of the Warriors and Warlock tribe, and she was right. She was tall and looked strong. She was dressed in the warrior uniform of leather trousers, jerkin and cap.

"I'm Maya," she said, recognising that Sofi was the leader without asking. "Follow me, please." The chief seemed confident, calm and comfortable with her command. She was young, not much older than Finn the Deep, but her bearing and her expression said that she'd left her youth behind a long time ago. Sofi dared hope that they had found a useful ally.

"I'll come with you, Sofi," said Wulf.

"If you like." Now that they were closer to The Meadows,

Sofi was less keen to indulge Wulf with a share of the command. It was possible the best course of action might result in some of their own people's deaths. She wasn't sure he had the mettle to give those orders.

While the others went with the warlock who'd been talking to Finn, Wulf and Sofi followed Maya through the tent and lean-to camp. Perhaps one in five people wore the Warrior or Warlock tribe's garb. Many of the others were injured, and there were several large groups of children being looked after by just a few adults. Sofi didn't want to ask Maya where the parents were.

"Who are the people who don't look like warriors or warlocks?" she asked instead.

"We're a mix of many tribes now," Maya answered. "Anyone is welcome so long as they don't bring disease or a bad attitude."

The chief led Sofi and Wulf into a large leather tent.

It was surprisingly homely. Two flamboyantly decorated and skilfully made water jugs sat on a table with four plain, earthenware cups, and there was a low bed on each side, each covered with subtly patterned rugs. A large flap above the table was open to flood the room with air and light and give a view across the Valley of the Gods to the red, white and green mountains on the far side.

Maya gestured for them to sit on one of the beds and poured water for them.

"Tell me everything," she said.

Sofi and Wulf did.

The chief listened and nodded, interrupting sometimes for clarification. Sofi had no qualms telling Maya about her vision quest and the coffin. She trusted the woman.

Maya confirmed that two warriors matching the description of the men Sofi had seen in her vision quest had disappeared when the paradise of The Meadows had died and the disasters had started.

Sofi didn't tell Maya about Janny and his people and neither did Wulf. It seemed he agreed with Sofi that there was no point burdening Maya with everything.

"So," said Maya when Sofi's tale was done, "it was our fault. We knew it was the Warlock Queen causing all this horror, but we didn't know why. It is unfortunate that it was caused by one of us, but that doubles my resolve to help you end it. What can we do?"

"We have to get the coffin and Ottar the Moaner to The Pyramid," said Sofi.

"Why?" asked Maya.

"We suspect," said Wulf, looking at Sofi as if for confirmation, "that the Warlock Queen intends to kill Ottar and give his body to her own child."

Sofi nodded sadly.

"I see." Maya shook her head. "Do you have any idea how you'll crack her?"

"Not a one unfortunately. I heard that you'd tried before?" said Wulf.

"Our last attempt was ten days ago. There was a cold spell and I hoped the monsters would be docile. Fifty of us set off down the Virgin River. We got to the point where the Virgin River flows into the Red River. The first canoe hit the Red River and dissolved. Its crew screamed, then they were gone. The next three boats back-paddled, but too late. The current was strong and they went down, too. Three boats, including mine, reached the bank. Thirty warlocks and warriors were reduced to a bloody foam floating off down the Red River in a heartbeat. With our numbers so badly reduced, we didn't press on. Four more were killed by monsters on the way home, another five badly injured.

"It is not something I look forward to attempting again, but we caused this and will do all we can to help you."

"Thank you," said Wulf. "How far from The Meadows does the Virgin River meet the Red River?" asked Wulf.

"One day's easy walk. In normal circumstances."

"So I guess we start with a boat ride and stop before the Red River."

Maya, Sofi and Wulf debated, came up with a plan and agreed to leave as soon as everything was ready.

# Chapter 3

## Virgin River

The sun sank behind the red and white mountains as Sitsi Kestrel walked with Keef the Berserker out of the Valley of the Gods. Marred as it was by the giant flash flood's debris, Sitsi was sad to be leaving such a beautiful place.

Ahead of the Wootah and Calnians, some holding burning torches, were several dozen warriors and warlocks. Sofi had told her the plan. She couldn't see how it could possibly work, but all the same it was good to have help.

She could hear Ottar and Freydis larking about behind her. She'd worked it out. She wished that she hadn't. She was pretty sure Sofi knew. They were taking Ottar to his death. They had to be. He'd be killed and the Warlock Queen's son would take his body.

She blinked. Maybe she was wrong. But she wasn't often wrong. Sitsi looked back at the lovely valley, trying to take her mind off the subject.

She hoped she'd be able to come back to the Valley of the Gods with Keef the Berserker. Maybe they'd settle here? Why not? She didn't feel bound to the Owsla any more and she was pretty sure Sofi would let her go. Maybe Sofi would stay with them?

No. Sofi wouldn't settle. She'd do her duty. She'd go back to the Green tribe, pick up Ayanna's son Calnian and take him back to Calnia to rule. She'd need help with that. Thinking about it, Sitsi would never be happy letting Sofi go off and face the danger alone. And Keef would love the adventure. He was no readier for domestication than she was.

The only certain thing about her future was that it was unknown. It was frightening and exciting. However, if they were taking Ottar to his death, that would cast a pall over the rest of her life. Surely there had to be another way?

Time was that she'd known the future. She was Calnian Owsla. She would fight until she was too old or she was killed. If she survived, she would train others until she was too old for that, then she'd sit around and knit, embroider, sing and gossip until she died. That had been her life plan. She'd never thought that Calnia as she knew it would come to an end, nor that she would find love.

It all changed the day they'd captured Keef, cut off his ear and gouged out his eye. Had she fallen in love with him then? No. But she'd liked him. She remembered standing on the bridge, listening to him being brave and funny. What was it he'd said? *Don't take my eye, you don't want a captive with no depth perception.*

It was the first time she'd ever liked an enemy and, perhaps more importantly, the first time she'd ever questioned the actions of the Owsla.

*Oh, Innowak*, she called after the great swan that had flown behind the mountain, *please let us live through the attack on The Pyramid. Please let all of us live.*

That was never going to happen.

*If we don't all make it, please let Keef the Berserker and me live*, she added, feeling guilty.

They reached the spot where the Virgin River resurfaced from the flood debris. Chief Maya directed the preparation of the canoes. There wasn't anything for the Calnians to do. It was wonderful.

She watched a warrior toss a squirrel into the Virgin River.

The rodent swam ashore, seriously pissed off but otherwise unharmed.

Sitsi waited with the others for a while. The mood seemed both sombre and fearful. They were heading into a battle they might not win. She wondered if any of the Wootah had worked out Ottar's role. She suspected that Keef had. He'd been the only Wootah to understand that killing Pook was the right thing to do. She hoped he would be as understanding about the sacrifice of a child. Their child.

Right then, Ottar was the most relaxed of all of them, sitting on a log, puffing out one cheek and then the other.

Sitsi had to look away.

Paloma Pronghorn ran alongside the Virgin River. They'd decided it was safer to travel by boat at night. She didn't know why and she didn't care. She would never be safer in a boat.

She tore up a mountain. Caught up in her thoughts, she misjudged it. It was pretty much a cliff for the last hundred paces. Relentless gravity pulled at her as she neared the peak. She strained as hard as she was able – something she very rarely did – leapt the last couple of paces and was on safe ground again.

She'd made it. Phew. Falling backwards down a mountain would have been a seriously dumb thing to do.

She stood on the cliff edge. The boats wound downstream along the grey river below like little black beetles. All her friends were in those boats, heading towards probably the most dangerous place in the world. They looked very vulnerable from her high perch.

Which of them would make it out alive? She hoped they all would, she really did. She may have messed things up a bit by snogging Finnbogi and then ignoring him, but they had a tolerably awkward relationship now. She was with a group of diverse characters who made her feel comfortable and valued, and, what was more, she valued every single one of them. Even Finnbogi.

So she really didn't want any of them to be killed.

Who would she pick, she wondered, if she had to choose one of them to die? They were her friends now and that probably wasn't a normal thing to be thinking, but who said she had to become normal just because she had friends now?

An image of Thyri Treelegs' sulky face popped into her mind.

Yup, definitely her. But she'd still be upset if Thyri died. She'd even risk her own life to save her.

She'd changed.

Paloma sighed and ran on. Moments later she was happy again. At least she still had running, and she would still have running after whatever happened at The Meadows. Assuming she made it through. *Who was she kidding?* she thought as she tore down the hill, freaking out an owl that was flapping along a narrow passage of woodland. She was Paloma Pronghorn. Of course she was going to live.

She'd do her best to make sure the others did, too.

Erik the Angry awoke, rolled his head around and heard his neck crack.

"Good morning," said Chogolisa without turning.

They had a canoe to themselves, away from the children they'd been carrying so often. Wulf had insisted on it, even though it meant that his own canoe with Freydis, Ottar, Thyri and Sassa was a little crowded. Erik was grateful and embarrassed by the kindness, and tried not to think that Wulf was giving them some time together because he thought one or both of them was going to get killed.

"Why don't you get some sleep now?" he asked Chogolisa.

"I'm fine," she said quietly. "We'll sleep during the day."

"I can never sleep in the day."

"I can. So sleep now and guard me when we stop."

That seemed reasonable to Erik. The current was swift enough to carry the boat without paddle power, but there were no serious rapids so she'd be fine piloting the craft alone.

"Okay," he said, settling back. He'd been worried about Chogolisa, and himself for that matter. The coffin seemed to exude some kind of melancholy miasma. Now that the warlocks and warriors had taken if off their hands – they were currently towing it in its own canoe a good way behind them – they'd both perked up a lot.

Erik liked the Warlocks and Warrior tribe, particularly Maya, their chief. He'd told her that being too near the coffin made you feel shitty. She'd listened, nodded and asked him what he thought they should do. That was why it was being towed in its own boat.

He liked it when people were clever enough to listen to him and do what he recommended. Kobosh, his old friend and chief of the Lakchans had been like that.

Erik wondered if he'd ever see him again.

Moments later he was dreaming about his bear friend, Astrid. She was towering on two legs, paws on hips, angrily asking where the Hel he thought he was, and when he was coming back.

He was woken what seemed like a couple of moments later by a bang and a splash of water on his face.

"Erik?" said Chogolisa. She was paddling hard.

"Yes?"

"Might need a bit of help."

Erik sat up, but was knocked back as the canoe surged down what he guessed was a small waterfall.

He gripped the sides and hauled himself up.

They were in a canyon. The sky was beginning to lighten. The boat turned sideways to the current and he could see past Chogolisa. The river was churning.

Erik grabbed his paddle. "Ready. Just tell me—"

"Hard on the left, hard on the left. Don't ease up until I tell you." He paddled, hard. "Ease up . . . now!"

The canyon was deep and majestically meandering. The canoe bucked and slid, plunged and rocked along the vivacious current. Chogolisa shouted instructions and they paddled, leant from side to side, sometimes guiding the boat along with the flow, sometimes fighting the current.

Erik was so wrapped up in his work that he'd forgotten the others, until a couple of high-pitched screams rang out behind them.

He turned, expecting to see a smashed boat and heads bobbing down the treacherous tumult, but it was Freydis and Ottar, squealing with joy.

"Wooooo-tah!" shouted Wulf, paddle aloft.

"Wooooo-tah!" he yelled himself as they flowed over the next low waterfall.

"Wooooo-tah!" he heard Finnbogi shout.

Erik smiled. For all its hardships, this trip hadn't been all doom and gloom because, quite simply, the Wootah were a lot of fun. So were Chogolisa, Paloma and Sitsi now, but it had taken exposure to the Wootah to bring it out of them. Even Sofi was good company – and he'd be dead at the bottom of a canyon without her, of course.

He wanted to go on more adventures. He really hoped they lived through this one.

"Left paddle, left paddle!" cried Chogolisa. She was enjoying it now as much as he was.

He was looking forward to a life with her more than anything.

It was almost a shame when they rounded a bend and found several warriors standing bravely in the fast channel, gripping canoes and shoving them towards a shingle beach.

Chogolisa stuck her paddle forwards to the left and, with one mighty swoosh, sent their canoe surging through the water towards the beach with such force that Erik fell backwards.

She held out a hand to help him up and out of the canoe. By the way she'd driven the craft ashore, she could have piloted it alone through the rapids without a bother. She hadn't needed his help. She'd just wanted to enjoy it with him.

He smiled.

Chogolisa stood, hands on hips, watching upriver for the others. She could have strode into the current and proved her strength by hauling in the boats like the warriors, but showing off wasn't her thing.

She was so lovely, so kind, so powerful, so pretty. What did she see in him? He didn't need to ask her whether he was just a fling to distract her as they travelled. Paloma Pronghorn might have done that, but not Chogolisa. He was pretty sure she was the type who mated for life, just like he'd always wanted to be.

Suddenly, Erik's breath was short and he felt a little sick and faint. He sat on a boulder. Was this death coming? He was over forty years old now. People his age often just died. It did happen.

But he didn't think he was dying. Thinking about how much he loved Chogolisa and the rest of them, he was suddenly very, very afraid. He could feel the fear in his *elbows*, for the love of Tor.

He knew they had to go into The Meadows, that they had to return the dead boy to his dead mother at The Pyramid. But he didn't want to do it. He didn't want Chogolisa to be in danger ever again.

The others came ashore and Erik recovered enough to stand up and fake a smile. The Warriors and Warlocks made breakfast as the sky lightened, but, other than bringing them food, kept their distance from the Wootah and Calnians.

Maya wandered over when they were eating. "I hope you don't think we're being aloof," she said, "I just know you've had a difficult journey and thought you could do without having to make polite conversation, so I've told the others to leave you alone."

"That," said Sofi, "suits us very well."

After eating, Erik and the others turned their canoes upside down to make shelters against the grass bank. The sun wasn't over the canyon's sides yet, but the day was already heating up. Erik made sure that Chogolisa's spot in the lee of their boat was comfortable then sat on the other side, leaning against the canoe.

He never knew if Chogolisa did actually sleep, because as soon as he sat down, even though he'd slept a good part of the night, he himself fell into a deep, dream-free slumber.

He woke around midday. It was so hot in the deep canyon, even by the rushing river, that it was difficult to breathe. He went to check on Chogolisa. She wasn't under the boat.

He panicked for about four heartbeats then spotted her sitting upstream making a garland from the flowers that hung in clusters from the riverbank.

"If there's any snow on the mountains upriver—" he said.

"Then this heat will have melted it already and it will be on its way downriver," she said. "I was thinking that, too. We should have camped on top of the bank, at least."

"Shall we get everyone to move?"

"No, let them sleep. Let's sit here and keep an eye on the current."

A warrior appeared out of a bush.

"What are you doing? Get back under cover!" he barked. It seemed the warriors weren't all as charming as Maya.

"We're keeping an eye on the current," Erik explained, "in case there's a flash flood."

The warrior puffed out his chest like a fluffy bird trying to attract a mate. "And you didn't think we were capable of thinking that?"

"That wasn't our main motivation, no," said Chogolisa. "It's so hot that—"

"That snowmelt might cause a flash flood." His tone was patronising and mocking. "What do you think I'm watching for?"

"I don't know," said Chogolisa, cocking her head innocently, "maybe for a decent character to come bobbing along the river, so you can swap if for the fucking bellend one Innowak gave you?"

Erik glowed with pride. *Fucking bellend* was one of his expressions.

The warrior looked her up and down as if deciding whether to attack her, then said: "Get back to your shelter and stay there. The size of you, any passing monster will spot us."

Erik did not much like having Chogolisa's size mocked. He stood, Turkey Friend in hand. Chogolisa put a hand on his shoulder. "It's quite secluded, our shelter, isn't it?"

"It is," he answered.

"Let's go back there. I'm sure we'll find something to do."

They set off again at dusk.

Finn the Deep had loved the rapids that morning. His boat mates Keef the Berserker and Sitsi Kestrel liked to take the fun routes rather than the safe ones. It wasn't what Finn would have done himself, but he was glad they had.

This next section of rapids, however, was considerably more treacherous. It didn't help that it was getting darker every moment. Finn managed to whack his own paddle into his lip, which bled, then Keef yelled at him for paddling on the wrong side. *We are going to drown*, he thought after they'd made a particularly brazen route choice and plunged over a waterfall higher than he was tall. Moments later, however, they popped out of the canyon into a gently rolling valley. The river widened and the current slowed.

The moon was bright. Crazily bright. Mountains to the east and a monumental mesa to the west were silver and black.

He counted the canoes ahead and behind, then counted again to be sure.

"One boat missing," he reported grimly.

"Did you count ours?" asked Keef.

"Ah, no. We're all here then."

They stopped for a meal on a rare stony section of bank. Finn didn't know what meal it was. Hardworkers hadn't had a name for a meal in the middle of the night. Everyone in Hardwork had slept through the night to prepare for another day of indolence.

Finn wasn't hungry anyway. He walked upriver, alone.

He wasn't sulking. He was overjoyed for everyone who'd found love. He really was. It was wonderful that Sitsi and Keef had got it on. They were so well suited. Wulf and Sassa had been a great couple for years. He didn't mind that his father and Chogolisa didn't have time for anyone else – they were new lovers heading into a dangerous situation. And he was glad that he'd accepted Thyri would never be the one for him. She was becoming more introverted and moody every day. If they were a couple he'd have to deal with that. How tiresome would that be? *Imagine the sex, though,* said a voice in his mind. *No, I won't,* Finn argued back.

*Play with the stones you receive,* said dead Gunnhild, *not with the ones you wish you had.*

*I'll give it a go,* Finn replied.

He sat on the shingle and threw stones into the dark swirl. A fish leapt and flashed silver.

And Paloma? Was his campaign of aloofness working? He had no idea because she seemed to be operating the same campaign towards him.

He stopped throwing stones into the river and started to throw them at his own feet.

He'd denied his child and left it to be brought up by another man. He didn't deserve love. He'd probably die attacking The Meadows but if he did survive he was destined to walk the world alone.

*Worse than any disease is not to be content with yourself*, said Gunnhild.

*I'm sure you're right*, thought Finn. *But what if yourself is a prick that you hate for leaving its baby?*

*Just cheer the fuck up, it's happened.* That didn't sound like Gunnhild, but Finn was glad to take the advice.

It would be okay, walking the world alone. He'd be a craggy wandering hero, then one day he'd find his child, and they would –

There was a footstep behind him. He jumped to his feet and turned in one move, pulling Foe Slicer free of its scabbard.

"Please don't kill me," said Paloma Pronghorn with the hint of a smile that said *I know I'd kill you a thousand times out of a thousand.*

She looked vibrant. Finn was tired and his arse was wet and itchy from the canoe.

"I've been practising," he said.

She nodded. "I'd like to talk before we head into The Meadows."

"Sure." Finn's voice cracked only a little. He sat back down on the stones. Paloma sat next to him.

*I am a very cool man with a mighty sword*, he told himself, hoping he wouldn't be sick.

"Finn," she said.

He nodded. It wasn't a very happy sounding "Finn". He

almost welcomed disappointment. Hope was becoming unbearable.

"I am not the one for you."

*There you go.*

"Oh."

"I wish I was. It would have made logistical sense to hook up with you, and seeing the other smug couples cuddling and giggling makes me want to gouge my eyes out and stuff them in my ears."

"Me, too." He picked up a stone and threw it across the river. Two ducks shot out of the reeds, quacking angrily. "And tear my nose off and ram it up my arse so I can't smell their contentment. There's no chance that we—"

"No. You're a good-looking chap, Finn. You're clever and you're kind. You're funny and you're brave. A lot of women will find you attractive."

"But not you."

"I do think you're attractive, Finn. If you were my age I'd be all over you like a pox at plague time. But you are not my age."

"Erik must be fifteen years older than Chogolisa."

"She likes older men. It's not unusual. I'm the same. Or at least I'm not attracted to younger men."

"I see."

"When this is done, I've no idea where we'll go. Maybe back to Calnia to install Calnian as emperor. Maybe we'll go to the Badlands now that Rappa Hoga is in charge. Point is, we'll go somewhere where there will be a lot of women your age. And you, my conquering hero, will have to beat them away with a shitty stick."

"You think?"

"I know. Finn the Deep, the exotic adventurer from across the Great Salt Sea. A lot of women will fall for you."

"So why hasn't Thyri?" *Why haven't you?* he thought.

"Not all women, Finn, just a lot of them. Some won't

because some women like other women. Some women like
clever men – warlock types. Some are more into strong but
stupid – your warrior."

"I don't think all warriors are stupid."

"And not all warlocks are clever. It's a generalisation.
Point is, people like different types of people. You're not
my type and you're not Thyri's. But you are definitely a
lot of women's type."

They watched a red-tailed hawk fly downriver. It spotted
them, flicked its wings and headed for the hills to the east.

"I suppose you're right," said Finn. It was pretty much
what Moolba had told him. Was it that outlandish to believe
that the woman would be attracted to an exotic swordsman
who'd recently been on a quest to save the world?

*Who'd left his baby behind?*

"I don't deserve anyone."

He could feel Paloma looking at him but he didn't turn.
"Because you're the sort of utter shit who abandoned his
unborn baby?"

"Yes."

"We've all done shitty things, Finn. I've killed hundreds
of people and I don't hate myself. Both Bodil and that kid
will be happier with Olaf."

"You think Olaf will be a better dad than me?"

"No. He's a dick and you're a decent guy, or at least you
have the potential to be a decent guy. But you don't love
Bodil and he probably does in his weird twatty way, and the
child will be safer there than it would be with you. Arguably,
your desire to be important to your child is selfish. Sure, it
could do with a father, but that doesn't have to be you. And,
let's admit it, you'll get to adventure around without a tiny
child in tow. It is the best thing for everyone."

"But it's the *wrong* thing."

"Because your Aunt Gunnhild wouldn't have liked it?"

"Well, yes."

"Forget that. You have enough things to be unhappy about without getting wrapped up in somebody else's morality."

"Thanks."

"I mean it. Don't invent worries, forgive yourself for things you can't change and enjoy yourself. That's the Paloma way and it's the best way." She leapt to her feet and held out a hand. "Come on."

"When I beat these girls away with a shitty stick," asked Finn as they walked beside the rolling moonlit river, "what's the best kind of shit?"

"Badger."

"Badger?"

"It's the smelliest."

"Not skunk?"

"Not actually as smelly. But it will probably still keep your suitors at bay. Basic rule of thumb for shitty sticks is to use carnivore crap, never herbivore."

"So bighorn shit might actually attract women."

"It might, Finn. It just might."

They met Keef and Sitsi coming the other way. Sitsi raised an eyebrow.

"What the Hel are you two doing together looking so pleased with yourselves?" Keef demanded.

"We're good friends now," said Finn.

When they were past, Paloma punched his arm: "If we are going to be friends, you'll have to stop saying lame things like *we're good friends now*.

"I know. I was joking," said Finn, "because we're actually *best* friends."

Paloma punched his arm again, quite a bit harder.

Finn smiled.

# Chapter 4

## Valley of Fire

The sky was lightening when they stopped again. Finn guessed that the confluence with the Red River was ahead and they'd probably have to walk from here. Shame, he thought. His arse was so itchy from the constant damp that it actually hurt, but bobbing along with a painful bum was better than walking across a land that might turn into murderous monsters any moment.

Warriors and warlocks busied about, preparing food bags and water skins. Several were coiling ropes and slinging them over shoulders. Finn hoped they weren't going to have to climb anything with ropes. How steep was The Pyramid?

He saw one of the warriors headed downstream with a squirrel in one hand. *Where were they getting all the squirrels?* he wondered, following the man. He didn't have anything else to do. Was this the same squirrel they'd used to test the water upstream? If so, it was a very unlucky animal.

The warrior was a muscular man, bigger than Wulf. Finn had noticed him before because he'd been staring sourly at the Calnians and Wootah.

The sky was tinged pink at the eastern edge when the warrior reached a stretch of bank above the confluence of the Virgin and Red Rivers.

Finn listened out for the squirrel's thoughts, found them, and immediately wished he hadn't. It *was* the same squirrel that they'd thrown in the river upstream. It was not happy.

*Bite him! Bite him!* Finn told the squirrel, but it was too angry to listen.

The squirrel's rage turned to hatred as the warrior tossed it high and far. Hatred turned to terror as it fell, limbs waggling, towards the lighter water of the Red River.

The moment it touched the river's surface it burst in a cloud of fizzing steam. There was a flash of agony then its thoughts were gone.

The large man laughed.

"You think that was funny, do you?" said Finn, marching up the slope towards him, not sure what he was going to do.

"Yeah. I do," he said, looking down at Finn. His eyes were deep-set because his eyebrows were muscular. His *voice* was muscular.

He reminded Finn of Garth. Not looks-wise, but in the way he regarded Finn with amused contempt.

"You killed an animal when you could have chucked in a cactus pad and seen all you needed to see."

"So what?"

"So you're a twat." Finn's ears were hot. He knew he was being very stupid, but he was very angry. That squirrel had suffered.

The huge man swung a punch.

Finn ducked and danced to one side. He jabbed a fist into ribs and pulled Foe Slicer free of its scabbard as he passed, then leapt and smacked the flat of his blade across the man's arse cheeks with all his might.

The warrior stumbled away, one hand on his ribs, one on his arse. He looked at Finn, confusion knitting his meaty brow.

Finn slipped Foe Slicer back into its scabbard. "We're on the same side," he said, "we should be struggling together

. . . and not as we were just doing. I mean fighting the Warlock Queen and her monsters together."

"You called me a twat."

"And you took a life when you didn't need to. There's been far too much of that sort of thing and there's going to be more. We don't need to add to it."

The big man looked unconvinced.

"Tell you what," said Finn, "I won't call you a twat again if you don't throw any more squirrels into poisonous rivers. Deal?"

The large warrior looked westwards, then back at Finn. He was smiling. "Yeah. Why not? Deal. Come on, we've got to get back. We'll be heading off soon."

"But the sun will be up in a couple of heartbeats."

"I know. It's going to be a hot one, too. But I'm just a follower."

"Me, too."

"What's your name?"

"Zeg. Yours?"

"Finn."

"Pleased to meet you, Finn. Tell me about the bum-slapper you've got there."

"It's called Foe Slicer." Finn drew the sword and proffered it to Zeg, pommel first. "Have a hold."

Zeg rejoined the warriors and Finn went back to his lot.

"What are you grinning about?" asked Erik.

"Nothing," said Finn.

They headed off westwards up slickrock. They hadn't been going long when the sun rose over the horizon behind them.

"Tor's helmet!" said Finn to nobody in particular when he felt its heat. "It's like being pounced on by a burning dagger-tooth."

"Nicely put."

Finn jumped. Thyri Treelegs had sneaked up behind him. There was a gap behind her to where the children were walking up the stone slope with Erik, Chogolisa, Sitsi and Keef.

"Have you thought of becoming a storyteller when this is over?" she asked, falling into stride alongside him. "You could walk from place to place making up things to say."

"A sort of warrior-cum-storyteller?"

"Just a storyteller."

"Thanks."

She punched his arm and grinned. "I'm joking! Your dad would miss you if you went off alone."

"Would you?" he dared.

She walked on for four very long heartbeats, then said, "Yes, I would."

"Thyri," he said. "I don't know what Sofi and Wulf have got planned for this attack on The Pyramid, but I know we'll both be involved. We might die. There's something I need to tell you."

"You're going to tell me that you love me? Well, sorry, Finn, but I was never interested. And I don't think you do love me, I think—"

"It wasn't that," he said. "I was a kid when I thought I loved you. I've . . . changed. I wanted to tell you that Garth Anvilchin wasn't killed by Scraylings."

"What?"

"He tried to kill me when the tornado hit us, then again by the Water Mother."

"Why?"

"He said it was because I wasn't as clever as I thought I was."

"He was right."

"I know." Finn noticed a long-legged lizard on a rock, watching them walk by.

"If he'd tried to kill you," said Thyri, "you'd be dead. He was ten times the man you'll ever be."

"At the tornado he punched me and knocked me out. I would have died if I hadn't fallen into a trench."

"You just fell into the trench. Garth was nowhere near you."

"Do you remember that day? I was carrying Freydis. I was falling behind and Anvilchin came back to get her. That's when he did it."

"I didn't see. I was busy rescuing Sassa and watching my brother die."

"He hit me. He meant for me to die."

"And at the Water Mother?"

"He came at me with his axes. I pushed him off the cliff."

"Bollocks."

"He goaded me. He told me how you shagged. He said you begged him to do disgusting things to you."

"That's not true! He didn't say that. He couldn't have done because we never . . . You wouldn't have beaten him. You couldn't have done."

"You'd taught me how to block. That was all I needed. I blocked two blows, shoved him and over he went."

They walked on in silence, Thyri shaking her head. Finn remembered the sick feeling in his stomach when Garth had lifted him over his head and walked to the top of the cliff. He remembered Sassa's arrow, sticking out of Garth's mouth. Erik wiggling the arrow to pull it out of Garth's face. He remembered himself and his father rolling the heavy body over the cliff.

"Tell me what really happened, Finn," said Thyri. She was crying. "What can it matter now?"

"I pushed him off."

"Please, Finn, tell me the truth. I loved him. I still do and I always will. What happened? I deserve to know, especially if we're all about to die."

Finn sighed. He looked around. Nobody was in earshot. Sofi Tornado could probably hear him, of course, but she was as likely to sprout a second head as she was to gossip. And she probably knew anyway.

"Okay. Garth did try to kill me, during the tornado that took Chnob, and again at the Water Mother."

"The truth!"

"At the Water Mother, he lifted me above his head. He was going to throw me off the cliff. I was terrified. Sassa came. She had to choose between shooting him or letting him throw me off the cliff. He really was going to do it. She told him not to, again and again, and didn't shoot until he was halfway through hurling me."

"She chose your life over his?"

"I don't think it was an easy decision, I really don't. I think that's why she waited until the very last moment. It made more sense to keep Garth. He was far the better fighter and it was before we knew I could control animals a bit. But I guess she chose the would-be murderer over his victim. Maybe you'd have done the same."

"Sassa killed him," she said.

"Garth was holding me over his head. He was about to throw me off the cliff. She didn't have a choice."

"A choice is exactly what she *did* have."

Thyri stalked off ahead.

Finn was relieved. He hadn't enjoyed holding that secret. Thyri's anger wouldn't last. It was clear that Garth had been in the wrong and Finn had been a victim. Anyone could see that.

He chuckled to himself. Not long ago, his next leap of logic would have had Thyri leaping into his arms. He didn't expect that any more, and, he realised with mild surprise, he really didn't want it.

Had he manned up? No, that was a silly expression. Every woman he knew was tougher than he was, including Freydis. He'd just grown up. Better late than never.

They walked up a rocky crest. Bare red, orange and purple

rock stretched all around arranged in crazy crests and tumescent domes. All was silent. The sun hammered down, cooking the rock. It felt like a kiln and it smelled like a kiln.

They followed the warlocks and warriors off the crest and down to a valley. Despite the heat, the warlocks were still in their feather jackets and the warriors in their leathers. Finn guessed they were used to it. They walked along the valley's dry red sand floor. Walking on the sand was an arse ache, but the rock either side was a mess of fissures and craggy fins.

"Quite hard going, this sand," said Erik.

"Maybe running will be easier?" Freydis suggested.

"It's too hot to run," said Finn.

"Try!" She trotted off, knees high.

Finn copied her.

Running was a bit easier, strangely enough, and soon he and the girl had closed the gap on the leading warriors and warlocks to around fifty paces.

Finn was comparing the gaits of the two groups – the warriors were bandy-legged, the warlocks dainty – when a gigantic brown and white spider exploded out of the ground in a shower of red sand, grabbed a warlock, leapt backwards and disappeared, leaving nothing but a cloud of settling sand.

It happened so fast that Finn wasn't certain he'd seen it.

"Off the sand!" shouted Erik.

Finn grabbed Freydis's hand and pulled her towards the rock. The ground fell away ahead of them. A spider the size of a humped bear rose out of the ground. Finn froze. The creature looked at him with four small, round eyes in the centre of its head and larger oval double squashed-together eyes on the sides. It was covered in sparse, wiry brown fur, with darker bands around its legs and across its face. Its huge fangs, also furry, hung below its face not unlike a proud pair of breasts presented in a low-cut dress. As well as long legs, each ending in a small claw, it had little arms stretching around its fangs, presumably for pulling prey into its horrible maw.

Freydis hopped to one side, stringing her bow. Finn pulled Foe Slicer from its scabbard.

The spider advanced.

Freydis's arrow zipped into its bulbous abdomen. It did a weird little dance, then hissed – *hissed* – and kept coming.

Finn looked into its horrible eyes and froze.

Freydis ran round him and chopped at the spider's leg with her obsidian moon blade. The beast struck for her with its fangs, thrusting its head far enough forward for Finn to stab Foe Slicer hard, in the centre of its four eyes. The blade cracked through chitin and slid in.

Finn pulled his sword free and the beast collapsed.

"We beat it!" shouted Freydis.

"We beat that one," said Finn.

Dozens more – hundreds maybe – had launched from the sand and were setting about the warlocks and warriors. The bear-sized spider that Finn had killed had been a small one.

The warriors fought solidly. Legs wide, they swung their heavy spears like clubs. The warlocks had a lighter style, more like Sofi's jumping and spinning. Both were effective and many spiders were dying, but there were more and more emerging from the red sand.

Finn saw Ollia, the woman he'd talked to on the way into the Valley of the Gods. She was standing in the thick of it with a warrior, shooting arrow after arrow. A spider plunged is sharp leg through the other archer's neck and he fell. The monster clamped its jaws around his head and dragged him underground. Ollia stared for a moment, then skipped away backwards, shooting arrows into the giant arachnids.

"Wooooo-tah!" Keef the Berserker shouted, as he, Wulf,

Sofi, Chogolisa and Thyri ran past Finn towards the fight, weapons raised, kicking up red dust.

Paloma, who'd been off scouting as usual, came tearing across the slickrock from the east and leapt into the fray, killing stick swinging.

Sitsi and Sassa ran to a perch over to their right, a couple of paces up the rocky valley side and began to shoot arrows into the spiders.

"Finn, Freydis, over here!" Erik dropped Ottar from his shoulders next to Sitsi and Sassa, and pulled the coffin off the sand. Freydis ran to join them.

"You look after Ottar, I'm going to fight," Finn yelled to Erik, holding Foe Slicer aloft.

"No, Finn. Get off the sand."

"But . . ."

"Try and get into their minds! We can stop this attack!"

"But . . ." His father was right.

He skipped onto the slickrock as the others ran up the valley towards the beleaguered warriors and warlocks. He was still holding Foe Slicer. The sword seemed to twitch in his hand as the others reached the spiders. He wanted to fight.

More and more of the huge beasts were bursting from the sand. He saw Keef shear spider legs with Arse Splitter, then there were too many of the monsters and he could no longer see any humans. It was all a mess of sand, screams and hisses.

He closed his eyes and tried to reach the monsters' minds. He found them. They weren't angry or even hungry, they were simply filled with a dogged desire to kill humans.

*No, not humans, we must kill each other*, he thought. *Humans are good and we are bad. Spiders like us must die and –*

*BE GONE!* a huge voice shouted and all went black.

He woke. He'd been out for only a moment. Sassa, Sitsi, Paloma and Freydis were still standing on the slickrock shooting arrows. Ottar was jumping up and down, watching the battle and flailing his hands. Erik was sitting next to him, shaking his head and blinking.

"Same for you?" he asked Erik.

"Warlock Queen," his father replied.

"I guess so." Despite the intense sun Finn was suddenly cold. He had felt her power. She was a landslide and he was a spring flower in her path. If he tried to take over the spiders' minds again she would crush him.

"I don't want to . . ." he said to his father.

"No," agreed Erik. "Back to traditional means." He hefted Turkey Friend. "Ottar, stay next to Sassa, all right?"

The boy nodded.

"Finn, come with me."

Father and son ran down onto the sand, club and sword in hand, towards the melee of spiders and people.

A warrior staggered towards them, face bloodied. A spider leapt onto him, grabbed him with all eight legs, then flipped onto its back and tossed him about as it spurted thick silk from what looked like its arse. Two heartbeats later the man was wrapped in white web.

"Wootah!" shouted Erik.

"Wootah!" shouted Finn. He reached the spider first. There was a narrow join between its chest and its big bulbous arse part. Finn slashed and struck true. The beast fell away, split in two.

As Erik ran past, Finn severed the silk around the man's chest with his blade and the warrior struggled free.

Finn followed his father into the melee.

He saw Chogolisa with a warrior's hefty spear in each hand, beating at the beasts like a two-hammered blacksmith. A smaller spider clamped onto her shoulder but Thyri was there, slicing into its abdomen with her sax and flicking it away.

Wulf and Keef were back-to-back, Keef impaling with Arse

Splitter and Wulf whacking away with Thunderbolt like Tor himself.

Sofi darted past, hand axe and dagger-tooth knife held high, and leapt into a knot of spiders. Finn lost sight of her, but she emerged and all the spiders that had surrounded her – all of them – fell dead.

But there were still many, many more.

He shook his head. He had to stop gawping like an idiot. He saw a spider bat the spear out of a warrior's hand. He ran to help.

The warrior – it was Maya, the chief – slipped a coil of rope from her shoulders and beat the beast. The spider pressed. She tripped and fell. Finn jumped over her and slashed through the eight-eyed head with a backhanded upper cut. The spider fell back.

He helped Maya up and looked about for what to do next. The spiders didn't seem interested in him but Zeg – the warrior he'd called a twat – was separated from the rest, hard pressed by three of the buggers.

Finn raised his sword and ran. He was maybe halfway when one of the spiders clamped its fangs around Zeg's shoulder. Zeg yelped and whacked at the biter's head, but his strength seemed to fail and he dropped his spear.

Finn sped up as the other two spiders closed in. The ground disappeared and he fell, realising as it happened that he'd stepped into one of the holes that the spiders had emerged from. He lifted his arms and they thumped onto sand, preventing him from disappearing under the desert floor. He heaved, but was stuck firm, head in the air, torso clamped, legs dangling who-knew-where, tempting targets perhaps for who-knew-what.

The largest of Zeg's attackers grabbed the warrior's lolling face with its forearms and opened its great fangs.

"Someone help Zeg!" Finn shouted, struggling to get a purchase and heave himself out.

Erik steamed past a moment later, Turkey Friend swinging. He whacked his club down into the largest spider's abdomen, half crushing it. The beast fell away. Erik backhanded the other monster, cracking its head in two, then set about the spider clamped onto Zeg's shoulder. This one seemed tougher and took a good few whacks.

Finn managed to dig Foe Slicer into the sand and pull himself halfway out.

Another spider – the largest Finn had seen so far – appeared behind Erik as he tried to smash the beast off Zeg's shoulder.

"Dad!" Finn shouted.

His father turned to him, mouth open with concern. *He thinks I need his help*, thought Finn.

"No! Behind y—"

The gigantic spider punched a spiked leg up through Erik's back and out of his chest, then gripped his head with giant fangs.

Finn roared and pulled on the sword with everything he had. He finally came clear but the spider fell backwards, dragging Erik by the head. Both disappeared underground.

Finn looked about. Maya was behind him, finishing off a spider with her stout spear. Her rope was back around her shoulder.

"Maya! Tie the rope to my ankle!" he shouted.

She'd seen what had happened and knew what he intended. She ran to him.

Rope attached with Maya holding one end, Finn ran, leapt and dived at the spot where his father had disappeared.

The sand gave way and he was falling, first through loose sand and then air. He saw the ground coming and tried to roll, but he crunched down painfully. He struggled to his feet.

He was in a long, high chamber, lit red by sunlight punching through holes in the ceiling. Sand showered like red rain.

The huge spider was five paces off on its back, tossing a white, Erik-sized bundle in the air, trussing him with silk.

Finn ran in. He cut through three legs with one slice, then chopped through the narrow link between abdomen and thorax.

His bundled father fell to the ground. His head was free. One side of his face was a mess of blood and bone. He looked dead.

The rapid patter of gigantic arachnid feet roused Finn from his horrified trance. Dozens of the beasts poured into the chamber and headed for them.

Finn stood by his dad and circled, brandishing Foe Slicer. The spiders seemed to realise that the blade was dangerous and slowed their charge. They closed in with steady menace.

Finn dropped to the ground next to his father's trussed body, gripped him in his arms, then kicked again and again, yanking the rope attached to his ankle. He hadn't agreed a signal with Maya. He hoped she would understand.

The spiders advanced. The nearest one reared, pointed feet ready to stab. Finn pumped his leg like a madman. The spider struck. Finn dodged, but not enough. He felt a searing pain as the end of the beast's legs pierced his arm like a spear.

The spider reared again.

Finn closed his eyes and gripped his dad. He was going to die holding his father.

Next moment he was flying feet first across the chamber floor. He held Erik with all his strength as his leg whipped up and they were turned upside down.

Spiders ran in and slashed with sharp limbs.

Finn was sure they'd get him, but suddenly he and Erik were shooting upwards. Only the sticky spider silk gluing their bodies together prevented him dropping his father.

They rose through the sand and then they were out.

Something caught Finn. He choked up sand as strong hands laid him down.

He blinked sand out of his eyes and opened them to see Chogolisa running off, Erik cradled in her arms.

"Can you run?" Maya asked.

"I think so."

"Then come on. Get off the sand."

They reached the rock. Finn ran to where Chogolisa and Paloma were ripping spider silk off his father. He was vaguely aware that the battle must be over if Paloma was tending to the wounded. Or the dead.

Blood oozed from Erik's chest. His face was ruined. One eye was hanging on a string and half his teeth were bared like a dog's.

Finn stared.

"Out of the way, fast woman," said a sensible voice. It was Ollia, the warlock.

Paloma jumped clear and Ollia crouched, swinging her backpack onto the rock next to her.

"The spider's leg went through his chest from behind," said Finn.

"Help me roll him onto his side."

She ripped his shirt away and prodded the exit and entry wounds.

"Fast woman, come round this side and press your hand here," Ollia commanded. "Finn, put your pack under his head. Get that eye back into its socket, then fold his face back and hold it in place."

"What?" Finn asked.

"Move aside!" cried Chogolisa, running up.

"Back, Chogolisa," said Paloma.

"Get water, Chogolisa," said Ollia. "Lots of it."

Finn lifted Erik's gory head onto his pack.

He saw what Ollia wanted him to do. One side of Erik's face skin was folded back over his skull, still attached at his forehead. His eye was lying on his bloody cheek, a string leading back to the socket – or at least to a mess of blood and spurs of bone where the socket was meant to be.

As Ollia cleaned the wound on Erik's back, Finn picked up his father's eye between finger and thumb. It looked back at him.

"Wait," said Ollia. "Snap off any shards of bone that may puncture his eye before you put it back in its hole."

Finn laid the eye gently back on his father's cheek, grabbed the largest of the bone splinters around the socket and twisted. He felt a pop as the point of the bone pierced his skin.

"Fuck!" The ball of his finger was gashed and bleeding. He'd cut himself on his father's broken face bone. He heaved. Vomit filled his mouth. He swallowed. Erik probably wouldn't thank him for puking on his skinned face.

"Here." Paloma, one hand still pressed on Erik's chest wound, leant across and, with deft flicks, snapped off the shards from around the socket.

"Thanks," said Finn.

He picked up the eye again. Was it looking at him reproachfully? With his other hand, he poked the cord back into the hole, then pushed the eye down onto it. Cord was still sticking out on one side, so he lifted the eye and poked the cord further down into the hole. *My finger is in my dad's head*, he couldn't help thinking. Cord more neatly stowed, he pressed the eye in.

"That's upside down," said Paloma.

"Are you sure? How can you—"

"She's right," said the warlock.

Finn lifted the eye, twisted it half a turn and placed it back in its gory hole.

"Hold it there a moment," said Ollia.

He did and she tipped a skin of water over the skinless face.

"Fold his face back on now," she said, as another warlock handed her sinew threaded on a bone needle. She began to sew up his back wound. "Make sure you leave his mouth clear for breathing. I'll do his chest next, then sew his face back on."

Finn wasn't sure that his father was still breathing, but he gathered up the fatty flap and rolled it back down into place. He had to poke the eye about a bit and pull his cheek and eyebrow apart, but soon he had the eye looking out of the hole and all the rest of Erik's face in roughly the right place. Blood oozed and he didn't look good, but he looked a lot better than he had done.

Blood bubbled around his lips. He was alive.

They carried those who couldn't walk away from the valley of spiders to a clearing by a small pool in a rock cleft.

Chogolisa laid Erik down and knelt next to him. Finn stood, feeling useless and terrified. All around were moans and groans as the warlocks tended to the wounded. Sassa was a little distance away, sitting with Freydis and Ottar and holding their hands. Of the Wootah and Calnians, only Erik had been wounded. Finn could see the rest of them standing on higher ground with the warriors, weapons in hand and watching for more trouble.

He looked back at his father. Erik's face was bloodied and misshapen, but at least he looked like himself again. In fact he looked very peaceful. Very peaceful . . .

"Chogolisa, is he . . .?"

The strongest of the Owsla looked up, eyes wet with tears, lower lip wobbling.

"No," Finn managed.

Chogoslia shook her head. "I'm so sorry," she said. "Your dad's dead."

# Chapter 5

## Small Sullen Sheep

Erik the Angry blinked.

The land was cold, wet and green. The wind whooshed in his ears with an echo as if he was underwater. There were no trees, only a few leafless bushes bristling with thorns. Small sullen sheep nibbled the already short grass and paid no attention to the large, bearded man. To his right, a soaring black slab of rock towered over the dank scrub – a drabber yet more foreboding mountain than any he'd seen before. Off to his left and far below was an iron-grey ocean flecked with white. A wooden ship lay at anchor. Its mast was a cross and its elongated prow carved into a dragon's head.

There was a path running along the cliff top. Erik walked across the wet grass, then along the path.

Screaming grew louder as he approached the cliff edge. Thousands of seabirds, white and black, circled below and perched on the cliff, beaks open and yelling for all they were worth.

He followed the path, revelling in the salty tang of the cold wind and the moisture on his beard. It was a soggy, cold, alien land. But he felt at home.

The trail crested a hill to reveal more of the same – grey and black cliffs, treeless heath and more sodden sheep. Perhaps half a mile off was an enormous longhouse. High windows glowed orange and vented smoke up into the wet sky. The faint sound of singing drifted across the damp moor.

Erik noticed a man sitting on a rock, watching him. The man stood. How had Erik not spotted him immediately? He was enormous. He was a bigger, older, bearded version of Wulf – long blond, curly hair, a welcoming face and sparkling blue eyes. He had a hammer identical to Wulf's strapped to his waist.

"Greetings, Erik," said the man in a voice so deep and warm that it made Erik's arm hairs stand on end.

"Tor?"

"That's what some call me."

"So I am dead."

"It happens to everyone, my friend."

Erik blinked and looked around. It was pretty much as he'd expected. Apart from the sheep. "And this is Valhalla?"

"It is a Valhalla. It's your Valhalla. Don't worry, the weather will improve. We swim in the sea here for most of the year."

"And that hall is . . .?"

"Full of people like you."

"People who fell in battle?"

The god smiled. "Some of them. But I don't only choose people who die in battle. I really don't know where humans got that idea."

"Who do you choose?"

"My main rule is no twats. I'd happily sit next to every man and woman in that hall, or any of my halls, for the entirety of a feast. You will find the same. You belong here."

"So there's drinking?"

"There's a lot of drinking."

"Hangovers?"

Tor smiled. "Have you ever had a hangover when you felt a little slower, a little less clever, but filled with a warm sense of peace and happiness as you watch other people get on with the work?"

"Yes."

"That's a Valhalla hangover."

A nearby sheep bleated unhappily.

"Are there other animals?" asked Erik.

Tor pointed towards the longhouse. There was a lower but longer building next to it. Erik could have sworn it hadn't been there before.

"Many fine animals roam the island. Some spend their nights in that smaller building," said Tor. "These sheep are food for people and animals. That's probably why the wooly little bastards are so miserable. The island is large. You may go wherever you want, whenever you like. There are interesting things to see, but no dangers."

"Any bears?"

"Your friend Astrid the bear is not here, Erik. She's living next to the Rock River on her own, and she is pregnant. She is mostly happy, looking forward to having a cub, but she does pine for you in her quieter moments. She will die in three summer's time, after her child leaves her."

"So you do die when you die?"

"You do."

"And the Wootah? The Calnians? Chogolisa? My son? Will they come here?"

"I like them all, so yes, I should think so," said Tor. "Your son is interesting. I've enjoyed watching him. Many of the great people I've watched started off as idiots."

"Finn is bound for greatness?"

"I didn't say that."

"Well, is he?"

"I cannot tell you."

"You told me about Astrid."

"I made an exception. I'm a god, Erik. I can do what I want. I'm also not to be pressed." Tor opened his eyes a fraction wider and Erik felt a brief but intense flash of terror.

For all his surprisingly avuncular charm, Erik understood immediately that Tor was not to be fucked with.

"Sorry."

"Don't be. I *will* tell you that you'll find your friends Bjarni Chickenhead, Yoki Choppa and Gunnhild Kristlover in the longhouse, as well as the Owsla Morningstar and Luby Zephyr. They will be glad to see you. Everyone will be glad to see you."

"Gunnhild's here?"

Tor laughed. "There are few things I enjoy more than the look on Christians' faces when they pitch up here."

"So Gunnhild passed the twat test?"

"I'll be honest, she was borderline. Ottar the Moaner loves her though. Picturing his joy when he sees her swung it for me."

"Will Ottar be here soon?"

"That's enough questions for now."

"Can I ask one more?"

"You can try."

"Do we stay here for ever?"

"No. You will stay here a good long while, but not for ever."

"What happens afterwards?"

"That, my good Erik the Angry, is the next mystery. Life is better with a mystery. It's one of the reasons you fools make up gods. The Vikings are the only ones to get it right so far."

"The who?"

"I'll tell you all about them another time. We are not short of time. Come, let us join the others in the hall. You look like you could do with a mug of mead and some mutton. The sheep taste better than they look. And when I say a mug of mead," the god grinned just like Wulf, "I do of course mean many mugs."

Erik and Tor walked side by side down the hill, towards the enormous longhouse.

"I guess you won't tell me when the others are getting here?" asked Erik.

"I will not. But time is strange here, my friend. It won't seem long until you are all reunited. I am looking forward to it."

The singing grew louder as they approached the long-house. Erik the Angry recognised the song. It was the same one that Freydis had sung as she'd walked along next to him that morning in a different world.

# Chapter 6

## Let's Go

Finn had no idea how many warriors and warlocks they'd started with, but he counted fifteen still with them. Apparently well over half had been killed by the spiders, including Zeg, the man he considered to be his friend even though he'd laughed after throwing a squirrel into the Red River.

And his father.

He hadn't cried yet. He kept expecting to see Erik walking along next to Chogolisa. Instead he saw Chogolisa walking next to Sitsi, head down, pulling the Warlock Queen's dead child's coffin.

Wulf was walking next to Finn. He hadn't said anything. He was just there.

They headed on, across the baking, sun-smashed rock.

Finn wondered if any of them would make it as far as The Meadows, let alone defeat the Warlock Queen and walk away.

"We will be reunited in Valhalla," said Wulf as the path crested a rise and a new view of mountainous red desert opened up ahead of them.

"You will. You and Erik are dead certs for Tor's Valhalla." Finn had always assumed he himself would be sent to one of the lamer god's halls.

"As will you, Finn. You're a warrior."

*   *   *

Sassa Lipchewer kept one hand pressed over her bulge and carried her bow in the other, but they saw no more monsters that day.

The sun was near the horizon when Maya led them up a narrowing, stony but bush-choked valley, busy with yellow butterflies. Up ahead Sassa could see the mouth of a slot canyon.

"We're going to camp here," said Sofi, jogging back to them.

While the others made camp, Sassa led Wulf into the canyon. It was the narrowest they'd seen so far, with beautiful curves and patterns on its walls, as if it had been carved by a skilled and soulful sculptor. Her brother Vifil the Individual would have appreciated it, she thought.

"I can't believe Erik's dead," she said.

"He has left this world, Sassa," said Wulf. "But this world is not the end."

"So when you died . . .?"

"I saw nothing. I wasn't really dead, though. I know for certain that we carry on after this world, because it's impossible that something as wonderful, lovely and complicated as you could simply cease to exist."

Sassa wasn't sure whether to cry or vomit at Wulf's words, but she was distracted from both by spotting a great black wasp with red wings on the canyon wall. Wulf saw it, too, and crushed it with a flick of Thunderbolt. They looked around but there didn't seem to be any more.

"I do not want to lose you again," said Sassa. "And I don't want to lose our baby. There's so much danger ahead. Let's go, Wulf. Leave the rest of them to it. We'll make no difference."

Wulf took her in his arms and hugged her for a long while.

"You know we can't go," he said eventually. "This is our quest as much as everybody else's. We must finish it."

"But we'll die."

"We will not. We will prevail and we will spend the rest

of our lives knowing we saved the world. Our children will be brought up by world saviours." He grinned at her.

Of course he was right. Of course they couldn't back out now. And maybe they would both make it through whatever terrors were to come.

"You're not to get smug," she said, smiling herself.

"I'll change my name to Wulf Worldsaver."

"I'd rather live with the shame of abandoning our friends."

"Okay. If I promise not to change my name, will you come with me and finish our quest?"

Sassa closed her eyes. She remembered the spiders, tearing warriors and warlocks to pieces. She pictured Erik's bloody, disfigured face, and the worry and pain all over Finn's and Chogolisa's. She remembered the agony last time Wulf had died.

"Promise me you won't die again," she said.

"I promise." He jutted his chin manfully in a mock-heroic pose. "I will never die."

# Chapter 7

## Menagerie

They walked up through the slot canyon the following day, then through more gullies and along narrow valleys. It was hot, but not as crazily hot as it had been, and they saw no monsters and no tornados, firenados or other lethal horrors.

*Maybe*, Finn thought, *maybe the Warlock Queen was dead!* Or dead again . . . What did you call it when the dead died? Point was, maybe they were going to arrive at The Meadows and find it was all over.

And his father would have died for nothing. He almost cried. *No*, he told himself. *We don't mourn the dead.* He kept repeating the words to himself, willing himself to believe them.

Almost immediately after he'd dared think their quest was over, Finn thought he could hear something like animals crying and roaring in the distance.

He caught up with Sofi. "Can you hear anything?"

She nodded. "The monsters at The Meadows."

"But I thought we were still—"

"We're more than ten miles from the edge of The Meadows and there's a mountain between us and them."

"But they must be—"

"They are very big. And there are a lot of them."

She sped ahead. The conversation was over.

The noise became louder as they approached the ring of

mountains surrounding The Meadows, then climbed it. As they neared the top it was loud enough to make conversation difficult.

Everywhere else they'd travelled the vegetation was thicker as they climbed. Here it was all dead. The miniature pines that had cheered him on other parts of their odyssey were naked and twisted, bent twigs like the fingers of the dead snagging at the questers.

The only signs of animal life were bright white skeletons of birds, lizards and mammals, so thick on the ground that it was impossible to avoid stepping on them, crunching bone and desecrating little corpses.

Nobody spoke.

They climbed.

Finn walked behind Thyri's swinging behind. He tried to ogle her out of habit more than anything else, but he didn't have the energy or the will.

Fear sat in his stomach like a heavy ball of rotting meat.

He tried to listen to Thyri's thoughts, to take his mind off what was coming, but didn't get anything. He considered trying to listen to the minds of the monsters over the mountain, but after what had happened with the spiders, he didn't dare. He was sure the Warlock Queen would kill him the next time he tried to mess with one of her creatures.

He fell back to walk with Freydis and Ottar. They were already holding Sitsi's and Paloma's hands, so he joined at the end, holding Ottar's. He and Paloma swung the little boy in the air every few steps. By the way Ottar laughed, it was the funniest thing imaginable.

Ottar's unashamed and wholly natural laughter was a bright torch, dispelling the gloom on the dreadful mountainside and in Finn's heart.

\* \* \*

Finally, they arrived at the summit and looked out over The Meadows.

It was worse, much worse, than Finn had thought it could be.

Far away – someone had said it was a dozen miles – was The Pyramid. It was a great black triangle, high and solid as a mountain, rising from the desert like a spear point from a murdered man's back. A tornado – a tornado, for the love of Loakie – rose from The Pyramid's tip, slender at first, but wider and wider until it blended with the black, swirling clouds above. Lightning flashed down through the tornado, striking the tip of The Pyramid. The body of the tornado shifted sinuously but its point stayed fixed to the point of the man-made mountain.

The great basin of The Meadows stretched all around The Pyramid. At first glance Finn thought it was filled with a sea – grey-green and shifting. But then he realised that, no, all the land between their mountain and The Pyramid, all the land bound in by mountains more than twenty miles away to the south, west and north, was heaving with writhing, crawling creatures.

There were huge multi-limbed monsters with great claws, stings, fangs, branches, spikes, crests, fins and even long floppy tentacles. There were gigantic, sharp-toothed hairy creatures and others made of black goo that looked like they'd crawled from the deepest oceans. A group of giant scorpions caught Finn's eye. They were larger – much larger – than Beaver Man's Plains Strider.

Nearer were a couple of things hopping about that looked a lot like rabbits but were bigger than the church in Hardwork, and several bear-like beasts rearing out of the monstrous maelstrom.

Further away the largest of all the giants, much larger than even the scorpions, were great, glistening lumpen slugs, hills of shining flesh, with waggling, useless looking limbs and multiple mouths.

Above these beasts the sky was busy with impossible, bloated, flying animals. Something that looked like a fish with long, slender wings, perhaps a quarter of a mile long, opened its great mouth, folded its wings and dived. It plunged towards one of the slug mountains. The vast organism wobbled like a fat man's gut as the flying fish monster sank into it like a punching fist. The mountain of shining flesh splayed out then coalesced, closing around and enveloping its attacker. Moments later, a fish's face strained outwards from the shining wall of flab. The skin burst in an explosion of goo and the fish-bird's head emerged, screaming and screaming.

Its eyes widened and the screaming became gulps as it was sucked back into the body of the beast-mountain. Gooey flesh closed over it, and it was gone.

"Deep. Throat. A. Goat," said Sassa Lipchewer.

Next to her was Sitsi, mouth open.

At this distance Finn could see only the details of the very largest animals. There were many, many more smaller ones teeming about, if the adjective "smaller" could be applied to creatures larger than the thunder lizards. The quarter-mile-long fish-bird, for example, had been only one of many flying things attacking the ground-based beasts. All over shapes were plunging out of the sky at the animals below. It also looked like many of the land animals were fighting each other. A giant rabbit screamed and bucked as huge hairless dogs – like the ones they'd seen dead shortly after Finn had been stung by the wasps – bit at its ears and neck.

Sitsi Kestrel, of course, could see all of this with perfect clarity. Looking at her wide, horror-filled eyes, for the first time Finn did not envy her eyesight.

"They're killing each other," said Finn. "So if we wait, they'll die and we can walk to The Pyramid."

"They're being created as fast as they're dying," said Sitsi.

"They're growing out of the ground. They are the ground. It's all monsters. And we'd better act soon." She pointed to the north-west.

There, at the top edge of The Meadows, were six more black pyramids. "I thought there was just one—" Finn started.

He saw that they were moving. The six gigantic pyramids in the north were all, impossibly, swaying from side to side as they were carried on the backs of enormous beasts.

"The Warlock Queen means to spread over the world, creating new centres of horror," said Maya. "The disasters and death flooding from The Meadows are only the beginning."

Thunder boomed from the clouds above The Pyramid, making everyone jump, apart from Sofi who pressed her hands over her ears. The thunder reverberated around the basin as more silent lightning crackled above The Pyramid. The mass of monsters teemed and pulsed.

Despite the sea of beasts more extraordinary than anything from his wildest nightmares, Finn's attention kept returning to the great black pyramid in the middle of it all. He could feel its power. He wanted to go to it and he wanted to flee from it. He wanted to open his mind out to it, and he wanted to dash his mind out on the nearest rock from sheer terror of it.

He looked about for Erik to see what he made of it all, then he remembered.

"Can you see a door into The Pyramid itself?" Sofi asked Sitsi. "There should be one three-quarters of the way up."

"There's no way in," said a Warrior. "This has got worse, much worse. We should turn round now and—"

"There is an opening halfway up The Pyramid," Sitsi interrupted. "If we can get to The Pyramid we could climb it easily enough. It's steep but it's made of volcanic stone so it will be grippy. But that's all moot, because there's no way we can forge a path to it."

The captain of the Owsla glanced at Finn. "There is a way," she said.

Finn's eyes went as wide as Sitsi's. Why had she looked at him when she'd said that?

They walked back down the mountain.

"Well, that was interesting," said Keef to Finn. "A nice little sortie. If we keep up this brisk pace we'll be back in Hardwork in time for tea."

Finn wished they were going back to Hardwork. Instead they were walking back down the barren mountain to a relatively safe camping spot. Sitsi, Sofi and Wulf were in earnest conversation. Finn and Keef had walked ahead.

They were to attack at dawn. The monsters would be a little more sluggish then, according to Maya, and there would be enough light to see what they were doing. Finn couldn't decide if he was relieved that they weren't going to plunge into the basin of horror immediately or frustrated that they weren't just going to get on with it.

"This time tomorrow," said Finn, "we might be walking down this mountain on the way back to Hardwork, world saved."

"That's not going to happen." Keef sounded serious for once.

"You don't think we're going to make it?"

"I'm going to make it. Don't know about you. But we won't be walking down the mountain because there's a valley to the north-west we can walk out through once we've killed all the beasts. You don't climb a mountain when you don't have to."

They were forced to descend single file for a while, hopping down a dry rocky gully between dead trees. They emerged onto a stony hillside, dotted with red barrel cactus. They were the first living plants since the top of the ridge.

Finn jogged to catch up to Keef. He'd talked to Thyri and

Paloma. There was one more difficult conversation to have before they were all slain by the monsters.

"Keef," he said.

"Yup."

"How do you feel about Bodil staying with Olaf?"

Keef blinked. "I'm Hird, Finn. Not a girl. If you want to talk about feelings, find Freydis. Then ask her if she knows any girls a lot lamer than herself who want to talk about their *feelings*." He swung Arse Splitter around his head and brought it down with a "Yah!", bisecting a barrel cactus.

"Okay . . . Look, Keef. There's something I need to ask you."

"What?" he said, then "Wooo-TAH!" as he dispatched another barrel cactus.

"Why do you hate barrel cactuses so much?"

Keef stopped arseing about and looked at him. "Now that," he said, "is a much more interesting question than I was expecting. Is it really what you want to ask?"

"No."

"How disappointing."

"Do you know that Bodil's baby is mine, not yours?"

Keef gave him a look that could have deflated a field full of barrel cactuses. "What of it?"

"I wanted to thank you for looking after her, and being ready to look after the child."

"I didn't do it for you."

"I'm sure you didn't. I'm sorry, though, that you had to. I should have—"

"You should have."

"I was terrified and freaked out and, well, it was *Bodil*."

Keef stopped and looked at Finn with his remaining eye. The sky and the land behind him were blood-red. "Finn," he said. "I'll let that one go, but badmouth Bodil one more time and I will barrel-cactus you."

"You're right, I'm sorry. I wanted to say that I think I would have stepped forward by now, if she was still with us and hadn't stayed with Olaf Worldfinder, I mean."

The Berserker contemplated him an uncomfortably long while with his beady eye, then nodded. "That's easy to say."

"I think I would have done."

"I'm bored of this. What is it that you require of me?"

"I want to say I'm sorry."

"You want me to forgive you?"

Finn thought. "No, not that."

"Then what?"

"I just want you to know that I'm very grateful."

"Well, whoopee fucks for you. See ya!" Keef ran off down the hill, waving Arse Splitter around his head, jabbing, chopping and sending more barrel cactuses to barrel-cactus Valhalla. Finn walked after him.

They made camp in a dry stream bed overhung by dead trees which had probably been willowy once but were now skeletal.

People spoke only as much as was necessary, and then in hushed tones. Finn had nothing to say to anyone. It was all done. His father was dead. His grief had settled on him like drunkenness, confusing him and making it difficult to talk.

He wasn't the only one brooding. Everybody was in a sombre mood, apart from Ottar and Freydis. The boy was counting stones in and out of a pot, while Freydis was telling him a story she'd made up about Raskova, the friendly squirrel who lived on the world tree.

Finn walked a little way from the others and found a rock to sit on. The sun was setting. Would it be the last sunset he saw?

Raskova . . . Raskova . . . thought Finn. Then he remembered. Raskova the Spiteful and Marina the Farter had been twin daughters of Jarl Brodir the Gorgeous back in Hardwork. He shook his head. It had been only four moons before – the beginning of summer – when the Calnians had slaughtered the lot of them. He should remember them all; his Uncle Poppo Whitetooth, his sort-of sisters Brenna the Aloof and Alvilda the Shy, and so many more.

He'd been lucky to make it so far, to become a Wootah. Most of the people who'd left Hardwork after the Calnian attack were dead. He tried to remember them all. Frossa the Deep-Minded had been jumped on by a giant fish, Hrolf the Painter's throat had been ripped out by a black bear. Fisk the Fish had been torn to pieces by Erik's bear Astrid when he'd tried to kill Rimilla and Potsi. And Gurd Girlchaser! That dick! The only one of them that the Owsla had actually killed. It was the first time they'd seen any of the Owsla up close. Finn remembered being stunned by Sadzi Wolf's amazing athleticism and beauty, and the undeniably thrilling horror when she'd taken Gurd's axe from him and cleaved his face in two.

Next to go, and good riddance, had been Chnob the White, sucked up by the tornado. Then there was Garth Anvilchin, another one he'd been glad to see the back of. Did he mean that, he wondered? Had these intense few moons matured him enough to wish that Garth wasn't dead and he could have sorted out his differences with the man? No, not at all. Good riddance to the murderous fucker.

Frossa, Hrolf, Fisk, Gurd, Chnob, Garth. He wasn't going to miss anyone who'd died on the far side of the Water Mother. Funny how all the arseholes had died so quickly, he mused, not for the first time. It was almost like the gods had been smiting those who might hinder their quest.

Then they'd crossed the Water Mother and left the gods behind. Wonderful Bjarni Chickenhead had been an idiot and killed himself. Morningstar wouldn't have liked to admit it, but she'd become one of them and Finn had liked her.

That horrible reverser warlock had killed her. Lovely Luby Zephyr who he'd hardly known but already liked a lot, had been killed by the Badlander Owsla, then Empress Ayanna had thrown herself – well, had Chogolisa throw her – into the jaws of a thunder lizard to save them all.

Then Gunnhild. Was it the wasp sting or had she simply died? It was almost like she'd known how much tougher the journey would become and that she'd be a burden, so she'd just let go of life.

And then Erik. His dad was dead.

Finn squeezed his eyes but no tears came. He could accept Bjarni's death. He loved Bjarni, but with the man's lust for drugs and lack of nous it had always seemed like he had a tenuous grip on life. It was more than that, though. Why was Bjarni like that? Underneath all the zany bluster, he had been sad. He'd always been sad. Finn hoped Bjarni was now smoking, eating and snorting all he could find in Tor's Hall and wasn't missing this world at all.

It was the same with Yoki Choppa. Finn wished he hadn't died, and was grateful that he'd saved Ottar, but the warlock had seemed ready to go, free of ties to this world and ready to embrace whatever the Hel went on after life.

Gunnhild, on the other hand . . . the way she'd loved Ottar and Freydis, the way she'd loved Finn himself, she must be missing them all terribly. He couldn't see them from his rock, but he could still hear Freydis singing and Ottar chirruping along happily. How Gunnhild would have loved to have been here, fussing over the children and telling everyone else how to live their lives.

And Erik.

*You die when you die*, said Gunnhild in his mind. *Hardworkers do not mourn the dead.*

Fuck that shit, thought Finn. The Wootah do. But on the other hand, if anyone was going to enjoy Tor's Hall, it was Erik. And that's surely where he was now, having a marvellous time. That's what Finn was going to tell himself. It would make the whole thing a good bit easier.

Freydis asked to sit on Paloma's lap after the evening meal to listen to Sofi, Wulf and Maya's plan of attack. Paloma was pleased to let her. It was a bit much when Ottar cuddled up next to her but she couldn't really knock him back after she'd said his sister could. Especially because tomorrow was his big day. Tomorrow they were going to find out why Ottar was so vital.

Paloma hoped it wasn't what she suspected. It couldn't be, could it? Surely Sofi would have told her.

She held the warm little children on her knee as everyone gathered on the broad, dry stream bed. The sun had set but the moon was bright and it was warm. They could still hear the monsters in The Meadows roaring and screaming and they could also, Paloma fancied, smell them. Something smelled faintly of dirty monster arse, anyway. It might have been Ottar, now she thought of it. Left to their own devices, little boys were smelly animals, and nobody had been looking after Ottar much of late.

When all were assembled, Maya began.

"The warlock Finn the Deep—"

"I'm no warlock," interrupted Finn.

"You can enter the minds of animals?"

"Sometimes."

"Then you're a warlock. As I was saying, Finn the Deep will take over the mind of one of the creatures in The Meadows and—"

"But I can't." Finn looked flustered. "I told Sofi. When I tried to take over the spiders—" Finn stopped. He'd noticed the look on Maya's face. Like many chiefs, she wasn't a big fan of being interrupted. "I'm sorry, but I can't," Finn finished.

Maya continued: "You have to, because you are our only hope. To improve your chances, the warlocks and warriors will attack a couple of miles to the north and distract the Warlock Queen."

All the warriors and warlocks, Wootah and Calnians were looking at Finn. Paloma was kind of proud. Sofi gave him a single nod — her version of an encouraging hug.

"While we have her attention," continued Maya, "you will persuade a suitable animal to come to the edge of The Meadows. You, along with some of the Wootah and Calnians, will climb aboard with the coffin."

"Some of the Wootah and Calnians?" asked Sassa.

"You are pregnant," said Sofi. "You will stay behind. And Freydis is not needed."

"I'm coming," Sassa insisted.

"Sorry," Wulf shook his head. "Someone needs to look after Freydis."

"She can stay with the warlocks and warriors. I'm coming. My archery will be useful, as it was when we fought our way out of the Badlands, as it was when we defeated the wasp men, as it was when we battled the spiders. I've killed way more monsters than you have, Wulf the Fat, and none of them have killed me. Why don't you stay and look after Freydis?"

Wulf opened his mouth but had nothing to say.

"I'm very happy not to come," said Freydis, "and I'll be happy with the warriors and warlocks. I'm glad to hear I'm not needed. So which one of you has learned to talk to Ottar?"

"Ot-tar!" shouted Ottar.

"If he is as important as everyone keeps saying," continued Freydis, bobbing her head to some internal tune, "you need to know what he's saying."

Sofi looked at Wulf. "All right," said Wulf. "All the Calnians and Wootah will ride on the beast."

"Assuming we dupe a goddess with a trick which wouldn't fool Ottar," muttered Finn.

Maya ignored him and continued the plan. When all seemed done and Paloma was ready to get up – her bum was numb from the extra weight of the children – Maya said: "There is one more thing you Wootah and Calnians should know."

The way Sofi and Wulf looked at her, this was news to them.

"One of the Warlocks has seen treachery among you in his alchemical bowl. You should be wary of each other tomorrow."

"Which one of you has seen this?" demanded Wulf, looking towards where the warlocks were gathered.

An older man stood. He looked unsure of himself. One of his eyes stared off into the mid distance while the other looked at Wulf. Paloma breathed again. The guy did not look reliable.

"What did you see?" asked Wulf.

"Nothing solid. I felt one of your group killing one of his or her own. Perhaps more than one. That is all."

Paloma swivelled her eyes to look at Sofi. Was she still planning to follow Empress Ayanna's orders and kill all the Wootah? Sofi's expression, as always, was unreadable.

"Could it have happened in the past?" asked Sassa.

"I don't think so."

"The Warlock Queen is pale-skinned," said Sofi. "Could you have seen her death?"

"Yes . . ." said the warlock. "That could have been it." He did not sound convinced.

When they were done, Finn went to look for Chogolisa. He found her, sitting on her own a little way down the dry gulch. She looked up at his approach. Her eyes were wet with tears.

He sat down next to her. She took his hand in her own and he held it as she rocked and cried.

# Chapter 8

## Assault on The Meadows

The sky lightened. It would be a good while before the sun cleared the mountain behind them.

Finn the Deep crouched with Paloma Pronghorn a short way uphill from the edge of The Meadows. They were wrapped in a grey blanket that blended into the dusty land. Paloma was dressed in Owsla garb and pressed against him. Finn hardly noticed.

Monsters ruled The Meadows. The mountain shook with cries, groans and screams and the air was heavy with the stink of rotting meat, excrement, beast sweat and Loakie knew what else. The size of the monsters completed the sensual assault. Some towered high above where he and Paloma were hidden, a hundred paces up the hillside.

Of the six beasts with pyramids on their backs to the north of The Meadows, three remained. Finn wondered if the others had died and collapsed back into the monster mash. More likely, they'd gone to spread the Warlock Queen's misery around the world. How many more had gone before?

As they'd seen the day before, the creatures seemed to be held back by an invisible line and they did not stray up the hillside. It reminded Finn of the Hardwork confinement – the invisible boundary ten miles from the village of Hardwork which the Goachica had forbidden them to cross. The Pyramid was apparently around ten miles from the edge of The Meadows.

*Coincidence?* thought Finn. Yes, probably. *A life without coincidence,* said Gunnhild, *is more unlikely than the strongest coincidence.*

As the sky brightened further flying creatures emerged from the throbbing morass and screeched into the air. Some plunged back immediately, wailing hideously. Others circled, screaming hatred. Like the ground-based animals, they were noisy bastards. One breathed a great gout of fire. Finn's eyes bulged – all the Calnians and Wootah being burned to a crisp in an instant would be a serious hindrance to their plans – but then he saw that the fire-breather had set its own head alight. It plummeted, consumed by flames, and exploded on the monsters below. The roaring raged momentarily louder as dozens of beasts burned.

There were plenty more to take their place. The Meadows was a constantly evolving lake of creation and death. Monsters rose and sank; the living climbed over the dead, the dead fell onto the living.

A column of something that looked like snot rose rapidly skyward. It wobbled – tall, shimmering and aggressively green – and Finn thought it must collapse. Instead, all over the pillar thousands of rheumy eyes blinked open, shining with malevolence. *Then* it collapsed, to burst with a great splat, coating all the beasts nearby with mucoid goo.

As if taking that as a cue, the warlocks and warriors began their attack, two miles to the north. Thunderous booms rang out and light flashed. Maya had promised noise but Finn hadn't expected anything like this.

"All right," said Paloma. "It's time."

Finn opened his mind.

He'd expected the minds of so many and such huge creatures to hit him like a hurled bucket of water, but it was more like having shit-soaked moss rammed into his mouth, nostrils, eyes and ears. It was the mental manifestation of their smell.

He breathed deeply, calming himself and pushing back against the sluggish tide of semi-formed, primitive thought. He probed the sea of minds. They felt unimaginably ancient and dangerously stupid.

And, thank Oaden, no Warlock Queen so far. It was just possible that the Warlocks and Warriors' noisy diversion was working.

He began to find individual voices. The great globular hill of life with eyes wanted to consume other organisms and grow. The insects and the crabby beasts were in a frenzy of violent ravenousness. A couple of giant lizards, four-legged and low-slung, wanted to kill as many other creatures as they could, then eat them. There was a theme.

He spotted what he wanted — one of the giant rabbits. This one was cowering on its own, looking no happier in the crowd of carnivores as one would expect a rabbit to be. It was black, and mind-bogglingly huge. Had it fallen from the sky onto the village of Hardwork, it would have obliterated the village.

Was it prejudice, he wondered? Had he picked the warm-blooded, furry animal because it was more like himself?

He told himself to shut the Hel up and get on with it.

The giant rabbit, was terrified. Several lizard beasts were attacking it, but they couldn't bite through its fur, let alone its skin. The rabbit understood this, but also knew that there were larger beasts all around which would be able to hurt it. It was hunkered and shivering, believing that they wouldn't see it if it stayed still.

A giant blue-armoured beast came shambling towards it. Rivers of saliva flowed from a mouth that could have easily accommodated the rabbit's head. The rabbit held its ground. What else could it do? Underfoot was shifting and strange. It didn't want to run.

*Run here!* suggested Finn. *It's nice here.*

He heard the squeak of fear above the other monster grunts and felt the rabbit's terror at having another voice in its mind. It was more frightened of Finn than of the blue fucker that was going to eat it. It gripped the ground and shivered. Crouching further, it exposed tendons on its back foot. One of the relatively little lizard beasts managed to get a mouthful.

The rabbit redoubled its efforts to stay in the same place.

*Escape pain, escape pain*, Finn tried, attempting to be more encouraging and less commanding. *It's nice where the hill begins. The ground is still and the lizards won't get you.*

The rabbit stood, sniffing.

*Come onto the rock, away from the pain. Hop over here. It's good over here.*

The rabbit flicked a back paw and the buffalo-sized lizard which had been biting it flew, tracing a high parabola across the monster-filled sky. Still the rabbit stayed put, afraid to move across the shifting ground.

The big blue beast was heartbeats away, mouth agape and ready.

*Your feet are huge. You will have no trouble crossing the land. You are stronger than you know.*

The giant black rabbit leapt away from the predator and came hopping over the sea of monsters. Smaller beasts screamed as they were crushed by huge rabbit paws.

The armoured beast didn't even deign to watch the rabbit run, let alone chase it. Finn guessed there were plenty of other animals to eat.

The rabbit hesitated at the edge of the beast swamp. It wasn't meant to go on the rock.

*Safety here, warm rock to lie on. Nice rock.*

The rabbit hopped onto the mountainside a hundred paces down the slope and lay flat, nose twitching.

"He's done it!" shouted Wulf, a little way up the hill. "Come on!"

Sassa and the rest of them followed, bounding down the boulder-strewn slope towards the giant rabbit that they

intended to ride across the monster-filled Meadows to
The Pyramid of the Warlock Queen. Over to the right were
screams and great bangs as the warlocks and warriors
attacked the oversized, warped beasts with magic, might and
as much furore as possible.

*Just another Wootah day*, thought Sassa.

She wondered if Finn should have chosen something a
little more dauntless than a rabbit.

Chogolisa was by her side, holding Ottar clutched to
her chest with one arm and the coffin on her shoulder with
the other. Sassa could feel dark nastiness emanating from the
coffin. She felt bad doing it, since Chogolisa and Ottar
were putting up with the malevolence, but she slowed to
get some distance from the vile box. She had a child to think
about, she told herself.

Sofi ran past.

Wulf was worried that Sofi was going to turn on them.
He hadn't said as much, but Sassa could tell by his expressions when the Owsla captain was nearby as clearly as if
he'd shouted *I don't trust Sofi!* all night.

Sassa knew he was wrong. She knew it. Sure, there'd
been a time Sofi had been trying to kill them, but that
was following the orders of an empress who'd sacrificed
herself so that the Wootah could live. Surely that was as
clear a cancellation of her commands as anyone could ever
need?

Ahead, the others were making short work of scrabbling
up the rabbit. Finn was already sitting between its ears like
an elf in a saga.

The vast beast didn't seem to have noticed the human
invasion. Sassa reached its flank. Paloma and Freydis were
ten paces above, standing on the back of the big bunny.

Chogolisa placed Ottar gently down with one arm then
threw the coffin up to Paloma. Paloma caught it, disappeared
for a moment, then returned.

"Whheeee!" cried Ottar as he flew up the side of the rabbit, thrown by Chogolisa. Paloma grabbed him at the top.

Sassa pulled herself up next to Thyri Treelegs. The rabbit's fur was thick as rope but smooth as, well, rabbit fur.

"Lovely morning for climbing a giant rabbit," she said.

"Sure," said Thyri.

*What's got* her *back up?* Thyri had hardly said a thing since the battle with the spiders. She guessed the girl was afraid. Everyone took Thyri for granted. They thought that she was tough and that she could look after herself. Sassa knew different. Thyri was seventeen years old. She'd been brought up with a shitty brother and even more of a shit for a dad. She was as insecure as any seventeen-year-old. She'd never had support, but that didn't mean she didn't need it. Sassa resolved to do more to look after Thyri when this was all over.

She reached the rabbit's spine, looked over the sea of monsters and gasped, forgetting Thyri and finding her own fear again.

Sofi's plan was absolutely, totally, lever-a-beaver insane. The rabbit was huge, but, compared to many of the other animals, it was rabbit-sized. There were much, much bigger, much, much more ferocious beasts.

Ten miles or so away, past thousands of leaping, rearing and diving creatures, towered the black pyramid. Even at that distance, even with everything else around, she could feel the anger and danger pulsing from it.

How could they hope to make it that far? And how could they hope to prevail if they did?

"Keep moving," said Paloma, "sit behind its shoulders."

Sassa half crawled, half walked over slippery fur to where Freydis, Ottar and Chogolisa were sitting behind Finn on the beast's shoulders. Chogolisa had one hand on the coffin. Sassa sat down next to her.

The coffin leaked misery, but Sassa made herself stay put.

If Chogolisa was prepared to put up with it for the good of the group, so was she. For now, anyway.

"Here, let me help!" Paloma held out a hand to Sofi because she knew it would annoy her.

Instead of climbing the last pace up onto the rabbit, Sofi pulled hard on two thick strands of fur, flicked herself heels over head and landed on her feet next to Paloma.

Paloma smiled. Would she ever tire of mocking authority, she wondered? And would Sofi ever cease being irked by it?

She looked north to where the warriors and warlocks were attacking. Sitsi stood next to her.

"How's it going for them?" Paloma asked.

"They've killed several of the large beasts," said Sitsi. "It's amazing."

"And . . .?"

"A few of them are down. But the rest are still attacking. They've done—"

Both women crouched as the rabbit lurched "—well."

For a while, to Paloma's amazement, it worked.

The rabbit's feet were large enough to lollop across the living, shifting ground without sinking, and it was small enough that the truly vast mountain-of-flesh monsters didn't notice it. The Wootah and Chogolisa sat between its shoulders, gripping onto its thick but silky hair.

Sofi, Sitsi and Paloma stood, wind whipping their hair around their faces – because they could stand. That was the advantage of bare feet coupled with alchemically enhanced balance.

Sitsi shot down the flying beasts that approached. Freydis and Sassa had both loosed arrows from their seated positions, but neither of them had hit anything yet.

Paloma stood next to Sofi. She had thought she'd run

ahead at this stage, but the ground was made of creatures coming to life, dying creatures, and a huge variety of things that she guessed you could call creatures, waving multiple limbs in the air, scurrying or just flopping about. Paloma doubted that even she would be able to run on it. She knew she didn't want to. The noise was extraordinary. The smell of excrement and decay was eye-watering.

Still, Paloma was happy. They'd come nearly a third of the way from the edge of The Meadows to The Pyramid and it seemed like they really might make it. A few hideous fanged, clawed and tentacled beasts that were nearer the rabbit's size did chase it for a while, but their mount was faster. It looked like Finn had chosen well after all.

A tornado stabbed down between them and The Pyramid, sucking up thousands of flailing beasts. Finn steered around the vortex. He cut it fine. For a moment the sucking wind threatened to pluck them all from the rabbit, then they were past.

Paloma looked back as monsters, some larger than the rabbit they were riding, tumbled spinning up into the sky. A great slug beast rippled and wobbled but remained grounded as the tornado passed directly over it. It flung out clawed tentacles to grab animals flying past, then pulled them down and into its oily body.

They were halfway. The Pyramid was huge now and Paloma could see the opening on its side. She began to dare to think they'd make it. They passed a great, fat animal on flippers with a head very like a wolf's. It was a lot bigger than their rabbit.

Paloma felt like the wolf-seal's yellow eyes were looking into her soul and not liking what it found. It bent down, plucked up something that looked like a feathered dagger-tooth cat and bit down. The feathered cat burst like an overripe fruit.

*Please don't chase us*, thought Paloma.

But it did. The wolf-seal whirled its great flippers around and slid across the mess of monsters on its massive belly, crushing some, annoying others. It was fast. Faster than their rabbit.

"Finn!" Sofi shouted.

The rabbit turned tight to the north, swerved around a mountainous slug then skidded back onto its westward course, kicking up showers of smaller beasts which screamed as they flew broken through the air.

The seal-wolf barged the slug aside and swung round behind them, closer now. It snapped at the rabbit's rear and missed. Sitsi shot arrow after arrow into its yellow eyes, but it blinked them away.

The rabbit jinked to the left.

The wolf head came closer and closer, but the seal body didn't. For a moment Paloma thought the head had become detached and was flying after them, but then she saw that a long neck was growing out of the bloated torso.

The massive jaws champed at them again, missing the back of the rabbit by a pace. The ground around was still a writhing mass of beasts snapping teeth and claws, stinging with barbed needles and generally killing each other. And The Pyramid was still several miles ahead.

Finn headed for one of the giant scorpions. The wolf-seal leant in and bit a chunk out of the rabbit's hind quarters.

Their mount squealed and stumbled. Paloma, Sitsi and Sofi crouched. Chogolisa gripped the coffin and both children. Sassa held Wulf. Thyri, who'd been standing like the Owsla, would have fallen off if Keef hadn't grabbed her.

If the rabbit fell and tossed them all among the morass of monsters . . . well Paloma didn't know what she'd do. Try to save Ottar, she guessed, but it would be hard enough to save herself.

"Down!" shouted Wulf. Paloma dropped and gripped fur

as they shot between the scorpion's legs then underneath its abdomen. She looked back in time to see the wolf head appear between the scorpion's legs, buck, and throw the huge beast over its back.

The manoeuvre had bought them maybe half a heartbeat, which the wolf-seal made up more or less instantly.

Their pursuer reared its head to strike. It wouldn't miss this time.

"Shall I?" Paloma asked Sofi.

"Go," said Sofi.

Paloma sprinted to the front of the rabbit, gripped the handle of Finn's sword Foe Slicer and whipped it clear of its scabbard. Finn was too focused on controlling the rabbit to notice.

"Chogolisa, throw me!" she commanded. "Top of the head!"

The big woman didn't hesitate.

Paloma caught Freydis's eye. The girl was biting her lip.

"You can be Freydis Pronghorn now!" Paloma yelled as Chogolisa grabbed her by the heels, swung her round once, twice, then hurled her at the striking wolf-seal's head.

Chogolisa's aim was a little off.

Paloma flew, Foe Slicer out in front of her, directly for the beast's gaping, blood-dripping maw. Not what she'd hoped at all. It might still work, but she hadn't meant to be flung quite so certainly to her death.

*Top* of the head, she'd said. *Oh well.*

When she was only paces away from the dripping fangs, the wolf-seal lunged at the rabbit again, dipping its head. Paloma pulled Foe Slicer behind her and whumped into the huge nose, rolled over and struck down with the sword, into the beast's muzzle.

The monster reared again. Paloma was thrown flying upwards. She peaked, hung in the air for a moment (which was a wonderful feeling), then plummeted, sword first, all her strength and weight put into driving the blade into the beast's skull.

Its head was a great deal softer than she'd expected. The sword sliced through flaccid bone and into brain. Her hands, arms, shoulders and head followed the sword into the soft matter. She felt like screaming, she felt like vomiting, but she managed to swirl the sword around inside the animal's soupy mind.

She felt herself shooting upwards again. She was thrown high as the beast stretched its neck and unleashed a horrifying scream.

Then she was falling.

She landed on the beast's body. She sprung onto all fours and wiped gore from her face. Her view of the rabbit was blocked by the bulk of the seal-wolf. She could see The Pyramid, though, and reckoned the rabbit must be between her and their goal. She gripped the sword free and sprinted across the dying animal's head with all her power.

She leapt.

This time it was her aim that was a little off.

She flew, arms and legs working as if she were running. She had the distance, but the rabbit was forty paces further east than she'd gauged. Wootah and Calnians watched her, shock-faced. She felt a bit silly, soaring through the air, forty paces off track, about to plunge to her death.

The rabbit lurched to the right but it was far too late. Paloma's momentum failed and she fell towards the writhing mass of monsters.

Was it possible to land well on a pile of animals, she wondered?

If it was, she didn't manage it. The air was punched from her body. Her face slapped onto something leathery. She pushed herself up on her arms, but her hands stuck to the gooey skin of whatever vile beast was below her. She saw the rabbit's huge cotton tail bouncing away, then her view was blocked by a hairy, giant semi-human rising out of the animal soup. It swung a lumpen fist. She tried to pull her hands free but they were stuck fast.

The blow knocked her sideways and down into the gloop. She realised her hands were free but before she could use them, something impossibly heavy fell on her. Teeth or possibly a claw bit into her shoulder. She kicked uselessly as she sank into the sea of beasts. Teeth clamped into her ankle. Hot wetness enveloped her other leg and something rough licked her face. She was stuck, she couldn't breathe and she was sinking.

And she was enraged. This was not how she was meant to die.

# Chapter 9

## Treachery

S assa Lipchewer's elation at the stopping of the seal-wolf turned to horror as she watched Paloma plunge.

"Go right!" shouted Sofi.

The rabbit swerved. Far too late. Paloma fell into the sea of monsters and disappeared.

"Hold the coffin," said Chogolisa, standing.

"Turn the rabbit!" called Wulf.

"No," Sofi ordered.

"But—" said Sassa. There was nothing to say. If they went back, the chances of them all being killed multiplied greatly, and they'd seen Paloma disappear under the tide of murderous beasts.

Far to the north Sassa could see only two of the great beasts with pyramids on their backs. The rest had left The Meadows to spread the Warlock Queen's madness and death around the world.

They had to get the coffin and the boy to The Pyramid.

The rabbit ran on. More animals gave chase. Beasts leapt at the giant running mammal. It dodged some and kicked others away. Running across The Meadows had made it bolder. Paloma would have appreciated that, thought Sassa.

The Pyramid loomed larger and larger ahead of them. It was a regular triangle, clearly made by human hands – an awful lot of human hands. The tornado at its summit was paler and cleaner than any of the tornados they'd seen, including the two that were raging right then in the west of The Meadows. Perched as it was fifty or so paces above the top of the peak, The Pyramid's tornado wasn't sucking up any debris. Or people. Not yet anyway.

Sassa looked back, expecting to see Paloma bouncing along over beasts, ready to leap back onto the rabbit's back with a quip and a smile. There was no sign. But something caught her eye to the east.

There were thousands and thousands of flying beasts coming for them. Wasp men.

Sitsi stood ready with her bow.

"Wulf, hold my feet!" Sassa shouted, leaping up. Wulf, lying on his front, clasped her ankles to hold her steady. Freydis jumped up with her bow. Ottar wriggled free from Chogolisa's arms and grabbed his sister's feet to secure her.

Keef stood, bow in hand, then stumbled as the rabbit lurched to the left. Sofi grabbed him, then sat down behind him, holding his hips as the Wootah man stood, arrow strung.

They could hear the familiar wasp men screaming now, over the noise of the other beasts.

Sitsi shot. A wasp man fell, one tumbling from the multitude.

Sassa waited. She had only two dozen arrows and she'd have to kill a wasp man with every one of them. Keef and Sitsi had the same, Freydis had ten. So that was . . . eighty-two arrows.

She had no idea exactly how many wasp men were headed for them but it was a lot more than eighty-two.

They flew in, screaming hate. Sassa shot, Keef shot, Freydis shot. Wasp men fell, but it was like trying to hold back the rain by shooting a few raindrops.

They were twenty paces away. Ten. Their yellow eyes were unsheathed and glowing. Sassa could feel the foul wind from their leathery wings. They were clacking claws, clenching and unclenching their human-like hands as if to show how they were going to rip the Wootah and Calnians to pieces.

"Can you go faster, Finn?" shouted Sassa.

The rabbit swerved to the left and Sassa nearly fell. Finn had turned to avoid a grey-green beast rising out of the ground ahead. It was more hill than animal. Smaller monsters tumbled down its shiny flanks as it grew.

The sudden change in direction flummoxed the wasp men but only briefly. As Finn brought the rabbit back on course for The Pyramid, the wasp men were maybe fifty paces behind and closing fast again.

"Wow," said Keef. Dozens of bulges had appeared on the vast, shiny flank of the new monster and were forming into frog-like faces. As Sassa watched, open-mouthed, one of the faces opened its own mouth and spat something enormous and pink at them.

It was a tongue. She had seen frogs hurl their sticky tongues at beetles. The fat end of the tongue enveloped the helpless beetle and sucked it back into the frog's mouth.

"Speed, Finn, now!" she shouted.

The rabbit bucked forward and the tongue – a colossal ball of pink, shiny flesh on a thick and veiny grey rope – fell to the ground behind them.

There was already another one coming, this one aimed a little high. Keef hurled his bow aside and pulled Arse Splitter off his back. He swung the long axe overhead and cleaved the tongue in two. A shower of grey goo drenched him. The split tongue fell away.

"Ya!" shouted Keef, then looked about for his bow.

"You threw if off the rabbit," said Chogolisa.

"Why did I do that?" said Keef.

"You probably thought it would look more dramatic."

"That does sound like me."

Sassa raised her bow and aimed at the nearest wasp man, but a tongue hit the creature first, enveloping it and hauling it back into a giant frog mouth.

More and more tongues lashed out from the frog faces on

the grey monster's flank. They whacked into wasp men and sucked them back shrieking into the body of the monstrosity.

The swarm of wasp men screamed and turned, diving at their attacker. Sassa saw several of them spray poison on the frog faces, then they were out of sight around the flank of the monster.

"I think we're through," said Sofi a short time later. Indeed, the monsters were thinner on the ground as they neared The Pyramid. Soon the rabbit was sprinting across bare, baked earth, smashing aside dead, burned trees.

Sassa could see why there were no monsters. The Pyramid loomed ahead, higher than even the largest of them – so much larger than it had looked from a distance – black and terrifying. It wasn't just the tornado, swirling and roaring at its summit. The very air thrummed with the power of the thing. Nobody, nothing, with any sense would go anywhere near it.

"Good rabbit," said Sassa, patting their mount as it drew to a halt at the base of The Pyramid and lay, shivering.

They slid down. There was no need to say anything. They began the ascent of the rough, black sides of The Pyramid.

Although if you'd fallen you would probably have died, it was – as Sitsi had said it would be – an easy climb. The Pyramid was less steep than it had looked from a distance, and the black rock was grippy. The gale howling around the man-made mountain up towards the tornado at the top actually helped to pull them up. Even Ottar and Freydis were scampering with relative ease, and Chogolisa Earthquake was managing admirably with the coffin on one shoulder.

Sassa kept glancing back, as did everybody else. She expected to see Paloma tearing across the sea of monsters towards them, and was almost surprised every time she didn't. Paloma *could not* have died. There was no way a life that burned so brightly could be snuffed so suddenly.

But there was no sign of the speedy Owsla woman, just monsters, tornados and great gouts of fire pluming out of who knew what.

Soon Sassa reached a platform. She, Thyri and Finn were last up. Several hundred paces above their heads the tornado howled. Sassa panted. It was hard to breathe.

The platform was maybe twenty paces by five, cut into the side of The Pyramid two thirds of the way up. The entrance, a square doorway three paces high seemed to be open, but such was the blackness within that it was hard to tell.

A long way below, back in The Meadows, the frog-faced mountain monster had almost sunk back into the mess. Wasp men hovered above it like everyday wasps over rotting fruit.

Still no sign of Paloma.

"Let's go," said Wulf, leading the way with Sofi.

Sassa waited until last, still hoping that Paloma might appear. A six-legged monster with a long nose, the largest animal she'd seen so far, was walking west to east, heading for the valley that led out of The Meadows.

"Sassa!" someone shouted. She turned. Thyri Treelegs was standing between her and the entrance, sax in hand, red-eyed, tears running down her face. Everyone else had disappeared into The Pyramid.

"Why did you kill Garth?" Thyri shouted over the roar of the tornado.

"To stop him killing Finn!" Sassa yelled back.

"So you *did* kill him!"

*Shit on a tit.* She'd walked into that one. "It was him or Finn! Thyri, this is not the time. When we've got the coffin—"

"Who were you to decide?" Thyri raised her sax. Her tanned face was mottled purple. The veins on her neck looked like they would snap.

"Not now, Thryri!" Sassa shouted, walking nearer. "When we've —

Thyri's arm moved in a blur and Sassa saw a flash. She felt a blaze of pain across her neck. She opened her mouth to say something but only a horrible gurgling groan came out.

*Fuck a mother-fucking duck!* she thought. *She's slit my throat! Thyri, you dick!*

She put her hand to her neck. Warm blood pulsed between her fingers.

Finn followed Chogolisa into The Pyramid. He couldn't see past the big woman and the coffin on her shoulder, which was annoying. He should have nipped in ahead of her, but he'd been busy watching for Paloma to come running. She wasn't dead. She'd catch up soon.

He touched the wall. It was the same rough black rock as the exterior but it glowed with a weird light that he could only describe as black. He tried to look around Chogolisa again. No. He could see nothing but big, muscular and magically lit Owsla arse. The tunnel, as far as he could tell in the dark light, was as wide and high as the door that had led into it. The air was dry, and he guessed it was usually odourless, but since Wulf and Keef were ahead of him, the primary smell in there was sweat.

The passage seemed to be sloping gently downwards. It turned. It kept turning and heading downwards. The pulsing that had been thrumming in Finn's head since they'd approached The Pyramid strengthened into a throbbing headache.

*I'm dying*, he heard.

Where had that come from? Was it part of The Pyramid's nastiness? Was the Warlock Queen dying? He dared hope.

*I'm dying and my baby will die.*

Sassa! Why would she . . . Thyri and Sassa had been the last people outside The Pyramid. He spun round. They weren't behind him.

Without thinking what he was doing – without thinking to tell anybody else what he'd heard – Finn set off at a sprint, back the way they'd come.

*I'm dying and my baby will die*, Finn heard again.

The journey back up the spooky passage seemed a lot, lot longer than the walk down. *Was it some kind of magic?* he thought. Was he doomed to be running for ever upwards, trapped by the Warlock Queen? Finally, there was a square of blinding light ahead and then he was out, blinking in the sun.

Sassa Lipchewer was kneeling, eyes closed, breathing quickly and snottily through her nose, hands clasped around her neck, trying to staunch the blood that was seeping out around her fingers. Thyri Treelegs was looking down at her. She saw Finn and turned to him, sax raised. Her face was a mess of tears.

"Step away, Thyri," he shouted. "You've made a mistake, but we can mend it. Let's stop the bleeding."

"No." Thyri came at him, weapon in her hand, like she had so many times in their idyllic evening training sessions, back when he'd been so in love with her.

Finn grabbed for Foe Slicer's hilt. But his scabbard was empty. Paloma had Foe Slicer.

"No!" Thyri slashed at his head.

He ducked the sax and whacked a balled fist into her wrist.

Her mouth opened and she bent forwards.

He punched her hard on the nose with a left.

She staggered.

He hit her jaw with a swinging right.

She reeled.

He swung another punch.

She leapt clear.

"You're no match for me, Boggy," she yelled, straightening and raising her sax. "You don't have the balls!"

*I'm dying and my baby will die*, he heard again

Sassa was dying. He loved Sassa like a sister. He'd find balls.

He ran at Thyri. She swung her blade. He jinked back to avoid the cut, then surged forwards and shoved her two-handed in the chest.

Thyri Treelegs staggered two steps backwards, then gasped in horror when the third step met thin air. She waved her hands in circles, trying to stop herself from falling.

Maybe Finn could have reached out and grabbed her. He didn't try.

Thyri fell backwards, off the edge of The Pyramid. She screamed as she bounced down the rough rock side.

Finn rushed to Sassa. She was lying on her side, eyes open now but staring blindly. He gripped her wrist and felt for a pulse. He didn't find one.

Finn the Deep stood and looked over the edge. Thyri was lying on the baked soil a few hundred feet below, limbs splayed and misshapen. The giant rabbit hopped across and bent its head as if to sniff her. Mother rabbits sometimes ate their babies, Finn found himself thinking.

*No*, he commanded.

Perhaps he was too far away. Perhaps he didn't really mean it.

The rabbit lifted its head and hopped away. Thyri was gone.

# Chapter 10

## Raiders

Sitsi Kestrel took the lead with Sofi Tornado and Wulf the Fat. The Warriors and Warlocks had lashed torches and flints to the coffin for them to use in The Pyramid, but they didn't need them because the ceiling, floor and walls of the rock-hewn corridor gave off a freaky glow.

Not that there was much to see. The passage wound downwards in ever enlarging spirals. There was no sign or sound of anything alive, but she had an arrow strung. She had only three arrows left. Hopefully she wouldn't need any. They'd find the dead Warlock Queen and leave the coffin and that would be that.

As if it was going to be that easy!

The corridor wound down and down. Sitsi was convinced they must be under the earth by now. Her suspicions were confirmed when the corridor straightened out and stretched off a long, long way into dimness. It seemed to be narrowing and curving slightly but it was hard to tell. She'd tried to keep track during the spiral descent but it had been impossible. She had no idea which direction they were heading. The corridor turned a few times more, as if to reinforce her confusion, then began to slope upwards.

They walked along, everybody silent, not even a wisecrack from Keef.

"Who's missing?" said Sofi a short while later.

"Sassa?" asked Wulf.

No answer.

"She stayed back with Thyri, looking out for Paloma," said Chogolisa. "Finn did, too, I think."

"Finn!" Sitsi called quietly. "Finn, Finn, Finn," echoed back from the vibrating walls.

"He's always a dawdler," said Keef. "He probably stopped for a—"

"Shush," said Sofi.

"Sofi, my wife is missing," said Wulf. "And so is—"

"Shut up!" barked Sofi.

Wulf saw sense and did so.

Sitsi strained to listen. Behind the constant hum of The Pyramid was a louder hum. A rumble even.

She looked up the corridor. Nothing. But the rumble was getting louder . . .

A great boulder dropped from the passage roof some hundred paces ahead. It slammed to the floor and rolled towards them, glancing off the corridor walls.

"Run!" Sofi shouted.

Sitsi sprinted, but she could feel as much as she could hear the boulder charging ever closer. There was no way they were going to outrun the rolling rock.

*Crushed by a boulder deep underground the Desert You Don't Walk Out Of,* she thought. Had someone asked her to guess how she was going to die, it would have taken her a while to pick that one.

Paloma Pronghorn felt something furry prod her exposed midriff. She jabbed with Finn's sword and it desisted.

The beast that had bitten into her shoulder had let go, but she'd been trapped in the shifting sea of monsters, churning around with them, for what seemed like an age. She had no idea which direction was up, let alone how she might head that way.

Something clamped around her ankle. It felt like a gummy

mouth. She kicked at it but the grip only tightened. Something warm and wet licked the underside of her foot and the lips around her ankle sucked hard, pulling in her bare leg so the grip was around her knee.

She kicked and tried to bring Foe Slicer down to chop at it, but she couldn't move her arm in the press of beasts. A sharp suck from what she was now pretty sure were lips, and the mouth was around her thigh. She writhed and struggled and yelled even though she knew there was nobody to hear her cries. She was panicking. It seemed reasonable, given the circumstances.

Paloma managed to get her fingers around the lip of whatever was trying to eat her leg and push. It pushed back, hard. She was driven along, through the pile of monsters.

And suddenly she was clear – free of the monster morass, rising into the air, a monster's mouth still clamped around her leg. It was some kind of huge worm or snake, she guessed. Whatever it was, she was now unencumbered and able to chop Foe Slicer into the bastard animal.

It went limp and she fell onto a pile of writhing fuzzy things with teeth. She pulled her leg free of the mouth and leapt up. The worm – a great thick purple-blue thing with a gummy mouth, now leaking from a gash across what one might call its neck – shot back under the seething, beastly surface.

*Ha!* thought Paloma.

Thirty paces away creatures tumbled as a great round thing rose from their midst. It was like a spider but had far too many legs . . . It wasn't a worm that had gripped her, it was one of this creature's tentacles.

More of those disgusting mouth-ended tentacles reached for her.

She looked about for The Pyramid, spotted it and ran, leaping from beast to beast, running along wet, whale-like flanks, sprinting up long necks and leaping off heads, and sometimes lopping off smaller heads with Foe Slicer as she flew by. It was a lovely weapon. Some wasp men flew towards her but she left them behind. She was too quick for wasp men.

Soon she was running around monsters rather than across them. Then the land was free of creatures, apart from the great black rabbit that the Wootah and Calnians had rode in on. It was chewing something. *Was that blood dripping out of its mouth?*

Paloma ran past it, towards the black pyramid with the tornado at its peak. She felt an urge to turn back. There was something very wrong with this man-made mountain. But there was something a lot more wrong with the sea of monsters behind her, and her friends were ahead. She sprinted up the rough stone side and reached the platform in a few heartbeats.

"Hello, Finn!" she said.

Finn looked up, tears in his eyes, Sassa's lifeless head in his lap.

Chogolisa stopped. "Run, Chogolisa!" Sitsi yelled, heading towards her.

"You run. I've got a boulder to stop."

"You'll never do it, it's too big and too fast, even for you."

"Have any other ideas?"

Sitsi hadn't. They'd been walking along the upward-sloping passage for a long time when the boulder dropped. They didn't have a hope. But there was no way Chogolisa would stop it, even with her strength. At best it would slow down as it rolled over her large body, but it would soon speed up again.

Sofi stopped, too, as did Wulf. Sitsi turned to watch.

Sofi, Chogolisa and Wulf stood abreast.

The boulder was twenty paces away, then ten.

Wulf sprinted forwards.

He leapt, swinging Thunderbolt.

The boulder exploded around him. Sofi and Chogolisa turned, hands over their head, as stones and shards whacked into them, followed by a wave of dust, followed by Wulf the Fat, walking nonchalantly and swinging Thunderbolt by its leather lanyard.

"That," said Chogolisa, "is no ordinary hammer."

"Boulder's stopped!" yelled Sitsi to Keef, who was still running down the passage, a child under each arm.

"Yeah, I know!" he called when he was nearly back to them. "Just practising my double child run and carry!"

Sassa Lipchewer's neck was bleeding but not jetting. Paloma took her wrist.

"I tried that," sniffed Finn. "She's dead."

Paloma pressed the tips of her fingers into Sassa's artery. There was quite a strong pulse.

"If I'm ever injured and you're the only one around, Finn," she said, "go and find someone else to treat me."

She looked at Sassa's neck again. If that bleeding didn't stop, she would be dead soon.

Paloma leapt to the edge of the platform, placed Foe Slicer's edge against the stone and sawed with all her strength and speed.

"What are you—"

"I'm sawing The Pyramid in half."

"What?"

Sword and rock started smoking. Paloma pumped her arm all the faster. "Get her ready!" she called to Finn.

"Sassa," Finn said, "I'd like you to prepare yourself. You're about to have a very hot—"

"Not emotionally ready, dickhead! Make sure I can get at her neck with the blade, and hold her very, very tight."

Paloma leapt back and pressed the red-hot blade against Sassa's neck.

There was a sizzle followed by the sharp tang of burning flesh. Sassa screamed, then whimpered.

"You can do the emotional support stuff now," said Paloma.

"Shall we wait for Sassa, Finn and Thyri?" asked Chogolisa.

"We press on," said Wulf. "We have to assume they're okay. Our priority has to be getting the coffin to the Warlock Queen."

Sofi Tornado was glad that Wulf had said it.

Without the constant thrum of The Pyramid, she might have heard what had happened to the others. As it was, she had to strain to hear the footsteps of the people just a few paces behind her.

They walked on, along the apparently never-ending corridor. She could hear something ahead now, something large scraping on rock as it moved, but she didn't know what it was. It wasn't an immediate threat and they had to keep going. So there was no point mentioning it to the others.

In her vision quest the queen had been an actual person. Were they going to meet her at the end of this underground journey and hand over the living boy and the dead boy?

And how far was the journey? The corridor was curving to the right. Only slightly, but they'd come a long way. Sofi had been trying to keep track. By her reckoning, they weren't far from where they'd started.

Sitsi was next to her, scanning ahead. In the vibrating corridors Sitsi's sight was a lot more use than Sofi's hearing.

Wulf had fallen behind. She glanced back. He was holding Ottar's hand. Keef was holding Freydis's. A few paces behind them Chogolisa was carrying the coffin. It was a poisonous burden. Chogolisa would never say as much, but Sofi could tell the coffin was weakening, even sickening her. It would be good to be rid of it.

Sofi had her own burden. The Wootah were not going to

like it when it was time for Ottar to die – nor were Sitsi and Chogolisa, come to that. Presumably someone as powerful as the Warlock Queen wouldn't give them a choice. Chances were she was going to kill them all. Why not? She clearly had utter disregard for human life. Sofi considered the idea of dying in a few hours, or maybe even a few minutes time. She didn't feel too bad about it.

The beast, or whatever it was ahead, was getting louder.

"The passage widens," said Sitsi. "And I think there's . . . it's gone. I saw something move. Something big."

They walked on and into a large room. Its walls glowed with the same shadowed luminescence as the passageway, but Sofi couldn't see the roof.

The monster heard them and turned. Standing hunched on two thick legs, it was maybe four paces tall. Its lumpen, one-eyed head was set to one side, as if it had originally had two heads but one was missing. One arm was as thick as the thickest tree trunk, but cut off at the elbow. The other, more slender but still marvellously muscled, ended in a metallic looking club. It was this club that Sofi had heard dragging along the ground.

It was the most humanlike of the Warlock Queen's creation that Sofi had seen so far although, had it stomped into your village, you wouldn't have said to yourself *oh look, here comes something humanlike.*

"Hello!" said Wulf, striding forward. "We mean you no harm!"

Sofi blinked. She meant it harm. She hadn't considered trying to befriend the thing. Perhaps it would work.

The giant watched Wulf approach. For all its deformity, it did not look aggressive.

"Shall we?" asked Sitsi taking a step forward.

"Hold," said Sofi, "but be ready."

Wulf raised an arm. "We are the Wootah and the Calnians," he said softly. "We are here to return the Warlock Queen's child. I say return. We didn't take the boy. We'd never have done that. But we are bringing him home."

The giant cocked his head as if studying him. It opened its larger arm in a gesture that seemed to say *you may pass.* Then, with all the indifference of someone sweeping an ant off their leg, it swung the arm back and sent Wulf flying. The Wootah man hit the wall halfway up with a crunch and dropped to the ground.

Sofi charged, Chogolisa and Sitsi at her side. Sitsi's bow was unstrung, brandished like Paloma's killing stick.

The giant raised its stubby arm and pointed it at them.

Sofi had a heartbeat to wonder what it intended, then something shot from the end of the arm at the speed of lightning and knocked her off her feet. She landed in a sitting position, but she couldn't move. Her legs and arms were bound in what looked and felt like spider silk. She could hear Sitsi and Chogolisa struggling next to her.

The giant shambled towards them, raising its club arm.

She heard running behind her, then Keef was leaping over her head. He jammed the point of his long axe into the stone floor, leapt up in a somersault, swung his weapon round and jammed the leading edge of the axe's blade into the beast's one eye.

The giant lifted its head to the invisible roof and screamed. Keef landed, then leapt again, swinging Arse Splitter. The sharp metal blade sliced through the thick neck like a flint knife through a wet reed. The giant's throat gaped open. It fell.

Keef sashayed back to the wrapped Owsla, swinging his axe around his head. For a moment Sofi thought he was going to kill them – they were embarrassingly helpless – but he sliced them free. Ottar and Freydis helped to untangle them.

Wulf, recovered from hitting the wall, walked over with a sheepish grin.

"Well done, Keef, you're better than the Owsla!" yipped Freydis, jumping up and down on the spot.

"Well, obviously," Keef replied.

The passage continued at the far end of the room. They headed on.

"Did anyone bring any food?" asked Freydis after a while. "Ottar's hungry."

"Sorry," said Chogolisa, "I don't think anyone thought it would take this long."

Ottar moaned.

Soon Sofi could hear running water. The passage opened up again, this time to a much larger chamber with what looked like a wide drain running across their path, perhaps a hundred paces across and ten deep. The sound of running water was loud but the drain was dry. There was a dark square in the softly glowing wall opposite them.

"The passage continues on the other side," said Sitsi.

"Let's get across quickly," said Sofi. It wasn't just the worry of a flash flood. She'd been able to hear something following them for a while, but with the strange vibration of the walls it was impossible to tell what it was.

They were almost halfway across when she heard something heavy and wooden move against stone, followed by a surge of water. Lots of water.

"Run!" she yelled. She snatched up Ottar and sprinted for the far side.

The water struck.

Sofi was swirled upside down, around and around. She let the boy go. He was a better swimmer than her.

She gasped for air but sank immediately. She struck out for what she thought was the surface, but a current caught her legs and whirled her around.

Sofi surfaced and thought she saw someone climbing out on the far side, or possibly the side they'd come from.

She thrashed, but the current pulled her down. The water was calmer now, the roaring in her ears quieter. She could see light, she could see which way was up. She flailed her arms and kicked her legs. No good. The current was holding her under.

*Should have learned to swim as a child*, she thought as her vision blurred and her mind clouded.

She could not die like this. Not before the quest was done. But her arms were weakening. What was it the Wootah said about death?

Something gripped her shoulders.

*Rescue!* she thought.

It wasn't rescue.

Whoever or whatever was dragging her down, away from the light.

Her ears squeezed painfully, as if she'd descended a mountain in a heartbeat, but then she was launching up and up and up and . . . out!

She gulped air.

She was on her back. Whoever had pulled her from the depth had one arm around her chest and the other holding her chin out of the water.

"Sorry if I freaked you out," said her rescuer, "but there's an undertow. I had to take you down then launch off the bottom."

It was Finn the Deep.

He pulled her to the side and she climbed out onto the rough, black, glowing stone. She held out a hand to help Finn from the water.

"Thanks," she said.

He nodded, then flopped down onto the stone and lay panting.

The rest of them were already there. She could see Paloma and Sassa watching them from the far side, Sassa with a white bandage round her neck.

"Paloma!" Chogolisa shouted with joy. Sofi felt herself smiling. It took more than being buried under a few thousand monsters to stop Paloma Pronghorn.

"Are you all right, Sassa?" Wulf shouted across the channel.

"She's got a cut neck!" shouted Paloma, "but she'll be okay."

"Where's Thyri?" Keef yelled.

"Ah," said Finn. "I killed her."

"*What?*"

"She tried to kill Sassa."

"Why?"

"Because Sassa killed Garth," said Wulf.

"How do you—" Finn started, but Chogolisa interrupted him.

"Can we talk about that later?" she asked. "I lost the coffin in the flood."

Sofi looked over the dark, swirling water. "Sitsi, can you see it anywhere?"

"I can't. I think that—"

Sitsi was interrupted by a rushing whoosh. Suddenly the water was draining away as quickly as it had come in.

The moment the water was gone, Wulf climbed down and ran across to Sassa. Keef and Finn clambered down and dashed to where the water had disappeared.

Sofi stayed where she was. The channel might flood again.

They couldn't find the coffin. Keef reported that the water had drained through a series of holes just about large enough to fit the coffin.

"I'll go down one of the holes if you like," he said, "but there are half a dozen and I don't know if they all go to the same place."

"No," said Sofi. "We'll have to carry on without it."

Wulf climbed out of the wet but empty channel with

Paloma and Sassa. Sassa looked even paler than normal above her white bandage.

"Are you all right to continue?" Sofi asked her.

Sassa nodded.

"If there's any point, now," said Keef.

# Chapter 11

## Freydis

They walked and walked along the humming, glowing tunnel. Finn the Deep didn't know whether it was day or night. He was hungry. He kept picturing Thyri's face as he pushed her off The Pyramid. He kept thinking about his father's dead face. The children trudged behind. Chogolisa was carrying the weakened Sassa on her back. Finn was a little embarrassed that he'd thought she was dead, but he was used to being embarrassed about something most of the time so it didn't trouble him too much. Killing Thyri, on the other hand, did.

It was a long walk. Finn had no idea how long, but he noticed after a while, first that his clothes had dried, second that they seemed to be heading upwards in ever tightening circles, and third that there was an ever-louder roaring sound.

Finally the passage came out into the open air. Finn blinked and looked around. There was a tornado *above* them. They were in a square yard, maybe two hundred paces across, with walls five paces high all around. It was made of the same black rock as The Pyramid.

They walked into the middle, looking around and up at the base of the tornado.

"Where . . .?" said Finn.

"We're at the top of The Pyramid," said Sitsi.

"But we're not. We walked for ages. We can't be back in

the same place. And the top of The Pyramid is a point," Finn argued.

"Not any more."

"Paloma, see where we are," commanded Sofi.

Paloma ran to the side, scaled the wall like a squirrel and came back moments later.

"Sitsi's right," she said.

"But—" said Finn.

"*You* may not have noticed anything unusual yet," said Keef, "but this is quite a strange place. Not being quite where we thought we were is not the most unusual thing about it."

"The monsters?" Wulf asked Paloma.

"Still doing their thing."

They looked around.

"Is this it now?" asked Keef. "We've lost the coffin and there's no Warlock Queen. Time to go home and pretend we never tried? Call a rabbit, will you, Finn?"

"Should we get a rope and try to retrieve the coffin?" asked Sassa.

"Ottar, what should we do?" asked Wulf.

"Dunno," said Ottar.

"He doesn't know," said Freydis.

"Hang on," said Sofi.

Could she hear something? Because Finn could *feel* something. It was like there was something alive under their feet.

"Follow me!" called Sofi.

They ran to the edge, then watched as the centre of the square collapsed. A dark shape emerged, rumbling and shaking, dust and debris cascading.

Walking towards them out of the dust – striding in fact – came a woman. She was wearing a leather jerkin and trousers, similar to the warriors' garb, and a golden helmet with a crest running from front to back.

Most strikingly of all, as Sofi had seen in her vision quest, the woman looked like a Wootah. She had blonde hair sprouting from her helmet, pale skin and blue eyes.

As the dust settled behind her, Finn saw a stone table. On it was the coffin they'd carried from Wormsland. The lid was missing.

The Warlock Queen stopped ten paces from the assembled Wootah and Calnians. Finn almost had to look away. You could feel the power flowing from her.

"Give me the boy," said the Warlock Queen, pointing at Ottar. Her voice was cool and quiet.

Finn noticed a long, curved scabbard on her belt.

"Will you stop your monsters and destruction if we give you the boy?" Sofi asked.

"If you don't give me the boy I will take the boy."

"We have to know," said Wulf.

The Warlock Queen raised an eyebrow. "You will give me the boy and you will leave The Meadows. Then I will stop the destruction. If you, or any others enter The Meadows again, I will bring it all back."

"But you are a human," said Sitsi. "Why would you want—" Sitsi grabbed her own throat and fell to the ground, eyes bulging. Keef ran to her, but she waved a hand at him to say that she was okay.

"It's a long time since I was human," said the Queen.

"Why do you want Ottar?" asked Finn.

"Oaden's tits," said Keef. He strode towards Finn, shaking his head. "I worked this out before we'd even left Hardwork. She wants his life to give to her long-dead kid. How could it be more obvious? For someone who's meant to be clever, you are thick as the crust on—"

He turned and flung Arse Splitter at the Warlock Queen. She lifted a hand. The hurled axe twirled around and shot back at Keef. The blade slammed into him. He flew and landed on his back, the leading point of the axe's blade deep in his chest.

Sitsi ran to him, wrenched out the axe and pressed her hands over the wound.

"Slain by my own throw," said Keef. "I will be the laughing stock of Valhalla." He closed his eyes.

Sitsi stood and turned to the Warlock Queen, stringing her bow. Sassa strung hers. Wulf raised his hammer. Finn put a hand to his sword hilt but he didn't know what he hoped to achieve. The others seemed unsure, too.

"Lower your weapons," commanded Sofi. Finn took his hand from the hilt. Whether the Warlock Queen had some sort of power over them, or whether they all saw the hopelessness of attacking her, it seemed that the fight had gone out of them.

"Give me the boy," said the Warlock Queen.

"I'll bring him to you," said Sofi. "Come here, Ottar." She held out her hand. Ottar looked very unsure.

"Take me instead!" Wulf pleaded.

The queen looked away, dismissing him without a word.

Sassa took a step forward. "You will not take the boy, Sofi."

Sofi held her gaze. "She just slew Keef with a thought. She can do the same to any of us. She is a goddess. We do not have a chance. We give her Ottar and walk away. Or she kills us and takes Ottar."

"I'd rather die."

"And take your baby with you? Think, Sassa. One boy in return for the world is no price at all. I lost six of my Owsla on this quest. You lost almost all of your tribe. He is one boy. We swap him for the lives of millions upon millions of children – those alive today and those to come."

Sassa's head slumped.

Finn sensed movement and looked up. A gigantic, winged snake was flapping overhead, between them and the base of the tornado. Surely if that weighty horror dived onto the Warlock Queen it would end her?

He reached out to find its mind.

Something burst in his head.

He didn't know he was falling until his knees hit rock.

"Finn, what is it?" Paloma asked.

"I'm okay."

He wasn't. It felt like his mind was leaking out of his ears, eyes and nose. "I tried to control one of her monsters. She hit me in the head. I'm not going to be much help." He lay on his side and tried to wish the pain away. Was he dying? Would it count as dying in battle? Would Keef be waiting for him in Valhalla, ready to take the piss? Would Erik be there? Thyri?

He opened his eyes. The tornado was darkening. The sky all around was getting darker. Was it going to rain? He didn't want to die in the rain.

Paloma Pronghorn crouched next to Finn. His breathing was shallow and his pulse weak, but he was alive.

Sofi was right. It was a sad choice, but it wasn't a hard one.

Wulf and Sassa looked desperate and angry enough to fight Sofi, but surely they could see reason? *They've got to make a fuss so they can leave here with clear consciences*, said the most cynical recesses of her mind.

"Your time has come to an end," said the Warlock Queen.

"No," said Wulf.

"We have to," said Freydis quietly.

She stood, small, blue-eyed and blonde. Tiny, weak and bravest of the Wootah.

"I don't want anyone else to die," said Freydis. "Ottar, go to the lady."

Ottar looked up at Wulf, confusion on his pink-cheeked face. His huge blue eyes were wet. So were Wulf's.

Wulf tried to speak, but couldn't. Sassa knelt and took Ottar's hands. "Ottar, you have to do something that you shouldn't have to do. That none of the rest of us can do.

You have to go to the lady, and she will take you. We will remember you every hour of every day for ever more. When we meet in Valhalla we will sing of your heroism every day and we will drink Tor's mead hall dry."

Paloma blinked tears. It was suddenly darker. She looked up. The tornado was sucking in storm clouds.

"Go to her," said Freydis. "That lady with the funny hat."

"Af to?" Ottar asked his sister.

"You do. Go now."

Ottar nodded, turned and walked away. Freydis' older brother was only eight and very small for his age, but he looked even tinier than usual as he walked alone to his doom. The Warlock Queen took his hand and together they headed for the stone table and the coffin.

Freydis came over to Paloma and raised her arms.

Paloma picked her up and held her tight.

*Freydis remembered coming to be – woven together from plants and soil then left in a forest glade. The Forest Goddess had created her in the same way as the Warlock Queen had created her monsters, but luckily the Forest Goddess had taken a little more time and care over it.*

*Nearly nine years before the Wootah and Calnians reached The Meadows, Holger the Dumpy had punched Aud the Manic in the stomach in an effort to kill the unborn Ottar. He'd failed, but he had damaged the tiny boy's mind. Ottar had been born, but it was soon clear that there was something wrong: Holger the Dumpy told everyone that he'd punched Aud the Manic's stomach. The Jarl sentenced Holger the Dumpy and Aud the Manic to death, but they'd fled with their baby before the sentence could be carried out.*

*The Forest Goddess saw Holger the Dumpy and Aud the Manic enter the forest with baby Ottar. They were Hardworkers who had been given everything by the Goachica and never looked after themselves, so they had no idea how to live in the forest.*

*Even though it was summer, in just a few days they were nearly dead, as was their baby.*

*The Forest Goddess created baby Freydis to help Ottar, and left her for his parents to find. The hungry Hardworkers' first instinct had been to eat her, but they desisted when the infant spoke to them. She showed them which fruits could be eaten and how to dig for tubers. She taught them to make fires and build shelters.*

*Aud the Manic and Holger the Dumpy became used to the idea of a baby telling them what to do, so when Freydis said that they should return to Hardwork after two years, they did. Freydis wanted to return to the town because it would be better for Ottar. Although she persuaded them otherwise, she knew that Aud the Manic and Holger the Dumpy would be executed.*

*Theirs were the first deaths that Freydis caused.*

The Warlock Queen lifted her dead son from the coffin and placed him on the table. Ottar stood, watching. Paloma held Freydis all the tighter.

The queen said something. Ottar nodded, then clambered up onto the table to lie next to the dead boy.

It was exactly what Nether Barr had done for Wulf. Paloma hadn't minded that one jot. But this was simply awful. Paloma wasn't crying yet but she was pretty sure that afterwards she was going to cry for the rest of her days.

*The Jarl executed Aud the Manic and Holger the Dumpy as expected. Freydis had not been sad about it for a moment – they deserved it for what they had done to Ottar. Gunnhild Kristlover took in Freydis and Ottar. She loved them and looked after them as if they were her own. Uncle Poppo Whitetooth made them laugh and was kind. Gunnhild Kristlover's daughters had been aloof and Finnbogi the Boggy – as he'd been known – only noticed the children when they got in his way.*

*Because of the noises he made trying to speak, the Hardworkers*

had dubbed Ottar "The Moaner". Freydis had not called him
The Moaner. Not once, ever. Every time she said a Hardworker's
name she'd used the full title − Finnbogi the Boggy or Sassa
Lipchewer − in the hope it would show the Hardworkers how
silly it sounded and that they'd stop calling Ottar such a horrible
name. But it hadn't worked.

She didn't mind being called Freydis the Annoying. They
could call her whatever they wanted; she was still a goddess
and they weren't.

When she judged people would think she was old enough,
she started speaking for Ottar. She didn't make it up to begin
with. She said what he wanted to say. Then she realised that
she could improve Ottar's standing in the tribe by having him
predict the future.

Freydis went into the woods, careful to avoid Finnbogi the
Boggy (who spend a lot of time out there in the woods alone)
and asked her mother for help. The Forest Goddess told Freydis
that she'd be able to see the future if she tried. Freydis, her
mother had explained, wasn't a particularly powerful goddess,
but the minor powers she did have could be very effective if
used cleverly.

It wasn't as easy as her mother had made it sound, but
Freydis had been able to see some things coming. She told the
others that Ottar had predicted the tornado, the beaching of
the sturgeon and a few other events.

People had begun to respect Ottar the Moaner, even love
him, and that had made Freydis happy.


The Warlock Queen raised her knife. Paloma Pronghorn
closed her eyes. When she opened them, the Warlock Queen
was walking around the table, chanting.

"How long is this going to take?" asked Finn.

"Are we keeping you from something?" Sassa snapped.

"No. I want it to be over."

"Can't we do anything, Wulf?"

"We can honour Ottar for the rest of our lives," he replied.

"Sofi?" Sassa tried.

Sofi didn't answer.

"Sofi?"

Paloma looked at the captain of the Owsla. She was shaking her head, face wet with tears.

*For a long time, all went well in Hardwork for Ottar and therefore for Freydis, but then it had all gone very wrong. Before the unusual weather began in Hardwork, Freydis's mother told her what the Warlock Queen was doing in The Meadows, west of west. The Forest Goddess told her how the Warlock Queen could be stopped and asked Freydis to do it.*

*Freydis couldn't tell the Hardworkers without revealing what she was and spoiling Ottar in their eyes. She tried to persuade them subtly. She'd thought for a while that Wulf the Fat and a few of the others were going to help her, but in the end they'd been too happy where they were to leave.*

*Then she saw that Calnians were coming to kill them all, so she made up Ottar's prophecy.* Save yourselves by going west of west to The Meadows. *They didn't listen, of course.*

*Freydis hadn't wanted them to die, not all of them.*

*She'd wanted most of them to die because most of them were lazy and useless. She was concerned only for Ottar and they were not nice to him. She would have killed some of them herself, if she'd been able. But she was only a forest goddess, and not even a major forest goddess. She could only do so much.*

*She hadn't wanted Uncle Poppo Whitetooth to die, and she had wanted Garth Anvilchin and a few of the others who'd survived to be killed, but that couldn't be helped.*

Sofi let herself cry freely. The brave boy deserved her grief. She made her decision. If the Warlock Queen let them walk away – which Sofi thought unlikely – she wouldn't kill the Wootah.

Through her tears she watched the Warlock Queen walk around the table. She stopped and raised her knife.

"Dink?" Ottar said. "Tirsty."

"I'll get you a drink soon," said the Warlock Queen, "if you lie there quietly for now."

"'Kay." Ottar lay back down.

The queen resumed her pacing, presumably put back a little in her chanting by the boy's request for a drink. Sofi thought about charging when her back was turned, but as soon as she thought it the Warlock Queen looked up and fixed her with an iron gaze.

Sofi Tornado stood and cried. It was all she could do.

*The Calnians came and killed nearly everyone and the survivors set off. Freydis found Yoki Choppa's open mind in Calnia, and communicated with him, pretending to be Ottar. The warlock already knew about The Meadows. Freydis told him how Ottar was vital to defeating the force there. Their plan to unite the Owsla and the Wootah began before the Owsla left Calnia.*

*Freydis managed to communicate with Erik and send him ahead of them, then called him back when she realised that they needed him.*

*She didn't actually kill any of the Hardworkers who'd survived the Calnian massacre herself, but not through lack of trying. She set the bear on Hrolf the Painter because he was slowing them down (and he was nasty), and the fish on Frossa the Deep Minded because she was so horrid, but Sassa Lipchewer had finished off Hrolf the Painter – much to Freydis's delight – and Sofi Tornado had finally killed Frossa the Deep Minded after the fish had failed.*

*Freydis had nothing to do with Astrid killing Fisk the Fish, nor Sadzi Wolf killing Gurd Girlchaser, nor Sassa Lipchewer killing Garth Anvilchin. She was glad they'd all died, though. All the Hardworkers who'd died between Hardwork and the Water Mother had deserved it.*

*Then, west of the Water Mother, the wrong people had started dying. She would have saved Bjarni Chickenhead, Morningstar, Luby Zephyr, Gunnhild Kristlover, Nether Barr, Yoki Choppa and of course Eric the Angry if she could have done.*

*So chances were she wouldn't be able to beat the Warlock Queen. But she wasn't going to let her kill Ottar without trying.*

Paloma watched the Warlock Queen pacing and chanting. She hugged Freydis, feeling sick.

"Put me down in a moment, please, Paloma Pronghorn," whispered the girl. "Then, when I say *now*, run as fast as you can, get my brother and keep going until you're on the wall on the other side. Then stay there and watch. Whatever happens, whatever you see, stay there with Ottar and keep him clear. If we all get killed, please run away with Ottar and keep running and look after him for ever."

Paloma put Freydis down and nodded even though she didn't have the slightest clue what was about to happen, or why she was obeying a six-year-old girl.

Wulf, Sassa, Chogolisa and Sitsi were staring at the Warlock Queen and Ottar. Keef lay still. Finn was out cold at Paloma's feet. She moved a little to the right so he wouldn't be in the way when she started her run.

She wouldn't be much faster than Keef's hurled axe and she had a lot more ground to cover. But if Freydis thought it should be done, she'd do it. She loved that little girl. And she trusted her.

The black clouds rotated above, ever larger, spinning around the top of the tornado. There was something strange about them. The clouds around a tornado usually looked part of it, as if the tornado was an extension of them. These clouds looked like they were closing in on the tornado, full of violence.

The queen stopped chanting and raised her long golden knife.

"Now," said Freydis.

Paloma sprinted.

The Warlock Queen turned and raised a hand.

*Here we go*, thought Paloma.

But the queen was distracted by something above and Paloma ran on. She jumped, somersaulted over the stone table, grabbed Ottar on the way, landed on her feet on the other side and sprinted. She felt the lightning slam into the Warlock Queen half a heartbeat later. She ran on, leapt to the top of the wall with Ottar in her arms and turned.

The stone table was smashed, the coffin obliterated and burning. A small, smoking skull was rolling across the stone. Ten paces away lay the figure of a woman. Nearby, a golden helmet rattled around on the rock in a sad circle.

*Freydis?* thought Paloma.

Freydis stood on the far side of the basin, looking like nothing more than a six-year-old girl. Wulf, Sassa, Sofi, Sitsi and Chogolisa stared at her. Finn was back on all fours, shaking his head.

"Well, Ottar," said Paloma to the wide-eyed boy in her arms, "I guess that explains a couple—"

The Warlock Queen's arms moved.

*Oh, bollocks.*

She climbed up onto one knee.

"Can you do it again, Freydis?!" Paloma shouted.

The girl shook her head.

The Warlock Queen stood. She raised a hand and a nearby boulder lifted off the ground. She flicked her hand and the boulder flew at Freydis. Freydis froze. Chogolisa dived and got two hands to the flying boulder, changing its course so it missed Freydis by a hare's whisker.

Sofi, Wulf and Chogolisa charged the queen. Sassa and Sitsi raised their bows and loosed.

*Whatever happens, stay there with Ottar*, Freydis had asked her. The girl had just called a lightning bolt to strike the thousand-year-dead Warlock Queen. Chances were she knew what she was talking about. Paloma stayed put.

The queen flicked a hand. Sofi, Wulf and Chogolisa were sent flying to lie dazed against the black wall.

Sassa and Sitsi's arrows flew upwards, into the tornado. The women shot a couple more each, but the Warlock Queen kept flicking their arrows up into the heavens as she walked towards Freydis. Then they were out of arrows.

Sassa fell into a sitting position and her head slumped. It was understandable. She had had her throat slashed not long before.

Sitsi stood, clearly not sure what to do.

Freydis waited, nose poked pertly at the approaching goddess.

Finn lay on the ground a couple of paces from Freydis, hands on his head, shaking.

The goddess raised her knife.

Freydis ran.

The Warlock Queen chased her.

Freydis, trained by Paloma, was a lot faster than anyone would have thought. Paloma actually smiled to see the speed at which she pelted away from the goddess. But, all too soon the goddess caught the girl, grabbed her by the hair and lifted her into the air.

*Stay where you are Paloma*, said Freydis's voice in her mind. *Whatever happens, please save Ottar.*

Freydis didn't struggle. She hung as if she was already dead. The Warlock Queen raised her knife to strike. Paloma tensed to run and try to save her, but Freydis had been clear. Her duty was to rescue Ottar. She would run with the boy as soon as the Warlock Queen killed Freydis.

\* \* \*

*I've failed, thought Freydis.*

She'd used all her power on that one bolt of lightning. She wouldn't be able to do anything like that again for a couple of moons. Even if she could, it clearly wasn't enough.

Freydis had really hoped the lightning would kill the evil hag, or at least knock her down for long enough for Sofi to brain her with her hand axe. With hindsight, she should have asked Paloma to attack after the lightning struck. But that would have meant leaving Ottar to be killed by the lightning. Given a choice, Freydis would have let everyone else in the world die to keep Ottar alive. Unfortunately, it now looked like Ottar was going to die along with everyone else.

The Warlock Queen did not look happy that Freydis had blown the corpse of her child to smithereens. What mother would?

Then Freydis saw something flying towards them.

"Wait," said Freydis. "There's something you need to know."

The Warlock Queen stayed her knife and held Freydis up by the hair with one hand so their faces were level.

Paloma ducked as something whooshed over her head.

A giant, winged snake zipped across the black yard at head height and grabbed the Warlock Queen's head in its jaws without slowing. It shot up sped out over The Meadows, then turned in a tight arc and soared towards the tornado with the queen dangling from its mouth.

The Warlock Queen still had Freydis held by the hair.

Movement caught Paloma's eye. Sitsi had saved an arrow! She loosed, the arrow zipped upward and skewered the Warlock Queen's forearm.

Freydis fell.

"Don't go anywhere," Paloma told Ottar as she set him down. She ran across the black pyramid top, leapt and caught the falling girl.

She landed and rolled with Freydis hopefully protected

in her arms. She finished up on her knees, holding Freydis at arm's length.

"Thank you, Paloma Pronghorn," said Freydis.

"You are a very special little girl."

"I'm not really a girl. And don't be too happy yet. It will take more than a little trip with her head inside a giant snake's mouth to kill the Warlock Queen."

They both looked up.

Paloma could just make out the flying snake and little figure in its jaws, high above them in the middle of the tornado. The clouds all around were really going crazy now. Faster than she knew clouds could move, faster even that she could run, great masses of black cloud zoomed in from all sides of The Meadows.

"Everyone look away!" screamed Freydis. "Close your eyes!"

Moments later there was a light so blinding that Paloma could see it even through her eyelids, followed by an explosion that knocked her flat.

She braced for more, but nothing came. Eventually, ears ringing, half blinded, Paloma looked up.

The sky above was blue and empty, as if the tornado, the storm clouds, the giant flying snake and the Warlock Queen had never existed.

"Freydis," Sassa asked, "was that you?"

"It wasn't. Can you go and get Ottar, please, Paloma Pronghorn?"

The boy was still sitting on the wall on the far side of the square, swinging his legs.

"He'll be okay for a moment. Is the Warlock Queen dead?"

"Yes."

"Was it you?"

"No. I did make the first bolt of lightning, but that didn't work. I don't know why the sky exploded."

"You defeated the Warlock Queen, Freydis." Paloma wasn't far off weeping with pride.

"But I didn't. She was going to kill me. Whoever persuaded that monster to grab her by the head and fly up into the tornado defeated her and saved me."

Paloma looked around.

Finn the Deep was climbing to his feet. He smiled sheepishly.

# Chapter 12

## End of the Tornado

"Ook," said Ottar, pointing behind Paloma as she leapt up to join him on the wall.

Paloma looked.

A cross-shaped monster with dozens of gigantic human-like heads hanging from one arm reared skywards. It wobbled then toppled, the heads screaming in rage or possibly terror. Maybe both.

Apart from that, things were pretty quiet in The Meadows. The monsters that weren't dead were flopping about uselessly on their last legs – or flippers, tentacles, sucker feet and so on.

Paloma smiled.

It looked an awful lot like their quest was done.

She ran back with Ottar to the others.

They were all bent over Keef, apart from Freydis who was sitting on the ground, smiling to herself.

Paloma put Ottar down next to his sister and went over to console Sitsi.

She didn't need to.

"It takes more than an axe to the chest," rasped Keef, "to kill the Berserker."

"No talking, you idiot," said Sitsi.

"He's a tough fucker," said Paloma.

"Yes. He should live."

"Good. The monsters in The Meadows are dying," she reported. "Everyone else okay?"

Sassa, Sitsi, Wulf, Finn and Chogolisa nodded. Sofi shook her head.

"Sofi?" asked Paloma.

"Sorry. I'm fine. It's just . . . I'm fine."

Paloma had never seen Sofi like this. It was almost a relief when, as soon as Sofi stopped talking, The Pyramid started rumbling and shaking and gave Sofi something to do.

"Finn, see if your rabbit is still alive," the Owsla captain commanded. "If not, find something else to carry us out of The Meadows. We'll get everyone up the wall first, then Chogolisa carry Keef, Wulf take Ottar, I'll take Freydis. Paloma, once we're up the wall is there a clear route down The Pyramid?"

"There is. It's the same as it was before, just with the top lopped off."

"Good. Help others up the wall, then make sure the route is clear."

"Rabbit's alive and on its way," said Finn.

"Let's go."

Finn the Deep climbed the wall – well, Chogolisa pretty much hurled him up the wall – then he helped the others.

For ten miles in every direction gigantic monsters were dying. But Finn couldn't stop staring at Freydis.

While the Owsla were lifting Keef up the wall, he turned to her.

"Um, Freydis."

"Yup, Finn the Deep?"

"What was that?"

"What was what?"

"You know."

"She can tell you later," said Sofi, looking up from where she was laying Keef on the stone.

Chogolisa leapt, gripped the top of the wall and clambered up. She stooped to pick up Keef.

"Let's go," said Sofi. "Hold my hand, Freydis."

They headed down the black slope. It was steep but so grippy that they could hop down it carefully.

Finn followed behind Sofi.

"I need to know some things, Freydis," said Sofi.

"I'll tell you whatever I can." The girl's voice sounded the same to Finn, yet completely different. It was high and girly but it had a weight – a power.

"What are you?" Sofi asked.

"I am a forest goddess."

*Of course you are*, thought Finn.

Sofi nodded as if her expectations had been confirmed. "Did you know you were taking Ottar to his death?"

"I hoped it wouldn't come to that."

"But you were happy to risk him?"

"I wasn't happy to do it. But I didn't know any other way to save the world. I knew the Warlock Queen would want him and would let him – and me – get close."

"Why did she want him?"

"It didn't have to be him, but he was very right for her. He is the same age as her son was."

"I could have got you a boy that age," said Sofi, as if they were talking about a new shirt. Finn shivered.

"Yes," Freydis sighed. "And I would have liked that to save Ottar, but the way Ottar's mind is . . . it would have been easier for the Warlock Queen to make him her son."

"She didn't exactly make it easy to bring him here."

"She did. She could have stopped us at any time. She could have opened up the earth below us then closed it again. Or sent some of those fire-breathing things to get us. Or—"

"But the worms, the wasp men, the firenado – everything else."

"She set those off but she wasn't controlling them. They weren't personal attacks."

*They seemed pretty personal*, thought Finn, keeping up so he could hear what was being said.

"So you used your brother to get close enough to kill her," said Sofi.

"Yes, but I failed. I thought the lightning would kill her. It was Finn the Deep who killed her, not me."

*Yup*, thought Finn, *I saved the world*.

"It was the explosion in the sky that killed her," said Sofi.

"That wasn't me either. I think it might have been her, killing herself because her son was gone so there was no point any more. But maybe it was another god. I don't know."

"And Finn's abilities with animals? Did you give him those?"

"No, that's nothing to do with me."

They reached the bottom of The Pyramid. The others started climbing onto the rabbit.

Sofi paused and faced Freydis. "Did you bring Wulf back to life?"

"No. I went to see if I could help, but I couldn't."

"Did you make Yoki Choppa tell us not to kill the Wootah and to help you come west?"

"I told him what I was doing and why. But he made the decision. I couldn't make him do anything he didn't want to do."

"So when he rescued Ottar?"

"That was nothing to do with me."

"Okay." Sofi nodded. "Finn, stop skulking around behind us and get up the rabbit. Paloma!"

Paloma's head appeared over the side of the rabbit.

"I'm going to throw Freydis up to you."

"Ready, boss!" shouted Paloma.

\* \* \*

Sassa Lipchewer sat on the rabbit as it lolloped across the plain of rotting monsters, one hand on her stomach, one hand on Keef the Berserker. Sitsi sat on his other side.

"What will you do now?" Sassa asked Sitsi.

"I think we should all go back to the Valley of the Gods. We can discuss what we're going to do next while we wait for Keef to get better. I think we should all stay together, though, don't you?"

"I do, but won't you do what Sofi tells you to do?"

"Look back at The Pyramid, Sassa," Sitsi said sadly, without turning herself.

Sassa turned.

The Pyramid stood stark and flat-topped out of the sea of dead monsters. Standing at the top, legs wide, hands on hips, was the tiny but unmistakeable figure of Sofi Tornado.

Sassa looked about on the rabbit. Sofi really wasn't there. She'd stayed behind.

"Why?" asked Sassa.

"Because she failed," said Sitsi.

"We didn't fail!"

"She was ordered to kill all Mushroom Men. She decided not to."

"That's a good thing . . ."

"Yes. But I think maybe not killing you really made it strike home that she could have questioned previous orders. She's killed hundreds of men, women and children. Perhaps she realised that she didn't have to."

"But you were drugged. And you were taught from childhood that it was what you were meant to be doing." Sassa looked from Sitsi to Paloma to Chogolisa.

"Yes," said Sitsi. "We three can blame the killing on the rattlesnake, and the conditioning, and forgive ourselves, or at least I hope we can."

"Why can't Sofi?"

"Because she knows she would have done it without the rattlesnake."

Chief Maya and four other warriors were waiting for them at the edge of The Meadows.

Finn the Deep thought that Maya looked great.

"Is the Warlock Queen dead?" she shouted up to them.

"She is!" Wulf called back. "Is this all of you?"

"No. We lost two. The rest are making camp."

They climbed down the rabbit. The furry beast hopped off back into The Meadows, presumably to die with its fellows. Finn tried to say farewell and thank you to it but its mind was already gone.

"Are you all right to walk?" asked Maya. "The rest are at the top of—"

There was a deep rumbling.

A great geyser launched from the top of The Pyramid and shot impossibly high into the air. It kept coming, an incredible jet of water. It finally reached its high point and water started to fall, southwards. More and more water was jetting out from The Pyramid – or from the ground where The Pyramid used to be.

Finn opened his mouth to ask Sitsi if Sofi had somehow got clear, but she'd turned away and her eyes were closed.

They headed up the mountains on the edge of The Meadows as The Pyramid spouted billions of gallons of water.

They found the rest of the surviving warriors and warlocks at the top. Wootah and Calnians sat, resting, eating and drinking and watching The Meadows fill with water. Soon, only the largest monsters in The Meadows were visible, then they too were covered by swirling, brown water.

Finn wanted to question Freydis further, but he was too tired. And besides, she was asleep, sandwiched happily between Chogolisa and Paloma.

Keef the Berserker was also asleep, snoring softly. Sitsi Kestrel sat next to him, stroking his strange short hair.

Ottar was asleep, too, curled on Wulf's lap. Sassa was leaning on his shoulder.

Chief Maya was sitting alone, a little way off from the others.

Finn walked over.

"Do you mind if I sit here with you?" he asked.

She looked up and smiled. Finn had never seen her smile before. She had a lovely smile. "Please do," she said.

# Historical note
# and
# Acknowledgements

My books would not exist without my wife Nicola who is, as our sons Charlie and Otty would attest, the finest person in the world. Otty, in case you're wondering, is really called Ottar and he is named after Ottar the Moaner. He'll be at least four years old by the time you read this, which shows you just about how long it takes to get a trilogy from head to bookshop.

Thanks very much to all at Orbit on both sides of the Atlantic – a great copy-edit from Richard Collins, wonderful organisation from Joanna Kramer, fantastic publicity from Nazia Khatun and Ellen Wright and magnificent editing as ever from my editor Jenni Hill. Thanks very much also to all those other Orbiteers who've helped make this book a real thing.

Thanks also to my agent Angharad Kowal for her tireless agenting.

My beta readers Amy Dean and my brother Tim have been invaluable for all my books but this last one in particular, so huge thanks to them.

Massive thanks to Sean Barrett for reading the audiobook so well. I'm only slightly annoyed that his reading rates slightly higher than the books themselves on audible.com (both the West of West and Age of Iron audiobooks rate astonishingly highly. It's where I go to read reviews if I'm ever questioning my writing abilities at the start of a writing day).

And big thanks to America. I'll be back in the UK by the time this book comes out after two marvellous years living in, arguably I know, the finest country in the world. I certainly like it here.


## Native Americans

A thousand years ago in the middle of North America near modern day St Louis there was a large, planned city. With a population of 25,000 people, it was bigger than both London and Paris at the time. These days we refer to it as Cahokia, or, in this book, Calnia. Seven hundred years ago it was abandoned and nobody knows why.

A little over a thousand miles away across the Rockies (or Shining Mountains), while Cahokia was thriving, stone towns were built into great cracks in cliffs at what we now call Mesa Verde in south-west Colorado. The largest of these – the Cliff Palace (or Cloud Town) – housed about 250 people. It was abandoned about the same time as Cahokia and – guess what – nobody knows why.

Point is, Native Americans were a great deal more advanced and diverse than most people know. There was an awful lot going on that we have no idea about on the wonderful continent of America before the Europeans came across and killed around ninety-five per cent of the indigenous population (by unintentional introduction of new diseases as well as intentional murder). We know about Cahokia and Mesa Verde only because the former has left behind pyramids and the latter stone buildings. Were there other huge settlements made of skin and wood that let no trace? Pretty much definitely. And what great wars, crazy adventures, huge love affairs and amazing encounters with animals (both hilarious and fatal) must have taken place in America, both north and south, all the time?

It's been a real joy learning about this period of American history, visiting the locations and running a story through them. Perhaps there weren't alchemically enhanced women and wasp men back then, but I'm certain that there were brave, sassy, fun, funny and groovy people who might well have had adventures not too dissimilar from the characters in this book.

It is a huge mistake to think that pre Columbian Native Americans were all craggy faced, monosyllabic sensible types in feather headdresses sitting on horses. They didn't have horses, for a start. Hopefully this book will encourage some to reassess their ideas about Native Americans and even do a little research themselves.

I strongly recommend a visit to Mesa Verde. I haven't actually been to Cahokia, but I'm sure it's excellent. Having said that, perhaps a better thing to do is drive into a National Park, State Park, National Recreation Area, National Monument or any of the wonderful landscapes of North America and wander around, wondering what went on there before the Europeans poked their big, destructive noses in. Perhaps you'd like to picture Sofi and gang leading Wulf and his lot through the land, or – probably better – you'd like to make up your own stories.

To recreate the journey in this final book, drive over the Rockies from Denver to Las Vegas. It's one of the greatest drives in the world. The national parks are amazing and the bits that aren't national parks are awesome too. If you'd like to know the exact route that Sofi and the gang took across America, including the Paloma, Freydis etc. diversion, give me a shout on Twitter or Instagram or it's easy enough to find my email address. (The route for the whole trilogy is Chicago to Las Vegas. That's a bit more of an undertaking, as the Ocean of Grass – now all very neat farmland – gets a little samey after the first few hundred miles, but I will be happy to tell you the whole route. I love talking about this stuff and the idea that a reader might visit the wonderful places I've been fills me with joy.)

## Vikings

The Vikings reached North America about a thousand years ago. The two Vinland sagas – the Saga of Erik the Red and the Saga of the Greenlanders – describe the voyages. Plus there's a place in Canada that is definitely a Viking settlement – L'Anse Aux Meadow in Newfoundland. So Vikings found America about 500 years before Columbus sailed the ocean blue.

No evidence has yet been found that the Vikings got any further than that village, and the sagas don't have them going very far. However – and it's a big however – the vast, vast majority of what the Vikings got up to is not covered by the sagas, and did not leave any archaeological trace. Add the fact that the Vikings were about the bravest, most adventurous people who ever lived and you can be pretty certain that they went a lot further into North America.

It is not outlandish to imagine that sailing, paddling and a little bit of boat carrying took the Vikings by river and lake to the shore of Lake Michigan just north of modern day Chicago, which is where I placed Hardwork (in what is now the Illinois Beach Nature Preserve).

From there, they really could have crossed the continent to The Meadows (interesting fact (or a fact anyway) *The Meadows* in Spanish is *Las Vegas*).

Perhaps they didn't team up with super warriors or get

chased by Tyrannosaurus Rexes, but it really is possible that people called Wulf, Erik, Freydis and Finnbogi walked on the red sand of the Great Basin Desert west of the Rocky Mountains a thousand years before I did.

# extras

www.orbitbooks.net

# about the author

**Angus Watson** is an author living in London. Before becoming a novelist, he was a freelance features writer, chiefly for British national newspapers. Features included looking for Bigfoot in the USA for the *Telegraph*, diving on the scuppered World War One German fleet at Scapa Flow for the *Financial Times* and swimming with sea lions in the Galapagos Islands for *The Times*.

Angus's first historical fantasy trilogy is Age of Iron, an epic romantic adventure set at the end of Britain's Iron Age. He came up with the idea for West of West while driving and hiking though North America's magnificent countryside and wondering what it was like before the Europeans got there.

Angus is married to Nicola. They have two young sons, Charlie and Otty, and two cats, Jasmine and Napa.

You can find him on Twitter at @GusWatson, Instagram at @angus_watson_novelist or find his website at: www.guswatson.com.

Find out more about Angus Watson and other Orbit authors by registering for the free monthly newsletter at www.orbitbooks.net.

# if you enjoyed

# WHERE GODS FEAR TO GO

look out for

# THE GREY BASTARDS

by

# Jonathan French

*BRING ON THE ORCS . . .*

*Jackal is proud to be a Grey Bastard, member of a sworn brotherhood of half-orcs. Unloved and unwanted in civilised society, the Bastards eke out a hard life in the desolate no man's land called The Lots, protecting frail and noble human civilisation from invading bands of vicious full-blooded orcs.*

*But as Jackal is soon to learn, his pride may be misplaced. Because a dark secret lies at the heart of the Bastards' existence – one that reveals a horrifying truth behind humanity's tenuous peace with the orcs, and exposes a grave danger on the horizon.*

*On the heels of the ultimate betrayal, Jackal must scramble to stop a devastating invasion – even as he wonders where his true loyalties lie.*

# Chapter 1

Jackal was about to wake the girls for another tumble when he heard Oats bellow for him through the thin walls of the brothel. Ugly, early sunlight speared through the missing slats in the decrepit shutters. Jackal jumped from the bed, shaking off the entangling limbs of the whores and the last clouds of wine swimming in his head. The new girl slept right through, but Delia groaned at the disturbance, raising her tousled red locks off the cushions to squint at him with naked disapproval.

"The fuck, Jack?" she said.

Laughing quietly, Jackal hopped into his breeches. "There is a large bowl of porridge calling my name."

Delia rolled her bleary eyes. "Tell that big thrice to hush. And come back to bed."

"Would that I could, darlin'," Jackal said, sitting on the bed to pull on his boots. "Would that I could."

He stood just as Delia's fingers began to coax at his back. Not bothering to find his brigand, Jackal snatched his belt from amongst the girls' discarded garments on the floor, buckled it on, and adjusted the fall of his tulwar. He could feel Delia's eyes on him.

"Hells, you are a pretty half-breed!" she said. The sleepiness was gone from her eyes, replaced by a well-practiced look of hunger. Jackal played along, purposefully flexing as he gathered his hair back and tied it with a leather thong. Giving Delia a parting wink, he threw open the door and hurried from the room. The corridor was dim and abandoned, still clinging to the bleak stillness of dawn. Jackal walked through to the common room, not breaking stride as he stepped around the pitted tables and over-turned chairs. The sour stink of spilled wine and sweat were all that remained of the night's revels. The door leading outside was cracked, the bright, intruding light already promising a sweltering day. Jackal stepped into the morning glare, clenching his jaw and eyelids against the assault of the sun.

Oats stood by the well in the center of the yard, the slabs of muscle on his broad back shining with water. Jackal jogged up and stood beside his friend.

"Trouble?"

Oats lifted his chin slightly, pointing with his spade-shaped beard down the dusty track leading to the grounds. Jackal followed his gaze and saw the shimmering shapes of horses approaching. Putting a hand at his brow to shield his eyes from the sun, he looked for riders and was relieved to find them.

"Not horse-cocks."

"No," Oats agreed. "Cavalry."

Jackal relaxed a little. Human soldiers they could handle. Centaurs might have meant their deaths.

"Ignacio?" he mused. "I swear that pit-faced old drunk can smell his payment from all the way at the castile."

His friend said nothing, continuing to scowl at the ap-proaching cavalcade. Jackal counted eight men, one clutching a banner that no doubt bore the crest of the king of Hispartha. That blowing bit of silk meant little in the Lot Lands and Jackal kept his gaze fixed on the man up front.

"It's Bermudo," Oats said, a second before Jackal picked out the captain's identity through the dust.

"Shit."

Jackal found himself wishing he had not left his stockbow under Delia's bed. Glancing over, he noticed Oats was completely unarmed, the half-full bucket from the well still clutched in his meaty hands. Still, the brute's appearance was often enough to discourage a fight. As was said amongst the members of the hoof, Oats had muscles in his shit.

Jackal was no stripling, but his friend was a full head taller. With his bald head, ash-colored skin, corded frame, and protruding lower fangs, Oats could pass for a full-blood orc as long as he hid the Bastard tattoos that adorned his powerful arms and back. Only his beard marked him for a half-breed, a trait Jackal had not received from his human half.

As the riders fanned out around the well, Jackal grinned. He might not be able to pass for a thick, but he was big enough to give these human whelps pause. Their clean crimson sashes, brightly polished helmets, and petulantly brave faces marked them as fresh arrivals. Mustachios must have been in fashion in the courts of Hispartha, for drooping from every upper lip was something akin to a furry horseshoe. Every lip except Bermudo's. He looked like one of those long-dead tyrants found on the old Imperium coins, all long nose and close-cropped hair.

The captain reined up.

He took a moment to survey the yard, his attention lingering on the stables Sancho maintained for his guests.

Jackal lifted his chin in greeting. "Bermudo. Breaking in some new boys, I see. What, did they demand proof that a man can still get some quim in the badlands?"

"How many are with you, Bastards?"

It was an offhand, almost lazy question, but Jackal did not miss Bermudo's concern.

"Not here to ambush you, Captain."

"That is not an answer."

"Certain it is."

Bermudo turned to catch the eye of one of his riders and flicked a finger at the stables. The chosen cavalero hesitated.

"Go check the stables," Bermudo said, as if instructing an idiot child.

The man snapped out of his puzzlement and spurred his horse to the west side of the yard. His compatriots watched his progress. Jackal watched them. All held demi-lances and round steel shields, with scale coats for further protection. Five of them had grown tense, betrayed by the tautness in their reins. The last one looked bored and produced an overwrought yawn. The errand runner had dismounted, tied his horse to the post, and now strode into the stables. A moment later, Sancho's stableboy stumbled sleepily into the glare. The cavalero followed not long after.

"Three hogs and a mule team," he reported when he rode back.

"The team belongs to three miners," Jackal told Bermudo. "From Traedria, I think. They're not here to ambush you either."

"No," Bermudo said. "They have dispensation to prospect in the Amphora Mountains. I know because I issued them the writ. You, however, have no such dispensation."

Jackal looked at the empty surrounding sky with awe. "Oats? Did Sancho's place get spirited into the Amphoras while we slept?"

"The peaks look smaller than I remember," Oats said. "Invisible, even."

Bermudo remained humorless. "You damn well know my meaning."

"We do," Jackal said. "And you damn well know Captain Ignacio allows our presence here."

"Did he assure you of that before leaving here last night?"

Oats's face clenched. "Ignacio wasn't here last night."

It was true, but Jackal would have preferred not to give that away just yet. The captains hated each other, but that didn't explain Bermudo biting at Ignacio's name as if it were bait. It also didn't explain his presence at the brothel. The noble captain did not employ Sancho's girls and was rarely seen this far from the castile.

Jackal attempted fresh bait. "Don't let us stall you from getting inside. Sure you're all eager to relieve some spend."

Bermudo sniffed.

"Observe, men," he said, his gaze resting on Jackal and Oats while also ignoring them, a skill only noble-born humans could master. "A pair of half-breed riders. From the Grey Bastards hoof. You will learn to distinguish them by their hideous body markings. Some you will come to know by their absurd names. Despite the allotments, they all think this entire land belongs to them, so you will find them in places they do not belong, like this establishment, blatantly ignoring the fact that it rests on Crown land. It is within your power to expel them in such instances. Though it is often best to allow them to sate themselves and move on. Unlike a pair of rutting dogs, it takes more than a bucket of water to discourage half-orcs in heat. They are . . . slaves to their base natures."

Jackal ignored the insults. He looked beyond Bermudo and smiled at the cavaleros arrayed behind him. "We *do* love whores. Pardon. We enjoy seeking our ease with willing company. Reckon that's how you'd say it up north. Either way, Sancho and his girls are always hospitable."

Bermudo curled his mouth with distaste, but it was the yawning cavalero who spoke, his mouth now settled into a comfortable sneer.

"I would never pay for a woman willing to lay with half-orcs."

"Then you best start fucking your horse," Oats rumbled.

Jackal smiled as the eyes of the new cavalero grew wide. "He's right. You won't find a whore in the Lot Lands who hasn't been spoiled by us. I'm sure they would take your coin, but don't be offended, lad, if they fail to notice your pink little prick is even in."

The man visibly bristled. Looking closer, Jackal noticed his mustachio could not quite conceal a harelip. The other six were casting uncertain looks at the back of Bermudo's head, searching for guidance. The captain's helmet was hanging from his saddle, and he carried no lance, but his hand had drifted to the grip of his sword.

"Make trouble," Bermudo said, his face turning flinty, "and I will drag you behind my horse all the way back to your lot, whatever arrangements you have with Ignacio be damned."

Jackal hooked his thumbs in his belt, getting his hand closer to his own blade. He could posture as well as the captain. "There is no quarrel here."

"Not unless you make one," Oats put in.

Bermudo's eyes flicked between Jackal and Oats. Was he actually considering spilling blood? Would this arrogant ass risk a feud just to save face in front of a gaggle of outcast nobility with new saddles and wet dreams of heroism?

Bermudo's jaw bulged as he chewed on his pride, but before he came to a decision the harelip rode up to the well.

"You there," he said to Oats, gesturing with his lance. "Fill yonder trough."

Jackal let out a snort of derision and watched as a ripple of uncertainty passed through the recruits, every eye on their outspoken comrade. Bermudo shot the man a warning look. "Cavalero Garcia—"

The youth waved him off. "It is all right, Captain. We have half-orc servants at my father's villa. They have to be kept well in hand or they turn mulish. Clearly these two have gone undisciplined for too long. A lack of humility that is quickly remedied. It is all in how you address them." He looked languidly down at Oats. "I said fill the trough. Step to it, mongrel."

Jackal heard the strained creaking of wood as Oats's knuckles paled against the bucket. This was heartbeats from coming to blood.

"You want to get your new arrival in hand, Captain," Jackal said. It was not a suggestion. "He might not know what an angry thrice-blood can do to a man."

Bermudo's haughty manner was showing cracks at the edges. He saw the situation turning ill, same as Jackal. But he set his jaw and allowed the insubordination.

Shit.

Nothing to do but control whose blood was spilled, and how much.

"So, Captain," Jackal said, "what did this fop do to be banished here? Gambling debts? Or, no, Oats had it before, didn't he? Your man got caught with his father's favorite stallion. Riding it without a saddle. Inside the stable."

The smug cavalero stamped the butt of his lance into Jackal's face. He did it so casually, so lazily, that Jackal had plenty of time to avoid the blow, but he let it land. Pain overtook his vision and he reeled back a step, snapping a hand to his throbbing nose. He heard Oats snarl, but Jackal reached out blindly and laid his free hand on his friend's trunk of an arm, stopping any retaliation. Spitting, Jackal waited for his head to clear before straightening.

"You will keep a civil tongue," Cavalero Garcia told him. "Speak with such impudence again and I shall have you horsewhipped in the name of the king."

Jackal looked directly at Bermudo and found nervousness infecting his face. But there was also a creeping look of satisfaction.

"King?" Jackal said, sucking the last film of blood from his teeth. "Oats? Do you know the name of the king?"

"Such-and-Such the First," Oats replied.

Jackal shook his head. "No, he died. It's So-and-So the Fat."

Oats gave him a dubious squint. "That don't sound right."

"Wretched soot-skins!" Garcia exclaimed.

Jackal ignored him, throwing his arms wide in a mock flummox. "The name escapes us. Anyway, he's some inbred, overstuffed sack of shit that weds his cousins, fucks his sisters, and has small boys attach leeches to his tiny, tiny prick."

This time, Jackal caught Garcia's lance as the man thrust and used it to yank him from his mount, angling him to collide with the well's roof on the way down. The horse shied away, whinnying. Garcia floundered in the dirt, sputtering wordless rage as he tried to stand. Jackal grabbed the cavalero's cloak, pulled it over his head, and punched his face through the dusty cloth. He fell flat.

The horses were balking at the disturbance, but the men were stilled by shock. Bermudo had visibly paled.

Jackal motioned at the fallen Garcia. "I think that's a good lesson for these virgins, Captain. You agree?"

Bermudo was no fool. He saw the chance being offered. With a curt nod, he took it.

Garcia, however, was still conscious. And less wise. Sitting up, he yanked the cloak from his head, revealing a mouth dripping blood and venom.

"Captain," he seethed, an accusing finger sweeping between Jackal and Oats. "I demand these two be brought back to the castile and hanged."

Jackal laughed. "Hanged? You're not dead, frail. A trade of insults, you bust my nose, I smash your teeth. That's it. It's done. Now go inside, get your cod wet, and forget it."

Garcia was deaf to good sense. His vengeful stare shifted up to Bermudo.

"*Captain?*" He spoke the rank, but it sounded far from the respect due a superior.

Jackal and Oats shared a look. What was this? Certainly not the first time cavaleros and hoof riders had come to blows. It happened at Sancho's more often than anywhere. It was time for everyone to ride on.

A gem of sweat studded the center of Bermudo's upper lip. He looked torn, chewing on a choice that was making him angry.

"Bermudo . . ." Jackal tried to get the man's attention, but was shouted down by Garcia.

"You will languish here forever, Captain!"

It was a threat. And it made up Bermudo's mind.

"Take them!" he commanded.

Bermudo tried to draw his sword, but the bucket took him in the brow before the blade was half free. Oats had thrown with such force that not a drop of water spilled until the bucket smote the Captain's skull. He fell from the saddle, unconscious before he even struck the dust of the yard.

Jackal kicked Garcia under the chin, sending him sprawling before he could squeal further. Rather than intimidate the other riders, the violence against their comrade steeled their courage and all six lowered their lances. Jackal drew his sword and tossed it to Oats in one motion, keeping hold of Garcia's lance and leveling it against the impending charge.

Before the cavaleros could spur their horses forward, their gazes snapped up to stare wide-eyed. A voice rang out from behind Jackal's head.

"Think twice, you prickly lipped eunuchs!"

Jackal smiled. The voice was ill-humored, commanding, and familiar. The cavaleros were lowering their lances, every mouth agape.

"Perfect timing, Fetch!" Jackal called over his shoulder. He gave the men a gloating smile before turning around. A moment later, his own jaw fell open.

Fetching stood upon the roof of the brothel with a stockbow in each hand, both loaded and trained on the riders. She was stark naked.

"You're bleeding, Jack."

Jackal managed a grunt and a nod. He had known Fetching since childhood, but neither of them were children any more.

Her pale green flesh was flawless, lacking the ashy grey tones found in most half-orcs, and smooth save where it rippled with muscle or swelled with curves. She had both to spare. Her dark brown twistlocks were unbound, falling to her shapely shoulders. She held the heavy stockbows steadily, the points of their quarrels unwavering between the prods. It was an impressive sight. And based upon the stunned silence behind him in the yard, the cavaleros thought so as well.

Clever Fetching, always using every advantage, though she needed few.

"You're bleeding," Fetch repeated, "and I am awakened very early. Someone is going to die."

Garcia had managed to stumble toward his fellows and pointed with a quivering finger.

"You filthy ash-coloreds!" he shrieked through his swollen lips. "You will all dangle from a gibbet! Take them, men! Take them!"

"That one," Oats grunted.

"That one," Fetching confirmed, and shot Garcia through the eye. He fell backward stiffly, the fletching of the quarrel blossoming from his left socket. The cavaleros cursed and struggled to keep their shying horses under control.

"I got one bolt left," Fetching announced. "Who would like it?"

There were no volunteers.

Jackal spun on the cavaleros.

"Before any of you say anything fool-ass, like, 'My father will hear of this!' remember – no one cares a fig for you back north in whatever civilized jewel you called home. If they did, you wouldn't be here."

Jackal swept every man with a steady gaze, noting which ones looked away.

"What are you, third-, fourth-born? At least one of you is likely a bastard. You were all fobbed off here to be forgotten. To patrol the borderlands and watch for orcs. You have no station, you have no privilege." Jackal tossed Garcia's lance onto his corpse. "*He* forgot that. Don't make the same mistake. If you want to survive your first skirmish with the thicks, you best begin to look kindly on us half-breeds. We are what keep you safe. Bermudo's right. We claim this land as our own. But we aren't the only ones. The orcs call this land Ul-wundulas. They think it's theirs. You won't prove them wrong by believing you're better than they are. Your fathers can't help you here. The king, whatever his name is, can't help you here. Only we mongrels can help you here. Welcome to the Lot."

Stepping back, Jackal gave Oats a nod. The brute picked the unconscious form of Captain Bermudo off the ground as if he were a child.

"Didn't take more than a bucket of water for you, 'Mudo," he said, and slung the man over the back of his horse. He handed the animal's reins to one of the cavaleros.

"Take him back to the castile," Jackal told the men. "Tell Captain Ignacio that Cavalero Garcia defied Bermudo's orders and struck him. He fled on horseback rather than face discipline and was last seen heading into centaur territory. The Grey Bastards have volunteered to go searching for him. But we're not confident he'll ever be found. When Bermudo comes around, he will want to remember it that way. You all will. Unless you want a war with the half-orc hoofs."

No one responded. Each face had gone pale and placid.

"Now is the part where you all nod!" Fetch called down from the roof.

Every helmeted head bobbled up and down.

Jackal extended a guiding arm toward the track. Within minutes, the cavalcade was a shimmering smudge on the horizon.

Jackal found Oats staring at him and shaking his head.

"What?"

"Nice speech, Prince Jackal."

"Suck a sow's tit, Oats."

Jackal probed at his nose while Fetching jumped down from the roof, the well-developed muscles in her long legs absorbing the impact.

"Next time you go out to make pretty words with the frails, don't forget to bring a thrum," she said, tossing Jackal the spent stockbow.

"And next time you come to our rescue, you should wear that," he retorted, sweeping a hand at her nakedness.

"Lick me, Jack!"

"Didn't one of Sancho's girls already do that?"

"Yes," Fetch replied, turning her back to head for the door of the brothel. "But like all the whores, she would rather have had her head between *your* legs."

Jackal stared brazenly at the dimples above Fetch's pert backside until she disappeared into the shadows of the whorehouse.

A cuff from Oats on the back of his head brought him around.

"We need to get back."

Jackal scratched at his chin. "I know. See to the hogs."

Before Oats could head for the stables, the same door that had so recently enveloped Fetching now disgorged the brothel's proprietor. The pleasant swell in Jackal's cod immediately withered.

Maneuvering his corpulence through the jamb, Sancho came heavy-footed into the yard, his small mouth held in an oval of witless alarm. What little hair the man had left was already soaked with sweat, a slick black stain across his head. Sancho stared at the cavalero's corpse and shook his head slowly, causing his ill-shaven jowls to jiggle.

"I'm ruined."

Jackal snorted. "Don't tell me that this is the first man to die here, Sancho."

"The first cavalero!" the fat man said, his voice sounding choked. "And not even one of Ignacio's commoners, but a fucking blue blood! What have you done?"

"Rid you of a future troublesome guest," Jackal told him. "Fair wager, that piece of hogshit would have beaten your girls."

"That I can handle! But the body of exiled gentry is not so easily managed."

"It is. Contact the Sludge Man." Jackal gestured at Garcia's sprawled carcass. "Let him dispose of our deceased friend."

The whoremaster's large, moist face went pale at the mention of the name.

"He and our chief have an understanding," Jackal said before Sancho's panic fully took root.

"You sure you want to involve him?" Oats put in, an uneasy look on his bearded face. Jackal wasn't sure who he meant, their chief or the Sludge Man, but he didn't bother to clarify. This was the way through.

He kept his attention on giving Sancho instructions. "Send a bird. When he gets here, give him the body and the horse. Tell him it's for the Grey Bastards."

"And what about me?" Sancho demanded. "What do I get for being your agent in this?"

Jackal took a deep breath. "What do you want?"

"You know," Sancho told him.

"I do," Jackal conceded. "Fine. I'll tell the chief."

The whoremaster eyeballed him for a moment, then nodded. Giving the cavalero one final, grudging glance, Sancho stomped back inside.

Oats clenched his jaw. "Claymaster won't be pleased."

"Our days of pleasing him are almost over, so he better start getting used to it," Jackal replied, breathing out hard through his sore nostrils. "Get ready to ride."